# CURSED KNIGHT

## Elmon Dean Todd

Games & Collectibles

CURSED KNIGHT
GODSHARD CHRONICLES: VOLUME ONE


Copyright © 2021 J-Cat Games and Collectibles, LLC

ISBN: 9781091847385


Book and Map Design: Matt Todd (@m_todd58)
Cover Art and Illustrations: Chris Koh (@Zamberz)
Editing: Anne Hamilton

Published by
J-Cat Games and Collectibles, LLC
www.godshard.com

J-CAT GAMES Trade Paperback Edition May 2019
Printed in the USA

# ACKNOWLEDGEMENTS

I would like to thank Chris Koh for breathing life into the Godshard Chronicles with his magnificent art, especially his lustrious character designs.

My thanks to Matt Todd for giving the Kingdom of Ordonia a proper map and sorting out the book cover.

Special thanks to Michael Beeman and J.C. Todd for their long, arduous hours of proofreading in such a short time frame, along with their creative feedback and input. Thanks also to my cousin, B, who provided the inspiration behind Squire Shah and the Mana Knight Academy.

My eternal gratitude to my editor, Anne Hamilton, who ensured that the world of Alban remained coherent.

I would like to thank James Blanchard for his world-building contributions to the Kingdom of Ordonia. For without them, there wouldn't be such things as star-apples, Dwarfside, Pariahs, Sir Agama and the Trial of the Chair.

And most of all, this book is dedicated to the memory of Jason Dubose. Although he no longer lives among us, his journey in Alban will continue on.

# Author's Notes

This book is written in British (UK) English.

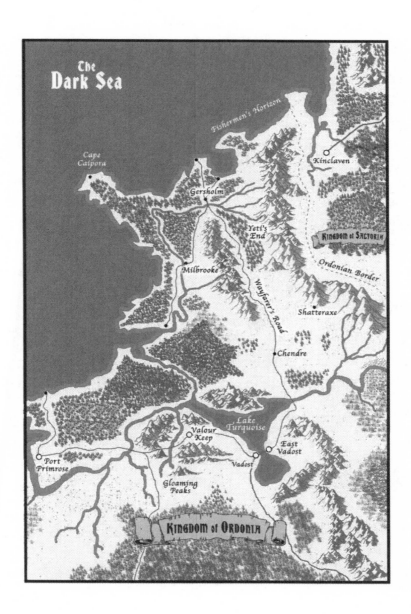

The Dark Sea

Fishermen's Horizon

Cape
Caipora

Gersholm

Kinclaven

Kingdom of Saltoria

Yeti's
End

Ordonian Border

Milbrooke

Wayfarer's Road

Shatteraxe

Chendre

Lake
Turquoise

Valour
Keep

East
Vadost

Vadost

Port
Primrose

Gloaming
Peaks

Kingdom of Ordonia

# Part One

## Journey Across the Sea

# CHAPTER ONE

### Logres

*When the gods warred amongst themselves, they supposedly destroyed everything except the land of Logres. Beyond Logres lies the sea. Beyond that, more sea. There is nothing beyond the sea except death, for those who ventured out beyond have never returned.*

Lothar, Chieftain of the Lothar Clan

**A** heavy fog crept into the village.

The Einar elders claimed that the fog came from the god, Rudras, who sent it to collect the souls of the dead for the netherworld. On this particular day, the god seemed eager for a new soul. It was spring, but the chill air felt like winter.

Kairos stood in the middle of the village centre, facing his enemy, who was the same age, but stood a head taller with broader shoulders. Kairos gripped his wooden sword with his left hand, and round wooden shield in his right. He was dressed in padded leather, ready for a fight. His enemy before him wore the same, waving his wooden sword in a taunting manner and leering.

It wasn't a duel to the death, but everything in Kairos's short fifteen years of life teetered on the outcome of this fight. He had to win.

The village centre was a field of mud large enough for spectators of the entire Azel clan. Even a few members of the other Einar clans came to watch. The crowd stretched back to the houses, which were made of wooden beams, insulated with mud and wattle, and roofed with clay tiles. The mud they stood in was ankle deep, rutted by carts and fouled by the wretched livestock that roamed free. The fog made everything sticky and damp. Nobody cared, because if there was one thing the Einar race loved, it was a fight.

Kairos had two family members in the crowd. Karthok, his father, stood behind him. Known to all the Einar as 'Karthok the Cruel', his father had some grey hairs on his beard, but despite his age he towered over many of the other villagers with his broad frame and seven-foot height. Kairos did not need to turn around to see the glower on his father's furious face. His father frightened him. Frightened him much more than the enemy standing before him, because Kairos knew the consequences of losing. His father did not tolerate weakness.

Next to Karthok the Cruel was Thylar, Kairos's older brother. He was nineteen years old, yet like their father he towered over most of the clan. Kairos was not frightened of him. Unlike Karthok, Thylar often trained Kairos, always offering a warm smile and words of encouragement. Kairos loved his brother more than anyone.

In the bleak land of Logres where only the strong survived and the weak perished, Thylar was the shining light of hope in Kairos's world. Their mother had passed when they were young, leaving their father to raise them hard because a man must be hard. The land of Logres was full of violence and death, and one needed to be prepared to rise above it all. Karthok rose above it all, because he was chieftain of the Azel clan, and he expected glory and triumph from his sons.

Unfortunately, Kairos did not meet those expectations.

Now, he waited, poised with his wooden weapon before him. He tried his best to appear strong, but only quivered in nervousness. No one was impressed.

'Kairos the Coward,' his enemy taunted. 'Why don't you come at me already?'

Kairos said nothing.

'Or is it because you're about to piss your breeches?'

'Shut up,' Kairos answered.

The truth was that Kairos was scared. He was so scared that his hand holding the wooden sword shook uncontrollably. His enemy took notice and laughed. Kairos knew his adversary was toying with him. He would lose like he always had, and the result would anger his father beyond measure.

'Why don't you fall to your knees and grovel?' the enemy said, 'And I'll let you off with a minor thrashing.'

'Piss off,' Kairos said, knowing that was something his father would say.

And that was when the battle started.

His enemy charged, slashing his weapon towards Kairos's head. Kairos raised his shield, and the blow almost knocked him off his feet, sending him staggering back a few steps. Laughter rippled across the crowd, and Kairos's face flushed with shame. Even the crowd knew the fight was one-sided.

The enemy in front of him was his cousin Keng, son of Uncle Vinh, and Kairos had to defeat him in order to sail with the Einar fleet. It was a voyage for the salvation of the entire Einar race. Kairos wanted to seek glory like everyone else in the clan, but there was only one spot left on Karthok's longship, and Uncle Vinh recommended Keng. Kairos's father wanted both of his sons to go. There was only one resolution. 'Let them duel to decide,' Karthok had said, frowning.

His father had a reason to frown for Kairos never won duels. He was considered the weakest boy his age in the village. Even now, Kairos could see the villagers placing bets against him. They knew he would lose. He always lost. His cousin noticed the stakes in his favour and laughed. The only two cheering for Kairos were

Thylar and an older man aptly called Mad Mavos, who was considered to be quite daft.

Kairos could not back down. He had to go on the voyage across the sea with his brother and father. If he stayed behind, he would have to live with Uncle Vinh, who hated him beyond reason. His uncle was taller than even the massive Karthok, soaring at the height of seven and a half feet, but he was much slenderer with a sly and sinister face, and protruding front teeth like a grinning rat. Even now, Kairos could see his uncle's rat-like grin, cheerfully anticipating his downfall, and he shuddered at the prospect of what would happen to him once his father and brother were no longer around.

Feeling hopeless, Kairos sought an opening in his enemy's stance. He found none. He knew that his attacks would be cast aside. They always were. His opponent had him bested in strength, speed, and skill. The only thing Kairos had left was luck. He squared his shoulders as his enemy readied to attack. Well, if the odds were against him, he could give his enemy less time to think. Less time to attack.

Forcing his shaking hand to stop, Kairos walked purposely towards his cousin. A murmur of surprise spread through the gathered crowd. For a moment, his cousin looked surprised, too, but he quickly composed himself and began laughing.

'Is that nervous laughter? Perhaps you are the one who is afraid of losing?' Kairos said, trying to display a bravado he did not feel.

'Have you gone mad, cousin?' Keng shouted, looking around the crowd to soak in their reactions. Several chortles broke out. Keng laughed again.

That was what Kairos had wanted. Seizing the moment of his adversary's distraction, Kairos leapt forward at Keng, whose laughter soon turned to a gasp of surprise as he barely had enough time to raise his shield. Kairos anticipated the move and dropped down, striking a blow to Keng's shin near the knee. Had it been a blade made of iron, Keng would have never walked again. But the blade was wood and Keng howled in pain and fell back limping. Kairos noted that he favoured his other leg.

Hope surged through him. Maybe he had a chance! Behind Keng, Kairos saw his father nod his head in approval.

'Kairos, you sheep-swiving coward!' Keng screamed. 'You dare strike at me when I'm not looking?'

'You were open,' Kairos answered in an even voice.

The crowd laughed, but this time not at him. Kairos trembled at the feeling. He had hurt his opponent. Not much, but it was enough to show that Keng was not invulnerable. Throughout his life Kairos had been smaller than the average Einar, much to his father's dismay. No one wanted a runt for a child, and Kairos was a runt. All of the other youth were bigger and could beat him in a fight. This affected his reputation as a warrior amongst the Einar clans. Most called him 'Kairos the Coward' or 'Kairos the Craven' when Karthok and Thylar were not around.

So the fact that Kairos scored a hit against Keng, a renowned fighter in his own right, was delightfully entertaining to everyone present.

'A lucky strike, cousin,' Keng growled. 'But you'll pay for that with your blood.'

'Come take what blood you can,' Kairos said, edging backwards in the muck.

As Kairos tried to keep his distance, Keng hobbled towards him. When his cousin drew close, he lunged forward, flailing with his wooden blade. Kairos took a step back, avoiding the swing.

'What's wrong?' Kairos asked, flashing his teeth. 'You're not so fast now.'

Keng said nothing and continued advancing, his mouth set in grim determination. Kairos backed away from the blows and kept his distance. He knew that as long as he kept his distance, he could hope to tire out his opponent and end the fight.

The break came soon enough.

His cousin stumbled forward in the mud. Kairos saw the opportunity and rushed forward to attack. Just as his wooden blade was coming down onto his cousin's head, Kairos saw the wicked smile and realised his mistake. His cousin was feigning his limp. Kairos's blade missed as his cousin twisted away, countering with his own wooden blade. The blow struck Kairos in the ribs, sending him reeling. Kairos tried to regain his balance, but sprawled forward into the mud, crashing atop of his shield. Keng leapt onto Kairos instantly, pinning down Kairos's sword hand with one arm and raining blows onto his face with the other. He had abandoned his wooden sword in favour of beating Kairos to a bloody pulp with his fists.

'Make a fool of me, you bastard!' Keng screamed. 'I'll kill you, Kairos.'

Kairos could do nothing but writhe and twist in the muck. He tried to break free, but his cousin was too strong. Each blow ignited blinding, painful flashes in his vision.

'That's enough!' a voice boomed. Kairos vaguely recognised it as his father's.

The blows ceased. The fight was over. His father shoved Keng aside and jerked Kairos to his feet. Disoriented and dizzy, Kairos wiped his face and looked at his hand. It was covered in blood and grime. His head throbbed, but he knew this was nothing compared to what was in store for him later. One look at his father's thunderous face promised a severe beating.

Kairos sighed in disappointment and summoned all of his willpower to fight away the tears that were beginning to well up. He was already in enough trouble. There was no need to make matters worse by letting his father see him cry. Crying was a show of weakness, and the Einar had no place for weakness.

Now he would stay behind with Uncle Vinh whilst the others embarked on a journey for the Einar's salvation. A journey across the sea.

As long as any on the isles of Logres could remember, no one had ever travelled across the sea. Kairos heard legends from the elders that the Einar had originally come from faraway a long time ago. They came with dwarves and settled on the isles of Logres – until they decided to kill the dwarves off, leaving only the ruins of the dwarven fortresses. Now the Einar clans lived on the isles and fought each other, and would have continued doing so until the end of time.

Until the land began to die.

The Einar called it the 'Blight' and it started shortly before Kairos was born. Thylar said that the isles were once covered with birch, rowan, and yew trees, but by now most of the trees had died, and the only ones remaining appeared pathetic and withered. The animals were affected, too. Most died off in masses, and those that survived looked plague-ridden.

Only the Einar remained unaffected. They made the appropriate sacrifices to Rudras to stave off the Blight, but nothing worked. In the end, they counted themselves blessed with their resilience to it, and reasoned that they could resort to eating fish if all of the land animals perished. Yet, the supply of fish around Logres began to dwindle, and the Einar had to sail out farther and farther to sea for them. Most of them preferred raiding the other clans for food. Kairos even joined some of these raids, but his father made him watch from afar.

After much bloodshed, the Einar elders and leaders set aside their differences long enough to hold a council in Karthok's mead hall. One elder, Mad Mavos, proposed sailing across the sea as told in the legends. This brought about laughter until Uncle Vinh suggested that finding new land would bring the most glory an Einar could possibly attain. After much more deliberation, the elders and leaders decided to use the remaining precious wood to construct three longships. The Einar would finally work together at last.

And now Kairos could not go. He would have to watch his father and brother leave whilst Keng embarked on a quest for glory. But that was the least of his worries, as a quick cuff from his father brought him back to his present predicament.

'You bastard,' Karthok growled, 'you weak, pathetic bastard. You're no son of mine.'

'Father...' Kairos began.

'I'm not your father,' Karthok snarled, dragging Kairos along by the arm back to their mead hall. 'You're not my son. No son of mine would lose to some snivelling shit of a boy.'

Kairos wanted to point out that Keng was no easy adversary. His cousin could easily defeat most of the other boys of the village, but Karthok would have none of it. He wanted another son like Thylar – a powerful and brave warrior. In his father's eyes, he proved to be the exact opposite.

The fog was impenetrable by the time they arrived at the mead hall. Several of Karthok's house warriors looked up from where they sat at the long tables. At the sight of their enraged chieftain, they quickly abandoned their meals and shuffled out. Karthok slammed the door shut and threw Kairos onto a table, smashing food and crockery.

'Father...' Kairos pleaded. He looked around for Thylar, hoping that his brother's presence would calm his enraged father, but there was no sign of him. He was on his own.

'You're not worthy to be my son,' Karthok shouted. 'You have brought nothing but shame to my bloodline! How could a runt like you ever come from my loins? You're a disgrace. A mistake.'

Kairos clambered wetly from the table, dripping chunks of food. He backed away as his father approached him with clenched fists. Judging by the wild look in Karthok's eyes, all reasoning had long fled from his father's mind. This punishment was going to be one of the worst. His father grabbed Kairos's tunic with one hand whilst rearing back with his other. Kairos feebly raised his small arms to shield himself. Maybe his father would beat him too severely this time and end his miserable existence.

At that moment the door to the mead hall burst open.

Father and son both turned. Thylar stood in the open doorway, wisps of fog looming hauntingly behind him. Kairos almost felt relief, but the look on his brother's face unnerved him.

'What's the meaning of this, Thylar?' Karthok shouted, though Kairos noted that his father's anger had dissipated.

'Kairos, prepare for the voyage,' Thylar said in a solemn tone. 'You're coming with us.'

'What do you mean?' Karthok demanded. 'Kairos lost to Keng. Kairos is staying behind.'

Thylar shook his head. 'Not anymore,' he said. 'Keng is dead.'

\* \* \*

'What really happened to Keng?' Kairos asked.

Thylar's smile, wide as the ocean that surrounded them, vanished as he stared out to sea. Kairos had asked this question several times before, and each time, Thylar changed the subject. Kairos knew his brother was the only one with Keng during the time of his cousin's death. His brother called it 'an accident', but Kairos was not so sure. There were whispers amongst the other Einar that Thylar had murdered Keng, but no one dared to ask or confront the chieftain's eldest son. Except one person.

'Well?' Kairos prompted.

Thylar remained silent, the look on his face resembling their surroundings.

A fierce storm was brewing, blanket of clouds hung low and dark over the sea. The spray of the frigid waters flew like an arrow shower down on the decks of the three longships. They raced each other in the pelting rain, riding the treacherous waves as the men aboard called insults to each other. These ships were the *Wolf Fang*, the *Sea Serpent*, and the *Grenda*. They had been sailing for over a month, and still there was no sight of land. Their food supply was dwindling, but the Einar needed competition to keep their spirits up.

'They would have killed you, Kairos, if you didn't come along with us,' Thylar said at last, as he gripped the steering oar of the *Grenda*, fighting the waves. His hair was long and dark and plastered against his head and back. The padded leather tunic he wore under his coat of mail was soaked through. Being Karthok the Cruel's second-in-command, Thylar was the only man trusted with manning the tiller in such a storm.

'Who would have killed me?' Kairos asked in surprise.

'Shhhh!' Thylar glanced askance at the other fifty-eight men aboard the *Grenda* to see if anyone had overheard. No one had. They were too busy rowing, for Karthok had ordered the sails down due to the buffeting winds. 'Not so loud!'

'Who would have killed me?' Kairos repeated, leaning towards his brother.

'Uncle Vinh.'

'Uncle Vinh?'

'You're an obstacle because you're the chieftain's son,' Thylar said, his muscles bulging as he pulled on the tiller. 'Uncle Vinh wants to be chieftain if something happens to me or father, so I had to make sure that you came along with us.'

'But you didn't have to…' Kairos began. 'Keng…'

'It was either him or you,' Thylar finished, 'and I made sure it was him. Don't look at me like that. It's the Einar way. The weak die and the strong survive.' He gave a good-natured slap on Kairos's shoulder to ease the tension.

It didn't work.

Kairos stared at his brother in horror. He did not like the 'Einar way'. The Einar always slaughtered each other, and for what? More power, more authority. His father did not earn the title of Karthok the Cruel through peaceful rule. Even as malicious as Keng had been, the thought of him being murdered sickened Kairos. He couldn't believe his brother would do such a thing. He was about to press for more details, but a shout interrupted him.

'Ship ahead!'

The rowing ceased. The men on the rowing benches craned their necks for a better view. After over a month of monotony at sea, they finally had some excitement. They had travelled across the deep sea where the serpents dwelled, past the furthest any Einar in history had ever sailed. This was unknown territory. An unknown ship.

Kairos also wondered who or what was aboard that lone ship. Living on Logres for countless generations, the Einar had never encountered another intelligent race. Kairos knew that dwarves had once lived on Logres, but since the Einar had supposedly slaughtered them all long ago, the only trace of them remained in songs, and in their fortresses the Einar now inhabited. Kairos didn't suppose they were fellow Einar. No, the ship looked too strange. Whoever was on it was probably doomed, he thought sadly, looking at his father.

Karthok the Cruel eyed the ship hungrily and grinned in anticipation. He planted his feet in the bow of the *Grenda* – named after his late wife. He wrapped his muscular arm around the wooden neck that swept up in a graceful arc and ended fifteen feet above his head with the fang-bearing head of a serpent. The serpent head was a frightening sight, its frozen visage roaring its defiance to the storm, only complemented by Karthok the Cruel's leering expression.

'Row faster!' he bellowed, his voice carrying above the lashing rain and tempest. 'Rudras has dropped us a gift from the heavens, ripe for the taking, and you lazy whoresons are going to let it float away!'

The Einar resumed rowing with renewed vigour, and the bow of the *Grenda* soared over a wave, followed with a plunge into the trough. Seal-hide ropes creaked as the port side dipped into the sea, scooping up the seawater like a ladle. The water rushed in, crashing against the mast, against dozens of sea chests lashed to the deck, and against the well-muscled warriors. The *Sea Serpent* and the *Wolf Fang* followed closely behind. Everyone was eager to raid.

Except for one man.

Mad Mavos stood up from his bench and shouted, 'Turn back! Turn back!'

All heads aboard the *Grenda* turned toward the older Einar, who despite his age still looked like a formidable warrior. However, he was 'touched by Rudras', the elders claimed, and his outburst began to unsettle the crew. Many of the Einar, Kairos included, believed that those who were touched by Rudras had the gift of foresight.

'Turn back!' Mad Mavos continued.

Whilst still clinging to the serpent's neck of the ship, Karthok the Cruel faced Mad Mavos with a look of barely contained fury. He pointed and yelled, 'Sit down and shut your mouth, you old fool!'

Mad Mavos ignored the command and pointed ahead. 'That ship... Bad omen.'

'Throw him overboard.' Karthok commanded.

The men around Mad Mavos readily complied, picking up the older man. Mad Mavos shrieked and thrashed about in protest, but the other warriors overpowered him and tossed him over the starboard side of the ship. He bobbed up to the surface for a moment and then disappeared into the storm-tossed waves. Everyone aboard the ship began rowing again, eager to leave the old man and his ill-fated auguries behind. No one wanted bad luck.

Karthok burst into a loud guffaw, joined by the rest of the *Grenda*'s crew.

Only Kairos cast a rueful glance back at the spot where Mad Mavos was last seen. He muttered a quick prayer to Rudras when he thought no one was watching. He really liked old warrior. Mavos had trained Kairos and was one of the few of the Azel clan who never treated him poorly. He looked at his father, who was still laughing, and felt nothing but loathing for the man. A man who used violence to solve everything. He vowed to be nothing like his father.

'How are you feeling, brother?' Thylar asked, his voice full of concern.

'I'm fine,' Kairos said tersely, still staring at the spot where he had last seen Mavos. He wanted to help but didn't know how.

'You look like you're about to shit your breeches.' Thylar used his forearm to wipe the water from his eyes. 'Don't worry about that daft old man. He can preach his madness to the serpents from the ocean bottom.'

Kairos grimaced. He was angry. Angry at his brother and father. But he was also terrified. Mad Mavos's warnings unnerved him, for the warrior was rarely wrong. He didn't like the look of the ship and wished his father would turn the fleet around.

'Do you know what's coming next?' Thylar asked.

'We fight.'

'That's right.' Thylar grinned. 'Though I was hoping for women!'

Kairos smiled wanly, his gaze still lingering where he last saw Mavos. Thylar was quite popular with the women of Logres and talked of them as much as battle, but he knew that his brother was trying to cheer him up and loosen the tension. He would have to mourn the loss of Mad Mavos later. He needed to focus on the upcoming battle.

'But if they're like us, then they've probably left most of the women behind,' Thylar said sadly, to which Kairos nodded, because many Einar considered it bad fortune to bring a woman on a ship to sea. Kairos did not agree, but he supposed that the women were key to the Einar's survival. Thylar's face suddenly brightened in the gloom. 'Or maybe it's a ship full of women wanting a good ol' rutting!'

Kairos now laughed despite himself. 'What if they're Einar?' he asked, looking at the ship in the distance.

'Then we'll know what to expect,' Thylar cried cheerfully as if this were just another fun-filled outing rather than a dangerous struggle in a storm. 'Either way, let's hope they have some good treasure.'

Kairos sighed. The Einar way: raid first and ask questions later. Sometimes he felt as though he didn't fit in.

The *Grenda* and the two other ships had the wind and seas behind them now, and were propelling down the waves stern-first. Kairos became more nervous as they approached. Unlike most of the other men aboard preparing for battle, he had no armour and very little experience. The idea of an actual battle against men with sharpened blades frightened him. His legs felt like buckling under his weight, and his belly seemed to climb into his chest. He expected to die.

As the small Einar fleet neared, the lone ship turned out to be larger than any ship that Kairos had ever seen. He counted three masts in contrast to the one mast on an Einar longship, and there was another deck stacked upon the rear of the main deck, which looked as if it could hold more men. The sails were furled and Kairos did not see any oars, and he suddenly felt a sinking feeling in his gut. This ship did not seem so eager to escape, and it sat there in place, riding the waves as if waiting.

'Thylar,' he began. 'Something doesn't seem quite right about this. They would've seen us by now, but they're just sitting there.'

'This is no time to be craven, Kairos.' His brother stared up at the looming ship. 'We have almost two-hundred of the best Einar warriors with us, and I don't see that ship holding more than a hundred at most. This battle is ours.'

Kairos was not convinced. 'What if this is some sort of trap? What if Mad Mavos—'

Thylar laughed. 'You think too much! You always have. This is a chance for you to slaughter something besides kobolds! Let's just hope they're carrying something more worthwhile than prayer beads and stinking animal hides.'

On the towering deck of the large ship, a large group of stout armed figures came into view and waited, prepared to fight. The Einar were ready for battle, too. Amidships men donned their mail and began freeing swords from sheaths and lifting shields from the gunnels. Others brandished spears. Kairos gripped the hilt of his seax, his treasured weapon and the only gift his father had ever given him. It felt clumsy in his hand, but he was proud to carry it.

Thylar grinned. 'Good. They're ready for a fight. Let's show them one. Now remember, Kai, hold back until our front lines cleave a way through.'

'I know, I know.' Kairos shrugged aside his brother's overprotectiveness.

Karthok the Cruel began howling like a madman, and the rest of the Einar on the other longships joined in, the noise carrying over the sound of the waves and the storm. It was meant to frighten the men on the other ship, though they stoically stood on their deck and waited in silence.

The *Grenda* was the first to reach that ship. Thylar heaved the tiller to swing the longship broadside to the larger ship. That was when Kairos got a good look at its occupants. They were not the maidens Thylar had wanted. They were dwarves, or what he assumed were dwarves since he had never seen a dwarf before. They were just as heavily muscled—if not more than the Einar— but seemed shorter and broader in stature. Even as their ship swayed violently on the waves, they stood on their deck in a solid line and held their shields in front like a wall, brandishing spears, swords and axes. Their faces appeared impassive as they braced for battle.

The Einar folksong told of dwarves and how they and the Einar fought for dominion over Logres long ago. The Songs portrayed the dwarves as cowardly weaklings who fell to the Einar blades. But as Kairos gazed upon those dour-faced warriors on the other ship, their fierce expressions showing no fear, he realised that the songs lied.

Those dwarves looked ready to kill.

\* \* \*

It was a slaughter that day.

The port side of the *Grenda* slammed against the larger ship's starboard. They struck hard, jolting everyone on both ships and causing the dwarven shield wall to momentarily waver. The dwarves had the initial advantage due to their ship's side being higher, which also served as a wall, so the Einar had to overcome that obstacle before thrusting themselves at the deadly shield wall on board.

Kairos had never been in a shield wall before, but he did not like the situation one bit. He knew of the battles involving the clash of shield walls with other Einar clans, and they always resulted in high casualties. A shield wall was a place where men died, where a press of bodies hacked away at each other leaving the ground littered with blood, faeces, and corpses. His father had always said that no man became a warrior until he fought in his first shield wall, never mind how many kobolds he had slaughtered. It took tremendous courage to face down that deadly, well-organised wall of men compared to the disorganised band of kobolds.

Kairos soon saw why.

The first few Einar who jumped the gap between the ships were quickly cut down. The archers aboard the *Grenda* tried to shoot arrows at the dwarves, but they thumped harmlessly into the shields. Karthok bellowed in impotent rage as the dwarves continued to hack away at the first unfortunate few, leaving behind a bloody mess. The rest of the Einar crew could not join because the waves lifted and dropped the boats with each passing, and the footing, unstable in calm conditions, was treacherous on this day.

'Grappling hooks!' Karthok roared.

The second Einar ship, *Sea Serpent*, came, slamming into the other side of the dwarven ship, causing the dwarves on board to stumble again, and Karthok's men to seize their opportunity. The archers aboard the *Grenda* loosened shafts into the dwarven line, allowing their allies time to bridge the gap. Two men from the *Grenda* managed to tie the ships together, and the rest of the crew began jumping aboard. Karthok was one of them, yelling a battle cry as he launched himself at the dwarven shield wall. The third Einar ship, *Wolf Fang*, closed in, but the man steering the longship appeared to have difficulty in navigating the choppy waves.

The Einar from the *Grenda* and *Sea Serpent* began to pack onto the dwarven ship and form their own formidable shield wall against each side of the dwarves. Kairos breathed a sigh of relief as he watched from the aft of his ship. A battle at sea was like a battle on a narrow strip of land. Two sides usually made their shield walls, and the most precarious part was crossing into the enemy's ship, which the Einar had just accomplished, except they now had almost two full crews of Einar crushing the dwarves from both sides in a deadly pincer attack.

It was brutal chaos. There were shields clashing on the wide enemy midship, swords and axes swinging. Men screamed and men died, more dwarves than Einar, for the Einar fought with a fierce bloodlust and had the advantage in numbers. It seemed that the Einar would emerge victorious at this rate.

'Looks like quite the battle,' Thylar said with a grin, maintaining his position next to the tiller.

'Look,' Kairos said in awe, 'their shield wall is breaking. We have won.'

'Not quite.' Thylar watched the outflanked dwarven warriors fighting with the ferocity to match an enraged cyclops. 'As a warrior, you must be prepared for anything and everything in battle. Always expect the enemy to have a hidden tactic.'

Kairos nodded, though he doubted the dwarves could turn this battle around. Their shield wall had collapsed, and now they had a serious disadvantage. Something else caught his attention, too. The other Einar ship, the *Wolf Fang*, lingered a distance away, making no move to join the fight. His cousin, Viklo, the eldest son of Vinh, and Keng's older brother, commanded the ship. Even at the age of fifteen, Kairos suspected treachery. As far as Kairos knew, Viklo was an angry, jealous man known for losing his temper, and he held little love for Thylar or Karthok, and even less for Kairos. 'Why hasn't the *Wolf Fang* joined the fight?' he asked, already knowing the answer, but wanting to hear confirmation from his older brother.

Thylar's expression darkened. 'Bloody traitors,' he snarled. 'They're watching and waiting for the outcome of the fight... Maybe they're wanting us to soak up the casualties and pounce on us when we're weakened. This all must be because of Keng's death!'

Kairos stared at Vinh's longship, but a flicker of movement in front of him caught his eye. He looked up at the deck above the dwarves and saw that they were not alone. 'Thylar!' he said, pointing.

Thylar looked and nodded, looking grim and uncertain. Kairos knew something was wrong, because his brother always looked cheerful and confident. Thylar relinquished the steering oar to Kairos. 'Wait here with the archers. Be ready to cut loose and steer if we need to retreat!'

'But I want to go–' Kairos yelled, knowing full well that he couldn't steer the boat even on a clear and calm day.

His brother shook his head. 'The Einar at home are depending on our success. No matter what happens, you must survive.'

'What do you mean?' Kairos asked, but his brother barked an order for the archers to stay with Kairos and leapt aboard the other ship with his sword drawn and joined the fight. Kairos looked up again and realised what was on the ship's upper deck: beasts. They had the body of an enormous feline, and the head and feathered wings of a majestic bird. On their backs, they carried men who weren't dwarves, but somehow, they did not resemble Einar, either. Kairos could not tell who or what they were.

The beasts – more than a dozen – took flight, though some struggled in the battering wind of the storm. They soared over the ships and the sea, and their riders did something that Kairos had never seen before. The first rider raised one hand, as his mount flapped furiously in the windy rain, and orange-coloured light flashed brilliantly against the backdrop of clouds. It was followed by a volley of glowing projectiles raining down onto the *Sea Serpent*, which was still on the other side of the enemy ship.

Kairos could not believe his eyes. The bards' songs discussed magic, but he'd thought it was a myth, a song to awe little children. Yet, here before him he witnessed the dreadful myth come to life as it shattered the *Sea Serpent*, sending wooden fragments hurling outwards in all directions. Those that remained on the boat did not have a chance. Kairos instinctively took cover behind a sea chest, and when he looked up, only splintered pieces of the ship remained, floating on the waves. A few Einar survived the blast by jumping into the water beforehand, but they soon sank, weighed down by their mail. Kairos could not help but feel sympathy for them. Drowning was a horrible way to die. He did not dwell on their fate for long, however. He had his own concerns.

The winged beasts and their riders were still out for blood. Some flew after the *Wolf Fang*, which was now sailing away back in the direction of Logres. Kairos muttered a curse at his cousin, Viklo, who was leaving his Einar brethren to save his own hide. He did not watch his cousin's ship for long, however, because the strange flying creatures were now veering towards the *Grenda*, his ship.

'Archers!' someone yelled, 'Kill the flying beasts!'

The Einar archers on the *Grenda* loosened shafts at the flying beasts and their riders. Their aim struck true, and three of the winged-creatures floundered in the sky as they fell helplessly into the dark waters.

The archers continued to loosen more arrows into the sky, but the remaining beasts flew out of range, and a faint glow began to radiate from each rider. Kairos knew what was coming next and he needed to act.

As the archers on his ship made one last futile attempt to shoot down the flying enemies, Kairos drew his seax and leapt across onto the larger ship's deck just in time to avoid the explosion that rocked the *Grenda*. The concussion of the blast knocked him off his feet, and debris flew past him. Before he could rise, Kairos knew that the *Grenda* had been destroyed. Kairos had no time to think about the fate of crew left aboard either ship. He stood up and went to join his comrades on deck, but as he looked around, he found that many of the Einar were dead or dying. There were many dwarven casualties, too, but Kairos stared in paralysed horror as the enemy moved in for the kill.

Mad Mavos was right, after all.

The Einar continued to resist, Karthok being one of them. The large man continued to wreak havoc around him. He did not rely on the shield wall, but charged the dwarves, shield slamming one way and his sword bringing death in the other. At one moment, he was overwhelmed by the dwarven warriors, but there was a shriek of fury, a clash of metal on metal, and Karthok came out of the mass of men, his blade red and swinging, looking for more men to kill.

The other Einar held out as best as they could, but they had learnt that the dwarves, too, could fight. The shield walls had dissolved into an all-out melee. Kairos looked for his brother in the chaos. No one took notice of him yet, a small boy standing on the edge of a vicious battle. Then he heard the familiar war cry. Thylar was fighting two dwarves near the mast, his sword and mail covered in blood. He raised his shield just in time to catch an axe coming down on his head. The axe embedded itself, and Thylar pulled the shield, dragging the dwarf, who foolishly held on to the axe handle towards the other dwarven opponent. Thylar thrust his sword low from under the shield, catching the dwarf on his thigh, and brought the weapon upwards to cut into the groin. The dwarf screamed a terrible scream, like a woman in childbirth, and Thylar was attempting to pull his sword out when the other dwarf lunged.

'No!' Kairos screamed.

The axe came down onto Thylar's left shoulder – his shield arm. His brother let out a howl of fury and swung at the dwarf who attacked him. It was a good slice, across the neck, and the dwarf pulled away, taking the axe with him. Blood poured out of Thylar's wound, and more dwarves swarmed in, and Kairos saw his brother fall under the mass of bodies.

'Thylar!' Kairos cried, his heart lurching in his chest. The one person closest to Kairos had now fallen. Cheerful Thylar, who always cared for him.

With tears blurring his sight, the battle lust finally filled Kairos, he charged at the dwarves surrounding his brother, swinging his seax at the nearest dwarf, slicing through the leather padding and into his arm. Kairos followed with another swing, but the dwarf instantly turned and parried the blow with his sword, not looking the least bit hurt. Kairos soon saw why. The padded leather armour took the brunt of Kairos's attack, and the wound was barely a scratch. The dwarf, wearing a helmet with a skull face-piece, drew back for the killing stroke. Seeing he was fighting a mere boy instead of a grown man, he paused and laughed. Kairos was pissing himself in terror, but he launched himself at the dwarf again anyway, slicing at the neck, which the dwarf parried with ease, causing the seax's blade to bend. The dwarf saw this and laughed even more, then punched Kairos in the head, sending him sprawling onto the deck in a daze and landing in a wet mess of gore and entrails of a nearby corpse. The dwarf stood over Kairos with the tip of his sword pointed down at his chest. He paused as he stared down at the boy. 'Sorry, lad,' he said in a heavy accent and a remorseless tone. 'There is no glory in killing a boy, but Malus says that you lot cannot reach our shores.'

'Malus?' Kairos asked in a daze. He tried to focus, but his head seemed to explode in pain.

'Besides, no one cuts me and lives to tell about it.' And the dwarf raised his sword for the killing blow.

At that moment, lightning flashed in the dark clouds above, illuminating everything like daylight, including the interior of the skull's face-piece. Kairos could see the cold, dark eyes beneath that fearsome helmet that bore into his soul, filling him with fear. He knew that an Einar was supposed to stay and fight until the very end, but he also knew that this was a futile fight. This dwarf scared him, much more than his father even. Kairos howled the Einar war cry in a broken voice that sounded like a desperate shriek and threw his bent seax at the dwarf, who nimbly swatted the weapon aside, causing it to clatter against the deck and slide overboard into the sea. The boy scrambled to his feet, hoping that he was quicker, and did what few Einar would do: he ran.

He did not get far.

Something flashed from above, striking Kairos straight in the chest, knocking him onto his back. He screamed in pain as the electricity jolted his entire body. He could not move. Every muscle contracted and pain consumed his every thought, surpassing even the most severe beatings he received from his father. Then the pain suddenly stopped. Kairos realised that he was still alive, and better yet, he could move again. But he did not. He looked up and saw the dwarf standing over him, sword at his side.

*This is it!* Kairos thought. *He's going to kill me.*

Instead, the skull face was looking up at the deck, the source of the lightning. 'I didn't ask for your help, Captain,' he yelled at the tall figure standing on the deck above. 'We can win this fight without you elves and your bloody magic!'

'Then finish him off,' came the reply, 'or I will.'

Before the dwarf with the skull-faced helm could react, a vicious roar cut above the melee behind him. It was Karthok. He had left a pile of corpses behind him and was charging towards the dwarf standing over Kairos, who turned to face his new opponent in surprise. Kairos was surprised, too, because he didn't know that his father cared about him.

'Run, you stupid boy!' Karthok shouted, charging towards the dwarf with the skull-faced helm.

As Karthok neared his opponent, a crackle of energy struck him from the deck above. Even Kairos felt the shockwave of the blast, and as the blinding light subsided, he saw his father lying face down on the deck and unmoving.

He did not wait. He took advantage of the dwarf's distraction and scurried to his feet, breaking into a run towards the starboard side of the ship. The dwarf took a brief moment to react, allowing Kairos a slight head start. But he recovered quickly and anticipating the boy's move, rushed to finish Kairos off, but he stepped on a corpse's spilled intestines, causing his right foot to slide sideways and his sword thrust to miss. Whilst the dwarf was unbalanced, Kairos leapt over the side of the ship, landing into the tumultuous waters. For once, he was grateful that his father did not allow him to wear armour, because he was able swim though the treacherous swells. He looked up at the ship and saw the dwarf pointing and screaming in frustration. Another taller being ran next to the dwarf and traced a pattern with his hand. Kairos saw flickers of orange light and knew, this time, what was coming. He took a deep breath and dived under, swimming as far as he could. He felt the water around him tingle as the magic spell narrowly missed him, and he swam until he thought his lungs would burst. Fear and adrenaline kept him going, propelling him as far away from this nightmare as he could manage.

He emerged, gasping for air and choking on some water. When he was no longer coughing, he managed a look back and saw magical flares raining down upon the area he had just been moments ago. He dived under again and swam further away. He continued doing this until he could no longer see the enemy.

Kairos struggled to stay afloat in the storm. He escaped one danger only to face another: drowning. He prayed to Rudras for a miracle, not really expecting one.

But a small miracle came.

It drifted nearby in the form of what remained of the *Sea Serpent*. Or what he assumed was the *Sea Serpent*, for it could have been the *Grenda*, such was its condition. It was a good chunk of the port beam, overturned and bobbing on the crest of each swell. Kairos used the last of his strength to swim to it. A portion of the rower's bench remained with a length of seal-hide rope attached, and Kairos found that he could hold onto it and ride the waves, giving his worn-out muscles their much-needed rest as he caught his breath and waited for the enemy to come and kill him. Even at this distance, he could see some of the flying beasts and their riders gliding over the waters looking for survivors. An occasional burst of magic over the water showed that they found a few.

He waited for them to come. He was too tired to care if they killed him now, even welcomed it. He preferred death by them to dying from what awaited him at sea.

The rain continued to pour, but no enemy came. A large swell tipped over the broken aft that Kairos was on, but he held onto the rope and pulled himself back onto the rower's bench. The minutes flowed into hours, and after what seemed like an eternity, the storm finally abated during the night.

As he floated on the open sea, Kairos did not see any signs of the enemy ship, nor traces of the other survivors. He could only see the stars above, and the occasional flickers of lightning in the far-off distance. Away from the danger, he was able to calm down and consider his situation. He thought of his brother and fellow Einar who were aboard that ship.

*Dead. Everyone is dead.*

One minute, they were all sailing together, and the next they were all gone. He would never see Thylar again. He would never hear his laughs, or that warm booming voice as he rambled on about women and battle conquests. Kairos did not have many friends, and he did not like his father much, but now that they were gone, he truly felt alone for the first time in his life. He began to sob as grief and self-pity consumed him. He was glad no one was around to see him now, whimpering like a weakling, his tears falling into the endless sea.

Kairos drifted in the darkness, waiting for the end to come.

\* \* \*

Stretching languidly from performing the Meditation of Mana, Malus smoothed his black robes, and walking to the window of the Kinclaven Citadel, stared down at the execution yard far below, his grey lips pursed, his brow frowning. As if aware of the dark elf's stark scrutiny, the black-garbed executioner looked up at the Citadel window from the platform of the chopping block and nodded, then resumed running a whetstone against a massive axe.

Malus looked at the prisoners in the queue for the chopping block, their wrists bound by manacles, shackled to each other in a line – a long line, prodded along by soldiers in dark-plated armour. The prisoners faced their punishment in front of a mixed audience of dwarves, elves, dark-elves, gnomes, and a few odd humans. One of the prisoners, a human, followed the executioner's gaze to the where Malus stood, and he spat. Malus's frown deepened in annoyance. A Mana Knight, he thought. He would watch this man's fate with immense satisfaction. He hated all Mana Knights, especially those who dared to venture into his realm to commit espionage, and most of all, one who dared spit towards him. Fortunately, the wait would not be long. There were only two men before the knight.

Not all of the prisoners had death sentences. The first man in line, an obese dwarf, committed the petty larceny of a cask of ale, so he was to lose his right hand. The rotund dwarf cajoled and pleaded as he was removed from the line, but the guards shoved him forward and bound his arm to the block. The axe came down, and the dwarf gave a high-pitched shriek as he clutched the bloody stump where his hand used to be. The executioner kicked the pudgy, lifeless hand off the platform and called forth the next criminal, causing Malus to chuckle in glee.

It was a very short elf – almost as short as the dwarf – with chestnut hair and a squinty face. The elf was naked. Malus's lip curled in disgust, because he knew why. The elf's charge was forcible defilement of a young maiden, and he was going to lose something more valuable and painful than a hand. The elf sobbed for mercy, but one of the guards kicked him, whilst the other grabbed him by the hair and led him towards the block. There would be no mercy for him today. Even the executioner seemed to cringe at what he was about to do.

A soft, self-deprecating knock interrupted Malus as the executioner raised his axe, causing the dark elf to look away from the window towards the door. 'Enter,' he said in a mild, pleasant voice, though he heaved a sigh immediately after, scowling as his glance went to the window. He'd missed it. The elf was already doubled over, clutching himself and making the most pathetic of squeals.

The scowl was gone by the time his visitor appeared in the doorway. The light from the window flashed off the man's black leather outfit, gilt in silver and designed to adhere tightly to the contours and bulge of the male form. Leather creaking as he stepped into the room, a pale-skinned elf with hair of flowing gold, bowed in greeting from the open door. He then shut it carefully behind him, crossed the floor and stood before the dark elf, cradling his wing-crested helmet in his left arm. 'Captain Hargonnas of the Grimaldi Flying Squadron, my lord,' he began with a flourish, 'I'm here to report–'

'Wait,' Malus said, glancing out the window just in time to see the executioner bring his axe down upon that accursed Mana Knight. 'Ha! Serves you right, you fool. See if you ever spit towards me again!'

Captain Hargonnas, unaware of the execution, looked at the dark elf in confusion. 'I beg your pardon, my lord?' he murmured.

Malus waved a dismissive hand, and poured himself a glass of wine, offering none to the visitor – a lethal insult in all elven cultures. 'Don't worry about it. You were here to report something, correct?'

'Yes, my lord.' Captain Hargonnas bowed again. 'I am here to report another battle.'

Malus sighed in exasperation. 'Let the generals handle this matter. I don't have time to meddle with every minor scrap or skirmish–'

'I again beg your pardon, my lord,' interrupted the elf, taking a step forward in his earnestness, 'but it was not the Mana Knights this time.'

Malus stared intently at the man's face and noticed, for the first time, the serious and solemn intensity. His expression grave, the dark elf set the glass of wine down on the desk and gave the captain his full attention. 'Proceed, then.'

'We engaged an enemy' – the captain hesitated, appearing to brace himself for the reaction of the dark elf – 'who came from across the Dark Sea itself.'

Malus regarded the captain in silence, his face darkening. Captain Hargonnas, a man not easily cowed, licked his lips nervously in the presence of the unpredictable dark elf. He had witnessed Malus at his worst and shuddered at being on the receiving end of that anger... and power.

'What happened?' Malus asked.

'It was as you foretold, my lord. Humans came from across the sea and arrived in the waters off Cape Caipora where we had one of our ships waiting,' the captain replied. 'We meant to attack them first, but to our surprise, they sailed their three ships toward us, boarded our ship, and fought like demons, matching the ferocity of our dwarven warriors with shield, sword and spear. They might have emerged victorious had my griffon squadron not been there.' Captain Hargonnas laid emphasis on mention of his squadron in hopes that Malus would notice and recognise his use.

Instead, Malus's frown deepened. 'Humans attacking dwarves with sword and spear,' the dark elf muttered, clenching and unclenching his grey hand, a habit he had. The captain, having seen it before, was always reminded of a falcon seizing its prey, and he involuntarily took a step back.

'Yes, my lord. It was human shield wall against dwarven shield wall. Neither my men, nor the dwarves, have ever seen anything like it. They were large and powerful humans, with strength to rival a well-trained dwarf.'

The brows eased, the displeasure receded somewhat. 'Did they use magic?'

The captain paused in thought for a moment. 'No, my lord. I do not believe so.'

The dark elf frowned again. 'Are you sure?'

'Yes, my lord,' Captain Hargonnas hastened to assure him. 'As a matter of fact, these humans seemed shocked when we used magic on them.'

Malus raised an eyebrow. 'Go on.'

The captain nodded and continued, 'They stared at our spells like a herd of hobs watching a light orb.' He wiped more sweat from his forehead with the back of his hand. 'But what happened when our spells hit them surprised us, too.'

'What happened then?' Malus was fascinated in spite of himself.

'They resisted our magic!' the captain said in awe. 'Lightning bolts that should have killed them only stunned them. Flames that should have charred their entire bodies merely singed them. Our magic only provoked their anger, and they fell upon us. If my griffon squadron had not destroyed their ships with half of their men on them, the battle may have not gone in our favour, my lord.'

'So our men were victorious, I take it?'

'Yes, my lord. But the dwarves suffered heavy casualties. More than half. And I lost three griffons and their riders, and another two were injured–'

Malus waved his hand in dismissal. 'What about the enemy? Any survivors?'

Hargonnas bridled. 'Possibly, my lord.'

'What do you mean by 'possibly'?'

'We captured two who were severely wounded, but they may not live for long.' The captain saw Malus narrow his eyes and hastily added, 'the others fought to the death, and it was only because these two succumbed to their injuries were we able to capture them at all, my lord.'

'Just how severe are their injuries?' Malus's voice grated.

'One has been disembowelled, and I fear the healers aboard cannot do much for him. The other is still unconscious. He has lost a lot of blood.'

The dark elf swore, causing the captain to flinch and stare at the floor with a clenched jaw. If Malus saw the small act of defiance, he made no mention of it. After a long, tense pause, Malus asked, 'Where are they now?'

'They're still at sea on my ship, the *Grimaldi*, approximately a few hours from the coast of Cape Caipora.' The captain was now profusely sweating; it dripped from his face and landed onto his leather outfit, running down his body in black, glistening trails. 'After the battle, I flew here immediately on griffon-back to deliver you the news, my lord.'

'I see.' The bristling brows eased slightly, the displeasure receding somewhat. 'Cape Caipora.' Malus brooded in thought for a moment, then frowned again. 'Were all the enemy casualties accounted for?'

'Er... no, my lord,' the captain said sullenly. 'I presume some of them drowned at sea, when they jumped into the waters. We tried searching for them, but the storm was fierce and I didn't want to lose my griffon squadron to the elements. There is little chance that someone can survive in those waters for long.'

'You presume?' the dark elf said, his eyes reproachful.

'The seas were very rough in that storm—'

Malus stood up immediately, causing the captain to wince, but he turned his back on the visitor and walked over to the window to gaze at the execution yard below. But the punishments were far from his mind when he glanced back at the captain. 'Captain Hargonnas,' Malus began, calling the elf by name for the first time, which further unsettled the warrior. 'Wouldn't you agree that there's a possibility that at least one of these mana-less humans could have somehow survived?'

'Yes, my lord,' said the captain. 'It's a possibility.'

The dark elf began to pace back and forth in front of the window. 'It seems to me, therefore, that at least one of these humans could have reached the shores around Cape Caipora.' Hearing no response, Malus took an exasperated breath and raised his voice. 'Thus, there's a possibility that one of these humans could enter Ordonia, the land of our enemy and home of the Mana Knights, without being caught.'

'My lord, we combed the seas after the battle—'

'Did you talk to the two survivors, yet?'

'No, my lord.'

'Then there was no way you could determine how many humans were on those three ships, and how many humans are unaccounted for.'

'No, my lord.'

'Do you remember my warnings about these humans across the sea, Captain Hargonnas?'

The captain's expression changed from discomfort to one of confusion. 'That they will bring disaster, my lord?'

'Not just disaster, Hargonnas… A calamity!' The dark elf spread his hands upward for dramatic emphasis.

The captain, now completely lost, could only stare at his lord. 'My lord, if I may?'

'Yes, Captain?'

'After fighting those humans, I don't think they have the capacity to cause trouble to our army as a whole.'

Malus turned back to face the captain, and affixed him with a ferocious gaze, causing the captain to shrivel under its intensity as the air in the room tingled with a fierce magical energy. Most men would have dropped to their knees in terror. The captain remained standing, though very unsettled. 'I will only make this clear one time, captain. You serve my army to follow *my* orders – not think for me. I do the thinking. Do you understand?'

The captain took a step back from Malus, bowed his head and held it there. 'Yes, my lord.'

'Do not underestimate these humans. They are the Cursed Ones. They caused our ancestors much grief long ago, but we almost eradicated them, and the survivors fled out to sea. Our ancestors made the mistake thinking they would die there, but as you can see, that is not the case,' Malus said, noticing the shock on Hargonnas's face. He continued, 'I will not make the mistake of our ancestors. If these mana-less vermin from across the sea reach Ordonia, then we will have a problem beyond the comprehension of that egg-sized brain of yours.'

'Yes, my lord.'

With a thoughtful, pensive air, Malus clasped his hands behind his back, and the magical aura emanating from him dissipated. 'Therefore,' he continued in a low, deadly tone, 'I think it would be best if you inform the other ships of the fleet, gather the other griffon squadrons, and organise a large search party at Cape Caipora. If that was the closest piece of land where the battle occurred, I want you to sift through those sandy shores, comb through the forests beyond, and scour the rocks and mountains for any trace of the Cursed Ones. They must not be allowed into Ordonia!'

'Yes, my lord,' Captain Hargonnas said, summoning what was left of his pride and dignity and straightening his posture. 'If I may, my lord?'

The dark elf waved, allowing him to continue.

'The Mana Knights have a small outpost on Cape Caipora. Surely they'll object to our presence there.'

'Destroy them. The outpost is a lighthouse that is barely manned, and we don't need a bunch of knights digging into our business.'

'And the humans across the sea, my lord? If we find any, shall we slaughter them?' The Captain sounded hopeful.

'No.' The dark elf frowned. 'Try all means to capture them first. If that doesn't work, then you can dispose of them. Be sure to bring me the bodies for confirmation, and tell your men...' Malus paused in thought, then smiled. 'Tell your men that for each body discovered, I will pay five golden crowns. And for each live one discovered, I will pay fifteen golden crowns.'

Captain Hargonnas gasped in surprise. It would take him a whole year to earn fifteen gold crowns, much less a common soldier. 'Yes, my lord! I will tell them.'

'Also tell them,' the dark elf continued, 'that if they bring me a human corpse that is not from across the sea, then they will join the prisoners at the chopping block below.' Malus gave a shooing motion with his hand. 'You are dismissed.'

The elven captain, happy to have survived, breathed a sigh of relief, bowed and shuffled towards the exit as quickly as his leather-encased legs would take him. He reached the door and opened it.

'Wait,' Malus called out.

The armoured elf paused, turned and swallowed nervously. 'Yes, my lord?'

'Don't you wear that ridiculous ensemble in my presence ever again. Understood?'

'Yes, my lord.'

'Now go!'

The captain did not require further prodding. In his hurry, he inadvertently slammed the door shut, causing Malus to jump and scowl. He did not like the captain at all, but he was powerful in the magical arts and was cruel and efficient enough to get the job done. Still, he could not erase the image of the captain in his skin-tight leather trousers gilt in silver lining. He shook his head to remove the disturbing image, stood up and walked back to the window to look at the yard below. Already finished with the first half of the prisoners, the executioner and his assistants were piling the severed heads and body parts onto a cart. The dark elf sighed, his mind wandering far away from the gory scene. The news from the captain disturbed him greatly and rid him of all joy he received from watching the executions. Moreover, he did not trust the captain. He returned to his desk, sat down, and pulled out a journal.

*And so, in the year 964, almost a millennium after the Celestial War, the Einar attempted to cross the sea to return to Alban*, Malus wrote in his journal. *If even one surviving Einar makes it, then I fear the worst for my empire.*

\* \* \*

Kairos drifted along the waves in the bright sunlight. He shivered in the cold water and felt weaker by the moment. All he needed to do was let go and give up. He was too scared to do even that. He feared drowning. The idea of inhaling water made him cling to the broken piece of the longship with reborn desperation.

Regret haunted his mind. He should have given his life with honour. It was the duty of an Einar to fight to the last man… Not run away like his cousin Viklo. The memory of the *Wolf Fang* fleeing from battle, leaving the rest of the Einar to their fate made Kairos seethe with rage. Viklo was a coward! *Yet, I'm no different.* He'd fled, too. The image of dying in that battle of beasts and magic seemed less noble after he had seen his comrades slaughtered. It was not like the bard songs at all. He heard the screams of pain. Smelt the blood and shit of spilt guts. He was lucky to be alive from that battle, but if he did not live through this ordeal at sea, all would be lost.

He looked around the open endless sea. Water everywhere… and not a drop to drink. Thirst threatened to consume him. Hunger left him weak, whilst the cold water tempted to pull him under. He wondered which of these he would succumb to first.

As the sun fell, the sky turned a purplish pink. To Kairos it sounded as if the ocean was speaking to him, softly urging him to let go and slip into its dark depths for a long rest. Perhaps it was Rudras coming to take his soul. His mind began to wander, and he thought of Thylar; his brother's face clear in his mind, smiling and beckoning.

Other faces floated through his vision. His mother. His friend, Jonick. Mad Mavos. His father. He would never see them again.

His thoughts turned to the events of the last few days. He had learnt so many things on this voyage, saw many new things: serpents, flying beasts, dwarves, and magic — and lost so much because of them. Where did they come from? Did they live somewhere across the sea?

He lifted his head suddenly and coughed. He must have dozed off, his head slipping underwater briefly. He looked around tiredly at the dimming horizon. He thought he saw something. It was far away. Maybe it was a vision. His brother's last words came into his mind, 'No matter what happens, you must survive.'

Cold, parched, and hungry, Kairos wouldn't live for long out here, but he wasn't going to give up, either. He muttered a prayer to Rudras to take him towards what he had seen. Out in the desolate sea, it was his beacon of hope in the darkness.

# CHAPTER TWO

### Cape Caipora

*Cape Caipora, named after the fox-like people who inhabit the region. The Ordonians have long considered the caipora a nuisance to humanity and have all but driven them to extinction. Those remaining caipora hide themselves away in the forests and mountains near Cape Caipora, and avoid civilised races at all costs. A few small Ordonians settlements have appeared in the region in the past few decades, but it is still an untamed wilderness far from civilisation.*

*A History of Cape Caipora,* Professor Jomur

**G**ulliver left his living quarters, an old cottage of flagstone walls and a thatched roof, at the tip of Cape Caipora and started towards the lighthouse, which overlooked the sea from its rocky crag. Gulliver had found it beautiful when he had first arrived. That was then. Now he hated the place, hated the ocean. He wished to be anywhere else but here. Sure, the storm during the previous night provided a splendid view of lightning and surging waves, and he saw mysterious lights, as well, myriad oranges and reds on the sea's horizon. That was the highlight of his week, and eventually the strange lights subsided, and he could see nothing else.

The sky was clear today, promising another day of counting the birds. Gulliver thought about the strange lights of the previous night. They were not lightning flashes, but like powerful magic spells. Perhaps they were part of his imagination? They had to be, because nothing happened here, and there was no reason why there would be someone out at sea casting magic. He pulled a handkerchief from his pouch and wiped his face. The humidity here always made him feel oily – another of his many reasons to hate Cape Caipora. And speaking of oil, he had to store his armour in an oiled sack to prevent rust. He never wore it anyway. There was no need, because nothing threatened him out here except boredom.

As a low-ranking Wolf Knight, Gulliver should have been taking on missions to slay evil creatures rampaging the countryside or meting out justice for the innocent. Those grand schemes came to an abrupt end a few months ago, when Gulliver crossed an archduke. He punched the archduke's son who was drunk and terrorising the local populace at a tavern. The son cried to his father, who had friends of position and power in the Knighthood, and they took retaliatory measures against Gulliver, which led to his reassignment in lieu of being discharged altogether. His new assignment was the lighthouse at Cape Caipora, and his main mission to watch the sea for anything coming from across it, whether it be Malus's army or 'anything suspicious' that might lurk in its waters, and report it immediately. He shook his head in disgust; it was the same as chasing fairy tales. Everyone knew that there was nothing across the sea. The lighthouse at Cape Caipora was as old as the Knighthood, but every knight knew that it was a whipping post, a place to send the unwanted knights as a form of punishment.

Indeed, it was a whipping post, Gulliver mused. There were no young damsels or citizens to serve. His only company were a fellow knight, Tanton, who did nothing but complain, and a hound named Max, who was more pleasant, but did nothing but lounge lazily about and beg for treats.

'Stop chattin' nonsense, willya?' Tanton said at the breakfast table on the ground level of the lighthouse. He was also a Wolf Knight who had been assigned to the lighthouse for almost a decade, a fate he seemed to accept with contentment, though he never admitted the reasons for being sent out there: 'We don't 'ave to do nuffin' an' the fishin's blinkin' great.'

Gulliver eyed Tanton in disapproval, noting that the older knight appeared to have eaten his fill of fish, judging by his protruding girth.

'We are supposed to keep vigil of the sea...' Gulliver began, knowing it was useless to talk duty to the older knight. 'Haven't you ever wondered why? There's nothing out here.'

'That's the best part – there's nuffink at sea! Wot the 'eck is there to complain 'bout? Just eat, sleep, fish, an' play hounds-n-jackals. An' the drink.' Tanton took a swig from the mead bottle and belched.

'We're not supposed to drink mead while on duty,' Gulliver said with stern disapproval. 'How did you get that out here anyway?'

'Relax, mate. I 'ave merchant friends. Besides, dontcha worry 'bout it. Now wot was yer name? Gully, innit? Why dontcha make yerself useful an' watch the sea instea' of gripe at me like sum ol' naggin' housewive?'

Gulliver bit back the answer that he wanted to blurt out, which was something to the effect that Tanton had never been with a woman to experience the nagging, but he had learnt that any retorts rebounded harmlessly off the older knight, and only earned him more chores. Tanton was the senior knight, after all, and that meant he was in charge. Better to just do his job, which was observe the seas, and avoid Tanton in the process.

'Yes, sir,' he answered, gritting his teeth as he turned away. He did not know how long he could tolerate the older knight, who was lacking in morals, motivation, and very much all of the positive traits that were supposed to embody a Mana Knight. At least watching the sea did not anger Gulliver. The water and the waves did not indulge in ill habits or order him around like a servant, so he resigned himself to another dull day of watching the puffins and the waves.

He wished something would happen out there. Anything!

He climbed to the top of the lighthouse to begin his daily vigilance over the sea, cursing the luck of his life. He thought about how his fellow knights from the Academy were faring. They were probably embarking on adventurous quests, saving lives, and attaining their own bits of glory, he thought, whilst he rotted away into oblivion on this narrow strip of land, watching the ocean. He sighed in self-pity and looked up. The sky looked clear except for some clouds in the far west. He gazed down at the shore and blinked. He leant forward over the stone wall.

Debris. From a ship. Pieces of shattered wooden planks littered the shore. A shipwreck!

He raced down the stairs of the lighthouse to the living quarters where Tanton lounged and excitedly explained what he saw.

Tanton listened with droopy eyes and yawned. 'Prolly a fishin' boat. Nuffink to worry 'bout. These things 'appen. You can go an' see if ya like. Lemme know if there's any fishin' rods!'

Gulliver snorted in disgust and went to the sandy shores alone. He saw an oar, a broken cask, and part of a ship's hull. He walked farther along the beach, his heart racing. This was the most excitement he had experienced since his arrival at Cape Caipora a few months ago. But the scene also troubled him. What happened to the occupants of the ship? He shrugged away the morbid thought, instead focusing on what he could find. He saw another oar laying in the sand, and a few planks scattered further beyond. Then, he saw the serpent's head, broken off at the neck as if howling in pain and anger. *This is no bloody fishing boat,* he thought, letting out an involuntary shudder. He made the sign of Zemus in an effort to ward off the evil of the serpent's visage.

'Whoever these people were, they worshipped an evil god,' Gulliver muttered.

Uncertainty began to seep into his skin as he trudged along the sandy shore past the reach of the lapping waves. He expected to find something more. A corpse? Treasure? He continued searching and suddenly froze. Fresh footprints etched a path on the sand above the ebb of the high tide, leading away from the lighthouse and towards the forest.

He paused. Was someone shipwrecked overnight? Why didn't Max bark? He gave an involuntary tremor at the thought that this unknown person could have killed him and Tanton in their sleep. He gazed nervously at the forest in the far distance, wondering whether to report to Tanton first. No, he thought, better to leave the drunk knight to his drinking. Tanton wouldn't budge anyway, so Gulliver set out towards the forest alone. He grimaced when he looked at the ground. The heavy rains from the previous night made it a quagmire, and before long Gulliver became plastered with mud, but the footprints were apparently made after the rain, which made them easy to follow.

By the time he reached the inland forest, his legs burned from the muddy slog, and heavy clouds began darkening the sky from the west, threatening rain. He was loath to enter alone, because even during the clearest of days, very little light filtered through the gloomy interior of the woods.

Gulliver hesitated. The few locals inland told tales of caiporas, the dangerous fox-like people the region was named after, living within. These tales told how people went into the forests and wound up missing, never to return. This was their territory, after all. Tanton told him not to worry about the caiporas because they were harmless. That was easy for Tanton to say – he never ventured into the forest.

Gulliver tried to remain courageous. But he imagined caiporas, treants, and other malicious creatures lurking in the shadows. The large boles of the trees creaked in the wind. Rainwater dripped from the leaves above, echoing eerily. He wished he had brought his mana lance, but he'd left it at the cottage. He was capable enough with magic, but spells took time to cast and were less effective in close quarters, when blades, fangs and claws ruled the fight. At least he had his dagger should his magic fail; he gripped the hilt reassuringly.

He continued slowly into the gloom, looking around nervously as he tried to follow the tracks. A raven flapped its wings nearby, causing Gulliver to jump in alarm. He swore inwardly, and glared at the raven, who stared back. Gulliver traversed the narrow path and looked back. The raven still gazed at him with its cold, beady eyes. He shuddered and moved on. This was starting to become a bad idea. Perhaps he should have persuaded Tanton to come along, though how the fat knight would keep up was beyond comprehension.

As Gulliver trekked further on, he noticed that the sounds of the forest became quiet. He slowed his pace, for once thankful for the recent rains because the wet leaves made no crunching sound as he trod over them. There was something or someone ahead. He stopped moving and listened. It seemed something was trampling through the underbrush, but he could not be sure. He realised that he was shaking uncontrollably. Surely this must be a trap by the caipora to lure him here, or some evil treant coming for his soul. Gulliver crouched behind a tree. He tried to convince himself he wasn't being cowardly, but merely cautious. He looked out from behind the tree and saw it.

At first he wasn't sure what it was. The shadows of the trees obscured the creature. Was it just a person from the broken ship or something else? Gulliver recalled the fierce visage of the serpent and swallowed. Whenever there was one, there were many. He was on the verge of turning to flee when his curiosity overpowered his fears. He moved from his hiding place and crept forward. As he peered at the creature, he breathed a sigh of relief. It was not an evil spirit or a treant, but a mere boy. The sound of something crashing through the underbrush earlier was the youth clumsily trudging along the forest trail. Judging from the way he walked, he looked weakened or ill. He stumbled and fell. The boy picked himself up with considerable effort.

Gulliver made the sign of Zemus, crossing both his arms. He waited and watched, half expecting the boy to notice him and become a sudden threat. One could never tell out here in the wilderness. The boy fell again. This time, he did not get back up.

Apart from the mud-stained kirtle and trousers, there was little to indicate where the boy was from, except that he appeared human. He was fairly tall and lean, broad-shouldered for a boy. Maybe he was a surviving fisherman, or a peasant.

Months of inactivity had dulled Gulliver's quick wit and he mulled over what to do. He thought about running back to the lighthouse to tell Tanton. That would be the easiest option. But the stranger seemed very ill, and if he went back now, the boy was bound to get worse by the time he returned. He was likely to wander further away, or perhaps even die given his current condition. Also, Gulliver wondered if he should really help him. Maybe this boy was part of Malus's army. It was uncommon for humans to join the dark elf, but there were rumours circulating the land that Malus now had a fleet patrolling the seas – though Gulliver had yet to see a single ship. Yet, that would explain the frightening serpent prow. Or the boy could be a fugitive, because fugitives loved hiding in the wilderness. No one else in their right mind would come here, Gulliver thought.

Then he remembered why he had become a Mana Knight. It did not matter who this boy was; he needed help and a Mana Knight's sworn duty was to help those in need. Gulliver may have been punished and sent to a lighthouse in Cape Caipora, but he would not fail his duty. Perhaps it was Zemus's will that sent this boy here today.

With new resolve, Gulliver approached the inert boy. Just as he was about to give him a gentle nudge, the boy's eyes flickered open. They were dark grey, but glazed with fatigue and fever.

'Relax. I'm here to help,' said Gulliver, hoping the boy would understand.

The fevered gaze turned towards the young knight and focused for a brief moment in alarm.

'Don't worry. Allow me to help. You have my word that I mean you no harm,' Gulliver said softly, offering his hand.

The boy did not reply, but stared back. For an instant, Gulliver thought that he would attack or resist, but a moment later, the boy nodded and accepted the hand. With considerable help, he managed to get to his feet. He wobbled unsteadily and ignored all of the knight's questions. Gulliver sighed and guided him back to the lighthouse in hopes that he could help this young stranger. As they made their way out of the forest, he wondered how Tanton would react.

* * *

Kairos awoke slowly.

His limbs felt like the muscles had melted away, and his head pounded with each heartbeat. He opened his eyes. A tallow candle burned nearby, casting dancing shadows on the flagstone walls. Kairos tried to rise.

'Don't get up,' said a voice in a strange accent. 'Your fever has broken, but your body still needs rest.'

Kairos let himself sink back on what he guessed was a straw mattress. He lacked the energy for defiance and the voice did not seem threatening. Kairos tried to speak, but only croaked in his dry throat.

'Here, have some water,' the voice said, its owner coming into view next to the bed. It was a young man with a friendly face, uncorking a flask. Kairos felt the bottle neck of the flask brush his lips, and he swallowed a little of the cool water.

'Thank you,' Kairos said, trying to study the man next to him. He did not look like a dwarf, but did not quite resemble an Einar, either. 'Where am I?'

'Cape Caipora. I found you in the forest an hour's journey from the shore, in bad shape, I might add. My name is Gulliver.'

'How long have I been asleep?'

'Two days. Your fever broke last night. I thought we had lost you several times, but I managed to have you drink an elixir to help with the fever and the dehydration.' Gulliver seemed pleased with himself.

'Thank you.'

'Where did you come from? I saw the ship. You're not with the dark elf's army, are you?'

'Dark elf?' asked Kairos, uncomprehending.

'Sorry,' Gulliver said. 'That was rude of me. You're human, so it would be unlikely that you could've been serving in his army, but we must maintain vigilance.'

Kairos felt weak and empty, and this talk of dark-elves and armies tired him further. 'Is there anything to eat?'

'Of course.' Gulliver stood quickly. 'I should've offered you something earlier. I'll fetch some food.'

Kairos grunted and closed his eyes. He heard the young man move away and then pause.

'What's your name?' Gulliver asked from across the room.

'Kairos… Kairos, son of Karthok.' Kairos closed his eyes. It hurt too much to look around.

'Well met, Kairos, son of Karthok. Now if you'll excuse me, I'll get you something to eat.'

There was a pause, and then he heard Gulliver leave the room.

Kairos lay there, thinking of the recent events that crept into his dreams. His nightmares. It was all one big nightmare.

What would he do now? Despair as dark as the shadows of the room filled his soul. The Einar fleet was dead. He had found land across the sea, and even people, but he was all alone. Why had he lived when the others had died? How could he tell the others at home? He could not fulfil his mission alone and without a ship. And even if he were to return home, his uncle would now oversee the Azel clan and would most likely kill him. Kairos thought of his violent father, a man who had always beaten him. Now he realised that without him, he was nothing. The pain of losing Thylar ached worst of all. Was this his fate?

He truly was cursed. Forsaken by Rudras.

He heard someone return to the room, returning his thoughts to his current circumstances. His gnawing hunger was primary amongst them.

Gulliver had brought back a tray with bread and broth – along with the fattest man that Kairos had ever seen in his life. He was so surprised by the stranger's girth that he momentarily forgot his predicament. The man resembled a walking pig as he wobbled, out of breath, into the room. He sat on a wooden chair, which seemed to groan in agony under the burden, and glowered at Kairos.

'This is Tanton,' Gulliver explained sullenly. 'He is my senior and in charge of this post. Here is your food.'

Kairos struggled to sit up on the mattress, gawking at the newcomer and wondering how much food one had to eat to become so large. Was this land truly plentiful in food, as the Einar had hoped?

As Kairos ate, Gulliver talked incessantly. Kairos listened in silence, finding the talkative man's voice a pleasant distraction from his own woes. He noticed the fat man known as Tanton watching him with a dour expression, only changing it to take a swig from a large bottle in his hand. Kairos heard Gulliver talk about the Knighthood and their duties at the lighthouse, which included watching for ships or anyone out at sea.

After Kairos had finished his broth and scooped up the last crumbs of bread that fell on the tray, he asked, 'Have any survivors from my ship come this way?'

'No, you are the only one,' Gulliver replied, casting a glance at Tanton. The young knight returned his gaze to Kairos. 'Were there more of you?'

Kairos did not answer immediately. He wondered what had befallen those Einar who plunged into the sea. He knew that most wearing mail would have drowned, but maybe some of the archers could have clung to a wooden plank. That was unlikely, though. These two knights had found only him. Everyone that he had grown up with was dead. Darkness threatened to engulf Kairos from within, and he felt tears welling up in his eyes. He turned away so the two strangers would not see him for how weak he was, but he was unable to stifle the sobs.

Instead of ridiculing him for his moment of weakness like most Einar would have done, Gulliver surprised Kairos by placing a gentle hand on his shoulder. 'If I may ask,' he began in a soft voice, 'what happened to your ship?'

It took Kairos several moments to compose himself, but for some reason, this knight's kindness reminded him of Thylar, and he felt the need to tell him. 'We were attacked.'

Gulliver shot an alarmed glance back at Tanton, whose eyes widened, before turning back to Kairos. 'Who attacked you?'

'Dwarves.'

'Dwarves?' Gulliver said, looking aghast. 'What happened?'

Kairos told them about the ship full of dwarves and armoured figures mounted on flying beasts. He described the deadly magic flashes of light destroying all three longships of his people. Gulliver and Tanton listened in stunned silence.

'That was why I avoided your tower and went into the forests,' Kairos said. 'I expected the enemy to be here.'

'We are with the Knighthood.' Gulliver spoke gently, 'and we are here to help you.'

Tanton gazed at Kairos shrewdly, obviously not sharing the younger knight's benevolence.

'Tell us more about these dwarves,' Gulliver continued, 'from the sounds of it, they sound like our enemies.'

'They mentioned someone named Malum, or Malsis—'

'Malus!' Gulliver said, paling. He turned back to Tanton. 'We must light the signal fire. He was attacked by dwarves and elves in the Dark Sea!'

For the first time since entering the room, Tanton spoke, 'Now wait a minute. We 'aven't seen nuffink for sure, yet.'

Gulliver clenched his jaw. 'This boy saw them, and his ship is wrecked here. That should be enough!'

Tanton shook his head. 'Think 'bout wot yer doin' now, 'cause if ya light the fire, we'll bring the Knigh'ood, and they'll be askin' questions. Let's keep it quiet here, shall we? Come on, this boy is imaginin' things.'

Gulliver stood up and snarled, 'I've had enough of your negligence. I'm lighting the signal fire. You can sit there and drink, but it's our sworn duty to report any suspicion, and this warrants such!'

Tanton sat there dumbfounded for a moment, then he stood up and stared down at Gulliver, but the younger knight wasn't intimidated, holding his gaze with his senior. Kairos knew the signs and expected a fight, but after a few seconds of tense silence, the older, larger knight stormed out of the cottage without a word. Kairos did not entirely understand what was going on, but this matter was between two strangers. He was too tired to care.

The fury on Gulliver's face eased away once the older knight left. He placed a hand on Kairos's shoulder and said in a soft voice, 'Tanton and I have important matters to attend to. You should rest now. We'll handle this.'

Kairos agreed. He was exhausted; both his mind and body had suffered terribly. He lay down on the straw mattress and let out a long sigh. He heard Gulliver walking out and muttering something about returning later to check on him.

Within a few moments, he fell into a sleep without dreams.

*   *   *

Kairos awoke suddenly in the middle of the night.

For a few moments, he was unsure what had woken him. His body felt weak and cold, and he lay unmoving, listening to the gusts from the sea, battering the shore and the building. But there was something else. He sat up quickly. Somebody was opening the wooden door to the cottage. By Rudras, he wished he had a sword, or at least his bent seax, which now lay at the bottom of the sea.

A dog barked. Kairos knew that something was not right. Danger was near. He reached for something in the darkness, anything, to use as a weapon, only to find a burnt out candle. The wooden door opened allowing enough dim light from outside to silhouette the shape of someone. Kairos prepared to attack; he would not be killed without a fight.

'It is I, Gulliver,' the figure spoke, urgent and in a whisper. 'We must go. Follow me.'

'What's happening?' Kairos demanded, standing from the bed, his legs stiff and unsteady from days of inactivity.

'Ships are arriving. I saw their shapes in the moonlight from atop the lighthouse. If they're the same ones who attacked you, then I believe our lives are in danger. Come, they're almost here.' Gulliver tugged desperately at Kairos's wrist, pulling him to his feet.

Kairos felt light-headed. His legs almost buckled from his own weight, but he held himself steady with the help of Gulliver. As if to emphasise the potential threat, the dog's barks grew louder, and frenetic, and then were cut short with a yelp. Gulliver pulled Kairos to the door of the cottage, and together they stumbled outside.

It was dark when he'd passed through the first time, but Kairos vaguely remembered the layout of the surroundings from the sea to the forest. He looked up and saw that a bright fire burned at the top of the lighthouse, guessing it was the signal fire Gulliver was talking about. Its light reached below to the sandy shore, illuminating the ships in the distance. A group of men were marching towards the lighthouse bearing torches. They were still too far away, but Kairos knew they were dwarves, and he felt anger stir within. The dwarves coalesced around the entrance of the lighthouse. There was shouting and then a crash. Wood splintering.

Gulliver hesitated for a moment as he watched, but then turned and pushed Kairos forward. 'Hurry,' he hissed. 'To the forest!'

They took off at a fast pace. Kairos thought he would trip or stumble in the darkness, but there was enough light from the lighthouse's fire for him to find his way. The open ground before the forest was now soft and dry, but Kairos felt exposed out in the open and hoped that the signal fire would blind the attackers.

When they reached the cover of the forest, they heard a shrill scream from the lighthouse. Gulliver shuddered, tensed, and shoved Kairos forward with more intensity.

'Was that—' Kairos began.

'That was Tanton,' Gulliver whispered. 'He refused to leave.'

The ground on the forest floor was rough on Kairos's bare feet, and he wished he had a pair of boots on as he stepped on sharp twigs and stumbled into hard roots. Just as he began to slow his pace due to increasing pain, another scream rent the night, and he grimaced as he quickened his stride against the pain. Kairos dared a look back and saw through the trees some of the warriors moving towards the cottage he had left moments before. He could only imagine what those dwarves would do to him and Gulliver.

They traipsed through the underbrush as quietly and quickly as they could into the cold night. Thylar's last words echoed in Kairos's mind over and over.

*No matter what happens, you must survive.*

They spent the night travelling as far from the lighthouse as they could. They had a headstart, but knew their pursuers would come, especially since ground before the forest was soft and left tracks for anyone to see.

They followed an animal trail, dense with undergrowth in some places, and Gulliver had to resort to cutting a path. This act alone surprised Kairos, because the knight carried a spear that he called a 'mana lance', only it was short and sheathed like a dagger until he took it out and wielded it. Then the mana lance became long, and the spear tip resembled a sharp gem with a faint glow that sliced through the vines and branches as if they were made of warm butter. Kairos had never seen such a weapon in all his life and instantly thought of many questions, but he kept silent in order to not expose any lack of knowledge or weakness.

He did not trust Gulliver, yet, and his mistrust only deepened with what he saw next.

A very dense patch of underbrush blocked their path in the forest. Kairos suggested backtracking, but Gulliver shook his head. Instead, he lifted his hand and traced a pattern into the air with his index finger. A glowing image appeared, and a sudden stream of air whipped forth from his hand, cutting a path through the thick vegetation.

Kairos could not stay silent any longer.

'W-what was that?' he asked as loudly as he dared.

'What was what?' Gulliver misunderstood the question, then saw that Kairos was staring at the cleared, narrow path. 'Oh, the magic? A minor windcutter spell. Easy to do, really. You could probably learn it in a few months with the proper study.'

Kairos froze. The enemy who killed his comrades could also use this 'magic.' Thoughts swarmed around his head. Could everyone in this land use such trickery? Could he learn it? Would it save his homeland?

'Are you coming?' Gulliver snapped Kairos from his reverie.

'Y-yeah,' he mumbled, shuffling along the newly cleared path, thoughts of magic on his mind. He did not dwell on it all day, though. He soon had other concerns.

As the sun rose, casting dim light through the thick foliage of the forest, Kairos now limped along, his feet aching, and he was hungry and exhausted. He continued due to sheer willpower and the fact that he did not want to appear inferior or weak in front of Gulliver. The knight saw his struggles, however, and instead of mocking him for his shortcomings, he took pity and called for a short rest, setting up camp beside a stream.

The site was a steep, wooded bank with an overhang of earth and tree roots that provided them with not only shelter, but cover from prying eyes should their pursuers venture near. They miserably hunched under their meagre shelter, eating dried fish and stale bread that Gulliver had brought along and drinking from the stream to quench their thirst.

There was no sound of anything else nearby, except the trickling of the stream and the chatter of birds, so Kairos risked a whisper.

'Why are you helping me?'

After travelling for so long in silence, the young knight jumped at the sound of Kairos's voice. 'What do you mean?'

'What's in this for you? I have nothing to give you, and I'm only slowing you down.'

'It's my duty as a Mana Knight to help you,' Gulliver replied.

That answer did not help, but Kairos did not persist. He assumed Gulliver wanted something from him; no Einar would ever help a total stranger from the kindness of his heart unless there was something to gain. So be it, he thought. If the knight wanted to use him, then he would use the knight. The first thing he would do was learn as much as possible from him.

'Where are we now? Cape Caipora, you called it. What sort of place is it?'

Gulliver nodded as if pleased to engage in conversation. 'Cape Caipora was the promontory with the lighthouse. The most north-westerly point of Ordonia, garrisoned by the Mana Knights, just me and Tanton, really.' His face sank and looked down. '*Was* garrisoned, I might add. Malus's army now holds it.'

Most of this made little sense to Kairos. 'What is a Mana Knight?' he asked.

The young knight gave Kairos a quizzical glance. 'You don't know much, do you?' Before Kairos could answer, he continued, 'Mana Knights are the protectors of the godshards, and the defenders of justice. We promote peace throughout the land by aiding those in need. Come on, mate. Even the most outlandish country bumpkin knows what a Mana Knight is! Were you born inside a mountain, or across the sea?'

Kairos flushed in embarrassment at his own ignorance but said nothing. He listened to Gulliver explain more about the Knighthood, yammering on about peace and justice, which sounded like an odd concept to an Einar's ears. No one talked about peace in Logres, where the love of battle was shared amongst all clans. Then again, this whole land seemed odd to Kairos. Everything from the vegetation to the animals and creatures. Even the way Gulliver spoke sounded different. Kairos couldn't quite place it, his words took on a lilting intonation compared to the Einars' sharp way of speaking. He wondered what kind of gods these people worshipped, and if they even knew about Rudras.

'I suppose the Mana Knights and Magmus's army are enemies?' Kairos asked. The enemy of his enemy could possibly be a friend.

'It's Malus,' Gulliver corrected, 'and yes, he has been our enemy for more than fifty years.'

'Fifty years!' Kairos gasped. 'He must be a shrivelled, old man.'

'Shhh! Not so loud,' Gulliver hissed. 'He's an elf. A dark elf. They live much longer than we humans do… You really don't know much, do you?'

Kairos ignored the question. 'Who's going to stop Malus? Where is the rest of your army?'

Gulliver looked uncertain. 'In Vadost. We can only hope they saw my signal fire…'

'Signal fire?' Kairos asked. 'Was that the large fire you had atop the tower?'

'Aye,' Gulliver replied solemnly. 'It's the Knighthood's way of sounding the alarm to danger. The other citadels see our signal fire and light their own. This continues until the knighthood sends us help. That is, if they even saw my fire before Malus's army extinguished it.'

'How long will it take for them to come?'

'At least a week, I suppose,' said Gulliver grimly.

'We'll be dead by then!' said Kairos.

'We can make it,' Gulliver said, clapping Kairos on the back reassuringly. 'We have to keep moving, otherwise they'll catch us.'

'Like the other knight?'

'Aye.' Gulliver's face paled at the mention of Tanton, but he shook his head and looked up. 'What about you? Do you have family?'

'I did,' said Kairos. 'They're gone now. I'm all alone.' He gritted his teeth, fighting back the tears. If his father were here, he would have cuffed him.

'You're not alone now,' said Gulliver. His teeth flashed in the gloom.

Kairos forced a smile, but deep inside he felt empty and lost.

The song of the birds in the forest ceased. Something momentarily blotted out the sun's light trickling above the canopy. Kairos peered up. A beast with a large wingspan soared over their campsite and across the stream. A rider sat on its back watching the ground below. Gulliver grabbed Kairos and pulled him further into the dark shadows of the earthen overhang on the bank.

'A griffon-rider,' the knight hissed. 'Get back or he'll see you!'

As soon as he uttered the warning, more griffon-riders flew over. Kairos willed them not to detect their hiding place. Gulliver held still in the corner of the overhang.

The griffon-riders flew so low that they almost brushed the treetops, and Kairos and Gulliver could smell the beasts, but none of them seemed to look in their direction. The sight of the winged beasts brought back the memories of Kairos's battle at sea, the fear he felt back then had now returned. His whole body trembled.

After some time, the pair dared to breathe again. They waited a while longer after the last griffon-rider flew by before cautiously venturing out of their hiding place and peering around. There were no signs of the flying creatures, and the birds had resumed their singing, but the pair feared it was only a matter of time before the dwarves caught up. They were both stiff. Kairos still felt weak from his fever and found it hard to stand. His breathing was laboured as he concentrated on overcoming his dizziness. 'Where shall we go?' he dared to whisper.

'Those griffons were heading east,' said Gulliver. 'Downstream leads to a settlement to the south, though it's a bit of a longer route to Vadost. It's called Milbrooke. We can replenish our food there, and walking in the water will mask our trail.'

'Vadost?' Kairos asked. He had heard Gulliver mention that word before, yet there were many words not making sense to him lately.

Gulliver sighed like a parent explaining something to a child. 'It's the second largest city in Ordonia. The Mana Knights have a strong presence in a stronghold nearby. Malus's army would not dare attack there, so that's where we need to be.'

Gulliver offered his hand to Kairos who was still unsteady on his feet, and together, they waded downstream. Kairos struggled to keep up with Gulliver. He wished he still had the boots he had left at Cape Caipora. The soft, sandy bottom of the stream provided some relief to his feet, which were beginning to form blisters on the bottoms, but trudging through the water slowed their pace significantly. Although it was difficult to walk, the wonders of the flora and fauna around him took his mind from the pain. He did not know that so much green could exist in the world. The birds even seemed happy. The Einar would love it here, he thought sadly.

They followed the stream for the remainder of the day, taking shelter in what Gulliver claimed was an abandoned Caipora den underground, still filled with primitive furniture, a bundle of furs, and some crockery that was apparently stolen from humans. Gulliver discovered the dwelling by accident after he tried unsuccessfully to catch a rabbit for dinner. In the furthest depths of the den, Kairos found the skeletal remains of a humanoid creature that was almost his size.

'Probably died of old age.' Gulliver prodded the skull with the tip of his mana lance, which was partially extended. 'It's very odd that it lived alone. Caiporas usually live in large families.'

'We should bury it,' Kairos suggested, 'so we don't anger its spirit.'

The knight paused and raised an eyebrow but shrugged. 'Very well. Where do you suggest?'

'Outside, since we're staying in here.'

Gulliver did not argue. They buried the skeleton in a shallow, sandy grave near the stream, and ventured back inside the den. Kairos found a dagger, which also seemed to have been stolen from humans, and took it for himself. The blade provided him a sense of relief and security, for any Einar without a weapon felt naked and exposed.

The pair spoke very little that night, since the day's journey had sapped them of their energy. Gulliver's plan to go south seemed to have worked for they heard no signs of the pursuers, but they dared not risk making more noise than necessary. Hunger was their immediate concern. They had eaten the remaining food Gulliver had brought along, and now their stomachs growled pitifully. Kairos feared starvation would kill them before their pursuers could. At least they had a bed tonight, if rather earthy, using the bundle of furs for warmth.

The following morning, they left the caipora den and resumed their journey south. Kairos wondered if the forest would ever end; it stretched further than the largest isle in Logres.

'We should be arriving at Milbrooke soon,' Gulliver said, as if reading Kairos's thoughts. 'We'll fill our bellies soon.'

It was late evening when they finally came to edge of the trees. Kairos's hopes sank as he smelt the smoke in the forest before seeing it. They emerged to a great expanse of rolling hills, which would have been beautiful on any other day.

'Dear Zemus,' Gulliver gasped, making the sign of his god. 'What happened?'

They saw the source of the smoke – the charred remains of what was once a thriving settlement.

Milbrooke was no more.

* * *

The small settlement – what remained of it – nestled in the bend of the stream. The buildings with walls made of finely hewn rocks still stood, though their thatched roofs had burnt away. The charred beams of the other buildings stood out like blackened skeletons, smoke billowing out from their remains. Only one dilapidated barn had escaped the flames, perhaps due to the attackers feeling it was already damaged enough on its own. The dead were heaped on the ground near the dwellings, some charred, others butchered. Some corpses lay on the outskirts of the settlement, a pitiful attempt to flee the attackers, but none had made it far. Whoever killed them was much faster.

'Dear Zemus,' Gulliver said again, covering his mouth.

War memories of Logres flooded Kairos's mind at the scene before him. The Einar attacked each other and razed settlements, but they did not wantonly slaughter the women and children like this. Instead, they took them as thralls to serve the victorious clan. As he saw the charred body of a little boy, a slow anger began to boil within him. This was butchery.

'Why do they kill the children?' Kairos asked.

'Malus and his army despise humans.'

Sensing no sign of the enemy, the pair entered the settlement in silence, both fearing what other atrocities they would find within. Gulliver walked past the corpse of a middle-aged farmer, cut in half. His torso, with its gut lines, soaked the earth whilst the legs lay nearby, bent at odd angles. The young knight hurried away a few paces and vomited. When he was finished, he gazed at Kairos in shock.

'W-what are you doing?'

'Taking his boots,' Kairos said. 'He doesn't need them anymore, but I do.'

Gulliver frowned, but said nothing as Kairos tugged the pair of boots off the dismembered legs. Kairos knew the knight disapproved of looting the dead, but the Einar had always looted corpses after a battle. Spoils of war. He tried on the boots and discovered that they were a little loose, given that the farmer was a grown man, but he could walk around fine and the lining inside felt comfortable on his travel-worn feet.

They went to the first large building. Its walls, made of stone, were now blackened from the soot. Near the entrance, the burnt bodies of a couple huddled together, embracing each other in death. Gulliver mumbled something under his breath, but Kairos couldn't make it out. He cast a glimpse at the young knight, whose tears had begun to roll down his scruffy cheeks, leaving salty furrows in the grime. Kairos looked away and back to the building they had just reached. It was getting dark now, and Kairos strained to see in the gloom. Nothing could have survived here. Whatever food there must have been was burnt.

'We shouldn't tarry here,' Gulliver muttered.

Kairos nodded. There was nothing here except death. He had been hungry earlier, but the sight before him made him lose whatever appetite he had, leaving only weakness behind. As the pair readied to leave, they heard a horse whinny from the dilapidated barn, causing both to jump at the sound.

Gulliver stealthily unslung his spear. 'Can you fight?' he whispered.

'A little,' replied Kairos, drawing his recently acquired dagger and wondering the same thing about the knight. For an adult, Gulliver's face had the soft look of a boy, and his body lacked the chiselled physical conditioning and size that the Einar took pride in. But Kairos would take any ally now than face whatever danger lurked nearby alone.

His hand shook. Was there an enemy still in the barn, waiting to ambush them? Or did the attackers simply leave a horse behind? He did not ask the questions on his mind, but silently moved forward with Gulliver; two cats stalking their prey. Kairos was not sure what the knight planned to do, but he felt his own blood rise at the anticipation of action. These past few days of travel and self-reflection wearied his soul, and here was a chance for him to do something – redeem himself, at least.

Gulliver's brows furrowed in pure concentration as he clutched his mana lance tightly. The tip of the spear was made of a blue stone, which gave off a faint glow as the entire spear lengthened to six feet. The knight no longer looked like a soft, innocent boy as he nodded for Kairos to move forward. They crept towards the barn, using an overturned cart and the boles of the remaining trees for cover, spreading out to approach the barn from two different angles. Another horse whinny gave them a heartbeat's pause.

Kairos did not think. The wave of battle lust descended upon him. If there was an enemy inside, he would take his revenge, thinking of Thylar, the crew on the *Grenda*, and the slaughtered villagers of this town. He didn't care if he was outnumbered, and he didn't care if he was going to die. He wanted there to be a score of dwarven warriors inside to fight, because if he could lash out at them, then each slash of his dagger would cleave away at the guilt that had been gnawing at him ever since he escaped Malus's army at sea.

Gulliver tried to motion Kairos to wait, but the young Einar ran into the barn, dagger ready for blood. Once inside the shadowy interior, he didn't find the dwarven warriors, a griffon, or its elven rider.

He found a girl around his age, huddling protectively over a smaller boy, who was next to a brown mare, all three looking fearfully at him.

* * *

Captain Hargonnas patted his griffon on the neck and congratulated himself for the successful raid on the town, which yielded a plump reward for his men. The townsfolk of Milbrooke did not put up much of a fight, and those that did were easily defeated.

Hargonnas had been itching for a fight. He wanted to prove himself to Malus by locating the boy from across the sea along with his knightly companion. There were only two settlements near Cape Caipora that those two could travel to within a week: Milbrooke and Gersholm. Captain Hargonnas anticipated that Gersholm, being closer, was the obvious route for the two fugitives, but his instincts told him they would go to Milbrooke, especially if they managed to see the griffons flying eastward from the forest.

'We shouldn't attack Milbrooke,' his Sergeant, Selkis, had warned him. 'We should conceal ourselves and observe. They will appear before long and we can capture them when they leave.'

The captain seethed at the memory. He was not going to allow some inferior to tell him what to do. Sergeant Selkis was jealous, because Hargonnas had managed to rise to the rank of captain despite being the son of a tailor and a light elf. Selkis was the son of a prominent dark elf lord, yet he did not command the magical power that Hargonnas did. He saw the hatred in the sergeant's violet eyes and knew who to watch out for when his back was turned.

So he attacked Milbrooke. His men were frustrated and restless after raiding the lighthouse to find only a paltry store of food and a fat, bloated knight who squealed like a swine before slaughter. He grovelled before Hargonnas and told everything he knew about the visitor from 'across the sea' along with his knowledge of the Knighthood – which wasn't much. Unfortunately, listening to the snivelling knight wasted time, and the other knight and the boy had escaped. His men's morale plummeted after scouring the forests in an unfruitful search. Therefore, the attack on the village cheered them up immensely, the loot and carnage applying a much-needed salve to the boredom festering amongst them.

The light elf also had logical reasons to back his decision. The young Mana Knight and the boy were probably hungry, and they would find difficulty in finding food or hiding in a charred and empty village. Moreover, the Mana Knights had probably seen the signal fire at Cape Caipora and sent reinforcements, so time was of the essence. Of course, he would have some explaining to do about raiding a village without Malus's approval, but the reward for capturing or killing the boy would far outweigh the consequences. Malus would soon see that.

This is the best course of action, he told himself.

'Captain Hargonnas, I bring news.'

The fair-skinned elf looked down at the scout below. A lithe, young man. 'What is it?'

'The boy and the knight have been sighted entering the village. It looks like they plan to stay the night in the barn. Shall we attack now?'

Hargonnas smiled, adjusting his helmet that was crested with raven wings, his leather outfit creaking in the process. 'Not yet. Let's give them a few hours to settle in for the night.'

'Yes, sir.'

This *is* the best course of action, Hargonnas told himself again.

He hoped he was right. He'd show them. But first, it was time to let his men have a little fun.

\* \* \*

'My name is Farina,' said the girl, who appeared just a little older than Kairos. 'And this is my little brother, Henrik.'

Kairos noticed that the girl spoke with the same lilting accent as Gulliver. The boy remained silent as his sister clung to him, both lost in grief that Kairos understood all too well as he thought of Thylar.

After barging into the barn and realising there was only a girl, a little boy, and their horse, Kairos suddenly felt sheepish. Gulliver entered a moment later with his spear extended and the spear point glowing brightly, causing the siblings to cower. Once he identified himself as a Mana Knight, they relaxed, and to Kairos's wonder, they looked slightly relieved. Did the people of this land look to the Mana Knights as their saviours? It seemed so, because Farina expected no danger from them, but she still seemed afraid.

'There's no need to worry,' said Kairos. 'I won't let any harm come to you.'

He felt foolish as soon as the words left his mouth. His face burned and he looked away, uncertain what to do; he didn't know why he'd said such a thing. But Farina placed a gentle hand on his arm.

'Thank you,' she said with a gratitude that reflected in her eyes.

He tried to think of something more rational to say, but nothing came to mind.

Fortunately, Gulliver broke the silence by offering to help tend to the dead first thing in the morning. He asked what had happened, and Farina told her story:

The griffon-riders had come a day ago whilst she and her brother were gathering berries in the forest. They heard the screams from far away and returned to find the village in flames. Hiding in the tree line, they saw elves finishing off the survivors. After the elves looted the village, burning what they could not take, they left on their griffons. Farina and Henrik waited a long time, but the elves did not return, so they entered the village and found the only survivor was the brown mare.

'Now we have nowhere to go,' Farina said, putting her arm around her little brother. He shuddered convulsively and began to sob.

Gulliver listened with grave concern, and Kairos clenched his fists with barely contained rage.

'How many griffons were there?' Gulliver asked. 'Which way were they headed?'

Farina looked puzzled. 'I don't really know. It seemed to me that the elves flew to the northeast.'

'We can leave for Vadost in the morning,' the young knight said. 'There is nothing here anymore, and it's too dangerous for just you two.'

Farina and Henrik nodded.

Gulliver looked around the barn. 'We'll stay here for tonight. Is there any food left?'

'I have these.' Farina pulled out the nuts and berries she and Henrik had gathered earlier. When Kairos held out his hand to take her offering, his gaze met with her pale blue eyes. For a moment, he forgot his anguish and stared at her in unabashed wonder. He had never before seen eyes of such colour; Einar eyes had darker hues, ranging from brown to amber.

He only came back to his senses when he dropped the berries she was trying to give him. 'Sorry,' he mumbled, immediately stooping down to gather them. 'Thank you, Farina… Thank you, Henrik.'

Despite her grief, Farina offered a wan smile. Henrik nodded.

They all sat down on the hay-strewn floor of the barn, and as they ate, they spoke of less unpleasant matters. Farina said that their father was a miller, and she and Henrik worked at the watermill, which now lay destroyed across the stream. Their ancestors were also millers, and they had founded Milbrooke, basing the village name on their profession and the stream running through the centre. Henrik listened in silence, watching

Kairos and Gulliver, as Farina explained how they had never travelled beyond Gersholm.

'I'm eager to see Vadost,' she said. 'We have nothing left here.'

Throughout the conversation, Kairos watched Farina, and he often found her looking back at him. Despite the grief that contorted her features, she was extraordinarily beautiful. She wore a green kirtle over a white dress and brown leather boots. Her long, strawberry blonde hair was pulled back with a matching green headband, and the flowing locks reminded Kairos of Vay, the golden orange moon. She looked completely different to any Einar girl Kairos had ever known; much fairer. He wasn't quite sure how to put it into words, but this girl had something that was lacking amongst the women in the warrior race – a sort of delicacy and elegance.

'Kairos has also lost his family from Malus's army,' Gulliver explained.

Farina shot Kairos a look full of concern, something else that was rare in Kairos's world: compassion. The only two people who had ever given him the same look were Thylar, and their mother when she was alive. Farina was about to speak, but stopped, placing her hand on his instead, her eyes welling up with tears.

'Perhaps the Knighthood can find the three of you a home,' added Gulliver.

'I can help you and Henrik,' Kairos offered, brightening at the idea of being with Farina. She, too, shared a similar degree of suffering and tragedy. His heart ached for her and Henrik, and he wanted to cheer them up.

Farina's eyes met with Kairos's. 'I would like that.'

Gulliver saw the exchange and cleared his throat. 'We should get some rest, so we can move out before sunrise.' His gaze flickered over to the open doorway to the outside as if expecting danger. 'The sooner we get to Vadost, the better.'

Everyone agreed. They finished eating and Kairos joined Farina and Henrik in rearranging the straw they gathered into makeshift beds, all the while stealing glances at Farina. Henrik was not oblivious to the attention his older sister was attracting, but clearly did not know how to stop it. Instead, he scowled at Kairos in silence.

As the night carried on, a light drizzle began to fall. Kairos was thankful for the meagre shelter the barn provided. There were many leaks, but they would remain dry tonight. Farina shared more of the berries and nuts foraged from the previous day. Her hand brushed Kairos's when she handed them over, warm and soft, causing his heart to flutter and his ears to burn. His brief encounter with Farina brightened the clouds of despair that had overshadowed his whole journey.

They readied to sleep, and Gulliver agreed to take the first watch. They finished the remaining food, and Henrik complained of being thirsty. Farina found a wooden pail and stood up to get water from the stream, but Kairos offered to go in her stead. The stream was on the other side of the settlement, and Kairos did not want Farina to venture out into the dark.

'Be careful,' she said. 'It's not safe at night.'

'I'll be fine.' Kairos brandished the dagger for extra show. He felt brave inside the barn, but once he ventured out alone, into the settlement that smelt of death, his courage withered away with the drizzling weather.

He went down to the stream to wash himself as best as he could. The bitterly cold water soon made his hands numb. He splashed the icy water on his face to remove the dirt from the days of travel. Now that he'd met Farina, he suddenly felt conscious of his appearance. He felt a strong urge to protect her, help her. In his dark world of violence, he would never forget that kind look she gave him. It was genuine, warm, and caring. So different from how the Einar had treated him.

Kairos had not been away for long, when he heard a shout and a scream pierce the night air. He jumped up and ran back. To his horror, he saw torchlights ahead and as he drew closer, he saw the armoured men swarming the barn.

The flickering light from the torches within illuminated a nightmare scene. He saw two men straddled over the struggling form of Gulliver. The torchlight made their faces distorted, monstrous, but Kairos realised that they were the griffon-riders – elves – with skin the colour of scorched wood, working on Gulliver's body with their knives. As Kairos watched in horror, one of the elves sawed at the knight's hand, then held up a severed finger in triumph, a look of malicious glee on his face. Gulliver screamed and thrashed, but the elves held him down.

Kairos looked towards the other side of the barn and saw Farina. She was pinned down against the ground by a grey-skinned elf. He held a dagger in one hand, and her long blonde hair in the other, as if preparing to saw away at her. She struggled against her captor, but the elf slapped her hard, and a trickle of blood poured from her lip. That was when she noticed Kairos.

Henrik cowered, wide-eyed in the corner of the barn. The brown mare was gone.

The elves had not yet noticed Kairos. He could have run. Escaped. It was his chance to evade his captors, and the Einar were depending on him to return. This land was lush and rich, perfect for the continued survival of his people. But was fleeing to survive a warrior's way? Gulliver had risked his life to help Kairos. Farina had shared her food with him. Was this how he would repay them? By leaving them to a grisly fate?

Farina's eyes pleaded with Kairos. Tears streaked her face, glistening in the firelight. Gulliver's cries of pain filled Kairos's ears. The elf over Farina lowered the blade against her, muttering something in his language. She clenched her eyes shut in an attempt to blot out what was happening.

Kairos thought of Thylar. His brother had tremendous strength, and had used it to crush his enemies and protect his little brother, not to thrive on violence against women and children. Not like these elves.

He could not allow this to carry on. He would never be able to face Thylar in the afterlife if he ran away and did nothing. He wasn't sure he'd be able to live with himself. Thylar had seen something in Kairos, enough to force Karthok to take him along for this voyage – an expectation to be a great warrior? If he was to live up to that expectation, be worthy of his brother's praise, Kairos had to act now.

Without hesitation to consider the consequences, he stepped into the barn, drawing the dagger he had found in the caipora's den. In his haste, he did not see the two elves waiting inside the doorway. Too late, Kairos realised it was an ambush. What a fool he had been! Of course, they'd know he was coming. The two elves reached for him and almost seized him, but he twisted away and charged at the elf standing over Farina, and lunged. The blade plunged into the side of the elf's grey-skinned neck, and Kairos slashed it outwards, tearing through flesh. The elf grabbed at his throat and made a gurgling sound as blood poured out of the gaping wound. One of the elves atop of Gulliver stood up to face him. Kairos felt the air around him change and knew it was magic. He had to act quickly.

Before he could do anything further, Kairos felt a jolt of pain tear through his body, followed by something crashing into the back of his head. His ears rang and his vision blurred. He fell onto the straw, struggling to get back to his feet. His blurry vision caught the shapes of several elves surrounding him. A swift kick to his side left him gasping for air. Another kick struck him full in the face, sending him onto his back. He tried to get up, but an elf kicked him back down and punched him in the face. He knew he was going to die, but at least he'd taken one of them with him.

'Look at me,' said the elf atop of him.

Kairos opened his eyes and saw the blurry vision of a blade levelled at him, the tip poking into his throat. The elf appeared to be the leader, judging by his wing-crested helmet, and he looked like a dark warlord death-bringer woven from a bard's story of nightmares.

'You killed one of my soldiers. Now I'll kill you.'

'No!' Kairos heard Farina yell.

Shaking free of her captors, she jumped onto the elf, knocking him off Kairos. A brief struggle ensued, but it was over quickly. The elf overpowered Farina and, in his rage, stabbed her repeatedly. Farina clutched her midsection where a crimson stain was growing on her kirtle. The elf stepped back as she crawled away from him, leaving a trail of blood in her wake. Kairos tried once more to rise, but another unseen kick to the head sent him back to the ground.

Farina crawled towards Kairos, and their eyes met. As his vision faded, his last thought was of her – and that he had failed her.

# CHAPTER THREE

## Gersholm

*D'Kari, the nation of the foul dark elves, and Salforia, the nation of the benevolent light elves, have been geographical neighbours from time immemorial. The dark elves are saturnine and glowering, aloof, and quite conceited. The light elves are pale of skin and fair of hair, quick with a laugh and very receiving of this scholar. Curiously, though diametrically opposed in everything, they have enjoyed a lasting peace. The light elves maintain this through military might, and the dark elves do naught but maintain neutrality. Although this scholar has yet to uncover the reason for it, this policy of neutrality has begun to shift in recent years.*

*Elven Culture and History: Vol. IX,* Lysandofer Galatius

**T**he next morning, Kairos awoke in agony. It was still very early, as the sliver of dawn was lighting the sky, and he was surprised to be alive.

He ached all over, his head pounding from the blows he'd received. His ribs felt cracked, broken, even. Each breath caused him pain. He could not move his arms much either, and realised they were bound behind his back. He slowly worked his way into a sitting position. There was a wall behind him, which he leant on. Straw, blood-soaked, was on the ground, and was wet from the morning dew. He looked around the barn and immediately saw the elves. Some were sleeping. Two were on watch sitting by the doorway. Then he found Farina.

She was dead. Her mutilated corpse was unrecognisable save for her bloodied clothes, and someone had scalped her beautiful golden red hair.

Kairos squinted his eyes shut, trying to cast the ghastly sight from his mind. But he couldn't. Even with his eyes closed, he could see *her* dead, unseeing eyes staring at him. Feeling the bile rise in his throat, he leant over on his side and vomited.

He didn't have long to recover, because the elf with the wing-crested helmet marched into the barn holding Gulliver's mana lance and yelled something in a language Kairos didn't understand. It sent the other men into a flurry of activity. One elf prodded Kairos with a boot to get up. No amount of prodding could get Gulliver up, and when Kairos looked, he gasped and saw why. The knight looked dead, his face plastered with blood, but the elves continued riling him and he eventually stirred. The elven captors lifted him up roughly and steadied him with strong arms.

Kairos's entire body ached, but he knew his pain was nothing compared to the knight's. Gulliver's eyes were swollen shut, his face coated in dried, congealed blood. Remembering the events of the last night, Kairos looked down at Gulliver's hands. He was missing the fingers of his right hand, crimson-soaked bandages covering the stumps.

The elves marched them out. Kairos chanced one last look at Farina. Tears flowed unchecked as he etched the ghastly sight forever into his memory.

\* \* \*

Later that day, Kairos found himself backtracking through the same forest he and Gulliver had just crossed. The young Einar walked morosely along, lost in a daze, tied to Gulliver and Farina's little brother, Henrik. He wished the elves had killed him. He could not understand why he lived.

Bruises covered his entire body. The back of his head seared with pain if he moved too quickly, and breathing still caused him to wince, although these wounds did not bother him as much as the wounds of his soul. He thought of Farina. Perhaps if he had submitted to the elves from the very beginning, they wouldn't have killed her. Had he caused her brutal death?

Brooding over the scenario kept him silent and obedient throughout the day.

By the evening, the elves set camp in a small clearing in the forest. They tied Gulliver and Kairos to a tree and set a guard a few paces away. Most of the griffon-riders had flown on ahead whilst the small squad traversed the forest. Some, including the leader, stayed behind with the prisoners in the camp. It became evident to the prisoners that the only reason they travelled by foot was because there was no room for them to ride on the griffons. The elves deemed their griffons too good for the likes of humans.

'What's happening to us?' Kairos kept his voice low so only Gulliver could hear.

'We're their prisoners,' answered Gulliver, his swollen, unseeing eyes facing straight ahead. 'I think they plan on taking us to Malus. They probably have their ships moored at Cape Caipora, so I reckon we're going back there. I don't know what will happen to you. As for me, I'm a Mana Knight. Low ranking or not, they'll have me tortured and executed...' His voice trailed off.

'And Henrik?' asked Kairos, looking towards campfire. The elven leader put a collar and leash on Henrik and made the boy sit next to him. Unlike Kairos and Gulliver, Henrik appeared unharmed.

'He's young enough. They'll probably enslave him if he's lucky. Or unlucky... I've heard that certain elven lords pay good money for human boys.'

They sat in silence. The chatter of the elves and the crackling of their campfire drowned out the sounds of the forest.

'How are you faring?'

Gulliver shook his head.

'Why did they cut off your…' Kairos could not bring himself to finish the sentence.

Gulliver sighed. 'To hamper my ability to fight. Now I'm less of a threat… though I don't suppose that I ever was much of one.'

A rock suddenly struck Gulliver in the head. It was a small rock and didn't cause any harm, but the elves around the campfire laughed. After a few moments they began talking of other matters and soon forgot about their prisoners. Gulliver sat in silence while Kairos contemplated the recent events.

He swallowed, trying to form the words to his next question. 'Did she… suffer for long?'

'A bit,' said Gulliver in a voice choked with grief. 'They left her for dead after she was stabbed, but she was still alive after they cut off my fingers. Then, they made Henrik watch as they removed her hair from her scalp. The one known as Captain Hargonnas finally cut her throat. I tried to help, but you can see what happened.'

'Why would they do such a thing?'

'Human hair is valued amongst the dark elf nobles. They use them as wigs.'

Kairos could listen no more. He turned away abruptly, causing his head to flare in pain, and spat. He glared at the elves around the campfire, his rage burning like the flames.

\* \* \*

Kairos dreamt of Farina that night. She was pleading with him to save her. This time, he leapt to her rescue, slaying all of her attackers with savage fury. He took her back to Logres where he was the hero who discovered the new land across the sea, and his peers marvelled at Farina's beauty. They held him in awe and respect. Somehow, Thylar had survived the battle at sea and returned to throw a feast in Kairos's honour. Farina sat by his side at the mead hall, smiling at him.

But then he awoke the following morning to his sad reality of being a prisoner. Her corpse was back at the barn, unburied, and the thought troubled him. Would her spirit rest in the afterlife?

Failure became the focus of Kairos's every waking thought. All of his rage and regret at the loss of his brother and fellow Einar and the self-loathing he felt at having failed to protect Farina seethed within him. Farina's murderers, the same men who slaughtered the Einar, stood in front of him gloating about their deeds. Kairos's anger burned throughout the day until it finally hardened into a steel-like resolve. He swore by Rudras that he would avenge Farina, Thylar, and his fellow Einar.

However, the men responsible for their deaths were many, and he was but one, tied up and helpless. He would have to survive, bide his time, until the right opportunity arose. For now, he would follow their commands and comply. He fought back the tears that threatened to flow and swallowed the knot in his throat. He would let none of his anguish show on his face. His captors did not deserve that satisfaction.

The elves broke their fast that morning, leaving the prisoners the unwanted leftovers, which was bread hard enough to break their teeth. As they left the camp, it began to rain, and they trudged along, miserable and sodden. The remaining griffons and their riders departed first, presumably to return to the ships banked on the coast of Cape Caipora to update them of the incoming prisoners. The one known as Captain Hargonnas stayed behind with the rest of his men, sending his griffon ahead. They were far from any settlements and no one was going to offer any resistance, Kairos thought. No one would save them.

A dull ache throbbed in Kairos's chest. It had begun after the battle at sea and intensified when Farina died. He shuffled along, unaware of his surroundings. His shoulders slumped as if carrying a great burden, and he tripped over an unseen tree root and sprawled onto the forest floor.

'Get up, you lout,' the guard said, kicking at Kairos's rear. The elf was lithe and had a severely upturned nose, reminding him of a sickly pig that Uncle Vinh once had.

GODSHARD CHRONICLES: VOL. 1

Kairos winced in pain from the guard's blow, which struck his already bruised and battered body. He wanted to fall and never get up, but he knew what would happen. And his pain was still nothing compared to what Gulliver faced. The young knight grew weaker by the hour, and he stumbled incessantly. Whenever he fell, the elven guard would shout and kick until the weakened knight picked himself off the ground and hobbled along. Kairos wondered how Gulliver managed.

Henrik walked in front of Kairos, streams of tears leaving streaks on his muddy face. He followed the elves' orders without hesitation and was left alone. Captain Hargonnas took a personal interest in him, and even made sure the boy was fed as well as the elves. Occasionally, Henrik turned and flashed Kairos a look of resignation, despair. That look wounded Kairos more than any blow the guards could muster.

Kairos wondered if the boy blamed him for his sister's death. He could not fault Henrik for that. He blamed himself, feeling responsible for everything. He should have been the one who died. Those elves would have never attacked Milbrooke if he had not come to this land.

Yet, despite his inner turmoil, he held onto that rage he felt for Farina's death. Whenever the guards were not looking, he slowly worked his way to loosen his bonds. To his grim amusement, Kairos noticed that the elf who bound him did not excel at knot-tying. Either that, or perhaps the Einar were more proficient, because he had himself free within a few hours, but he pretended that his restraints held until he found the perfect opportunity. He would probably die in the process, but he vowed to kill Captain Hargonnas before he went down. He saw Farina's hair hanging from the light elf's belt and vowed again to avenge her.

The opportunity came sooner than Kairos expected.

It was sometime around midday when Gulliver collapsed onto the ground and did not get up. No amount of painful motivation from the frustrated guard could get the wounded knight to stir. After a few kicks from the pig-nosed elf, another of his comrades muttered something and drew a sword. Kairos's heart lurched at the sight. Gulliver had risked so much for him, and now he would die in the forest like this. This was not the right time, but he had to act. He owed the knight that much. He would simply join Thylar and Farina much sooner.

Kairos slipped out of his bonds and took a step towards the pig-nosed elf, who was facing away from him towards Gulliver. He had a simple plan: take the pig-nosed elf's sword, kill him, and fight to the death. He reached for the sword's hilt.

'Kairos,' Henrik cried, 'Don't do it!'

The pig-nosed elf, along with every other elf in the squad, turned as Kairos's hand brushed the sword hilt. The Einar lunged, but the elf jumped away and within a second, the other elves drew their swords and closed in.

Kairos gave a long sigh. Henrik had unwittingly given him away. He resigned himself to fate.

Before the elves could make another move, something whirred past Kairos. The elf who was about to finish off Gulliver suddenly staggered backwards. Several jagged shards of stone protruded from him. The pig-nosed elf pitched forward, nearly landing on Kairos. The other elves turned in time to see another volley tear into them. In a matter of seconds, only Henrik, Kairos, and three elves remained standing.

Kairos did not know what to do, except crouch down to avoid the magical projectiles.

A dozen armour-plated men appeared behind Kairos, led by a tall man with sandy yellow hair and a flowing moustache. They brandished the shiny, blue-tipped mana lances like Gulliver had. Two of the elves took off, fleeing into the thicket, whilst the other one made a few sweeping gestures with his hand, causing an orange light to glow. Kairos, remembering the luminescent projectiles from his battle at sea, knew what was coming next.

The armoured men braced themselves as a fireball burst forth and struck them. To Kairos's astonishment, nothing happened. Were his eyes playing tricks? The fireball seemed to have struck an invisible force and dissipated harmlessly.

The leader of the armoured men stepped forward and traced a sign of his own. A much brighter light flared, and Kairos had to close his eyes from its brilliance. The explosion knocked him from his feet, and when he opened his eyes, he no longer saw the elf standing. The armoured men and their leader looked unscathed. Then he realised that the blast had flung the elf at least twenty feet away, his body was charred and his limbs twisted in contorted angles.

Kairos panicked. His captors were defeated, only to be replaced by a more fearsome group. They didn't look like elves, but in this foreign land, one could never be too sure. Were they Mana Knights like Gulliver? They carried the same weapons as he did and appeared human. Kairos had no time to consider the answer. Instead, he tried to run for the sword of one of the fallen elves, but some of the newly arrived men saw his intention and cut him off, reaching the weapon first. They screamed something at him, but the battle lust had taken over and he did not understand what was said. Instead, he focused on the fair-haired man in the silver-coloured mail, who wore a bemused expression. Kairos had seen that man use incredible magic and assumed he was the biggest threat, the leader.

There was a long branch near his feet, so Kairos picked it up and swung it at the moustached-man, who used his strange spear to parry the branch, and the wood snapped like a brittle twig. When the man saw this, he began to laugh. This enraged Kairos, thinking the man was humiliating and toying with him, so he charged again, this time with half the branch length, and beat at the man. He continued laughing and batted Kairos's hand with the spear, knocking the branch out of his grip. Unarmed, Kairos screamed and began hitting at the man with his fists, but the man thought it all very funny, as an unseen force repelled Kairos's blows. The man swept Kairos's feet out with the spear and several men rushed forward to subdue him as he flailed at them.

'Wait,' a guttural but weak voice – Gulliver's voice – said. 'He's with me.'

The men stopped, noticing Gulliver on the ground. They lifted Kairos to his feet and brought him forward to the fair-haired man who easily bested him. Kairos was puzzled. These men used magic, yet they fought the elves, and even though they had subdued Kairos, himself, they had not caused him any harm. Kairos could not be sure. Everything was backwards in this strange land. The leader, now chuckling to himself, came forward to look Kairos up and down, a twinkle of amusement flickering in his eyes.

And that was how Kairos met Galen Avenal, Dragon-class Mana Knight, one of the most powerful humans in Ordonia... whom he tried to best with a stick.

*  *  *

The Mana Knights had the element of surprise that day. They saw Gulliver's signal fire at Cape Caipora's lighthouse from the nearest watch tower in the mountains east of Gersholm, but did not light the subsequent signal fires to carry on the message to Vadost. Instead, they sent a messenger on the fastest steed to Valour Keep, the stronghold of the Mana Knights. The knights, in turn, despatched their best, Galen Avenal, along with his chosen men, to investigate. Vadost was a long trek away from Cape Caipora, but they made good time.

Galen had cursed under his breath, something he rarely did, when he saw the smoke from the direction of Milbrooke. First the signal fire, now this. He was on the verge of retirement, and his years of experience told him that this whole expedition was about to get very complicated.

And it did.

They arrived too late to help the villagers. Corpses littered the little hamlet. The enemy, Malus's agents, still lingered, and some of the younger knights wanted to rush in right away from their hiding place in the forest to take vengeance, but Galen held them in check. He understood their feelings, yet he hadn't become a

Dragon Knight by acting on pure emotion. *Watch and observe.* Thus, he and the knights saw the elves departing with captives.

Galen sent his scouts ahead and made his retinue of knights travel under the cover of darkness to avoid alerting the griffon-riders. He knew his knights could take on a patrol of elves and the dwarves, but those flying mounts would create quite the problem. More unsettling was the fact that the scouts returned and reported more of Malus's ships at Cape Caipora. Galen had not expected to find such a large fleet, especially as Malus had been quiet since his defeat twenty years ago, and whilst the Dragon Knight's force was formidable, he could not hope to attack an entire fleet that included griffons. This brought Galen to his next concern: *Why attack now?* First the lighthouse and now Milbrooke – all Ordonian territory. Malus was risking all-out war, and for what? These hamlets would earn him nothing, particularly not the godshard that his army desired. The dark elf was up to something and he was desperate; the knight was eager to discover the reasons.

Galen had hoped defeating the small regiment of elves and rescuing the prisoners would answer his questions, but he had more questions and no enemy captives. He sent his men to pursue the two elves who had escaped, and they came back empty-handed. Galen and the other knights buried the fallen elves and tended to the prisoners, especially Gulliver, whose injuries worried and angered all of the knights.

That was now several days ago, and they were in Gersholm, the other settlement near Cape Caipora. Due to the circumstances in Milbrooke, Galen used his force to fortify this small settlement against a potential attack. The knights could use the place as their base of operations, and when Galen was satisfied enough with the preparations, he would leave for Vadost. Gulliver was coming back once he was fit for travel. The little boy, Henrik, had family in the city.

There was one other concern, however.

As they sat in the tavern of the small settlement, Galen regarded the strange boy before him intently, and made a few deductions.

Judging by his rough, uncouth accent, in which Galen had trouble placing its origins, the boy was not from around here, and he had obviously grown up in an environment of violence. He also seemed extra skittish, flailing about when Galen tried to cast a healing spell on him; that could have been a result of his recent treatment from the elves, or perhaps from abusive parenting. Or maybe, Galen wondered, the boy had a mistrust of magic, which was an oddity for a non-dwarf, and often a sign of mental illness in humans. Either way, he felt a profound sense of pity for the boy.

'I'm Galen,' the knight said to him. 'What is your name?'

'Kairos,' replied the boy, 'son of Karthok.'

The boy's chest swelled with pride, and he looked directly at Galen as he spoke, though his hands trembled on the table. The older knight was impressed. He intimidated most young men, and they either stuttered or stared at the floor or their feet or anywhere except at him, as though they expected him to tear into them and eat them for dinner. Not this boy, though. He seemed to face his fears head on, despite being shaken.

'What a strange name. How old are you?' Galen asked.

'Fifteen. Almost sixteen.'

The boy held his dark grey eyes fixed and unwavering on the knight. They held too much knowledge, too much experience for fifteen years – too much travesty, too much pain. Galen thought of his daughter, who was close to the same age and wondered how she was doing.

'Are you hungry? Would you like something to eat?' Galen asked.

Kairos did not answer. He regarded the older knight with suspicion, as if expecting a tin of poison or a sudden attack.

'Did the elves wound your ears? Did the sound of my magic deafen you?'

'I'm hungry,' Kairos admitted.

'So you can hear after all,' Galen said. 'There's chicken here, bread, and cheese, and ale. Could you break off a piece of bread?

Gulliver says you were shipwrecked. It's obvious you're not from these lands.'

'Is Gulliver well?' Kairos asked.

'As well as he can be.' Galen's cheerful face took on a scowl as he took his piece of bread. 'My healing spells cannot regenerate severed fingers, but he will be fine otherwise. What about you? Where are you from?'

'Logres,' Kairos said.

'Logres?' Galen repeated the unfamiliar word. 'I haven't heard of it. Where is it?'

'Across the sea.'

Galen flashed Kairos a bemused look. He wondered if the boy meant some small island north of Ordonia or was conjuring up a lie. 'Tell me more about your home then.'

Kairos saw the look and glanced away. 'I'd rather not.'

'Fair enough, but I want you to know that I'm here to help. If you seek to return home, then I can aid you in that. And no, I'm not plotting something against you.' Galen saw the boy's expression contort into one of distrust. 'It's fine if you don't want my help. Just know that it takes several days of travel from here to any other settlement, and you don't seem to have the provisions or a single coin on you.'

Kairos licked his lips. His gaze dropped, fixed on his now-empty plate. The hands, long and slender, curled inward. 'My homeland,' he said in a flat voice, 'is very far away from here. We sailed for over a month, past the deep sea. Past the sea serpents. It's a place we call Logres, a land we share with kobolds and cyclops.'

The knight's eyes widened when he heard mention of the sea serpents. No Ordonian, elf, dwarf, or (as far as he knew) gnome had ever crossed the sea. He wanted to disbelieve the boy's claim, but somehow, the seriousness of those unwavering grey eyes spoke the truth. 'Go on,' Galen said gently.

'Our land is dying. The plants, the animals. It's the Blight. We've been living on mostly fish from the sea for several years, but we have to sail farther and farther out to get them.' Kairos lifted his gaze in defiance, ready to defend his claims. When he found the older knight regarding him with rapt attention, the boy relaxed and the words flowed out, as if a vein were cut open.

'Everyone back home thinks that Logres was the only land to survive when the gods warred amongst themselves. We never knew this place existed. Every day was a struggle to live, and we became desperate, so my father and brother...' Kairos paused and swallowed. He gritted his teeth, then continued, 'So they decided to embark on an expedition to find a new land. We had three longships. Everything was going well until we met *them*.'

'You mean Malus's army.'

'Yes,' the boy answered with a glint of anger in his eyes. His fists clenched on the table, more words flowing forth from the open wound. 'First we fought the dwarves. We would have won, but then those beasts – those griffons, as you call them – took to the air, and the elves used something we haven't seen before. It was loud, bright, and deadly, and it destroyed all our ships. I understand that part of fighting is to die, but what happened was a massacre without glory.' Kairos had lowered his voice, and Galen leant forward in his seat despite himself. 'Most of my people drowned. Those who didn't were slaughtered... I was the only who escaped.'

Galen lifted the wooden mug and drank, using the ale as an excuse to keep silent until he had regained control of his anger. It was a tragic story, one he had seen time and again. This poor boy was very much like the countless others. Malus's army attacked all humans in their path, wantonly killing them, seldom taking prisoners, and those who became captives often suffered a much worse fate. Some said that the dark elf's objective was the genocide of the human race. Others claimed he wanted to collect the godshards, and humans just happened to be collateral damage. Either way, Malus left behind death and destruction, and the survivors carried nothing but painful memories from their devastated homes. Few of them were able to rebuild their lives. Most either resorted to drinking to dull the memories or ended up as street beggars in the cities. Some couldn't drink enough to forget, and killed themselves from the insanity. This boy was just another victim who had to bear that heavy burden.

There was yet a chance to help him. Besides, there was something mysterious about this boy, but Galen could not quite place it. Malus was pursuing him for a reason. The dark elf did not waste time attacking rural settlements unless he had an objective in mind – though many others might disagree with Galen on this thought.

Something else this boy said bothered him: *The elves used something we haven't seen before.*

'You don't believe me, do you?' Kairos asked, taking Galen's silence for scepticism.

'My belief doesn't matter. You've seen what Malus's army tried to do to you.'

'Will you and your men do the same?'

The older knight laughed, but stopped immediately and cleared his throat. 'Of course not! We are Mana Knights. Our mission is to defend justice and protect the innocent. We strive to be honourable, unlike Malus's men who murder innocents.' Kairos said nothing, only listened. 'We also take quests to purge the land of evil,' Galen went on, biting into a piece of cheese. 'Beasts, fugitives, or searches and rescues... But the most important thing that Mana Knights do is preserve the godshards.'

'Godshards?'

'The crystallised essence of the fallen gods. Have you not heard? Everyone knows about them. That is what I believe Malus is after. He craves power.'

Kairos shook his head, becoming more confused. 'Fallen gods?'

'I see we'll have to work on your education.' Galen was becoming more confident that the boy did hail from across the sea. Even bumpkins from the most rural of farming hamlets knew of the godshards. 'I'll explain more at a later time. Are your people familiar with the gods?'

'Back in Logres, we worship Rudras,' Kairos said proudly, but the mention of home caused tears to well up in the boy's eyes. He angrily cuffed them away.

'Do you?' Galen said, impressed. 'I have heard of Rudras, though he is rarely mentioned in the texts. Very interesting. But enough about gods. We need to discuss your fate.'

'My fate?' Kairos blurted out.

'Yes. If you are from across the sea as you claim, then have you thought of what you plan to do from here?'

The boy shrugged as if he hadn't thought much of it at all. 'Go home, get more of my people, and take revenge on Malus and his army.'

'That sounds grand and all, but how can you get home without a ship or a crew?'

The boy had no answer.

'Even if you did have one, no one here has ever been across the sea,' Galen continued, talking through a mouthful of cheese. 'Even Malus, as far as I know, cannot cross it. Those sea serpents you have mentioned tend to destroy any ship that dares. They are attracted to our mana and attack without fail…' Galen saw the puzzled look on the boy's face and stopped. 'Why don't you accompany me to Vadost for now? The lands beyond here are wild and filled with monsters. I cannot force you, of course. It is your choice.'

Kairos didn't quite understand the offer. 'I cannot accept charity,' he said. 'My father said it's shameful to beg help from others, and it leaves you in their debt.'

'It's not charity,' Galen said briskly. 'I have a blacksmith friend who could use an extra pair of hands, and you can stay with him in exchange for work. I also have many questions about Malus's army, and perhaps you have answers. You've fought them. Been around them. We can help each other. Besides, any boy who has the courage to take on Malus's soldiers is a friend, in my eye. I'll get you a place to stay in Vadost until you can get your bearings and figure out what you want to do. In the meantime, I can try to enlist you into the Knighthood. We knights are fighting Malus, and could use another brave soul amongst our ranks. Gulliver says you killed an elven warrior with a dagger. That is impressive for one as young as yourself. I can only imagine what your potential could be with the proper training.'

Kairos contemplated Galen's words. 'And if I don't want to go with you?'

'Well, you're more than welcome to stay here in Gersholm, keep the locals company.' Galen shrugged. 'They can use another hand in the fields. Or perhaps help with the livestock. If that doesn't suit your fancy, the nearest settlement from here – excluding Milbrooke – is almost a week's journey by foot. You're sure to meet a hill giant on the way, or maybe a tribe of hobs. The wilderness here is not a place you can easily survive.

'And no, Kairos, I'm not trying to change your mind,' Galen interrupted himself, seeing the young boy scowl in anger. 'I am telling you the facts. The reality of your situation.'

Kairos looked down glumly at his food. 'What about my home? My clan? I need to go back.'

'I will help you with that in due time. The Knighthood may be able to help, as well.'

'But I need to go back soon,' Kairos replied. 'The Blight–'

'Like I said, that's not likely to happen without a ship,' Galen said gravely.

'How do I get a ship?' Kairos asked, the pitch of his voice getting higher as he became more agitated.

The knight did not immediately respond, but took a swig from his tankard and leant back in his chair, watching the boy with pity. *He has lost everything,* Galen said silently. *Family, friends, his people. There is nothing for him here, and there is no easy way to return.* The boy looked so lost that he wouldn't last a few days outside of Gersholm alone. Even if a wild beast or starvation did not kill him, the madness of desolation would consume him in the end. He needed help. A purpose to his life; something besides revenge – which would also destroy him. The Knighthood would provide that sense of purpose for a while. The training and discipline would be the shield that would protect this fragile boy, shelter him when he was weak or weary. Or the Knighthood might become the sword that cuts him, leaving him bleeding out and broken. Galen wondered uneasily if he was steering the boy on a path towards an early death.

'Why are you staring at me like that?' Kairos asked.

'I was thinking that you need a great amount of wealth,' Galen said.

'What?'

'You need a sack full of gold to buy a ship, and even more to hire a crew for such a dangerous voyage.' Galen then added, 'but you can acquire a ship by becoming a knight and rising through the ranks.'

Kairos glared down at his bread, which sat uneaten in his hand. 'How long will that take?'

'It can take years at best.' There was no sense lying to the boy.

'And I can fight Malus's army in the meantime?' he asked without looking up.

'If the occasion demands it,' Galen answered. 'Though new recruits do not engage in such tasks early on.'

The boy lifted his head and his eyes made contact with Galen's, filled with a burning passion that was lacking in most youth. 'I will go with you to Vadost, then.'

The knight nodded and set the tankard down. Reaching out across the table, he clasped the boy on the arm. Kairos flinched at the touch and started to pull away, but Galen held on firmly.

He didn't like to be touched, Galen realised, but he wanted the boy to understand the gravity of his words. 'Listen to me, Kairos,' he said, and Kairos stopped squirming and held still. The boy saw the intensity in the older knight's eyes. 'I'm going to be straightforward with you. The Knighthood will not be easy, nor will it solve your problems. It will test the limits of your courage, your resolve. Many people have tried to become knights and failed. Those that pass take on new problems, new pains. You will run towards dangerous situations that sane people flee from. You will take on incredible burdens that others abandon. Despite all of this, you may become a knight and never get a ship. Becoming a knight requires a lot of self-sacrifice.' Galen paused, tightening his grip on the boy's arm to emphasise his point. 'The Knighthood will try to break you down. The training is brutal. The leaders are strict. Those that are brittle of heart will break off and leave. Those that endure are rebuilt to become stronger and more resilient. Do you understand?'

'I understand,' said Kairos with solemnity.

'One more thing.' Galen still held the boy's arm, affixing him with a firm gaze.

Kairos did not move, only stared back transfixed.

'Do *not* tell anyone else that you come from across the sea. Do not tell them about Logres, the Blight, or about your people.'

'Why not?'

'Just don't,' Galen said, squeezing the arm and causing Kairos to wince slightly. 'At the very least, some will think you are either lying or mad. Others, like Malus and his army, may try to harm you. Promise me that you won't tell anyone! Not for now.'

'Okay. I promise.'

'Truly?' Galen released his grip.

'Yes,' Kairos said, holding his arm, but meeting Galen's eyes resolutely. 'I promise.'

The knight nodded, satisfied. 'Now do you have any questions for me, Kairos?'

The boy hesitated, not out of reluctance. He was wondering how to phrase his thoughts. 'I saw you kill those elves. Will the Knighthood teach me how to fight like that? I would like to fight like you. Can I?'

Galen frowned, thinking of his own daughter who had also said something similar. 'That depends,' he answered. 'Not everyone can use powerful spells. I don't know how *your* people are–' He focused on the boy, who suddenly looked down, as he said this– 'But it all really depends on how well you can hold yourself in battle, I suppose. Learning magic takes time. Some study and practise their entire lives and barely improve. Others just seem to have the gift.

'Everyone starts out as a squire,' the knight continued, seeing that the boy was still listening intently, even if he wasn't making eye contact. 'After a year of intense training, you take a test. Those who are not strong or practical enough fail. Some even die during the testing. The road is not easy. Those who pass must commit their lives to the Knighthood to become full-fledged knights. Even then, it still takes years of training and discipline to wield powerful spells.'

The boy's face contorted as if mulling over a very serious matter. 'What if...' He stopped.

'Go on,' Galen urged.

'W-what if I can never cast those powerful spells?' Kairos asked, actually sounding afraid. 'What if—'

'Do not trouble yourself with 'what ifs' and such,' Galen interrupted. 'If what Gulliver claims is true, the Knighthood could use a warrior such as yourself. There is more to the Knighthood than slinging spells around and commanding power.'

Kairos nodded, looking very serious, as he levelled his eyes with Galen. Determination replaced all traces of doubt.

'Now, Kairos,' said Galen, thinking back to the one troublesome thing the boy had mentioned. 'I have a question for you. Besides wanting to earn a ship and fight Malus, why do you want to become more powerful?'

The candlelight on the table glistened in Kairos's eyes. There was no hesitation in those dark grey eyes, only resolve. 'I'm tired of being weak and helpless. I want to become stronger to help those around me, and,' he made a fist and gazed at Galen fiercely, 'and make each and every one of those elves and dwarves pay for what they did.'

Galen, unable to hide his surprise at the vehement tone, looked closely at the boy to see if he were jesting.

Kairos was not.

The older knight gave an involuntary shudder, wondering if he was making the right decision by taking the boy back to Vadost.

* * *

Malus sat behind his desk in his elegant quarters in the Kinclaven Citadel. Though not as sumptuous as his home back at the D'Kari capital, the dark elf's chambers in the citadel were large and comfortable, containing a private bedroom, sitting room, dining room, and an antechamber for his secretary. The view from any of his rooms was magnificent, and he could look down upon the entertaining execution yard, one of his favourite pastimes. Gazing farther off, he could see beyond the walls of the citadel, into the forested countryside that stretched into the craggy mountains.

This morning, the dark elf's gaze was lowered, his eyes, if not his thoughts, on the execution yard. The executioner was providing a spectacular show of chopping the heads and limbs off of the convicted criminals — as if aware his most enthusiastic audience member was watching from above — thus he put on a dramatic show, ensuring that the screams of the guilty resonated longer and louder than usual.

It was, indeed, a gory day, and the main source of entertainment was a rotund Mana Knight, reportedly captured at a lighthouse, who was much larger around the waist area than any prisoner that had come before. He wore a brown, tattered robe, and was covered in cuts and bruises, and approached the chopping block sobbing and begging for mercy, much to the jeers of the members of Malus's army watching in attendance. No one felt sorry for him — elves especially detested obesity since most were slender. The executioner's axe bit into the big man's belly, and his guts spilled out onto the platform like a ruptured sack of slithering eels. The man wailed pitifully as the soldiers hooted and cheered.

Not so Dark Lord Malus. The executioner could have disembowelled a dozen Mana Knights for all the dark elf cared today. Or, Malus could have cancelled the executions indefinitely and sent most of the soldiers off on holiday. In fact, such would have suited his mood as he returned to his desk and sat down. His long, dark grey, bony fingers fidgeted over the polished wood, grabbing the quill pen, putting it down, pushing the ink jar, shuffling parchments, or rearranging the candles. It was his only outward sign of displeasure or frustration, for Malus's face was as impassive, his regal manner as composed as ever. The two armoured figures, Captain Hargonnas and Sergeant Selkis, standing silently before him, however, noted this fidgeting and knew the dark elf was in a foul mood. More so, when the red eyes caught sight of the Captain's tight black leather outfit – the very outfit he was told not to wear again –and narrowed slightly, causing the blond elf to wince.

The dark lord's hand suddenly slammed down on the oaken desk. 'I'm trying to comprehend,' his voice was tinged with a lethal edge, 'why it is that you, a so-called *elite* with your enormous magic powers, cannot bring in one boy!'

Captain Hargonnas and Sergeant Selkis turned slightly toward each other, exchanging worried glances. Then they faced Malus and the captain, his hands clasped before him, spoke. His strained and conciliatory tone contrasted with the stoic marble features of his face.

'I seek your pardon, my lord. If this boy were a normal human, we would have no trouble finding him. The fact that he is god-cursed makes it difficult. He has no mana, which makes him almost impossible to find.'

'I know that!' Malus bellowed. 'That's why you use your damned eyes and ears.'

'We have, my lord,' Captain Hargonnas dared to say. 'Our griffon squadrons scoured the land, and through due diligence, we had captured him. But Sergeant Selkis here–' the Captain gestured to the now horrified dark elf next to him, 'botched the job and left the men to the mercy of a regiment of Mana Knights, led by none other than the great Galen Avenal, himself!

'Now the boy is in the company of Mana Knights,' continued Captain Hargonnas, cutting off the sergeant's protest with an irritated wave of his hand, 'who now populate the Caipora region like ants pouring out of a disturbed anthill. The boy hides amongst these powerful men, whom we cannot approach without the risk of incurring casualties, and unlike other humans, we cannot trace him due to the lack of mana in his body.'

'Pfft!' Malus snorted. 'Excuses, excuses. Can't you use that filthy necrotic magic of yours to seek him out?'

Captain Hargonnas inhaled deeply, as though suppressing irritation. When he spoke, his voice was low and clear, a bad sign to those who knew him, as evidenced by Sergeant Selkis's greying face.

'My lord, the art of necromancy is attuned to the mana within the living and the dead. Those using the art, such as myself, can move among the people, casting out strands of magic as a fisherman casts a net. Whenever any being with mana – live or dead – comes within my range, those strands quiver with mana. This provides me the essential information about that being: such things ranging from their demeanour to their basic intentions and emotions.'

Malus rolled his eyes, and snorted again.

The Captain clenched his jaw, causing the sergeant to flinch involuntarily, uncertain what his superior might do. Though most ranked members of Malus's army were trained with strict discipline that encompassed more years than a human's lifespan, the Captain was known to speak his mind and lose his temper. Judging by Sergeant Selkis's discomfort, he would not have been surprised if the captain unleashed a barrage of magical energy that would vaporise the room like morning dew in the hot summer sun.

Captain Hargonnas restrained himself, however. Malus was not one to cross. 'With those who lack mana,' he continued in a controlled and strained voice, 'such as dwarves and gnomes, we have to readjust our senses to pick up on the small amount of life energy they emit, as opposed to the mana lacking in their bodies. Even though they can cast no magic, they still have a traceable energy that we can sense. But this boy – alongside the fleet he came with – emits nothing. I can sense nothing, feel nothing, and see nothing within the net I cast – even if he is inside the strands. To me, my lord, he merely passes through my net as though he does not exist! He could blend in with any group of Mana Knights and go wherever he pleases, and we would be unable to sense him.'

'That would be disastrous!' Malus said insistently, his hand upsetting the parchments on his desk.

There was a moment's silence, then a raised eyebrow from the captain. 'If I may, my lord, I fail to see how this boy could cause us so much trouble. He is powerless to do anything. I assume we can allow him to leave with the Mana Knights and go wherever—'

'You fool!' Malus said. 'I will not repeat myself. We *must stop* the boy! If you insist on knowing the reason, know this – the Pariah wants to use him to awaken Murasa, the Lost God. The boy is an Einar, a race that had once served this god before the Celestial War. Therefore, he is the only one on this side of the Dark Sea who can approach Murasa without being consumed. Do you understand?'

Sergeant Selkis gasped in awe. The silence was longer, more profound this time.

'Very well,' Captain Hargonnas finally answered. 'If that's the case, we must stop him, but how would you suggest I capture him when he is in the care of the Mana Knights?'

'The knights seem to be headed to Vadost, which is next to their stronghold, Valour Keep,' Malus remarked. 'Because of your blunder – and insolence – I am temporarily relieving you of your post as captain and reassigning you. You will undertake a covert operation into Vadost and help me locate this boy.' The dark elf held up a dismissive hand upon seeing the captain about to protest. 'Fail me in this and you will join the line in the execution yard.'

'Yes, my lord,' the now-former captain said coldly, his face darkening. 'If I may, once more: how shall I find one boy in such a place? Vadost is the second largest city in Ordonia.'

'I already have spies working there. Take your place among them and work together to find this boy. As for you, Sergeant Selkis,' Malus glowered at the hapless elf, 'it has come to my understanding that you are one who allowed the boy to slip your grasp.'

Sergeant Selkis lowered his head and cast a sidelong glance of hatred at Captain Hargonnas. 'I have no excuse, my lord,' he said acidly. 'I have committed a grievous error by pre-emptively taking the griffons back with me to Cape Caipora, and I will accept responsibility.'

Malus snorted. 'At least somebody knows their place. Very well, you are relieved of your post in the Grimaldi Flying Squadron. You will be reassigned to the new prison. You and your men will take charge of the prisoners, overseeing their labour, especially with their new project – the latrines.'

'Yes, my lord,' came the subdued voice.

'Both of you are dismissed,' said Malus, waving a hand. 'Now get out of my sight. Especially you and your black leather, Hargonnas!'

The elves exchanged glances, turned to leave, shuffling out of the room – or in Hargonnas's case, creaking, due to his tight leather outfit squelching with each step.

Malus watched the two leave. When the door shut and the sound of footsteps from down the hall ceased, the dark elf slammed a fist into the desk, upsetting the ink jar and scattering precious documents. Quivering in anger and fear, he sat at the desk for many hours, staring unseeing at the black ink seeping into the parchments, staining them with its darkness. His thoughts revolved around one topic over and over again.

*The Pariah and the Lost God.*

\* \* \*

The rolling hills became taller, growing into rugged mountains before shrinking back to rolling hills, which gave way to farmland. The clear sky had only a few wispy clouds, but showed no signs of griffons.

Kairos, Galen, and a small company of half a dozen knights rode along the road that cut through a mountain pass and made their way past the farmlands, stopping along a few farmhouses along the way. Kairos had noted that the knights asked for provisions rather than taking them, and paid for everything with coin. His thoughts drifted back to Logres, when the Einar raided each other for food and supplies. The enemies' reactions were either fear or anger, or a mixture of both. These farmers regarded Galen and the knights with a different look: respect.

So many things were different in this land, especially Galen.

Kairos rode in silence next to the armoured warrior, who treated him more like a son than his own father, Karthok, ever had. In fact, the knight had taught him how to ride a horse before they left Gersholm, cheerfully explaining the basics, and demonstrating calm patience when Kairos made a mistake or didn't understand something. Galen did not beat him like Karthok had, and much to Kairos's surprise, he found himself liking the older knight instantly. It was then, he realised, that he did not miss his father much. He was quite happy with his newfound company, though he did miss Thylar... and Farina. He tried not to think about them.

Kairos did not speak his thoughts, but listened to Galen or the other knights as they travelled, trying to learn about this strange land and its culture, and to occupy his mind from the recent nightmarish incidents. More often than not, his thoughts still drifted inwards, thinking about his future and the decisions he had made. His life had changed in ways he could never have imagined only days before. He was eating well and now, in the sunshine, with the cool breeze on his face, life didn't seem quite as terrible as it had been a few days ago. There was still an ache deep inside that threatened to surface at any moment, but he pushed it back down, focusing his attention to his next objective at hand.

Vadost.

Kairos needed to return to Logres right away to inform the Einar of this luscious land full of life and opportunity, but he had no choice in the matter. He felt helpless – and indebted to Galen Avenal. Regardless of what the knight said, an Einar always repaid his debts, and Kairos felt a debt of gratitude to the man who saved his life.

There was something else that bothered Kairos, as well...
Magic.

The knights used it everywhere. Kairos watched them wave intricate patterns of light in the air to create fires for cooking (though these were built in a pit for concealment), or set up alarm spells around their camp to protect against beasts or even Malus's army. The boy heard Galen caution his men on keeping spells to a minimum to conserve mana and avoid detection from enemies, but he clearly remembered the powerful spells that felled his elven captors. Malus's army also wielded this deadly power. These thoughts made Kairos feel even more dejected. The Einar never had a chance, despite being bigger and stronger than the people here. Even if they had arrived, they would have been at the whim of these superior forces.

For now, he would venture to this city called Vadost, and learn what he could about fighting Malus and his army. Maybe even learn how to use this magic. Then he could return to Logres with this new ability and guide his people to prosperity. And save them from the Blight.

# PART TWO

## ORDONIA

# CHAPTER FOUR

## Vadost

*Godshard. A small crystallised essence of a fallen god's soul that contains enormous magical power. It has the ability to create or destroy civilisations. The godshards are the only remaining evidence of the once-powerful gods.*

Ethelstan Crowley, Salforian Priest

**A**lthea Avenal looked ordinary enough. She sat on a large rock on the shore of Lake Turquoise. She had long blonde hair and soft blue eyes. Her face, cute with the promise of beauty, was etched in the lines of a frown. She threw rocks into the lake, listening to the sound of the higher splash when the rock hit, and the deeper splash when the water came back together to fill the void.

Earlier that day, a couple of boys and girls who were around her age – she was fourteen – had been making fun of her. They conjured gusts of wind and gouts of flame to show off their magical prowess. They called her a 'badger's tail' to make her feel bad. A badger's tail was the lowest of the low of those who wanted to become a Mana Knight. Although her father, Lord Galen Avenal, was a Dragon Knight, she barely had enough mana to light a candle. Yes, she looked ordinary enough, but she was a failure. Still, her father always seemed to be proud of her. He was supposed to be returning home later this evening from a two-month absence.

'Knightly business,' he always said. She never liked him to go, but she always liked him to return. He usually brought her some sort of present from his journey, a token from wherever he had been to show that she was always in his heart. He was gone so much that his recent gifts rarely appealed to her changing taste, but she would act delighted for her father's sake. She stood up, throwing the last few rocks, and turned towards home before they even hit the surface of the lake.

The distance from Lake Turquoise to her house took an hour, but Althea was glad of the long walk. She needed time to compose herself, for it would bother Stella if she came home with a long face. Stella was the dwarven housekeeper, and Althea's nanny, since her mother had died eight years ago. Not having any children, the dwarven maid fussed over Althea like one of her own. Stella was a woman most men feared and with whom few would pick a quarrel. She came from a rough upbringing in the dwarven homeland of Dvergar, and when she moved to Vadost, her pots and pans instantly became known to smash a few heads. She was quick to anger, and whilst she never raised a hand to Althea, the young girl had learnt to avoid conflict. Even her father, Galen, knew well enough to steer clear of Stella's wrath.

If Stella had witnessed what the kids had said to Althea earlier in the day, then she would have tracked them down and given them a walloping to remember. Althea knew she could not hide everything from the dwarf. She needed to say something about what had happened, just not the worst details. Stella had threatened other bullies before, but that only led them to further torment Althea.

By the time she got home, the street lamps were just starting to flicker to life. They were powered by the Sapphire Shard, one of the major godshards that was kept and protected in Valour Keep. Godshards were the last remnants of the gods. Most of them had perished in the Celestial War, which had been fought centuries ago for reasons only the gods and scholars knew. Godshards held mana, the power of magic. They could power an entire city – from the street lamps to the mana cannons mounted on the city walls – with their massive energy. Nations fought wars over the smallest of godshards. As a result, the Sapphire Shard made Vadost, the city near Valour Keep, a beacon of civilisation to neighbours and a target for enemies.

Althea thought about this as she walked. She had always been a good student. And with a father who was one of the five highest ranking Mana Knights, she had the very best education. She knew glyphs some of the instructors of Valour Keep did not know. She was good at writing, inscribing, and casting them, much better than those kids who picked on her. But her mana level was the problem.

She did not tell her father about her problems. He had other matters to attend to. According to the rumours circulating the kingdom, Malus's army had attacked several towns and cities throughout Ordonia, even taking a lesser godshard from the smaller kingdom near the border of Salforia in the process. These actions concerned the Mana Knights, resulting in more work for her father; even now, he was away from home, answering the call of duty. He had been gone for over two months, and she fretted over his safe return. No, she thought, she would not worry her father over her troubles. She softly closed the front door of her house, which in fact was a manor, behind her, and looked to her right. Her father's helmet – a sure sign he was home – was not hanging on the armour rack next to the door. Her hopes sank.

Stella heard the door shut. She knew something was wrong; Althea rarely failed to slam the front door. She came out of the kitchen, wiping her hands on her spotless apron, and saw Althea's neutral face and troubled eyes.

'Hullo, Stella,' Althea said simply.

'Oh, my! What's happened, lass?' Stella asked, concern etched all over her face.

Althea's brave face crumpled. 'Claudius and Vaughn called me a badger's tail. And Nacole said Father was embarrassed because I can't cast magic. I know loads more glyphs than those three together and I can cast them, too! But I just can't do much magic.' She finished in a whisper, leaving out the part where Claudius used the wind spell to raise her skirt, causing all the other kids to laugh. Stella would lose her head and probably have murdered the boy over hearing that.

Stella hugged the girl tightly and guided her to a chair at the dining room table. Althea was so close to a woman, but still as tender-hearted as a little girl. It was her blessing; it was her curse; it was what Stella loved about her the most. 'Oh, I know that hurt, Thea! They're just being mean because their hearts are hurting, too – though I have half a mind to go and sort them out right now, ya know. Let me get you a piece of star-apple pie. I baked it for your father's return, but he'll never know if a small piece is missing, and who knows when he'll be back.'

'Thank you,' said Althea. She dabbed at her eyes whilst Stella set off to get the pie. 'Stella?' Stella turned. 'You're the best. Did you know that?'

'Of course I do, lass,' she said with a wink that made Althea laugh. 'And your father couldn't be prouder of you, remember,' she added.

Althea's mood lifted as she sat outside on the veranda of the manor. Stella brought out a slice of star-apple pie for each of them, and they ate in companionable silence. The grey moon, Paollus, had already risen over the Gloaming Peaks in the west, and the evening was warm as the last rays of sunlight dyed the sky a violet hue. Althea enjoyed the view, one of the best in Vadost, due to her father living high on a hill that overlooked the city. She gazed at the hundreds of colourful street lamps dotting the cascading landscape, their reflection rippling on Lake Turquoise. Sounds of laughter carried from below, likely from the taverns which were beginning to come to life. The tantalising smell of roasted meat wafted up to them from time to time on the light breeze.

A pair of mounted men approached from the path leading to the Avenal manor. They passed under a street lamp, and Althea could see them better, though not clearly as they still were too far away. The lead rider was armoured, had a metal helm hanging from his saddle. A short staff — Althea knew it was a retracted mana lance — was slung over his shoulder strapped to a baldric. A Mana Knight. The second rider was accoutred differently, wearing the clothes of a peasant.

The Mana Knight rode up the path with a familiar gait, and even though Althea could not see his features from this distance, she knew who it was.

'Father,' she cried, leaning over the railing of the veranda and waving frantically.

Both riders looked up, and the armoured rider returned the wave and spurred his steed onward up the path. The second rider followed.

Before Stella could utter a protest about finishing the slice of pie, Althea jumped up and rushed through the manor to meet her father. He was galloping up the cobblestone path near the entrance as she bounded out of the house.

'Thea!' boomed a cheerful voice, and the tall figure of Galen Avenal loomed in front of her. The familiar jovial smile flooded Althea with warmth and melted her worries. Well, most of them. The stinging words of Vaughn and Nacole still lurked beneath the surface, but she suppressed them for now. Her father did not need to know.

'Father!' Althea ran to hug him as he dismounted.

Galen returned the hug with affection. 'So, did you treat Stella well while I was away? You didn't set the house afire again, did you?'

'Of course not! Set the house afire, I mean,' Althea added, wincing at the memory of when her fire spell actually did something for once, much to the chagrin of the entire household. 'What about you, Father?' Did you fight any monsters this time? Or travel to any foreign lands? What about a present? Did you find anything interesting?'

Galen Avenal beamed at his daughter. 'Slow down there, Thea. You need to breathe sometimes when you talk. And no, I wasn't able to bring you a present this time, but I do have a surprise.'

'Really! What kind of surprise? Is it the latest fashion in elven boots? Or perhaps a fae bracelet? I heard those grant you the ability to shrink. No goblin-tooth necklaces this time, please. Stella had to burn my dress because she couldn't wash the goblin stench out, and I really liked that dress!'

'I told you it was a surprise, not a present.' He gestured behind him.

From where she stood, Althea could now make out the lone rider straggling behind. She looked at the figure silhouetted in the darkness. As he rode up towards the manor and into the bright light emanating from a multitude of lamps (Galen Avenal often told Althea that a well-lit manor kept out the prowlers at night), Althea was able to pick out details as the rider dismounted and approached. He was a man with dark hair. He carried himself with the confidence of a full-fledged knight, but wore the ragged clothes of a peasant – no, even peasants dressed better – a street beggar.

'Father, don't tell me you hired another servant. Between me and Stella, we get the chores done—'

'He's not a servant, Thea,' Galen interrupted.

As the man got nearer, Althea studied him more closely. From afar she had thought him older. Now she could see that despite the hard edge on his face, he was probably around the same age as she was. Under the grime of long days of travel, his piercing grey eyes shone with a cold intensity.

With a start, Althea realised she was staring, and the boy's eyes had met hers. It wasn't like meeting the eyes of other boys like Claudius or Vaughn, who teased her mercilessly, but at the same time made flirtatious comments. This boy looked at her seriously, intently, the cold eyes piercing deep within her, touching something that made her catch her breath.

At that moment, Stella came outside and greeted them, though she had evidently been waiting from the open doorway for a few moments. 'Welcome home, milord! Have your travels been well? Eh? Who do we have here? A boy?'

Stella's appearance caused the boy to tear his gaze from Althea, but not before the dwarf had noticed the silent exchange.

'This is Kairos,' said Galen, clasping the boy on the back, and at the same time guiding him forward. 'Kairos, meet my daughter, Althea, and my trusted maid, Stella.'

Althea felt her cheeks redden. There was a pause, but the boy was no longer looking at her. Instead, he glowered at Stella.

'A dwarf,' he snarled. 'I don't like dwarves.'

'Quite the charming lad,' Stella replied in a caustic manner. She seemed to have much more to say but did not want to antagonise Sir Galen's guest with rudeness.

'Now, Kairos, not all dwarves are bad,' Galen admonished kindly. 'Stella has been a part of our family for several years. Address her as you would me.' The last words were spoken with warmth, but held the edge of authority that caused the boy to lose his rigid posture.

'Hail,' Kairos mumbled reluctantly.

He and the dwarf regarded each other coolly. Finally, Stella forced a smile, and Kairos gave a curt nod in return.

With that, Galen ushered Kairos forward and turned to Althea. 'It's been a long journey. Thea, would you mind helping Stella prepare dinner?'

Althea was more than eager to help, happy to be away from this strange boy. She kept finding herself drawn back to his piercing eyes. When he had finally turned away – his attention focused on Stella –Althea felt as though she had been released from one of the spells the Mana Knights used to ensnare outlaws. She immediately felt a surge of guilt. She should be more interested in talking to father when he had just returned from his trip, yet she wasn't expecting... this.

She followed everyone inside the manor and waited until her father had escorted the newcomer into the parlour, and when she thought both had turned away, cast a furtive glance at Kairos as Galen was giving him a tour of the house. As if the boy sensed her gaze, he turned his head. Their eyes met again for the briefest moments. Stella immediately interrupted, asking Althea for assistance in the kitchen. Grateful for the respite, she rushed into the kitchen to help the dwarf ignite the stove with her magic, convincing herself that the heat from the fire was what was making her face burn.

* * *

The sight of Althea, Galen Avenal's daughter, was enough to make Kairos forget his weariness from days of travel. Her beauty conjured the image of Farina to his mind. He felt a chill shudder through his body as he realised how similar Althea was to the ill-fated girl. They could easily pass for sisters. He couldn't help staring at her – it was as if Rudras had brought Farina back as a reminder of his failure to save her. Althea had seemed equally interested in him, which made Kairos all the more unnerved. During his introduction with Althea and Stella, Kairos struggled not to see Farina's scalped and blood-drenched face staring up at him from the hay-strewn floor of the barn. He still remained silent about the incident. He banished that secret to the darkest depths of his mind and sealed it away. But its presence lingered and burdened his conscience.

In contrast to the gloomy day of death and pain in Milbrooke, it was now warm and cheerful in the Avenal Manor, with the exception of the dwarven lady who continuously gave him suspicious looks. Althea bounced about with vibrancy, looking at him with a warm interest that both excited and scared him. By Rudras, she was gorgeous.

Kairos stole a quick glance at her as Galen was showing him the house. To his embarrassment, he found himself staring straight into her eyes. He quickly averted his gaze, but not before noticing the curves under her dress. He followed Galen, pretending to take an intense interest in a painting of a castle on the wall. His cheeks burned and they reddened further when he noticed Stella's disapproving stare. In an effort to divert attention away from him, he commented on the architecture of Galen's manor.

'Your home is impressive,' Kairos said, feeling more uncomfortable and very much out of place as he ventured through the manor, which with its magically glowing lamps and the silken cushioned couches offered more comfort than the most luxurious accommodation back in Logres. He was overawed at what he had seen of Vadost and its people, who seemed so far above him in appearance, culture, education, and... Magic. They might have been direct descendants of the gods themselves. He didn't belong here. He recalled when he had first entered Vadost, pointing and gaping at the magical splendours of the city with a naiveté and childlike wonder that made him a figure of fun to all observers; he saw their stares, their laughs and smirks.

Dinner at the Avenal Manor further disheartened Kairos's first impression of his new life. The 'table manners' of the Avenal family contrasted hugely with the Einar mead halls. First, Stella brought out a washing bowl, requiring everybody to wash their hands before eating. Then, the dinner table was a quiet affair. There were no shouted stories of grandeur, drunken toasts amongst warriors, or fights resulting in overturned tables. Even though he tried to copy Galen (because he would rather starve than mimic a single action from a dwarf), Kairos brought chaos to the table. When he grabbed the entire bowl of soup and began drinking directly from the bowl, Galen cleared his throat in an expression of disapproval and jerked his head towards Stella, who was eating the soup with a spoon. Althea giggled at these mishaps, though she turned red and looked down when Kairos glanced her way. Stella sighed in disapproval. Ashamed and embarrassed, Kairos sullenly finished his meal in silence.

Althea tried to speak to Kairos, but Stella hissed at the young girl whenever she did and sent her to her chamber immediately after dinner. The dwarf glowered at Kairos as his gaze lingered on Althea leaving the room. He instantly knew his enemy.

'He's not going to be staying here,' Stella said, casting Galen a fierce look as if that settled any dispute, 'It's improper, I tell you. Especially at their age. You're asking for all sorts of trouble.'

'It's only temporary,' Galen said.

Kairos listened quietly as they decided his fate. Although he wanted to be around Althea, Stella's presence bothered him, and he felt his temper rising the longer he was near her. His short experience with dwarves brought nothing but painful memories: Thylar, Farina. He immediately tried to forget them, but ever since he had arrived at the Avenal Manor, Althea's presence was a constant reminder of the Milbrooke girl. He also wondered what had become of Farina's brother, Henrik. Kairos felt a twinge of guilt intermingled with responsibility to help the boy. However, Galen said he was going to live with relatives and left it at that. Kairos did not dwell on Henrik's well-being for too long. He had his own concerns.

'He cannot stay here,' Stella said, ignoring Kairos as if he did not even exist at the table. 'Even if it's temporary.'

'It's just for tonight,' Galen said. 'I already have a caretaker in mind.'

Stella's eyes widened. 'Don't tell me—'

'Yes, it's Mr. Dubose.'

The dwarf slammed a hand on the table. 'You know he won't approve of this. You remember the last lad you brought over there. He didn't last two days!'

'Do you have any other suggestions? Or should he stay here, after all?'

'Absolutely not!' Stella said. 'Very well, to Mr. Dubose's house on the morrow, then.'

After dinner Galen expressed that he was worn out from his trip and retired early for the evening. Stella showed Kairos to his sleeping quarters, set the clean linen on the bed, and coldly bid him good-night. He did not deign to reply.

That night, he sat in bed thinking about his fate. He felt so helpless, subject to the whims of these strangers. Yet, that wasn't so different than living with the Einar, he supposed. No one called him 'Kairos the Coward' here. But he didn't belong in Ordonia. He belonged in Logres. This land was too different, and tomorrow brought even more uncertainty. He didn't know who Mr. Dubose was, and dreaded the thought that this man would be like Uncle Vinh. Either way, he was getting away from Stella. He had had enough of dwarves.

Just before he drifted off to sleep, his thoughts lingered on Althea. He would figure out a way to overthrow Stella's authority. He resolutely decided that he was going to see Althea again regardless of what that dwarf said.

\* \* \*

The next day was Zemdag, or Zemus's Day, though few in Vadost ever thought of it in those terms, considering the gods had long since vanished from the world. Some still paid tribute to them on this day, visiting the temples to pray and meditate; a few of them believed that the gods were still around and would reward the faithful. For many others though, Zemdag was a day of pleasure and shopping, because most of the schools and services were closed. Throngs of youth took advantage of this to crowd the marketplace and spend their parents' hard-earned money. Many of the adults relaxed till past noon, due to the late night drunken revelries of the prior day.

The Avenal family – not one to partake in spirits – was up with the dawn. They ate breakfast, everyone marvelling at Kairos's appetite; Stella muttering something about Mr. Dubose being 'eaten out of a house' as she watched the boy devour over half a dozen eggs and several scones whilst still wanting more. She also admonished Althea for wearing her best dress for such a simple outing.

Althea turned as red as the strawberries on the table and furrowed her brows. 'You're being such a fusspot,' she complained.

'Yes, you are fussing more than usual,' Galen added.

'I am *not* fussing!' Stella yelled.

Unlike Galen, the dwarf noticed Althea's flushed face and quickened breathing at the breakfast table. She saw that the girl avoided talking to, even looking at, Kairos. The previous night when Stella had voiced her concerns to Lord Avenal, he shrugged her off with a laugh, stating that Althea had several 'crushes' over the summer, and this was no different. But this boy *was* different, Stella surmised. Her guardian's eye saw what the doting father's had not: the immediate danger in his handsome good looks, which seemed only accentuated by the filthy grime that lingered despite his bath. He wore his long dark hair loose, the thick locks framing the stern jawline of his serious face, and his accent had a sharp exotic twang to it. As if these traits weren't enough to turn the head of any young girl, there was a sense of raw animalistic passion and serious purpose about the boy that was lacking in the typical Ordonian youth, and that Stella found particularly disturbing.

After breakfast, Stella told everyone that she was staying behind, despite many attempts of Galen trying to persuade her otherwise. She knew that Galen was going to take Kairos to his new home today – to Mr. Dubose's house. But how long would that take? Galen's nature was to spoil his only child, and Stella knew he would allow his daughter to run off unattended with this boy, and the thought appalled her. She had not watched over this lovely girl, the closest thing to a daughter, for the past several years for some urchin to whisk her off into trouble now. And this boy *was* trouble.

As she watched Galen, Kairos, and Althea travel down the cobblestone path that descended into the city of Vadost, Stella hoped that the boy would settle into Mr. Dubose's house and never come back ever again.

\* \* \*

Considered one of the most beautiful and magically advanced cities in the world, Vadost, meaning 'valley town' in the ancient tongue, started out as a humble monastery dedicated to the god, Zemus. The monastery attracted followers from around the world, and they settled the valleys surrounding Lake Turquoise. After the Celestial War, the Mana Knights erected the large tower called Valour Keep nearby in one of the valleys to house their newly acquired Sapphire Shard, which was rumoured to be a large essence of the fallen Zemus, himself. The knights and engineers discovered a way to harness the god-like power within the shard to provide an infinite supply of energy to the surrounding area, powering everything from street lamps to carriages to industry.

The land prospered. The keep became a large fortress. Merchants and craftsmen came to settle near Valour Keep, eager to ply their trades, and soon several small towns and villages sprang up around the lake, flourishing from the support of the Knighthood and the Sapphire Shard. More and more people moved away from the outside world of chaos and violence and into this area of peace and security, and the towns and villages eventually merged into the city everyone enjoyed today.

Kairos's attention took in the sights (when it wasn't focused on Althea) as Althea explained the history of the city to him. He had arrived during the previous evening when everything was dark except the street lamps and house lights, which illuminated the valley like a thousand fireflies, reflecting their myriad colour of lights on the surface of Lake Turquoise. Now he saw the city with a new coat of bright, daylight paint. He gawked at the surrounding architecture – the colourful stone houses and the clean cobblestone streets that neatly connected everything together. They contrasted with the crumbling stone fortresses, wooden cabins, and muddy roads that were common in Logres; trees, flowers, and well-manicured shrubs gave the city a luscious appearance, as opposed to the dreary, grey landscape of his home.

The people were also another source of wonder.

Townsfolk filled the city, good-naturedly engaged in the marketplace, eating at the restaurants, buying the latest fashions, bargaining with the vendors – or haranguing the gnomes, who were everywhere they didn't belong, tripping the taller humans, as they skipped carelessly into their paths.

The City Watch and a few Mana Knights patrolled the streets, keeping a watchful eye on the citizens, ready to intervene if there was trouble. Trouble seemed rare in Vadost, though. Unlike the Einar, Kairos noted, everyone conducted his or her business peacefully, and seemed more likely to resolve disputes with the sparring of words rather than blades. Kairos relaxed a little, but he was still glad he had his dagger concealed in the rucksack he carried over his shoulder.

An elderly man stood outside the door to his general goods shop, tracing a glowing pattern in the air with his wand to levitate a shipment of crates from the street into the second-storey window. He furrowed his brows in concentration as he guided a particularly large crate from the ground.

Kairos watched the whole process, mesmerised. Even the average citizen could use this power, he mused.

'Watch out!' Althea said.

Kairos was staring upwards at the levitating crate as he strolled forward – until he inadvertently bumped into the old man.

The spell fizzled and the crate fell, threatening to crush them both. The old man quickly traced a pattern, but equally quickly abandoned that idea and threw his arms above his head, his wand looking like a feeble stick compared to the cart-sized crate of imminent death that was descending upon him. Kairos did the same, knowing he could not move out of the way in time. Just as he thought he was going to become one with the street, the crate suddenly stopped, hovering a few inches above Kairos's face. Not understanding what was happening, he watched the crate slowly ascend upwards, depositing itself safely inside the second-storey window of the building.

Kairos looked around in wonder and saw a faint glow dissipating from Galen's hands, the knight's gaze directed upwards.

The old man stooped over, breathing heavily and clutching his chest as though he were about to have a heart attack. Once he recovered and realised he wasn't dead, he rounded on Kairos with fury. 'You bloody fool! Are you daft? Watch where you're going.

You almost killed us. Couldn't you see I was in the midst of a spell?'

'My apologies, sir,' Galen said, laying a gentle hand on the old man's shoulder. 'He's new here and admiring our great city so much that he forgot himself. I trust you can forgive him?'

The man's anger dissipated like steam in the wind. 'Lord Avenal! A blessed day to you, milord. W-why yes, there's been no harm, I suppose.' The man bowed. 'Don't tell me that it was you who saved us? It's an honour, milord.'

Galen dismissed the praise and, before it evolved into worship – so enamoured was the man of the knight – guided Kairos away. Galen was not wearing his knightly armour, but people here seemed to recognise and admire him, Kairos thought. In this regard, he was similar to Karthok, but Galen seemed to command respect with a warm and friendly demeanour, rather than the iron fist of fear and authority.

'You mustn't bother people when they're casting spells, Kairos,' Galen chided. 'That goes double when they're using levitation spells and moving heavy objects, mind you. It would be a shame for you to survive Malus's army only to be scraped up from the street, crushed by a wooden crate.'

'Can everybody here use magic?' Kairos asked, unfazed by the severity of his actions.

Galen and Althea paused and stared at him as if he had sprouted horns on his head. 'What do you mean?' Galen said. 'Of course they can.'

Kairos looked away, realising he had said too much. He did not want to reveal his weakness. The Einar weakness. It was only because no one had taught him, he told himself. He looked up at Galen, who was regarding him with a keen, knowing eye, as if the man could read his thoughts.

'Just where *are* you from?' Althea asked in a shy, innocent tone. 'I forgot to ask. Your accent sounds foreign.'

Kairos did not answer. He remembered Galen's words: *Do not tell anyone else that you come from across the sea. Do not tell them about*

*Logres, the Blight, or about your people.* He wondered if that applied to Althea. She was Galen's daughter, after all.

'Thea, please don't trouble him with such a question,' Galen answered instead, much to the boy's relief. 'He comes from afar, and he's been displaced as a result of Malus's army. It's not proper to bring up such bad memories.'

'Oh heavens.' Althea regarded Kairos with a look of genuine and profound sympathy. 'I'm sorry.'

They didn't walk far before the populace took note of Galen. Kairos was used to his father's popularity back in Logres, but that was miniscule in comparison. Kairos and Althea walked silently behind Galen as people called out to him.

'Greetings, milord!'

'Nice day, isn't it, Lord Avenal?'

'How fares the fight against Malus, milord?'

Kairos glanced at Galen uneasily. The knight smiled and greeted each person cheerfully in return. Althea, on the other hand, stared shyly at the cobblestone pavement beneath her, her skin burnished with a sheen of red.

'Is it always this way?' Kairos asked her in a low voice. 'Walking with your father, that is.'

'Yes,' Althea answered sadly. 'It's difficult to spend time with him. Everyone always wants his attention. Speaking of which, here comes Lord Cyr.' With an exasperated look, she added in a sarcastic tone, 'Duty calls.'

As the trio neared the Ivory Bridge, which led directly to the marketplace, a middle-aged man geared in a full suit of armour approached them. To Kairos's surprise, he was a big man, almost big enough to pass as an Einar. His armour barely seemed able to encase him. He had chestnut hair, tinged with grey and close-cropped. As he came near the trio, his attention fixed on Galen with a sense of purpose.

'Lord Avenal,' he said. 'You're just in time.'

As if anticipating what was to come, Galen Avenal held up his hands. 'I'm off-duty, Lord Cyr. Can't this wait?'

'But it's one of the dark elves, sir,' Lord Cyr said. 'Due to the recent string of events with Malus, some of the townsfolk are threatening to run him out of the city.'

'Who?'

'Sanctus.'

'But he's lived here for ages!' Galen said, his voice taking on an edge of anger. 'He's the best cobbler in the city.'

'I know, milord,' Lord Cyr said gravely. 'But there's a mob outside his shop and there are only a few of us. Perhaps you can reason with them. The citizens look up to you.'

Galen turned and gave Althea an apologetic look. 'Duty calls,' he said. 'Can we meet at the fountain later?'

'Go ahead, father,' she answered, looking glum.

'I'm sorry,' he said, pulling out a coin purse and handing Althea a few coins. 'Buy something for you and Kairos for now. I'll make it up to you later.' Galen hugged his morose daughter and followed Lord Cyr without looking back.

After watching the two knights run off down the street, Althea gave a long sigh. 'He always says that and rarely does.'

Kairos watched Althea stare after her father with a crestfallen expression. Her sad beauty made his heart ache. The good news in all of this was that they were alone now, away from Stella's cloying protectiveness. They could talk freely. But what would they talk about? He knew nothing of the girl, and she probably found him uninteresting, especially compared to the other boys he had seen in town, who were dressed much better than he was, and could use magic. He tried to think of something to say but couldn't. He wasn't used to talking to girls.

Suddenly, Althea's face brightened, and a large smile spread across her lips. 'Let's go,' she said. 'What would you like to see? The city square? The marketplace? Or maybe Lake Turquoise?'

'Everything.'

'Let's see.' Althea frowned in thought. 'We probably have most of the day. The lake is a bit cold in the morning, but the vendors should be up and ready at the marketplace. We should go there first before the crowds. Then we can climb the hill to the

Nobles District after that. There's a splendid view of the lake at the top. Shall we?'

'Let's go,' Kairos said.

More people filled the streets as the morning progressed and Kairos and Althea waded through mass of bodies. Carts rumbled past on the noisy street, most being pulled by oxen as their dwarven masters lounged comfortably in the coach seat.

Unlike the laid-back life in Logres, everyone in Vadost seemed to be in a hurry. Kairos was bewildered by the bustle and commotion. He gawked at everything, clumsily bumping into a cart before stumbling ankle-deep in what appeared to be a brown, muddy puddle. Althea tried to take his hand, but he snatched away. His hands were sweating profusely, and he didn't want her to touch them.

'I'm okay! It's just mud.'

'Um, that's not mud,' said Althea, looking a little hurt by Kairos's action. 'Have you noticed that it hasn't rained in a while? We'll have to wash those boots later. Ah, this is the marketplace. If you're looking for something, this is the place to be!'

Vendor stalls lined each side of the street for several blocks. Kairos had never seen so many different things for sale in one area. Here he could find anything that he had ever imagined and much more. The vendors were a variety themselves. A lone gnome plied his technological trinkets. Dwarves sold tools, weapons, armour, casks of mountain ale, and offered repairs on every item, especially the casks for customers who imbibed too much. Elves sold fashionable clothing, and Althea hurried to investigate one oddly-dressed elf in particular. 'He's new here in the marketplace,' she said, rushing towards the booth. 'He arrived just the other day, and he has the best clothing in all of Vadost!'

An elf with long golden hair and wearing a multi-coloured assortment of clothing bowed deeply to her. 'Oh, if it isn't the queen of beauty herself. How may I, Stephon, serve milady today?'

'I see you have some nice garments here,' she said excitedly, quickly losing herself in the racks of clothing.

'Yes, milady,' Stephon bowed, watching Althea peruse his wares. 'Ah, good choice. That exquisite gown is made with the highest quality elven silk... And that kirtle you're holding was imported directly from Kinclaven, my home city.'

Kairos stopped at the threshold of the booth, his muscles tense. He stared at Stephon's pointed ears, his large, round eyes, and skin that was pale and smooth with an ageless sheen. Watching the elf instantly brought back the gruesome image of the elves in the barn, Farina's corpse staring at him, blood gushing from the stab wounds in her torso, drenching her dress. Once again, her golden hair was missing, and great strips of skin had been flayed from her scalp; her mouth was open, dried blood caking her face, as though she were voicing the endless horror she had to endure... He felt an instinctive urge to rush in and shield Althea from this man.

Aware of Kairos's gaze, Stephon turned and looked. 'Why don't you paint a picture? It will last longer.'

'You're an elf,' said Kairos, glaring at Stephon.

'So I am.' Stephon rolled his eyes and heaved an exaggerated sigh for extra measure. 'I mean, what gave it away? It must be my good looks. Jealous, are we?' The elf turned to Althea. 'Piffle. Is this your friend? He's quite the rude one.'

Embarrassed, Kairos looked away. He tried to banish the anger that was threatening to surface. He knew it was wrong to blame this particular elf for Farina's death. But for some reason, Kairos still detested his presence.

'Please don't mind him, sir,' Althea said, mortified. 'He's not from around here, but he's staying with us for now.'

'No harm, my fine lass,' the elf said. 'I'm used to the occasional peasant who was raised by donkeys, though this one smells a bit worse.' Stephon leant forward and squinted at the boy in curiosity. 'Now that you mention it, though, he doesn't look like your typical human from around here. Especially with that dark hair. And he's not dark nor refined enough to be from Numidia. Interesting. So *where* are you from?'

'Piss off.'

'My, a feisty one! Definitely not refined. Milady, surrounding yourself with filthy low-class imbeciles like this—' Stephon sniffed at Kairos and, grabbing a handkerchief from a purple pouch hanging from his belt, put it to his nose. 'You have your work cut out for you, dear. Ah, never mind that. I see you have chosen a nice red bonnet. I have some matching boots that would look fabulous on you. The highest quality elven leather from the D'Kari, dyed and cured by the best and yours truly, Stephon the Great. See, I even added runes of protection – in a fashionable pattern, mind you – to prevent the usual wear and tear. These should last you for years.' The elf presented the red boots to Althea and bowed with a flourish.

'Splendid!' Althea held the boots up to admire them. 'How much?'

'For you, my dear, that will be a silver crown, and the rest on the house. Or perhaps I shall say, 'on the booth.' A gratuity for being a distinguished customer with the finest taste.'

'Really? No, I cannot take these for almost nothing. You worked so hard on them.'

'Ahem. Of course I did. But if you insist,' Stephon was appraising Kairos from head to toes with a look of disdain, 'then get that boy out of those rags and into something more, hmm, shall I say, more palatable?'

'What a lovely idea, Steph. Father did tell me to buy him some clothes.'

The elf suggested several tunics of exuberant hues and designs. Althea nodded with enthusiasm, but Kairos flushed with fury at the thought of wearing them. The tunics looked as though a peacock had exploded on them, so he refused one after another. Finally, the only tunic he settled for was a brown leather one with brown leather breeches.

'But these haven't even been dyed, nor have I graced them with my elegant designs,' Stephon said, aghast. 'For the sake of fashion, I cannot allow you to stroll the streets in such mediocrity.'

'These will do,' Kairos said, curtly. 'I don't like those other ones. Looking at them makes me want to vomit. Too many colours.'

'Ugh, no fashion or manners in this one,' Stephon sighed, wrinkling his nose and turning to Althea. 'My dear, you really should associate with someone of better class. He will only bring you down... That will be three silver crowns. I'll even throw in a cloth undershirt for free if that helps get rid of the stench. He can change in this stall. Be sure to close the curtain – I don't need you scaring away my customers. If you want to use the mirror, it's next to the stall. Don't stare at it too long, though, because I don't want your grime and filth to rub off on it!'

Kairos ignored the insults and entered the stall, slipping into his new clothes, which felt stiff and smelled like fresh leather; he took an instant fancy to them, nonetheless. Such attire would be worth a fortune in Logres. Upon exiting the stall, Althea showed her approval by clapping. Stephon merely grumbled, 'Well, it's an improvement, but you merely went from a filthy peasant to an average peasant.'

'Thank you, Stephon,' Althea said. 'Here, take three crowns. No, no! You must. Father would be quite displeased if I took something for a discount.'

Stephon gave another bow. 'Send your father my regards, milady.'

The pair left, Althea bidding farewell, continuing past the other clothing vendors. Kairos felt stiff, walking in his new outfit, but the elf was right. This was an improvement, though he was loath to admit it. He hated that elf. He hated all elves... And dwarves, too, he added as an afterthought, thinking of Stella. But he hated that elf more, he decidedly angrily when replaying the recent scene of insults in his mind. The only reason why he hadn't lashed out was because Althea liked him.

'Is something wrong?' she asked. 'You have an angry look on your face.'

'No,' Kairos said, then in an attempt to change the subject, he pointed to a building bearing a colourful sign of a girl with exaggerated curves holding a pint of ale. 'What's that place?'

'Ah, that's a tavern called the Pinch and Tickle. Father says I'm never ever allowed to go there. We're going over here. There's something you have to try.'

The next block had smoke full of all sorts of tantalising smells. They made Kairos's stomach growl even though he had had breakfast a short while ago. One peculiar aroma lured him to a stall occupied by a heavyset lady. Many spherical-shaped delicacies sat in arrangement on sheets of wax paper, and they smelled better than any delicacy back in Logres. 'What are these?' Kairos asked.

'Chocolate truffles,' Althea replied, her eyes aglow.

'What are they?'

'Oh, you would love them!'

The large lady gestured and announced in a throaty voice, 'She's right! These truffles consist of fresh cream and chocolate, rolled in powdered dwarven chestnuts.'

Althea nudged Kairos. 'Would you like to try one?'

He sniffed the air. 'I'd like to try two or three.'

'Okay, then four truffles, please!' Althea said.

'That'll be a half crown.' The lady took a small silver coin from Althea and wrapped the truffles in a sheet of wax paper, handing them over to an eager Kairos.

The pair trod along, eating. Kairos consumed his three truffles in an instant, remarking that they were the most delicious things he had ever tasted in his life. Chocolate covered his fingertips, which he licked, then wiped on his new leather tunic, consequently receiving a playful rebuke from Althea.

For the first time since he had arrived from across the sea, a genuine smile threatened to form on his lips.

\* \* \*

The city square, or Lazio Fountain as it was known, was the heart of Vadost. The fountain resided at the junction of four main roads of the city – including Merchants Lane – thus, serving as the place for families, friends, and merchants to rendezvous and relax. The youth of Vadost used the open square as a bastion of people-watching, which more than often resulted in flirting for the more daring.

The fountain itself was famous throughout the land for its remarkable beauty. Serving as both the backdrop and water source of the fountain, a statue of a dragon, standing at thirty metres high and portraying the avatar of the god Zemus, spread its enormous wings and was forever spraying a gout of water onto the boulders, the waters cascading down into the pool below. It was the largest fountain in Ordonia (though the dwarves claimed to have a much larger one in their homeland of Dvergar, but no human had ever measured it to confirm the exact size). On any given sunny day, many artists could be found, painting the majestic dragon statue and its fountain. On this day, many couples were having a picnic in the large shade of its wingspan.

The other pastime was casting a prayer spell. It was tradition with the Temple of Zemus to cast a spell transferring a small portion of the user's mana to the dragon when praying to the god. Now most Ordonians and tourists continued the gesture for novelty or good luck, though many superstitious merchants, mercenaries and knights would make sure to donate a portion of their mana along with a prayer on the eve of a risky expedition. In truth, this transfer of mana was what maintains the fountain's flow.

Spending time at Lazio Fountain was, next to flirting, shopping, and studying, Althea's favourite pastime.

Althea was well-educated – mandatory for a daughter of a renowned knight. Every morning was spent studying her lessons with Lady Beatrice, learning advanced theories and philosophies of mathematics, spellcasting, and history. Nothing pleased her father more than to look at her huddled over a book. And Lady Beatrice proved an excellent tutor. She ensured that Althea knew her glyphs and their constructs, and the various cultures of the world and their history. Their studies often stretched into the early afternoon, when Lady Beatrice suddenly noticing the time, would hurry out the door and towards her next appointment.

Occasionally Stella took over morning lessons, instructing Althea on the management of the household, raising of children, and the arts and crafts. Stella was an expert lute player, a skill she passed onto Althea. These lessons brought Althea a great deal of pleasure, along with filling the void of not having her late mother around. She and the dwarf spent a great deal of time tending the gardens and maintaining the upkeep of the manor. But, no matter how much she delighted in excelling at her studies or being with Stella, she looked forward each day to the end of the lessons when she would venture to Lazio Fountain, often with her friend, Cassie, to partake in her latest craze: boys.

Althea always enjoyed the serene atmosphere of the fountain, the sound of the water trickling down the rocks. Today she found a new appreciation of the fountain, as she shared its wonders and history with Kairos, who listened in silence, but regarded her with those intense eyes. They had visited many shops, seen several gardens, and gone to Lake Turquoise. As she watched Kairos take in the sights of Vadost through her words and eyes, she realised for the first time just how beautiful her city really was.

'I hope you enjoyed the tour of the city,' Althea said as they sat at one of the many benches facing the fountain.

Kairos nodded. 'I have. Thank you.'

'Perhaps after this, you can show some of your spells,' Althea mentioned. 'I'd love to see what type of magic you specialise in.'

To Althea's astonishment, Kairos's face darkened, his black brows coming together in a thick, hard line above his eyes. 'There's not much to see,' he said in a measured voice. 'I'm afraid I don't specialise in anything—'

'Of course you do,' cried Althea eagerly. 'Everyone specialises in something, except dwarves and gnomes, that is, because they don't have mana.'

'What do you mean?'

'Surely you jest,' Althea said with a smile, though Kairos regarded her with an odd piercing scrutiny that increased her discomfort. Seeming to feel the need for explanation, she added, 'Well, uh, you see… The country of Numidia focuses more on the water element. Light elves are the only race with schools of magic on the healing element. The farmers at Ordonia practise much of the earth element. Your homeland must focus on some type of element?'

'I'm sorry,' said Kairos in low tones, his eyes now wistful and shadowed. 'I'd rather not talk about my homeland right now.'

'Oh heavens,' Althea gasped, for the second time that day, recalling, again, her father's words. 'I'm sorry. Father mentioned your recent ordeal. How selfish of me.' She placed a gentle hand on Kairos's arm. 'If you ever feel ready to tell me later, then you can. Otherwise, I won't ask again.'

'Thank you,' Kairos replied, his eyes reflecting sincere gratitude. 'It's a very different world to this place. My homeland is harsh. I'll tell you more about it one day.'

'I would like that.' Althea cast a sideways glance at the water in the fountain. 'I've spent my entire life in here. I've never been outside of Vadost, unless you count Valour Keep. My father, on the other hand, has seen much of the world. That's one reason I want to become a Mana Knight – to see the world. And follow in his footsteps.'

'Your father made that very suggestion to me,' Kairos said. 'I'd like to become a Mana Knight, as well.'

Althea looked up at him. 'That'd be wonderful. Perhaps we could be in the Knight Academy together.'

The pair locked eyes. As they sat in close proximity, a delightful pain shot through Althea's heart. The look in the grey eyes was intense, more intense than the other ardent youth of Vadost. She saw the fierce determination, the sadness. Some part of her saw a cloud of darkness lurking beneath, too. Yet on top of the darkness, a flicker of a smile flashed in his eyes, if not on his face.

Kairos opened his mouth, thinking of what to say, but before he could say anything, a mocking voice interrupted them. 'You in the Knight Academy, Avenal? That's a laugh! Your fire spell can't even light oil afire.'

Althea sighed. She knew that voice anywhere. It was Vaughn. She slowly turned and saw that Claudius was with him. They regarded her with amused disdain.

'Who's your new friend?' enquired Claudius, the shorter of the two. He was lanky and had a gaunt, aquiline face, which reminded Althea of an angry falcon. 'And where did he come from? I ain't ever seen him before.'

'Yes, he's my friend,' Althea answered. 'And he has a name, you know.'

'Oh, he does, does he?' sneered Vaughn, the taller, heavyset boy. 'He doesn't look like much. Just another worthless git.'

Althea cast a sidelong glance at Kairos, whose face reddened. With clenched fists, he took a step towards Vaughn and Claudius, causing both boys to stiffen. Did she just see him reach for something in the rucksack he carried? She feared the worst.

Before anyone could make a move, a tall figure approached them from the side. 'There you are! I've circled the fountain twice looking for you two. What took you so long, Thea? You didn't stop at every shop along the way, did you?' It was Galen, much to Althea's relief. He flashed his quick smile at the two boys, measuring the situation immediately.

'Be easy on this lad. He's new in the city and not quite settled in yet!'

The taller, stockier boy laughed. The other one smiled in return to Galen's amused grin. All the tension vanished.

'Thea, come along. We're running late and need to hurry. Mr. Dubose will be quite cross with me if we show up during his evening meal.' Galen put his arm around Althea and Kairos's shoulders and led them away from Lazio Fountain.

When they were out of earshot of Vaughn and Claudius, Galen muttered to Kairos, 'You need to curb your quick temper. When I first saw you, you were making a suicide attack against well-armed elves. Then when you met Stella, the first thing you did was provoke her, one of the scariest and most violent women

I've ever encountered. And now you've been out with Althea for less than a day and you're almost fighting with Vaughn Akkitos and his friend Claudius, right in the middle of Lazio Plaza! I admit, you have some courage, but you won't live long if you carry on like this.'

'He's right, Kairos,' said Althea, as they left the city square, her heart still pounding in her chest at the threat of violence. 'Vaughn is clearly a buffoon, but he has an extraordinary mana level for his age, and he's the son of Lady Naiya Akkitos, who is a Griffon Knight.'

Kairos nodded, but said nothing. Althea saw that his hands were shaking and he was taking deep breaths, but she pretended not to notice. She was not used to being around someone who was so confrontational, and it took half an hour's walk for her nerves to settle. They were almost to Dwarfside, where Mr. Dubose lived, and she hoped that Kairos would not antagonise him or anyone else for the remainder of the day. There was one thought she kept to herself, however. The fact that Kairos easily stood up for her brought a sensation of warmth and joy to her soul.

# Chapter Five

### Dwarfside

*A dwarven residential district, or rather a small subterranean town, appeared in Vadost approximately two centuries ago when a dwarven miner, quite by accident, discovered a large deposit of hematite inside a cavern nearby the city. Subsequently, word spread and many dwarves, seeking a new life or escaping an old one, migrated to Dwarfside from their home kingdom of Dvergar.*

Autumn Greene, Vadost Oracle reporter

**W**elcome to Dwarfside,' Galen announced.

Kairos had never seen anything like it. He expected a tunnel, but instead found himself walking into a large open cavern that could house a small, bustling town. Street lamps illuminated the darkness, casting its ambient orange-red glow on the streets and buildings. That was another oddity – dwarves didn't have homes or houses, they had workshops they just happened to live and work in. Dwarven priorities, Kairos assumed.

The limestone streets bustled with activity. The sound of hammers pounded away from workshops, echoing along the streets in a cacophony of chaos. Dwarves stood about in groups, laughing and talking. Some of them cast curious glances at Kairos, Galen, and Althea as they passed, others rudely stared, and a few muttered comments. Apparently, humans did not pass through here often. Kairos clutched his rucksack closer, his hand instinctively reaching for his dagger. 'What's going on up ahead?' he asked.

'Ah, that is a very popular dwarven sport,' said Galen.

A large group of dwarves were gathered outside a tavern, which was also a workshop that happened to sell ale, making a commotion that rivalled the constant hammering. Kairos peeled away from Galen and Althea for a closer inspection and saw pair of dwarves engaging each other in an arm wrestling competition. Their muscles, thick as tree trunks, bulged with the strain. Small braziers of glowing embers sat on each side of the table, inviting the back of the loser's hand. Both dwarves turned red as blood vessels popped out of their foreheads and arms like tree branches. A drunken crowd clustered around to cheer and jeer. Kairos stopped to watch, content he was able to see over the heads of everyone.

Althea sighed. 'I don't understand the dwarves' fascination with this dull sport.'

'I like it,' Kairos said.

She raised an eyebrow. 'Really? That's quite odd.'

Galen paused too. 'Is arm wrestling popular where you're from?'

'Yes, but we don't use the burning coals. We use broken glass.'

Althea looked down and noticed a few scars on the back of Kairos's hand.

Both dwarves appeared on the verge of exploding from the exertion. Finally, one of them began losing ground, and the other seized upon the opportunity and wrangled his opponent's arm down in a shower of sparks for the victory. The defeated dwarf howled in pain and clutched his hand. A few cheers sounded, but a lot more curses rang out, followed by grumbling. Apparently, most of the crowd had placed their bets on the loser.

'Let's go,' Galen said solemnly, 'before a fight breaks out and we get caught in the middle of it.'

They left hurriedly, and not long thereafter, angry shouts, followed by the sound of glass breaking, came from behind them. A pair of armoured dwarves ran past them towards the melee.

The trio continued on until they reached the farthest corner of Dwarfside, where a lone workshop stood away from the street and the rest of the buildings. It was made of stone like the other shops; unlike the other shops, however, it was taller and wider. A placard above the doorway, which was level with Kairos's nose, read, 'Foreman Dubose.' Halting, Galen gave a booming knock. There came a clatter from inside, as of something shattering.

'You whoreson!' yelled an irritated voice. 'You've made me drop my bucket of corzite! What on Alban do you want?'

Galen grinned, winked at Kairos. 'I have your new apprentice, sir. The one I mentioned in the letter.'

'I'm through with apprentices,' the voice shouted. 'Send him away... Wait. Don't. He can clean up this mess.' There came the sound of footsteps and a door bolt lifting. The heavy oak door swung open with a creak.

'Meet the master blacksmith, Jace Dubose,' said Galen.

Upon hearing the word 'blacksmith,' Kairos expected an old man, or at least an older dwarf. Back in Logres, the Einar became blacksmiths when they could no longer fight effectively in a shield wall and keep up with the younger men in battle. Then they picked up the hammer and fired up the forge to make themselves useful for their clan. At the sight of the blacksmith standing in the doorway, glaring up at him, Kairos's impression of blacksmiths changed quite drastically.

The dwarf was, of course, short, but he came to Kairos's shoulder and was almost as tall as Althea. What he lacked in height, he made up for in muscular bulk; his rippling arms made the arm-wrestling dwarves at the tavern seem like amateurs. He was relatively young, appearing in his thirties in human terms, given that there was not a single grey hair on his head or in his beard – though that said little about the dwarf's true age. He was broad-shouldered with ham-fisted hands, which explained why he dropped the bucket. He had a swarthy complexion, with eyes whose darkness was emphasised by the menacing scowl on his face.

But it was not his fierce and mighty looks that caused Kairos to stiffen. The blacksmith was a dwarf. Galen never mentioned that Mr. Dubose was a dwarf. Now that Kairos thought of his current location, though, what else did he expect? A human living in Dwarfside seemed very unlikely, but he was too enraptured by his surroundings and too absorbed in his own dilemma to have given his future much thought. One thing was certain though: Kairos could have no respect for this dwarf.

He was subsequently surprised and irritated to see his own contempt reflected right back at him.

'Ugh, by Thelos's hammer, I should've known it was you, Galen,' Mr. Dubose growled. 'And you've brought me a damn human. A boy at that.'

The words frustrated Kairos, but not enough to miss the lack of respect towards Galen in the dwarf's tone. Ever since he'd met the knight, he'd heard everyone address Galen as 'Lord Avenal,' or 'milord.' This dwarf dropped the fancy titles.

'Well, what can you do, boy?' The dwarf's frown seemed to droop even more with the beard.

Kairos glowered in response. He would not answer such disrespect.

'Probably not much of anything, judging by those spindly arms.' Mr. Dubose answered his own question. 'Most of you humans rely on your piddling magic to start a fire or lift a boulder.' Turning to Galen, the dwarf said, 'Why'd you bring him here? He can't be an apprentice. The recent bloke couldn't last three days, and he was a dwarf and three times this kid's size. What makes you think this boy will do?'

'He has no choice for now,' Galen admitted. 'A victim of Malus's armies. He has no family and no home. I'll try to enlist him into the Knighthood with Althea, but he needs work, and a place to stay for now. Please consider it as a favour for me.'

The dwarf bridled, looking indignant. 'Do I look like a charity? How about *you* take him in if you want to help him so much!'

Althea's face brightened at the prospect. 'Of course,' she said. 'That's a splendid idea. We have that extra guestroom and–'

'Stella has already forbidden it,' Galen interrupted. 'She says that 'it's improper.' She also suggested that Mr. Dubose is the right candidate.'

Mr. Dubose's features softened for a moment. 'Stella said that?'

'He has nowhere else to go, Mr. Dubose,' Galen said. 'Please consider it?'

'All right!' the dwarf thundered. 'I'll do it! You don't have to beg me. Now if you'll excuse us, this boy has some work to do.'

'Yes, sir, Mr. Dubose.' Galen bowed and turned. 'Come on, Thea. Let's go.'

The young girl lingered behind. 'Shall we meet again?' she asked Kairos.

Kairos's voice faltered. He turned to look at her, trying to see whether she was in earnest. Her eyes were bright, and her cheeks were flushed. He swallowed hard. 'Yes. I'll come by your house when I can.'

'Do you remember how to get there?' she asked, looking worried.

'Thea, let's go,' Galen commanded, though there was a flicker of amusement in his eyes, and the girl reluctantly walked away with her father, but not before turning back to hear Kairos's answer.

But before he could respond, Mr. Dubose grabbed hold of his arm, yanked him through the doorway with a jerk that caused him to bump his head on the wooden frame, and slammed the door shut behind him. Kairos rubbed the new bump on his head, the pain overtaking any angry retort he had in mind. When the pain subsided, he looked around at his surroundings in apprehension. The house was a dark and shadowy workshop, illuminated by the glowing embers of the forge. Various weapons hung on the wall: bludgeons, hammers, maces, spears, a sword that strongly resembled Thylar's, and some other weapons Kairos did not recognise. At the opposite end of the room, a doorway led to another dimly-lit room containing bookshelves filled with books.

Mr. Dubose let go of Kairos and regarded him as if he were appraising a vegetable at a grocer's stall. He obviously found what he saw lacking.

Kairos began to seethe with rage beneath the offensive scrutiny.

The dwarf took a step towards Kairos, and leant forward, the dark beard and glowering dark eyes giving him a menacing, wild look.

'I am Jace Dubose. That's *Mister Dubose* to you, boy.'

'My name is—' Kairos began in a chipped tone.

Mr. Dubose waved a dismissing hand. 'I don't care what your name is, boy. I don't want to know. The last apprentice I had only lasted two days, and I didn't know his name, either. You little bastards run off after a few chores, so it's a waste of time getting to know you.' The dwarf's eyes moved away from Kairos. 'Now what's in the bag?' he said, snatching it with startling speed.

Kairos was too impressed and shocked to object to the dwarf rummaging through the contents of the rucksack.

'I see you brought a dagger.' The dwarf pulled the blade out. He held it up to his face, squinting as he peered at the etchings. With a meaty hand that seemed far too large for the handle, he held the dagger and made a few slashes in the air, almost slicing Kairos in the face.

Mr. Dubose returned the dagger to the rucksack, which he tossed aside on the floor. 'A fair dagger, but not well-cared for. See how tarnished it is?'

'I found it,' Kairos said, seeming to feel the need for explanation. 'In a caipora den.'

'Damn right, you found it,' Mr. Dubose barked. 'That's a dwarven-made dagger. And a caipora den? That's a drab lie if I ever heard one. Are you sure you didn't steal it? These things don't run cheap, and it's illegal for humans to carry blades out in Vadost, except for the knights and the City Watch. And I doubt either of those two are enlisting little runts like you. I suppose you don't know how to use it properly, do you, boy?'

Kairos was too appalled to reply. Steal it? His explanation dismissed as a 'drab lie!' True, he hadn't trained with daggers back in Logres, but he knew some basics—

'Yeah, I thought so,' said Mr. Dubose. He turned away, walked over to a stone table and sat in an iron-framed chair. He placed his large finger on a blueprint that lay on the table. 'A day's work all gone. I suppose I'll have to get more corzite and start over again.' Mr. Dubose motioned to an overturned bucket surrounded by shattered fragments of a blue-coloured stone. 'Clean up that mess, boy. There's a broom in the corner.'

Kairos had had enough, his anger exploded. 'No!' he shouted, stamping his foot to emphasise his wrath. 'I will not clean up your mess, you bloody dwarf. I am *not* your servant, or your slave, to be at your beck and call. I refuse to take orders from you, or any damned dwarf, for the matter. You lot, along with your elven leader, Malus, can all rot—'

Mr. Dubose could move very quickly for a stocky, musclebound dwarf. One moment he was seated on the chair, the next he appeared right in front of Kairos like a serpent bursting out of the Dark Sea.

'Listen to me, boy,' Mr. Dubose said, jabbing his thick finger into Kairos's face. 'First, you do not tell me what to do. I tell you what to do. If I tell you to lick shit off the floor, then you lick it clean and savour the taste. Second, you will refer to me as Mr. Dubose, or Mister, or sir. Third, don't you *ever* lump me together with Malus's army. Anyone who serves his army is my enemy. I've fought against Malus with Galen many years ago and would do so again if that dark elf were to so much as thrust his ugly grey head into Vadost.'

He moved the finger from Kairos's face to his own neck, tilting his head so Kairos could see the scar. 'One of his elites shot a spell through my neck like an arrow.' Mr. Dubose took a step, leant forward so that his neck was nearly touching Kairos's chest. 'Missed my spine, throat and artery. Galen's magic patched me up.

I have fought against Malus's army. Fought against fellow dwarves. I lost my wife to them.' The dwarf took another step and glared up at Kairos with unflinching intensity.

'I have also fought against Malus's army,' said Kairos coolly, standing his ground, 'and I have lost everything to them, including my brother and father, and...' He almost uttered Farina's name, but realised he was sharing too much with this... this *dwarf.*

Stillness as tense as a heatwave radiated between them. They stared at each other, perhaps sharing the same thoughts.

'Have you truly fought against Malus's army?' Mr. Dubose asked. 'You would swear an oath to this?'

Kairos hesitated. He detested this dwarf and silently cursed Galen for abandoning him here. The promise of a small hovel would have lured him out of that workshop in an instant. And now the dwarf was asking him to swear an oath. For the Einar, an oath was one's sacred word of binding. All Einar believed in standing by an oath, to break it was to dishonour one's own name and reputation forever, and Kairos assumed that the dwarf viewed oaths in the same way, judging by the gravity of his tone. In that last question, Kairos detected a subtle change in the dwarf's tone – a shared experience, a shared pain. A kindred spirit. He didn't quite understand it, but somehow deep down, he knew that he and the dwarf were alike in many ways. But he still hated the bastard.

'Yes,' said Kairos gravely. 'I give you my oath.'

Mr. Dubose nodded. 'Then it's settled.' He went to the corner, grabbed the broom, and handed it to Kairos. 'Now, boy,' he said, pointing to the scattered fragments on the floor. 'Start sweeping.'

Kairos took a deep breath and began to sweep half-heartedly.

'Wait.' Mr. Dubose stopped him immediately. 'What are you doing with that broom?'

'What does it look like I'm doing,' Kairos said in an exasperated voice. 'I'm sweeping.'

'No, that is not sweeping.'

'Everyone has a different method of doing things,' the boy answered. 'This is my method of sweeping.'

The dwarf raised an eyebrow. 'Different method? No, there's only one method, and then there's horseshit. Guess which one you're doing.'

Kairos groaned, briefly wondering if he would have been better off dying at the hands of the elves.

\* \* \*

For Mad Mavos's rundown, leaking hut, Kairos would have left the workshop, his new apprenticeship, and his vision of becoming a Mana Knight. He had spent the first night – or what he assumed was night since Dwarfside was underground – in his new home staring into the darkness, listening to the echoing sounds of incessant hammering and speculating on his options. Living with dwarves was unbearable.

Kairos had swept up the shattered corzite, which made him curious about the strange shiny stone. It gave off a blue glow, and Mr. Dubose mentioned that it helped channel mana. It proved as resilient as steel, once tempered, which the dwarf had been about to do prior to dropping it. After he dumped the broken stone into a bin, Mr. Dubose had taken Kairos to view his sleeping quarters.

His bed was more luxurious than his campsites with Gulliver. It was not comfortable, but it was an improvement over leaves or hay spread around on the cold earth. His feet stuck out over the edge of the bed, though, an inconvenience he remedied by placing a chair at the end of it.

'Everyone needs a blacksmith,' Mr. Dubose had told his new apprentice before bed. 'You can go to any town, anywhere in the world, and find work. And if you're a warrior or a knight, you can save yourself some money by doing your own repairs.'

Though he was beyond tired, Kairos could not sleep. Mr. Dubose snored so loudly that Kairos could feel his bones rattle. He wondered if the neighbours could hear, as well, but no one came to complain.

Near midnight, he had resolved to leave the next day. He would return to the Avenal Manor and ask Galen for help. Althea had mentioned having the guestroom, and the thought of being around her set his blood afire… No, Stella would not allow it – of course, it was a dwarf who thwarted his good fortune. But, where else could he go? He would never survive in a place like Gersholm, and the city of Vadost was so large that he did not even know where to start a life here. He was at a disadvantage until he could study the magic that these Ordonians used.

Kairos tossed and turned in his short bed. Lying there, he realised suddenly that the dull ache in his heart had diminished. He had felt homesick and lost before he had arrived in Vadost, like he wanted to die. The mental anguish of losing his brother, the Einar, and Farina pushed against his mind, like a tightening vice.

He pondered this. *Is the dwarf's work actually distracting me from my sadness?* he wondered. Since his arrival, he had performed a constant barrage of chores, and even though the work was gruelling, his mind was at ease. Perhaps it was because he was not dwelling on himself.

In the early morning hours, Kairos decided to stay. At least he might be able to learn some blacksmithing skills from Mr. Dubose; he conceded it was a useful skill to have. Also, the Einar were not quitters. He vowed to see this mission through, no matter what the dwarf threw at him. Decision made, he fell asleep to the dwarf's thunderous snoring and the clanging of hammers in the night.

That morning, Mr. Dubose cooked breakfast, which consisted of fire potato hash browns with goat blood sausage. 'Eat, boy. It'll put hair on your tongue and a fire in your eye.'

The fire potato scorched Kairos's mouth as soon as he tasted it, and he began to cough. 'I can't eat this,' he complained as soon as he caught his breath again. 'Do you have something else? This is spicy!'

'Excuse me? You're skipping around molten lava, boy,' Mr. Dubose barked, looking up from his plate. 'This is my home and my cooking. You and I are not equals. Here's me,' he said, putting his hand high above his head, 'and here's you.' He stomped his foot onto the floor. 'If I want to serve you only fire potatoes till the gods return, you will sit there every day and eat them like you've received Thelos's holiest of blessings and ask for more!'

'Why would I ask for more if they're rubbish?'

Mr. Dubose told Kairos to leave the table and wash the plates and clean up around the forge. Or at least that's what the boy assumed, because the dwarf was screaming with a mouth full of goat blood sausages, the juices dribbling down into his beard.

Kairos performed the chores around the workshop, while Mr. Dubose finished his meal in fuming silence. He did not mind the cleaning, as it took him away from the dwarf and brought him near the assortment of weapons hanging on the wall. He was impressed by their craftsmanship, especially the sword. None of the blacksmiths on Logres could produce weapons of such quality. He wondered if the dwarf made them all, or was able to use them.

Kairos discovered his answer the next moment when the dwarf appeared at his elbow.

'Admiring my collection, I see,' Mr. Dubose said. 'I bought most of them from a friend at a bargain. His wife made him get rid of them because she didn't want weapons in the house. What a nag. Anyhow, I thought they'd look good on the wall, but I tire of cleaning them.'

'Why do you keep them, then?' Kairos did little to mask the frustration in his voice. Look good on the wall! These weapons were a treasure hoard even his father, the most powerful man on Logres, would envy, and this dwarf was treating them as mere furniture.

Mr. Dubose flashed his teeth. 'Sell 'em for a profit, I guess.' Removing the sword that resembled Thylar's from the wall, he waved it around disrespectfully. 'I reckon I could get a gold coin or two for this one. That's more than I paid for the whole lot. A good investment, if I say so myself.'

Kairos stared, aghast. His hands yearned to pry that sword away from Mr. Dubose, to rescue it from such maltreatment.

'Well, enough of this,' Mr. Dubose said, carelessly hanging the sword back on the wall. 'It's time to begin your blacksmith training. You need to earn your keep around here.'

Kairos nodded, expecting to learn how to make a sword. Maybe he would have something that rivalled Thylar's weapon. Excitement tingled throughout his body.

'Now the first step is to light the forge fire.' After a brief demonstration, Mr. Dubose handed Kairos the bellows. 'Oh, and put on a leather apron before you burn yourself.'

The boy pumped the bellows into the forge as the dwarf had shown him, a wave of heat washing over him with each heave. He was pleased to see the satisfying glow from deep within the mound of charcoal.

'Now watch closely,' Mr. Dubose said, and placed a metal rod into the charcoal for several moments. When he took it out, it was glowing a bright orange. He hammered the rod, and sparks flew. He turned it using the tongs in his left hand and beat it again. 'And we continue doing this until it's straightened.' After several more hammer blows, he regarded the sharp point with a scrutinising eye, nodded in satisfaction, and plunged it into a bucket of water. The rod, now a sharp spike, hissed briefly as a tuft of steam rose from the bucket.

'What's that supposed to be,' Kairos said. 'It looks too puny to be a spear point.'

'A nail,' Mr. Dubose answered. 'And you're going to make hundreds of them.'

'A nail?' Kairos repeated, unable to hide the disappointment in his tone.

'That's right,' the dwarf said cheerfully. 'You can never have enough nails, no matter if you're a human, dwarf, or elf – everyone needs nails. Always. Someone, somewhere, is constantly building or fixing something. Believe it or not, these make me the most money.'

'But I thought we were making swords–'

'Ho, that's rich!' Mr. Dubose chortled. 'Who will I sell a sword to? Maybe the rare Mana Knight or City Watchman who can actually *use* a sword. Most of them prefer to twirl their fancy spells and poke at things with their mana lances. That leaves the dwarves as the sole customer base, and Dwarfside isn't at war with anyone.' Mr. Dubose picked up a rod and shoved it into Kairos's chest. 'Besides, forging a sword is complicated work. You're starting with the basics – the nail.'

Grimly, Kairos repeated the process the dwarf had shown him. He pulled out the glowing metal rod and began hammering away with his left hand. Mr. Dubose watched quietly as Kairos used the tongs with his right hand to rotate the nail. He finished the nail and plunged it into the bucket, reaching for another metal rod.

'Stop right there,' Mr. Dubose said.

'What is it this time?' Kairos asked, his irritation rising with the continuous criticism. 'Are you trying to make me quit? Because I won't. I'll show you that I'm better than a dwarf.'

Mr. Dubose just gazed at Kairos with a speculative eye. 'You're left-handed,' he observed.

'Is that wrong?' Kairos asked, feeling the need to be defensive.

'Not at all. That's a good thing, especially when it comes to fighting, but we'll get to that later. Now try using the hammer with your other hand.'

'Why?'

The dwarf glowered in response.

Kairos saw the look and expected an incoming blow. That was what his father did if he questioned him. He braced himself, but nothing came. To his surprise, the dwarf chuckled.

'It's training,' he said with a grin. 'To train both arms equally. We'll do the same with weapons, but for now, alternate using the hammer with each hand. I can't have an apprentice with one arm the size of a log and the other the size of a twig. Now we need to build you up some more. That means switching arms...Can you read and write?' the dwarf added.

'Yes, sir.' Kairos thought of Mad Mavos. The crazed and shunned Einar of the Azel clan had taught him the basics with the few precious books lying around. Most Einar considered reading and writing a waste of time, especially when that time could be better used for gathering food or training for battle. They preferred passing down stories in poems and songs. But Mad Mavos had told Kairos that these poems and songs would change through the generations, whilst the words in a book remained the same. Though Kairos liked reading, he had never found much use for it until now.

'Good, because I'll leave you a written list of chores every morning before I go out,' the dwarf said. 'You can have a quick lunch after you complete two dozen more nails. I don't need you passing out on me in the middle of work.'

'Yes, sir,' Kairos said. 'Let's make that three dozen.'

The dwarf nodded approvingly. 'That's more like it, boy.'

'I do have a name, you know, sir,' Kairos said modestly, pausing after delivering a series of hammer blows on a glowing nail.

'We all do, boy,' said Mr. Dubose, slapping him on the back. 'Now hurry up and finish that nail before it cools off. I have loads more work for you after lunch.'

\* \* \*

'You may enter,' said Malus from behind a desk cluttered with parchments, maps, and books.

He had barely left his quarters at Kinclaven Citadel during the last few weeks. The sudden turn of events throughout the world required his attention, so he had an endless number of letters to write, orders to give, and military commanders to meet – not to mention those pesky ambassadors from various countries who came to negotiate terms for peace, often bringing a payment of gold so he would not attack. Sometimes he took the gold and attacked anyway. Humans were so stupid.

All except the one who now entered the room.

A tall figure in hooded grey robes, he stood in the doorway, approached the desk and bowed.

'Greetings, General,' Malus said, returning the bow, which was more of a slight dip of his head. Those who knew the dark elf, however, would recognise the gesture of respect.

'Greetings, Dark Lord,' the hooded figure replied.

'Don't call me that,' Malus said. 'You know how much I hate that title. Please be seated.'

The General bowed again and lowered himself into a velvet-cushioned chair. 'My apologies. I've been away a while.'

The dark elf opened a book and traced a glyph, causing the pages to glow. 'What's the news from Vadost?'

The General began his report. As he spoke, his words appeared on the pages of Malus's book, traced in a brief orange glow. 'The atmosphere is tense,' he said. 'The Ordonians are anxious about your army's movements, and word has spread throughout the kingdom of the attacks on Milbrooke and Cape Caipora. Even the *Vadost Oracle* reported these events. The guards at the gates require passes from all travellers now, which is not so much of a problem for me. Also, one of our spies was discovered and imprisoned, though not necessarily for espionage.'

'What a fool,' said Malus, pouring his guest a glass of the exceedingly rare and valuable Vantarian wine, chilled to the perfect temperature. He poured himself a glass and took a sip, relishing the taste. 'What was his name again? Dunghill?'

'Dunhill, milord,' the hooded figure corrected. 'And you could say that he asked for it. He could report more on a woman's curves than the Mana Knights. He was spending most of his time in the taverns, harassing the barmaids every night. One night he followed one home from the Pinch & Tickle and tried to assault her within her house. Fortunately for her, he was so drunk that he only managed to vomit on her and pass out. She screamed for the City Watch, and they came and took him away.'

'This is why you cannot trust humans,' Malus said with disdain, then looked up at his guest and added, 'present company excluded, of course... But you hate humans more than I do.'

'Of course, milord.' The hooded man nodded and sipped his wine.

'This is precisely the reason why spies should simply observe and report, only acting when necessary. I understand some spies get a little bored and like to indulge. But committing such transgressions draws unwanted attention. So, what happened to him?'

'The City Watch imprisoned him, milord,' the man said dryly. 'On that very night, I stopped by – undetected, mind you – and magicked his food so that it would choke him. We didn't need him talking before his trial. The jailor found him dead the next morning, and no one assumes foul play, nor do they care.'

'Good work, General,' Malus said in a warm tone. Despite his personal grudge against humanity, he had taken a liking to this human and had promoted him to the highest rank, much to the astonishment and puzzlement of the rest of his army. Many elves expressed their disgruntled jealousy in the taverns, but they were mindful to keep their opinions to themselves around their superiors. But even the whispers of rumours would reach Malus's ears, though he turned a deaf ear to them – for now. He didn't care what the others thought. This general proved reliable. 'What about the Knighthood? How goes the situation at Valour Keep?'

'You will be pleased to know that enlistment is at an all-time low,' the General said. 'This year, the retirees will far outnumber the squire enlistments. Furthermore, the number of errant missions has been on the rise. Beasts and bandits harass the countryside, and the knights have their hands full dealing with these. The recent appearance of our armies has added a burden to them. Therefore, they have become less selective in their recruitment process. And speaking of recruits, I have some information that may interest you.' The General paused, looking questioningly at his leader.

'Go on,' said Malus.

'It appears that Lord Galen Avenal has enlisted two recruits, using his own name as a personal recommendation. I understand that one of the recruits is, naturally, his daughter. The name of the second recruit has piqued the curiosity of those at the Academy. It's a boy, though Lord Avenal does not have any sons.'

'Is that so?' Malus edged forward in his chair excitedly. 'Does he live at the Avenal Manor?'

'I don't know,' the General said in earnest. 'I haven't bothered to check. I also cannot approach the manor too closely without raising suspicion, so my information at the moment is limited. Would you like me to investigate the home further?'

Malus shook his head. 'No need. It appears that the boy will come to you. Don't those knights have some sort of aptitude test before the Academy? He should show up for that.'

'True,' the hooded man said. 'Is there a reason to investigate him beyond his mere association with Lord Avenal?'

'Yes.' The dark elf made a page-long note in his book with a quick spell. 'You've been in Vadost a while, so I'll give you a brief summary. It seems that blithering jester, Captain Hargonnas, supposedly captured one of the Cursed Ones, and allowed him to escape into the hands of Lord Avenal, who took him to Vadost.'

The hood twitched slightly. 'I see. Is the Pariah aware of this?'

'I don't know,' Malus admitted, frowning at the mention of the Pariah. 'We can only hope otherwise. I don't know if Lord Avenal realised what he had. We also lost sight of the boy once he entered the city… My spies within the city have reported sightings of Lord Avenal, but the boy is never with him. Therefore, if this new enlistee is the boy, then this truly is good tidings.'

'What would you like me to do, milord?'

'The same as before, General,' Malus said in a stern and solemn tone. 'Observe and report. He's not a threat yet, and your work in Valour Keep is too valuable to expose your cover.'

'And if he becomes a threat, milord?' the hooded figured asked gravely.

'Then you can dispose of him. But only if the situation warrants it,' Malus said. 'I sent Captain Hargonnas to Vadost, as well, so let him assist you and do the dirty work instead. He's more expendable than you are.'

'I am honoured you think so highly of me, milord,' the General said lightly.

'I don't.' The dark elf smiled back and poured another glass of wine for the guest and himself. 'Have you met with Captain Hargonnas, yet? He should be in Vadost by now.'

'No, milord.'

The dark elf scowled. 'When you do, watch him very closely. He tends to act on his own. Very unpredictable. If he didn't have his uses, I would have gladly had his head lopped off and sent to his parents as punishment for having the little puke.'

'I'll keep a close eye on him,' the General said.

'What about the dwarves in Vadost? They live in – ah, Dwarfside, right?'

'Aye. They are a bit different to the dwarves of Dvargerberg. Though they don't intermingle with humans so much, they don't bear hatred towards them. They tolerate humans as though they had forgotten the history of the Ordonians' conquest of their lands. Any dwarf who tries to convert them to our cause is turned away or ignored.'

'And the elves?'

'There are not many in Vadost. There's a grouchy dark elf by the name of Sanctus, but he's only interested in selling shoes. The rest of the elves are like him, even if the locals treat them poorly. They show little to no interest in our cause. Perhaps they've been living in human lands too long.'

'They're fools,' Malus told his General. 'They don't understand that this is for the greater good of the D'Kari and Salforian nations. For all elves, dwarves, and gnomes. Can't they see that humans cause trouble wherever they go?'

The General nodded in agreement, despite being a human, himself. 'Troublesome, indeed.'

'Do you have any other tidings from Vadost, General?' Malus asked.

'Nothing noteworthy. I still have not located any signs of the Pariah there.' The man sipped the remnants of his wine. 'Excellent vintage, milord. It takes me back many years… Where was I? Ah, yes – the Pariah. Are you sure he is with the Knighthood?'

'Yes, I am sure,' Malus answered coolly. 'I've intercepted a few of his messages. That is how I learnt of when and where to expect the arrival of the Cursed Ones. That is why I had my fleet sent to the Dark Sea to intercept and get rid of them, but Captain Hargonnas failed on his part with this particular one.'

'I can deal with the boy, milord.'

Malus grunted. 'That's not really necessary for the time being. Hargonnas's mistake may be a blessing, but first, I need you find out everything you can about this boy. If he is, indeed, the Cursed One, then the Pariah may come to him. We can use the boy as bait to lure him to us, and we'll effectively kill two birds with one arrow. However, I leave everything to your discretion.'

'One more question, milord.'

Malus tilted the glass towards his lips and made a beckoning motion with a flick of his other wrist.

'Are you certain that this boy is crucial to the Pariah's plans? I'm having trouble believing that a mere boy can cause such a threat to us.'

'From what I gather, the Pariah needs a Cursed One, an Einar, to interact with the Lost God, Murasa. Any Cursed One would do, since the 'curse' is what protects them from the devouring god's power. As Captain Hargonnas claims, these Cursed Ones have no mana or life energy to drain. And this boy is the only unaccounted survivor of the Einar fleet. Of that, I am quite certain.'

The General nodded gravely and bowed. 'I will keep a vigilant eye, milord.'

'I trust that you will. I must now tend to other matters locally.' The dark elf stood up, his signal to end the meeting. 'When is the next time I will see you?'

'It will be a while.' The General rose in turn. 'The Academy will start soon and I will be swimming in parchments, as the saying goes. If I cannot come here directly, shall I send word, instead?'

'No,' the dark elf said. 'Trust no one. We cannot trust for your message to *not* get intercepted. I would rather wait. If it's that pressing, you know what to do. Safe travels, General.'

The General bowed deeply. He straightened, and as he began to trace the glyphs for the teleportation spell, Malus stopped him. 'That boy whom Lord Avenal enlisted into the Academy… what was his name?'

It took the General a moment to consider the question, and another to remember the name.

'Kairos.'

* * *

'Listen up,' Mr. Dubose explained as they marched off towards Valour Keep from the city. 'If someone is being nice to you, and you don't know them, then tell them to piss off. No one is nice to you for no reason.'

'What if they're actually nice?' Kairos glanced back at the friendly-looking man who had offered them a tour of the city whilst staggering about and reeking of spirits. He'd fallen into a ditch and lay there unmoving.

'Well, they can take their happy arse and jump off a cliff.' Mr. Dubose, too, glanced back at the drunk. 'Or fall into a ditch!'

'What about Galen Avenal?' Kairos suppressed a grin. 'He was nice to me and I didn't know him. Then there's you. I suppose you should jump off a cliff, then.'

'I'm not nice to you!' the dwarf thundered. 'Besides, you're my apprentice. And that's *Lord Avenal* to you. Show some respect or I'll throw you into the ditch with that drunken nutter!'

Kairos turned away so he wouldn't laugh, but not before noticing the dwarf flush in embarrassment.

Three months had passed since Kairos arrived in Vadost, three months since he had seen Lord Avenal and his daughter.

He had turned sixteen in the meantime. The dwarf gave him a day off from work and asked him what he wanted to do. Kairos wanted to visit Althea, but Mr. Dubose refused, stating that Stella would castrate both of them for showing up uninvited.

Thoughts of Althea occupied Kairos's mind daily, and more so recently ever since Mr. Dubose informed him that they were going to meet today. Kairos felt a twinge of excitement, which started in the morning and only worsened as the day grew.

Mr. Dubose took notice and changed the subject. 'You've been hopping about the workshop all morning,' he said, 'like you've finished dropping the biggest turd of your life.'

'Yes, we were speaking of Lord Avenal. We're going to see him soon, right?' Kairos asked, oblivious to the dwarf's sarcasm.

The dwarf grunted. 'Somehow, I doubt you're this happy to see Galen – and if you are, then maybe I should reconsider your residence in my workshop.'

'What do you mean?' Kairos asked, feigning a look of ignorance.

'I've seen how you perk up whenever that girl is mentioned. You can't fool me, boy.' Mr. Dubose let out a loud guffaw. 'Well, I hate to break this to ya, but this ain't going to be a picnic. You're going to take the Badger's Trial.'

Kairos's newfound happiness extinguished itself instantly, replaced by a sense of dread. No one had ever said anything about a Badger's Trial. The Einar held trials back in Logres, tests of strength and bravery where those who failed died. Was that what he was doing today? He wasn't ready. Why didn't Mr. Dubose tell him earlier? He didn't have time to prepare.

As if reading the boy's mind, Mr. Dubose added, 'Don't worry. They're only testing your abilities to determine how much training you will need. It's not something you study or train for. They won't kill you... maybe.'

The boy and the dwarf arrived at the courtyard of Valour Keep by noon. The day was a hot one for late spring, and in the distance, clouds gathered on the horizon, hinting at rain by afternoon. Kairos stared with open-mouthed admiration at the keep.

The grandeur of the structure left him in utter awe. It was a large fortress, rather than a keep, built into the foot of a mountainside. Several minarets soared towards the sky, emitting blue streaks of electrical energy from their tops. The centre tower had the most energy coalescing into one magical swirling ball.

Kairos could almost feel the power radiating from the fortress, half expecting the magical energy to vaporise him at any moment. However long he stared, the streaks of blue light spun in place.

'Quit gawking,' Mr. Dubose snapped. 'You look like a Zemusian monk who just stepped into a brothel for the first time. Ah, there's Galen and his daughter. I'm going to have a word with him. You wait in line.'

Kairos saw the line of youth, most of them around his age, forming a column in the courtyard of Valour Keep. Several knights stood by, watching and waiting in the bright sunshine. To his dismay, Vaughn and Claudius, the two bullies from the fountain, stood in the queue. They noticed him, too, and began whispering to each other as they stared at him with leering grins. Kairos ignored them and went to the back of the queue. Much to his pleasure, Althea took her place behind him. They waited half an hour, during which some of those youth began to chat with their neighbours, Kairos and Althea amongst them.

'I was hoping you'd come,' Althea said. Then in a rush, 'I didn't know if you'd still be living with Mr. Dubose, considering how those previous apprentices quit. I didn't know if I'd see you again.' She looked embarrassed as soon as the words left her mouth.

'Oh, he's not bad,' Kairos replied. 'The work is hard, but he feeds me well. And even if he were intolerable, I have my reasons for staying.'

'And what are those reasons?'

'I talked to your father about becoming a knight. I suppose that would be the best course for me. At least until I can go back to my homeland.'

'Oh.' Disappointment coloured her voice. 'When will you go back?'

'I… I don't know. I'll figure it out someday, but for now, I cannot say.' He had not spoken to anyone about Logres since his conversation with Galen in Gersholm. This was as close to the truth as he dared tread. He did not know if she would believe him.

So far, no one else in Ordonia seemed aware that Logres even existed.

Althea looked at him seriously for a moment and then said, 'You mentioned more than one reason. What are the others?'

'Well, there's only one other, really,' Kairos admitted.

'And that is?'

The question took him by surprise. He did not know how to tell Althea how he felt. A girl as beautiful as her must have had plenty of boys tell her all sorts of clever phrases. Surely such a girl in Logres would not give him the time of day, given that he was considered the 'runt' there. But he wasn't a runt here. She also confirmed what he had suspected: that she was worried he would leave. He dared to believe for a second that she reciprocated his feelings towards her.

Kairos swallowed. 'You,' he answered.

Althea's face lit up and she grinned. Kairos felt warm, as if basking in her glow.

After that, the conversation took on the easy playfulness of that first stroll through Vadost. He wanted to talk to her more openly, but he felt the need to guard his conversation in the presence of her father, who stood nearby. Kairos could see Mr. Dubose muttering something to Galen, who bent down to listen. At once the older knight laughed out loud in a carefree manner and clapped the dwarf on the back.

'I have never seen my father laugh like that,' Althea remarked, watching the two.

'They must be really good friends,' Kairos said.

'I've heard they fought against Malus together twenty years ago,' Althea explained, 'and defeated him. Malus escaped and was quiet for some time. Since then, my father was promoted to a Dragon Knight, while Mr. Dubose gave up the sword and took up blacksmithing. But he always wanted to be a knight.'

'Mr. Dubose wanted to be a Mana Knight?' Kairos asked, incredulous. The dwarf had never mentioned such a thing to him. He regarded the blacksmith with a newfound admiration.

142

'You didn't know?' she asked. 'He tried to be a knight like my father, but the Knighthood won't accept dwarves.'

'Why not?'

'Because they have no mana. They cannot cast spells like we humans can. My father disagrees with this old-fashioned tradition, but there are those in the ranks, like Lady Naiya, who demand we follow it.'

Kairos had many questions about the Knighthood and was about to enquire more when a stir of commotion silenced the new recruits.

Instructor Jomur, a haughty ferret of a man, squint-faced with a receding chin, arrived riding on a donkey. The instructor was so tall, his feet almost dragged the ground. With a derisive shake of his head (which almost threw his glasses off), he eyed the recruits with disdain. Those in line who were on the verge of laughing at him fell suddenly and uncomfortably silent under his scathing scrutiny.

The instructor took his place in front of the recruits and pulled out a sheaf of parchment and a quill pen. 'Welcome to the Badger Trial,' Jomur announced in a monotone. 'I assume you're here because you want to join the Mana Knight Academy. Today's trial is to test you on your knowledge, mana capabilities, and physical fitness. When called upon, you will approach me and state your full name, age, and years of previous schooling. Then you will enter the training grounds to my right and wait for further instruction from Professor Argent and Professor Bumbershoot.'

The first in line, a swarthy boy of short stature, shuffled forward. He was pudgy, and his eyes had the dull look of a cow. He reminded Kairos of one of the farmers of Gersholm. 'Barnaby Shah, age sixteen, and sixteen years of schooling.'

'Sixteen years of schooling?' Instructor Jomur asked in disbelief, leaning forward. His glasses fell onto the tip of his nose, which he quickly pushed back. 'And you are sixteen, correct? May I ask what sort of school taught you whilst you were a baby?'

'My mother,' Shah answered. The recruits in the queue, along with the knights, who up till now had remained stoic, laughed.

Shah cringed and peered down, his face reddening, looking as if he wanted to dig a hole and dive in head first. The boy was obviously not a warrior, and Kairos wondered why he was even bothering with the Knighthood.

Instructor Jomur was the only one not laughing. He scowled, pointing to the training grounds and said, 'Go!'

The next person in line, a girl, approached Instructor Jomur reluctantly. She appeared to be on the verge of tears after watching Shah slink away in embarrassment.

'State your name and age,' said the instructor in a monotone voice. 'Years of previous schooling?'

One by one, the recruits dwindled. Instructor Jomur asked the same thing in the same monotonous voice. The process would have passed on quickly enough if every recruit was like Shah, but whenever someone claimed to have several years of advanced education, Instructor Jomur would perk up, impressed, and prattle on about his own studies.

Kairos soon formed a negative opinion of the man, and it only became worse when he was called upon to approach.

'Kairos, son of Karthok,' he said in response to the instructor.

'Son of Karthok?' Instructor Jomur sneered. 'That's not a family name. What are you? Some sort of barbarian? State your family name.'

The knights and the remaining students in the courtyard became silent, staring at Kairos in curiosity. His face burned with shame and confusion. The Einar never used family names. Everyone in Logres identified themselves by simply their name and their father, or mother in some cases. There was no other affiliation except the name of the clan… His clan, the Azel clan.

The instructor regarded him coolly. 'I'm waiting.'

Taking a deep breath, Kairos glowered at the instructor, summoning every ounce of patience within to not throttle the lanky man. His negative opinion now upgraded to loathing.

'Azel,' he answered. 'Kairos Azel, age sixteen.' The question regarding the previous years of schooling puzzled him. The Einar did not go to school. He recalled Mr. Dubose explaining the concept to him a week ago, but it sounded too strange. Reading, writing, books. How were these things important to becoming a knight? Yet, the instructor thought it all so, and he continued to stare at Kairos expectantly for an answer. So, he lied. 'I had a year of school.'

'A simpleton,' Jomur answered, scribbling away with the quill. 'Very well. Proceed to the training grounds.'

Kairos turned around and looked at Althea. She smiled, her eyes shining with encouragement. For an instant he saw Farina smiling, her hair cascading down her back in golden waves. He thought of Logres, the Blight, and the Einar.

With a determined step, Kairos walked towards the training grounds.

* * *

Althea stood apart from the other recruits as they introduced themselves after Jomur's brief interview. A boy with carrot-coloured hair glanced at her, as if wanting to start a conversation but Althea pretended not to notice. With nothing but boredom to occupy her mind, she fretted over what the Badger's Trial had in store. She avoided the carrot-haired boy's friendly gaze and searched for Kairos.

Just as she found him and tried to wave him over, one of the knights stood before them and brought them to attention, calling out a litany of rules for the Knighthood, including the infractions of the said rules, which would bring about every sort of dire consequences.

'Let the Badger's Trial commence,' yelled the knight. 'If you're scared, now's a good time to go crying to your mothers, because the Knighthood doesn't have room for cowards. And now Professor Argent would like to say a few words. Give him your full attention!'

The recruits quietened. Professor Argent took his place before them. He was majestic, sombre, his black coat gilt in silver swallowing him. His face, in spite of a long mane of silvery white hair, lacked the lines of aging. He affixed everyone with a penetrating gaze, taking in each recruit. Instructor Jomur stepped up and handed over the sheaf of parchment. Professor Argent studied the document, then looked up and made an announcement, which was direct and concise.

'When I call your name, you will come forward and accompany either me, Instructor Jomur here, or Professor Bumbershoot,' Argent gestured to an old man poking at an anthill with his cane, oblivious to his name being called, 'to the Chamber of Trials where you will demonstrate your knowledge of glyphs and spellcasting. The rest of you will wait here until called upon.'

Althea heard several names called out and jumped when hers came up. Her breathing quickened. There was no way she could cast a spell now – her hands were shaking too much and the mana in her body fluttered about, out of control. She looked up and saw Professor Argent was staring right at her.

'This way, Lady Avenal,' he said.

She followed him towards a nearby tower, nervous tears brimming in her limpid eyes.

* * *

The training grounds cleared out considerably after many of the recruits were called upon. Kairos still remained, sitting on a stone bench, wondering how he was going to demonstrate spellcasting when he had never once cast a spell in his life. He also didn't know a thing about glyphs. He sighed and thought of what Thylar used to tell him: *One step at a time.*

There was no use worrying. He would act when the time came.

'Hey, you!' a harsh voice called out, breaking him out of his musings. Kairos looked over and saw two boys and a girl lounging by the side of the building. He recognised two of them as the bullies from Lazio Fountain: Vaughn and Claudius, the boys he had almost fought. He did not recognise the girl.

'You don't look so tough without Lord Avenal around,' the tall, stocky one, known as Vaughn, said. 'Maybe you're spending time with his daughter hoping to get your prick wet.' He made a thrusting motion with his hips, stuck his tongue out, and rolled his eyes into the back of his head. His companions laughed.

Kairos ignored them and stood up to move away, but Vaughn stepped into his path, blocking it. The other two edged closer.

'Don't be so rude. Aren't you here to enter the Mana Knight Academy, too? Where's that bravado you had earlier?' Vaughn clenched his fists and puffed out his chest, imitating Kairos's actions from their previous encounter. 'Oh, that's right, Lord Avenal is not here to save you now. Care to finish what was started?'

Kairos could feel his face flush in anger. His hands clenched into fists at his side. But he remembered Galen and Althea's words. He must control his anger. He should not let this fool goad him, he would lose his only chance into the Knighthood. Maybe that was Vaughn's intention.

'You wouldn't behave so boorishly if your friends weren't here, Vaughn. I've heard that your level of mana would make you a powerful Mana Knight. You would do well to act as such. You demean yourself and the Knighthood.' Kairos made an attempt to sidestep Vaughn, but the tall boy moved again to block his path. His companions had stopped laughing now. The encounter took on a vicious edge. Vaughn put one hand on Kairos's chest and raised the other one, the fingertips glowing with energy.

'Watch it, boy,' he snarled.

'No, you watch it,' countered Kairos in a glacial tone. He stared Vaughn directly in the eyes. He had to raise his head slightly to do so. 'Take your hand off of me, or you'll regret it.'

The two stared at each other for a long time, neither giving in. Vaughn's companions shifted nervously and looked around. 'Um, Vaughn,' said the girl, who was Althea's age with long, chestnut hair. 'Someone's coming.'

'Kairos Azel!' A voice called out. It was Professor Argent. 'This way, please.'

Reluctantly Vaughn removed his hand and let Kairos pass. But he could not resist having the last word. 'You'd better quit the

Academy now, you git. Otherwise you're in for a long, painful time.'

As Vaughn's companions laughed, Kairos walked away with the professor to take the Badger's Trial.

* * *

'So what you're telling me is that you don't have any knowledge of glyphs or spellcasting?' Professor Argent asked in a mild tone.

Kairos thought he detected a glint of amusement in the silver-haired man's eyes. 'No.'

'No, *sir*,' the professor admonished gently.

'No, sir,' Kairos said.

Every muscle in his body tensed. His stomach churned and squirmed, and his heart lurched and pressed painfully against his chest. He tried to swallow, but his mouth was dry. His palms were so sweaty that they left wet streaks when he wiped them on his shirt.

The Chamber of Trials looked very different to what Kairos had imagined. It was like any other ordinary room – and neat, orderly, and clean. A few desks here and there, bookshelves along the walls, and a large stone table, which held parchments, a quill pen, and an ink pot. The only oddity in the room was a human-shaped figure suspended on chains, resembling the straw dummy that Mr. Dubose used for weapon practice in his workshop. This dummy, however, was made of blue rock. Kairos recognised it as corzite, the same material Mr. Dubose had.

The room was a disappointment for Kairos. He had envisioned vicious creatures, rampant sorcery, and other monstrosities greeting him. Instead, Professor Argent asked him to trace glyphs, which was needed for spellcasting, and to draw runes on a sheaf of parchment, neither of which he could do, both of which increased his anxiety.

When he failed each task miserably, the professor regarded him with a shrewd glance, his eyes narrowing. 'This test is of the utmost importance for entering the Knighthood,' the professor began. 'We give this test to every child who attempts to enrol prior to his or her entrance. It determines whether you possess the basic knowledge and fundamentals to fulfil the requirements the Academy will place on you. But in all my years, I have never met a child who has the magical knowledge of a dwarf. Are you making a mockery of this test, or is your education that lacking? Do you come from a farm in the middle of nowhere?'

Kairos looked away. He had never felt so much shame in his life, not even when he had placed last in the Azel Clan's arm wrestling competition, resulting in his father almost disowning him. At least then, he had known what he was doing. Here, he had no idea how to trace a glyph or cast a spell. He dared not say so, however.

Professor Argent's gaze softened in understanding. 'Try this,' he offered, raising a finger. 'Focus your mana into the tip of your finger and trace this glyph into the air. It's a simple glyph. A mere light spell, often the first spell anyone learns.' The professor's fingertip glowed faintly, and he drew a pattern in the air, which left a glowing afterimage. The pattern became a glyph, which flashed when completed, and a ball of white light flared into existence, hovering above the professor's hand and brightening the room. He extinguished it quickly. 'Now you try.'

Kairos turned inward, focusing on the very core of his being, to draw the energy out. He wanted this so much. He needed to become a knight. Galen said it was one of the few ways he could earn a ship, and Kairos could see no other method. He willed everything into his fingertip, which was glistening with sweat. He felt his body trembling under the strain to steady his finger, and somehow, he managed to trace the same glyph as the professor, or at least he thought he had.

Apparently, Kairos had imitated the spell perfectly. The professor's look soon turned to one of puzzlement.

Nothing happened. No glyph flashed. No ball of light appeared.

Grave disappointment flooded Kairos's being. Did he do the spell wrong? 'I can try it again,' he said.

'No,' the professor said. 'You performed the glyph well. Exactly as I have, in fact.'

'Then what's wrong?' asked Kairos. 'Why did the spell not work?'

The professor said nothing, instead he thrust his right hand into the fold of his robes and pulled out an object that resembled a short wooden staff with a transparent cube embedded on the end. Before Kairos could ask what the object was, the professor aimed it at him, and the cube flashed.

Kairos shielded his eyes with his arms. When he realised nothing bad was going to happen, he lowered them. 'What happened? What did you do?'

Professor Argent stared intently at his cube-topped staff, and for the briefest instant, his face took on a look of bewilderment, but he caught himself and his face resumed its original stone-façade.

'What is it?' Concern crept into Kairos's voice.

'My dear boy...' Argent began. 'It appears that you have no mana.'

# CHAPTER SIX

## Hammerfall Festival

*The Order of the Mana Knights formed during the Age of Chaos, the chaotic period after the gods' departure from Alban. The Knighthood's primary objective is to secure and protect the godshards. Secondary objectives include taking on quests to protect the weak and defenceless and abide by the code of chivalry and honour.*

*'The History of the Mana Knights',* Sir Edwin Rosal

J ace Dubose was pacing back and forth in the courtyard, eager to know the outcome of the Badger's Trial. He saw the recruits come out and greet their family members and friends, mostly with excitement, though some of them gave a firm shake of their heads as if deciding that knighthood wasn't for them. Althea finished her trial before Kairos and hugged her proud father.

The last of the recruits trickled out, and still no sign of Kairos. Galen and Althea came over to the dwarf, who didn't even notice them at first.

'Worried?' Galen asked.

'Me?' Mr. Dubose was appalled by the question. 'No! I'm bored. There's nothing to do but stand around and wait. A dwarf's worst nightmare, considering I'm the only non-human here.' He spat for emphasis, which caused a nearby knight to frown.

The dwarf was indeed worried, though he would never admit such a thing, even to himself. As far as anyone else was concerned, the boy just happened to be a good apprentice who, despite being human, worked as hard as any other dwarf from Dvergar. And he didn't want anything bad to happen to a good apprentice.

'How's the boy coming along?' Galen asked.

'Not as good as a dwarf, mind you,' Mr. Dubose answered. 'But he knows how to finish a job, I suppose. He's already started working on weapons.'

The knight nodded with a knowing smile. 'Do you have any plans for him before he starts the Academy?'

'We have the Hammerfall Festival coming up.' The dwarf tugged his beard in thought, and glanced at Althea who was hovering behind Galen, pretending not to listen. 'It's usually for dwarves, but I guess you're invited. Would you like to come along?'

Althea's eyes brightened. 'Yes!' she interrupted, a little more enthusiastically than she intended, caught herself, and blushed.

'We'll have to ask Stella,' Galen cautioned. 'You know how she fusses over your whereabouts.'

Althea grimaced, her hopes dashed. 'I know.'

'I'm sure the kid would like that,' Jace Dubose said. 'It's in three weeks.'

They talked for a while longer and made tentative plans, but the dwarf barely listened. Eventually the Dragon Knight and his daughter left, the sun began its descent, and Jace ran out of patience. He was about to enter the Chamber of Trials to find out what was bloody taking so damn long when Kairos emerged.

\* \* \*

As the sun dipped into the western mountains, Jace Dubose and Kairos made their way along the city road back to Dwarfside.

Kairos sulked and glared at the ground as if he held a personal grudge against the earth, kicking a loose stone here and there.

'What's wrong?' Mr. Dubose asked.

'Nothing,' came the cold reply.

'Horseshit,' said the dwarf. 'You came to Valour Keep happier than a stag in rutting season and came out looking as though the whole herd rejected you. Something happened in there, and I understand it bothers you.'

'No, you wouldn't understand,' Kairos said.

'Bah, you're sixteen… and a human. I think I can understand a damn sixteen-year-old human.'

The boy frowned and turned away. The dwarf saw the look, and his tone softened.

'Look, lad. If something is bothering you, then speak up about it. I may have a solution. Keeping these problems bottled up inside won't help either of us. I sure don't want to have you moping around my workshop like that. It's depressing me just to look at you.'

Kairos stopped, paused in thought, and told Mr. Dubose about the Chamber of Trials.

'What do you *mean* that you have no mana?' Mr. Dubose asked.

'Professor Argent said that I have no mana,' Kairos answered glumly. 'He compared my situation to dwarves and gnomes.'

The dwarf was astonished. Never in all his ninety-three years had he ever heard of a human with no mana. All humans had mana. Gnomes and dwarves did not. It was impossible for humans to intermingle with other races, so Kairos being a half-breed was out of the question – although why any race would want to mingle with an ugly human was beyond the dwarf's comprehension anyway. He suspected a prank at first, but another look at the boy's pale face revealed the truth. And, Jace thought, he had never seen the boy cast a spell during the past few months, or even demonstrate a sliver of magic. Something was odd about all of this.

'Look, I'm sorry kid,' said Mr. Dubose, gripped by profound sympathy. He once tried – with Galen's help – to become a Mana Knight, himself. The Knighthood rejected him based on two things: he had no mana, and he was a dwarf. One of the Dragon Knights at the time told him that the point of being a Mana Knight was to 'have mana.' The memory made the dwarf seethe. 'If the Knighthood won't accept you, there are thousands of other things to do. Look at me, for instance.'

'The strange thing is,' said Kairos, 'that they didn't reject me. Professor Argent told me he would put me in his class, along with the other squires who demonstrated low proficiency.'

This was another surprise for the dwarf. 'He did? How so?'

'Well, that puzzled me at first, too,' Kairos said, lifting his head up. 'But Professor Argent had received a letter of recommendation from Lord Avenal and Gulliver about how I killed an elven soldier from Malus's army. He said that based on my m-m-metal...' Kairos struggled to remember the word.

'Mettle,' Mr. Dubose offered.

'Right,' Kairos continued. 'He said based on that along with my willingness to fight Malus's army, I would make a great candidate for Knighthood. So, he made an exception and offered to teach me directly so I could succeed. He said I had promising skills for a warrior, and it would be a waste if I didn't make it, so he would like to help.'

'That's wonderful news!' the dwarf yelled, giving Kairos a slap of approval on the back that was so hard, it sent the boy pitching forward. 'Why are you so upset then? Oh, that's right. You have no mana.'

Kairos looked around in alarm. 'Mr. Dubose, please don't mention that so loudly. What will I do without mana?'

Mr. Dubose shrugged. 'The same thing you've been doing. That means you're just like a dwarf, all the same. We get along fine without mana. It may be a problem for you in the Academy, though.'

'Professor Argent said the same thing, especially if the other knights or instructors found out. Some of the tests require some degree of magic skill.' Kairos paused and stepped aside to allow a horse-drawn wagon to pass. The dwarf did likewise, and when the wagon was out of earshot, the boy continued, 'One other problem is fighting. How do I fight against those who use magic when I cannot?'

'Bah! Magic doesn't determine an outcome of a fight. It's merely a tool, just as your sword and shield are tools. As long as you know how to use them better than your opponent, you can win.' Seeing Kairos about to say something, the dwarf held up a hand. 'Of course, magic is a powerful tool, but some of those humans and elves get so caught up with wiggling their fingers and throwing spells around that they'd never see a punch coming.'

Kairos did not say anything. He walked alongside the dwarf, staring, with envy, at the townspeople going about their everyday lives. They used magic for everything, from watering their gardens to heating their stoves. Magic made everything convenient.

Mr. Dubose understood how the boy felt. All dwarves, at some point in their lives, felt the pang of not being able to use magic. He remembered his childhood of building forts and hurling imaginary spells at the other dwarven children. He heard many grown-up dwarves grumble about the 'useless' magic-users. He had done so himself, but deep down, he knew they felt the stab of jealousy and inadequacy, for if it were not for magic, the dwarves would not have lost the war and ceded most of their lands to the humans all those centuries ago.

'The professor also said something else,' Kairos began, as if reluctant to speak. His tone had taken on a sense of dread.

'Go on,' the dwarf said, fearing the onset of worse news.

'He mentioned the legend about the 'Curse of the Gods.' Have you heard of this?'

Jace Dubose snorted. 'I have, boy. It's just superstitious nonsense from humans who worshipped Zemus. An old wives' tale.'

Kairos dipped his head in acknowledgement but appeared uneasy. 'Yes. The professor said the humans with this curse could bring about the destruction of civilisation. He said that a group of these humans, working under a god named Murasa, wrought havoc before the Celestial War. That's why the Badger's Trial took so long. He was explaining all of this to me and told me not to tell anyone.'

Mr. Dubose snorted. 'Well, you're telling me!'

'You don't count.'

'I don't count,' the dwarf grumbled. 'Remind me to never tell you any secrets, then.'

Kairos stopped in the middle of the street and took a deep breath. 'Mr. Dubose, I am being earnest. You don't think I'm god-cursed, do you?'

The dwarf laughed, which caused Kairos to glare at him. 'I don't think this is funny.'

'You bringing about the destruction of civilisation?' Mr. Dubose asked, his voice full of mirth. 'Boy, you almost cut your own foot off when you picked up the sword the other day! I doubt you're much of a threat to civilisation. More like a threat to the civilisation of my kitchen, judging from the way you eat. Now what other silly nonsense did this human tell you?'

'He told me that I shouldn't tell anyone else—'

'Yes, you said that already!' the dwarf interrupted.

'Let me finish.' Kairos was chagrined at being interrupted. 'He said that I should keep this a secret for now because telling others would only lead to dire re...' the boy struggled over the word. 'Re... repair cushions.'

'Repercussions,' corrected the dwarf. 'And I have to agree with him on this one. Telling others about this, especially humans, would open you up to bullying and ridicule. Even some dwarves would find this a bad omen.'

They were nearing the great gated entrance to Dwarfside. It was almost dark and behind them, many colourful lights flickered throughout the city of Vadost.

'What shall I do then?' asked Kairos in despair. 'The Knighthood will expect me to cast a spell some time during the Academy.'

'I think I have a solution,' said Mr. Dubose, tugging on his beard. 'You see, I wanted to be a knight once, myself, so I've worked on a few things. Of course, the Knighthood never accepted me, but they'll take you.'

Kairos's miserable expression faded somewhat. Hope flickered into his eyes. 'You have? What is it?'

'You'll see.' The dwarf grinned. 'But for now, we need to prepare a feast to celebrate your passing of the Badger's Trial!'

'To celebrate *my* passing of the Badger's Trial?' Kairos said in surprise. 'But that's not even a trial! I passed without effort.'

'They failed me!' Mr. Dubose laughed, slapping the boy on the back again. 'But they fail all dwarves. Still, a celebration is in order, even though you didn't really do shit. It's also a good opportunity to gather the others in Dwarfside to talk about preparations for the upcoming Hammerfall Festival. Althea might be there, ya know.'

If Kairos had any lingering doubts, they were washed away at the mention of Lord Avenal's daughter. Mr. Dubose saw his face shine; he had learnt not to make fun of Kairos and his interest in the girl, but he couldn't help chuckling to himself.

As they entered Dwarfside, Mr. Dubose slowed his step. Kairos noticed and stopped and turned.

'What is it?'

'There is one thing that bothers me about all of this,' said Mr. Dubose. 'Why is this professor being so damned nice to you?'

Kairos shrugged. 'He likes me, I suppose? Maybe he's just nice.'

'Bah!' Mr. Dubose snorted again. 'Didn't you listen to me earlier? No one is ever nice to you for no reason. Are you daft, boy?'

'So why are you nice then?' answered Kairos with a glib expression.

Mr. Dubose was too embarrassed to provide an answer, so he glared at the boy in return and fumed in silence. Kairos laughed and began walking again. When the dwarf was certain that no one was watching him, he muttered a prayer to Thelos to watch over the boy.

He hoped that his misgivings were wrong.

* * *

Dwarfside was in chaos, preparing for the Hammerfall Festival.

By now, Kairos recognised most of the faces of the dwarves in the residential district, if not their names. Though Mr. Dubose criticised and berated him daily, he knew that the gruff dwarf praised him behind his back. It was evident from the way the citizens of Dwarfside treated him. They gave him small gifts, usually new clothes or food since the boy was known to 'eat like a growing dwarf.' When he wasn't working, many of the younger dwarves invited him to their games of arm wrestling, throwing axes, or smashing ore.

Kairos's erstwhile hatred of the dwarves had blossomed into a newfound camaraderie. He preferred their company over those of his fellow humans and found that they resembled the Einar in many ways – minus the plundering, pillaging, and ravaging. They expressed themselves in a straightforward manner, compared to the 'passive aggressive' behaviour (as Mr. Dubose termed it) of the Ordonians. Kairos enjoyed the contests of strength, the dwarven humour, and most of the cooking. The extremely spicy fire potato, a favourite of the dwarves, had grown on him since his arrival.

There was one dwarf that Kairos did not like.

His name was Togram. He arrived on the day of Kairos's Badger's Trial. He dressed and acted differently to the other dwarves, even the ones that came from their homeland, Dvergar. He shuffled into Dwarfside, entering the restaurant where Kairos and Mr. Dubose were celebrating. He bowed respectfully to Mr. Dubose, and greeted everyone with perfunctory courtesy, but did little to engage anyone in conversation, nor did he drink any ale or mead – an oddity for a dwarf.

Togram reminded Kairos of a viper in the grass, the look on his face calculating and menacing, slightly diffused by the abnormally large ears that stuck outward from his head like the handles on a jug. The dwarf's mannerisms brought back memories of Uncle Vinh, and Kairos felt a sense of discomfort as he watched Togram introduce himself to Jace Dubose.

'My name is Togram,' he said, 'and I am seeking to work in Dwarfside. I heard you were a foreman.'

'Why Dwarfside?' Mr. Dubose asked, frowning. 'Why not Dvergarberg, or the outlying areas where a dwarf can really prosper?'

'My father died and left me with a large debt, sir, so I had to sell the family business and even that wasn't enough to preserve our reputation.'

'Who was your father?'

'Alberich, sir.'

'Which Alberich?' Mr. Dubose asked. (Kairos had learnt that 'Alberich' was a common dwarven name and knew of three residing in Dwarfside).

'Alberich, son of Gimli, who is the son of Gloin.'

'Where was he from?' Mr. Dubose asked, cutting a slab of meat for everyone at his table, and passing a plate to Kairos.

'Fogvale, sir.'

'Never heard of it,' Mr. Dubose said. 'A mining town?'

'No, sir, we worked in carpentry and also raised horses.'

'So why come to Dwarfside, in human lands of all places?'

Togram shrugged. 'I've heard you were a great foreman to work for, but if you don't want me, I shall try my luck elsewhere.'

'Can you tend to the horses, Togram?'

'As well as a Dvergar whore can work her lips, sir.'

'You must be pretty good, then.' Mr. Dubose chuckled at the jest. He offered Togram a position as an ostler at the stables in Dwarfside and invited him to the feast. When Kairos said he did not like Togram, Mr. Dubose shrugged and said that dwarves took care of their own. They were sitting at the largest table in the restaurant, surrounded by Jace's colleagues. 'There is nothing worse, lad,' Mr. Dubose said, 'than a dwarf without a profession, a purpose in life.'

'I don't trust him,' Kairos said. 'He looks like he is running from the hangman's noose.'

'He probably is,' Mr. Dubose acknowledged, 'but Dwarfside doesn't discriminate against hardworking souls as long as they follow the rules here.'

Kairos soon forgot about Togram, and the devastating news of having no mana, in the midst of the upcoming preparations of the Hammerfall Festival. As the other dwarves scrambled to assemble the harvest and animals that would provide the food for the feast, Jace Dubose decided to teach Kairos the use of the sword.

The dwarf showed him several tricks and skilful manoeuvres he had learnt from a lifetime of fighting. Kairos had gleaned some aspects of combat from watching the Einar in Logres, but no one except Thylar and Mavos ever set aside time to teach him. His father, Karthok, said it was a 'bloody waste of time' teaching runts. However, the dwarf gave him his full attention, drilling him with thrusts, parries, and slashes from morning till dusk – though Kairos still could not tell which it was in the subterranean district.

They used wooden swords, which, although not deadly, left the boy covered in welts and bruises, and they continued the training for three weeks until the eve of the festival. Kairos, much to his delight, had added some bulk to his frame from the constant training, as well as the abundance of dwarven cuisine during his several months' stay. One time, he even managed to best Mr. Dubose during a sparring session. The victory was short lived. 'Beginner's luck' as the dwarf termed it, proceeding to beat Kairos down during the next several sessions to prove a point.

Despite being sore and battered, Kairos was happy for once in his life. He began to like Dwarfside much more than Logres. Food was plentiful and life was comfortable, and he earned enough to buy himself a new bed – a human-sized bed where his feet didn't stick out past the edge. Yet, no matter how many happy memories he created in a day, the grief of his recent ordeals lingered in his heart, and the professor's story of the 'god-cursed' infested his feelings further.

He thought of Farina, Thylar, and the Einar back home, and the dull ache would return in his heart. He felt the responsibility towards the Einar weighing down on him. He needed to return to his people one day to help them escape the Blight. Just when, he did not know, and guilt gnawed at him daily – he lived in pleasure whilst his people at home suffered. He couldn't do anything about it now, and the fact that he was the only human in Ordonia without mana, frustrated and tormented him. Kairos felt so helpless. He had always felt helpless–

He was so mired in his misery that he did not see the axe coming from his right.

'What's bothering you, boy?' Mr. Dubose asked, after using the blunt part of his wooden axe to bash Kairos into the mud. With a bored air, a nearby cow watched Kairos pick himself up. Today they were sparring on a farm owned by a dwarf named, Hothar, who had decided it was easier to raise cattle above ground in the sunshine and grass. 'You're lacking focus today. Had this been a real fight, I would've chopped into your groin area, and you would've bled out, squawking worse than these bloody hens.'

'I-I'm just not feeling well.' Kairos looked away. 'Maybe I'm sick.'

'Sick, huh?' Mr. Dubose walked up to the mud-coated boy, squinted one eye shut and leant forward, as if examining him for symptoms. 'Hmm, yes, it appears that you've come down with a severe case of horseshit. You're not sick. What's the problem here? I'm taking time out of my busy schedule to train you for combat, and you're whinging like some ninny who forgot her dress at a beauty pageant. Let's hear it.'

'I was thinking about what that professor said–'

'Look, boy,' Mr. Dubose began. 'You're *not* cursed by the gods.'

'Are you sure?'

'Yes, I'm sure the gods wouldn't bother with cursing a loiter sack like you.'

Kairos hadn't thought about that. 'I suppose you're right.'

'Besides, we dwarves don't use magic and we get along fine. I don't think of myself as cursed.'

'But I want to become a Mana Knight, and I still keep hearing that people with low mana cannot become knights.'

Mr. Dubose spat into the mud. 'That is nonsense. People with more mana, but less resourcefulness than you have become Mana Knights. And I've seen people with high levels of mana fail miserably at attaining knighthood. It takes courage and wit to become a good Mana Knight, and you may be a little daft from time to time, but you have some of those good qualities.'

Kairos gawked at the dwarf in disbelief. Mr. Dubose rarely, if ever, complimented him.

As if realising his error, Mr. Dubose flushed and coughed. 'I'm not saying you're courageous or intelligent, mind you,' he grunted, 'You just have a few more of those qualities than the other humans. As for your mana problem, I told you that I have a solution.'

'What's that?' Kairos asked, daring to hope.

'I left you a list of chores at the workshop. Finish those and meet me in front of the Grand Forge tonight. Don't be late.'

\* \* \*

Kairos was on his way to see Mr. Dubose, but he *was* running late. He had completed the chores, taking much longer than he cared for. Mr. Dubose had something to teach him – to help him become a Mana Knight, and to hide that he was cursed by the gods. The dwarf might keep assuring him that there was no such thing but Kairos wasn't so sure. He knew he had to make it to the Grand Forge in time.

The streets were easy to navigate; by now he knew his way around the subterranean district like he knew his own home. Several dwarves yelled greetings to him as he ran by. He did not stop, only waved in acknowledgement, even quickening his pace.

He had a reason for his unease. Somebody was following him.

The Grand Forge was still a block away. Kairos turned around a few times, but did not see anyone there. Instinct told him there was someone though. He circled the block twice just to be sure. Whatever it was, it stayed close by and out of sight. He quickly veered off the main street and went down an alley that seemed like a shortcut to the Grand Forge.

By the time he reached the halfway point of the alley, it was too late.

A silhouette stood at the end of the alleyway blotting out the dim red light from the streetlamps, just waiting for Kairos. It quickly traced a glyph. Kairos had nowhere to go. The glyph flashed as it was completed. With a loud hiss, a small fireball soared down the alley. Kairos had to jump aside, or else be burned.

The fireball struck the stone pavement behind him, exploding in a shower of sparks. Kairos still had no place to run, no weapon to fight, and his arms and shoulders were tired from the chores. He knew a bad situation when he was in one, and this was very bad. In very bad situations, one had to use very bad tactics, so Kairos did the least expected thing. He charged the silhouette.

The silhouetted figure began casting another spell, but Kairos was fast. He hit the figure, causing the glyph to fade before the spell could be completed. A sixteen-year-old human boy could not do much to an adult dwarf, yet the impact was enough to make the dwarf drop his staff. It clanked against the ground. Besides which, dwarves could not cast spells. Right then Kairos figured out that something was very off...

'All right! I give up!' Mr. Dubose shouted with a chuckle. 'I was just showing you how convincing my casting glove can be.'

The glove was way too small for Mr. Dubose's hand. He could only fit three fingers into it. Handing it to Kairos, he said, 'Here, you put it on.'

It fit Kairos's hand perfectly, like a glove.

'Now touch your thumb and index finger together while moving your hand about.'

Kairos did so. An orange line of light followed from where his fingers touched, hanging in the air just like the glyphs he had seen some Ordonians cast. When he opened his fingers, the line winked out.

'If you squeeze your fingers a bit harder, the mana line flashes, like when an Ordonian casts a glyph.'

'Where did you get this?' Kairos asked.

'Get it? I made that, boy! I didn't 'get it' from anywhere.'

Kairos didn't realise he had just called into question Mr. Dubose's dwarven craftsmanship, a serious insult, but he did realise he had offended him. 'Okay! I'm sorry. I didn't mean anything by it. I-I just haven't seen anything so brilliantly made before.' He hoped that was the right thing to say.

Jace Dubose beamed. Kairos decided it was.

'Aye! It's crafted of two layers of supple leather that hide and protect the runes,' he said, turning Kairos's gloved hand over. 'The condenser is concealed in the back of the hand. There's a small assemblage integrated into the glove that captures kinetic energy to keep the condenser saturated. Oh, and I reinforced the knuckles — for when things get messy. And a battle always gets messy.'

Kairos did not understand what the dwarf was saying, but he tried out the glove again. He cast the light glyph he had seen Professor Argent use during the Badger's Trial. It looked convincing!

'But I see others using one finger.' He frowned. 'I have to use two to use the glove.'

'Well, that's something you'll have to work out. Besides, who's to say that's not your technique from your homeland?'

'Wait. How did you make the fire?'

'Ha! That's where this staff comes in,' Jace said, reaching down to pick it up. It was an ordinary-looking staff made of brass, but with hand grips at the midway points of both halves. Unlike most staffs, this one had a hole at one end with evidence of soot. Mr. Dubose held the staff out to Kairos. 'This beauty combines the same dwarven ingenuity found in your glove, with gnome powder to fire a small exploding projectile – like the fireball you've just seen. An Ordonian would have figured out that it's gnome powder if a dwarf used it, but a human boy like you is another story.'

Kairos took the staff and clutched it in wonder. It was no beauty, and it would probably win a contest for the ugliest staff in Vadost, but Kairos did not care. This staff would help him become a Mana Knight. Give him an edge in battle. And conceal the fact that he was a Cursed One.

Mr. Dubose slapped his large hand on Kairos's back, which sent the boy tumbling forward. 'All right, boy! Now let's go back before someone gets the wrong idea about us. We have to prepare for the festival, and after that, I'll show you the other interesting 'magic spells' that your staff can do.'

* * *

The day began full of excitement for Althea, who was eager to display her best dress. She always loved the festival, which was full of fine-crafted dwarven jewellery that the Ordonians loved and cherished. She hoped to find a new necklace or a brooch. Her friend, Cassie, was going as well. She could meet with her and together they could sample the variety of food and exchange the latest gossip. But the thing that excited her most about this year's festival was the fact that Kairos was going to be there.

She wasn't sure what she would do if she met the boy.

Stella was going, too, guaranteeing to spoil much potential excitement, but Althea had no choice in the matter. The dwarven housekeeper insisted on accompanying her to the festival (despite Althea's repeated assurances that she wasn't going to get into trouble – especially as far as boys were concerned). It wasn't fair, Althea thought. She was fourteen, ready to enter the Academy of the Mana Knights, yet the dwarf treated her as if she were a child!

'Boys are nothing but trouble, lass,' Stella warned her, waggling a disapproving finger to emphasise her point. 'And the purpose of this festival is to have appreciation for a good year in the fields, not for gallivanting with the lads.'

Althea had heard the phrase many times over already. The Hammerfall Festival was not only a celebration of another excellent year of harvest, it was also a celebration of the dwarves' honouring their ancestors. But she wasn't a dwarf, so what did it matter what she did there?

There were some thirty or forty vendors – mostly dwarven – at the festival, plus various venues for entertainment: ale tents and food vendors, games of strength, games of chance designed to part the naïve from their silver, bards, and performers.

Althea was sorry to have gone without her father, but the Mana Knights had despatched him yet again. She was used to it, so the pain of his absence wasn't as fierce as when she was younger, but she had been looking forward to going to the Hammerfall Festival with him. The last time they had gone to a festival together was three years ago. Stella would have to do, she supposed. The dwarf treated her well enough when she wasn't being over-protective.

Althea sampled the wares of several food vendors whilst Stella griped about how much better her cooking was. Althea agreed but continued to hop from one stall to the next, her favourite being the dwarven 'chocolate ores'. Stella paid for everything and even bought a few chocolate ores for herself when she was sure Althea wasn't watching.

It didn't take long for Althea to run into people she knew. Most were from her school classes. Vaughn, Claudius, and Nacole were there too. They stopped when they saw Althea, but they quickly averted their eyes and shuffled away when they saw Stella with her. Nobody dared cross the dwarven housemaid. What she lacked in magic, she made up for in causing a scene, and no sane person wanted that embarrassment. Althea was relieved to see them go, but dreaded encountering them later.

Stella noticed everything. 'What's wrong, Thea?'

'Nothing.'

'Do you want me to talk to them?' She rolled up her sleeves.

The thought of Stella confronting Vaughn and his friends appalled Althea. They would never let her forget it. 'N-no. Please don't! Let's just go.' Although the image itself was rather amusing – like a small hound nipping at the heels of three horses.

She soon forgot about them when she encountered Cassie, who was watching a bard sing and play a lute on a wooden stage. Cassie saw Althea and ran up to hug her, whilst Stella scowled and said nothing. Althea knew why. Stella had lectured her many times on how bad an influence Cassie was.

Cassie acted very wayward and outlandish compared to the reserved Althea. According to Stella, she caked herself in a layer of makeup that would rival a serving wench at the Pinch and Tickle. The young girl fluttered her eyelashes and unconsciously preened herself when she caught the stares of the other boys, which she tried to do at every given opportunity. Althea's ribs began to hurt from the suppressed laughter of seeing Stella fume whilst Cassie flounced about the festival with them.

Finally, they arrived at Jace Dubose's booth, much to Althea's delight and apprehension. He sold necklaces, rings, kitchen utensils, and pans. At the moment, he was less interested in selling and more interested in talking to Stella, who tried to keep an eye on Althea, but did not want to be rude to Mr. Dubose.

Usually interested in the jewellery, Althea ignored the wares on the table and glanced in Kairos's direction, instead. He stopped rummaging through the inventory, looked into her eyes and flashed a wide grin.

The exchange did not go unnoticed by Cassie, who made an appreciative croon. 'Was this the boy you told me about?'

'Cassie!' Althea hissed, her face becoming warm from a fierce combination of her friend's brash comment and Kairos's intense eyes. 'H-hi,' Althea mumbled to him.

'Hi,' Kairos said cheerfully. 'You came!'

'Yes.' Althea flushed even further. She couldn't think of anything to say.

Cassie thought of something for her. 'Hi, I'm Cassie. Althea's friend. Nice to meet you.' She offered her hand, which Kairos looked at, unsure of what to do. 'You should come with us.'

Kairos cast a quick glance at Mr. Dubose, who shook his head. 'I can't now. I'm working.'

'Oh.' Althea tried to hide the disappointment in her voice, but failed. Perhaps she had the wrong idea or got her hopes up for nothing.

Kairos smiled again. 'I have to work for a bit, but shall we meet later?'

'Yes,' Althea found herself saying a little too suddenly. 'I would like that.'

'Where did you have in mind?'

'Shall we meet by the bard's stage in an hour?' She sounded breathless, as if shocked by the audacity of her own words. She looked back at Stella to see if she had heard, but the dwarf appeared to be looking elsewhere.

Kairos paused, only staring at her. He nodded. 'I'll be there,' he said.

No sooner had he said this than Stella swooped in, spun Althea around and pushed her away from the booth. 'Althea! What are you doing dawdling with that good-for-nothing boy? I turn my back for a moment and here you are misbehaving. I'll not have this boy remove your virtue under my watch! Tis not proper, you foolish girl!'

As Althea was whisked away, she looked back at Kairos and mouthed the words, 'See you there.'

'Come on,' Stella snapped. Turning to Cassie, she pointed a finger. 'And you, as well. Move along. I'm sure you've had a hand in this, too.'

Althea looked up at the evening sky and smiled. It was starting to get cool, but she felt very warm. She shared a knowing look with Cassie.

* * *

The Hammerfall Festival was a big event for the dwarves, an entire day of food, fruit and vegetables from the summer harvest (though they were short of star-apples this year), ale, mead, games of chance, competitions, fights, and drunken dwarves vomiting after engaging in all the above. The dwarves gathered in the field, apart from the Ordonians, and there were arm wrestling matches, competitions in throwing axes, and Kairos's favourite, sparring with wooden staves where each combatant stood on a platform above a mud pit.

Kairos worked with Mr. Dubose all day, assisting the dwarf with managing the money and supplying the inventory. The dwarf conducted all of the business transactions, since Kairos had little skill in engaging the customers. The one time Mr. Dubose allowed him to try, he inadvertently offended a nobleman and his wife by mentioning how wearing one of Mr. Dubose's necklaces would complement the greying hair of the lady. Besides that sordid encounter, he had a great, but tiring day, and the dwarf decided to let Kairos off early so the he could enjoy the festivities.

He wanted to partake in some of the games, but wanted to see Althea more, so he walked to the wooden stage where they agreed to meet. The dwarves formed a half circle around the stage and listened to the performer, supposedly a famous bard from Dvergar, singing songs that spoke of the glory days when Thelos roamed Alban, and how he created the mighty dwarven race destined to rule the mountains and all the land. The crowd listened solemnly. Kairos recognised a few dwarves from Dwarfside: Calev, Alberich (one of them), and Togram. He caught the latter watching him from the crowd, but the large-eared dwarf nodded and walked away upon being spotted.

The next song launched into a light-hearted story of a brothel in Dvergar, and many of the dwarves listened to the song's rhythm, occasionally repeating a phrase and laughing. Kairos sat a distance away with his back to a tree and waited. He followed the song, initially with rapt interest, but grew bored when the bard continued on with similar lyrics and rhymes.

Some time passed and the sound of the bard's lute and baritone voice helped soothe his mind, drawing him into the sleep that usually eluded him during the night.

It was dark when he awoke to the touch of a hand on his arm. Alarmed and befuddled, he slapped the hand away and sprang to his feet, ready to fight. The bard was now singing a song about some glorious battle.

Althea let out a gasp, and fell backwards, sitting down hard onto the grass.

Kairos's head cleared quickly. 'I'm sorry,' he stammered. 'Are you all right?' He helped her up.

'I'm fine,' she said, examining her dress and dusting herself off. She frowned when she discovered grass stains on the white fabric. 'I shouldn't have startled you.'

'I wasn't startled,' he said, embarrassed, 'just asleep.'

They both smiled at each other.

'I wasn't sure you would come,' Althea said. Then, in a rush, 'After you went to live with Mr. Dubose, I haven't seen you in so long. And after the Badger's Trial, I wasn't sure if I would see you again.' She flushed and looked down, feigning intense interest in the grass stains on her dress.

Kairos grinned. 'Mr. Dubose keeps me extremely busy.' His expression became serious. 'Though I thought about leaving on that first night.'

'Why didn't you?'

'Where else could I go?'

'Don't you have any family?'

'They are all dead. I had a brother and a father. Malus's army killed them, and now I'm alone.'

Althea reached out and placed her hand over his. Her touch made him breathless. 'What do you plan to do?' she asked.

'I have sworn to avenge them. But first I need to become a Mana Knight, because they're the only ones fighting Malus.' Kairos dared not tell her more — about the Einar, about the fact that he may be god-cursed. He did not want to frighten her. 'What about your family?' he asked, trying to change the subject.

'Father has always worked a lot ever since I was born. Mother died when I was little. I was very close to her and sometimes I dream that she's at home again, showing me a new spell or cooking for me.' She went silent for a moment, watching the dwarves sing along to the bard's new song. 'My father hired Stella, who is like family. So it's just us now.'

At the mention of Stella's name, they both looked around.

'We should take a walk,' she said. 'I ran off from Stella when my friend, Cassie, distracted her. She'll be looking for me here. If she finds me with you, she'll be furious.'

They traipsed off into the crowd. Dwarves from various booths called out aggressively to them to play their games, offering prizes. 'Only a silver crown to play!'

'How 'bout a prize for the lass?' another cried. 'It'll bring you *luck* tonight, if you know what I mean!'

Kairos ignored them. Mr. Dubose had told him that most of the games of chance were rigged in favour of the vendor. Still, they looked fun. 'Where shall we go?' he asked.

'Do you want to play a few games?' Althea asked.

He did, as he felt a need to impress Althea and win her a prize. With the money he earned from today's work, he tried his hand at throwing axes. One of the prizes was a silver necklace that she said 'looked pretty.' He managed to embed the axe into the wooden target two out of three times, just one shy of winning the prize.

'Not bad, lad,' the dwarven vendor said, deeply impressed. 'Especially for a human boy. Care to try again?'

Kairos answered by slamming another silver half-crown onto the table with determination. So much for heeding Mr. Dubose's warning about not playing these games.

The dwarf took the coin and jerked a thumb towards the wooden board which served as a target. 'Go grab your axe, then.'

Kairos walked over to the wooden board and stooped to pick up his axe. He found that the axe head was a little loose on the handle – which was probably why he had missed. He looked around and saw another axe lying on the ground and leant over to pick that one up instead.

Something whirred over him and struck the target with a *thud*. Kairos stood up in alarm. An axe was embedded into the board behind where his head had been a moment earlier. Someone had almost hit him!

'No throwing axes without paying!' the dwarven vendor screamed, scanning the crowd for the culprit.

'Are you all right?' Althea asked in a voice full of concern. She was deathly pale.

'I'm fine.' Kairos looked into the crowd. He could only see a mass of humans and dwarves. Most shuffled by without even glancing their way. 'Did you see who threw the axe?'

'No,' she answered. 'It came from behind me.'

The dwarven vendor, obviously not wanting two distraught customers loitering around his booth, handed Kairos the necklace. 'Here, lad. Just take it and go. It was probably a damn drunk.'

Kairos, with necklace in hand, left the booth with Althea. He scanned his surroundings, but all he found were – as the dwarf termed it – a bunch of 'damn drunks.' He led Althea to a secluded area at the edge of the festival, at the foot of one of the many mountainous hills surrounding Vadost, and they sat down on a cold rock.

Kairos placed the silver necklace around Althea's neck. It had a crescent moon on the chain and was cheaply made, he realised bitterly, cheaper than the silver crowns he had spent to earn it. Mr. Dubose would have griped about the poor quality. Still, Althea beamed as she wore it, and her smile filled him with a pleasant, newfound warmth.

'Thank you,' she said, looking into his eyes.

He stared back, watching the reflection of both moons. The image of Farina appeared in his mind. How Althea so much resembled the unfortunate girl! Another sudden rush of guilt flooded his being. More guilt for surviving when the others like Thylar and Farina had not. Somehow, he felt he didn't deserve all of this.

'What's wrong?' Althea asked worried.

'I-it's nothing,' Kairos said. 'I'm just... just really glad that I met you.'

Althea smiled and their eyes met again. She moved closer, her hand brushing his, and the proximity made Kairos's blood hotter, burning away the guilt and sadness.

'Thea!' a distant voice rang out. 'Thea!'

Althea jumped up. Kairos felt a stab of loss as her hand left his.

'I have to get back home,' she said. 'I've been gone far too long, and Stella will be furious.'

Kairos didn't protest. He knew she was right. 'Where can we meet next time?'

'I'm not sure. I don't think Stella will allow you to come to our house.' She looked back towards the festival where they could both hear the dwarf calling her name. 'Don't walk back with me. If she sees you, she'll only be angrier.'

'When can I see you again?' Kairos asked.

Althea paused in thought. 'Maybe at the Academy. We should have some classes together. If you can wait until then?'

'That's a whole month away...'

Stella's voice rang out in the distance again, this time more urgent and irate.

'I have to go,' Althea said hurriedly.

'Very well then. I'll see you at the Academy.'

Despite her apparent nervousness at the prospect of Stella's anger upon her return, Althea leant in quickly to Kairos and kissed him on the cheek. 'I can't wait to see you again,' she whispered, her breath warm against his ear.

Without waiting for a response, she turned and walked away as quickly as she could.

Kairos watched her leave. The sway of her hips and the warmth of her kiss made him ache for her.

\* \* \*

Kairos sat alone for some time. For once in his life, he didn't feel unlucky or cursed. He revelled in the night's events, replaying the conversations with Althea over and over again in his mind. He especially revisited the memory of her kiss.

The night was getting colder, and a gentle breeze rustled the leaves of a nearby tree, carrying the smells of roasting meat from the food vendors. Kairos smiled as he caught the timbre of another bard's voice, rising through the noise of the festival.

He stood up. It was time to go back and check on Mr. Dubose, maybe even help him pack up the stall. He walked back to the festival grounds, slowing his pace and skirting around a couple entwined on a blanket. He pressed on, suppressing a smile, finding a stone path that led directly into the heart of the festival.

As he neared the lights and sounds, he stopped. He thought he heard something behind him. For a moment there was nothing beyond the buzz of the merry-makers at the festival. A pair of lovers groaned in ecstasy somewhere off the path and Kairos was about to move on when he heard something again. It was close. The sound of footsteps on the stone path.

The back of his neck bristled, and his body tingled. He peered into the darkness behind him. Another sound. Directly from the direction he came. There was someone skulking nearby.

Kairos turned and faced the unknown adversary, taking a fighting stance. He felt naked without his dagger and newly acquired staff, but Mr. Dubose was adamant about leaving weapons behind at the workshop.

The footsteps drew closer. It was a tall and stocky man. No, a boy. 'Why are you posturing like that? So eager to fight me, are you?'

It was Vaughn's voice, slightly slurred by drink. A sliver of moonlight filtered through the trees above and illuminated the wooden tankard in his hand.

Kairos could smell the drink from several paces away. He sighed and turned away. He was still in a good mood from his meeting with Althea and didn't want to ruin it with this.

'Where are you going, coward? I have some unfinished business with you!'

Kairos moved away, closer to the festival where the lights were brighter. He could barely see Vaughn here in the shadows. If they were to fight, he wanted to see his hand movements.

'I'm not a coward, Vaughn,' Kairos said, edging towards the festival. 'I don't want to fight you. You're drunk. It wouldn't be a fair fight.'

Vaughn continued approaching. The path became brighter as they neared a magical street lamp, its ambient light revealing Vaughn's angry face, his eyes shadowed. 'Fair fight?' He laughed, staggering. 'I think you're just too scared to fight. Now prepare yourself, you git.'

The tankard fell onto the stone path with a wooden clatter, splashing its contents on Kairos's boots. He watched as Vaughn's fingertip began to glow and knew he was casting a spell. Kairos tensed. Vaughn had full intention of hurting, possibly killing, him. 'Stop, Vaughn!' he yelled. 'There's no need for this.'

'Oh, but there is!' Vaughn traced a glyph. 'You don't slight me and get away with it.'

Kairos jumped back, unsure of what to expect. Vaughn was drunk, but Kairos knew the boy was deadly with magic.

The glyph flashed, and a gout of flame burst forth, threatening to sear his skin. Kairos saw it coming and spun away, avoiding the flame by a hand's width. He felt the intense heat of the spell and could only imagine the consequences of getting struck. Kairos knew that he had to end this fight quickly.

'Give it up, Vaughn. I don't want to hurt you.'

Vaughn scoffed. 'You don't want to hurt me? No, I'm going to be the one hurting *you*!' He drew another glowing pattern before him. Despite swaying on feet, his spells seemed deadly enough.

Kairos, feeling the battle rage overtake him, surged forward towards Vaughn. He reached out and grabbed the hand tracing the glyph, snuffing out the spell. At the same time, he pulled Vaughn towards him and swung a vicious haymaker that connected directly on the nose. There was a crack, and blood burst forth.

Vaughn fell onto his back, dazed. There was no fight left in him.

Kairos couldn't stop now. Pent up fury overflowed in his veins. Fury at his recent failures. Fury at Vaughn, who had repeatedly provoked him and threatened his life. He would make this boy pay dearly.

He dropped onto Vaughn's chest and began raining blows on him. Vaughn feebly used his arms to shield his face, but Kairos's punches connected again and again. Each blow bashed Vaughn's head into the stone pavement. The blood, black in the ambient light, covered his face. Still Kairos continued.

After some time, strong hands pulled him away. Kairos twisted out of the grasp and turned to fight the newcomer. Stella stood there. A stout, sombre, yet calming presence. 'Easy there, lad, you're about to kill him,' she said.

Althea stepped past Stella and touched Kairos gingerly on the arm. They must have both approached during the fight. Behind them, the light from the magic street lamps illuminated more people gathering to see the spectacle.

Kairos glanced down at his hands, which were covered in blood. He began to shake.

\* \* \*

The audience hall of Vadost was crowded. The magistrate, several counsellors, nobles, and representatives from Valour Keep had come to see what would happen to the foreigner who had so brutally assaulted Vaughn Akkitos, son of Griffon Knight, Lady Naiya Akkitos. Many craftsmen and merchants of Vadost were present, and more dwarves than necessary filled the hall. Physical violence not involving magic was rare amongst humans, and everyone in the crowd hoped to see something memorable.

Vaughn had a solid reputation across Vadost and Valour Keep for his promising talent in magic. Almost everyone in the hall – even the dwarves – knew his mother, for her heroic deeds spread as far south as the kingdom of Numidia. Most saw his defeat as an affront on the Knighthood itself. If a young boy could best such a fine candidate for the Mana Knights, especially without magic, how would that hold up for the authority of the chivalrous order?

On the other side of the coin, a few citizens complained of several knights and their immediate family members abusing their authority. Vaughn was a primary example of someone who walked around the city and intimidated those who crossed him, whilst facing few to no repercussions due to his mother's rank. The dwarves obviously sided with the boy who lived in Dwarfside, because he was a human who bested a powerful mana-user without magic. And according to the rumours, the boy had no choice but to fight Vaughn.

The doors opened and Kairos walked in, escorted by two guards of the City Watch. All eyes turned to stare at him, as he strode towards the end of the hall where the magistrate sat.

Kairos studied the magistrate and the amassed groups of nobles. To his surprise, he recognised Instructor Jomur and Professor Argent, who sat with the representatives of Valour Keep in the row in front of them. His eyes met Jomur's, and he saw condescending amusement there.

Kairos lifted his chin in defiance. He had done nothing wrong. Vaughn had attacked him, and he had tried, initially, to walk away. Yet, he was not so naïve as to believe that he would get away with harming a renowned Griffon Knight's son without consequences.

The magistrate stood. The crowd hushed.

'Speak your name for all to hear,' the magistrate said.

'I am Kairos, son of–' He paused, remembering Instructor Jomur's disdainful reaction, and corrected himself. 'I am Kairos Azel, your honour.' Pride dictated that he act bold, but Mr. Dubose had cautioned him to address the magistrate with politeness.

'You are summoned here because you attacked Vaughn Akkitos, a soon-to-be squire of the Mana Knights, and son of Griffon Knight, Lady Akkitos. Is this true?'

'It is not true, your honour,' Kairos said with a hard edge of defiance in his voice. The audience began muttering amongst themselves. Kairos raised his voice to be heard above the noise. 'I did not attack Vaughn. He attacked me with magic, so I defended myself.'

The magistrate leant forward, adjusted his glasses and squinted at Kairos. 'You have no injuries,' he observed. 'Yet Vaughn is unable to leave his bed and attend today. He is beaten beyond recognition and is awaiting the services of a healer. It appears that you attacked him like a brute with the element of surprise, and once you gained the upper hand, you continued your course of action.'

Kairos clenched his jaw, fighting to suppress his churning anger. Mr. Dubose had also cautioned him not to lose his temper, and that he could not win an argument against the magistrate. He knew Mr. Dubose was right and he took a deep breath, dousing the fiery words before they could explode in outrage.

'That is not true, your honour. He challenged me. I attempted to walk away. He then attacked me with magic—'

'What kind of magic?' The magistrate gave him a shrewd look.

'It was fire, your honour.' Kairos dared not say more. He knew very little about magic.

The magistrate nodded. 'Continue.'

'I dodged his attack. He began casting another spell, and that was when I attacked him. I know nobody here will speak up for me. I am new to the city. I have no reputation, but I am no brute.'

The magistrate stared at Kairos for a long time, and Kairos returned the gaze. Murmurs ran through the hall.

'Do you have any witnesses to the entire incident?' the magistrate asked Kairos. 'The only witnesses who came forward saw just the aftermath of the fight.'

'No, your honour.' Kairos's voice was steady. 'We were alone on the outskirts of the festival when the fight started. No one else was around that I know of.'

The magistrate frowned. 'That is unfortunate then, Mr. Azel, because I have heard Vaughn's story earlier this morning, and he said that you attacked him. Due to your conflicting stories and lack of witnesses, I can only make a conclusion based on the given evidence, which is Mr. Akkitos's injuries. Therefore, I find you guilty of assaulting a prominent citizen of Vadost. As a result, you will face the penalty of—'

A commotion rippled near the entrance to the hall, cutting off the magistrate's verdict. The back of the crowd parted to allow someone through. Kairos turned to see Stella pushing her way forward.

'I will speak for Kairos,' said the dwarf in a strong voice.

\* \* \*

Stella waded through the crowd and stepped forward to address the magistrate. She had not come here to help this boy. She did not like him. But Althea had been weeping since the City Watch hauled him away to confinement.

When Althea had slipped away the night before, Stella scoured the festival looking for the irrepressible girl, shouting her name like a madwoman — much to the dismay of the other festival-goers, and much to the embarrassment of herself. When Althea finally appeared, the dwarf was so enraged that she swore to confront the youth and put an end to this nonsense. Telling Althea to stay put, she retraced the girl's path to find him, and that was when she witnessed the incident with Vaughn from beginning to end.

Stella would have thought nothing further of it once the boy went to jail, continuing on with her business, yet when Althea heard he was to appear before the magistrate, she begged Stella to intervene on his behalf. Stella disliked the idea of Althea courting the young boy. He carried a sense of intense purpose that she found particularly unnerving for a youth, especially a human, that age. But the dwarf realised during the night that if she stood against Galen's daughter, she would lose her. Stella had seen the way the girl sat with him, soothing him with her voice until he had stopped trembling. Althea cared for the boy, and if he was hurt, she would suffer horribly, so Stella had agreed to speak for him.

Besides, she told herself, she knew that Vaughn was in the wrong and was only going to speak the truth. Nothing more.

'The boy speaks the truth,' Stella began, all eyes on her. A tense silence stretched over the audience hall as everyone hung onto her words. 'I witnessed everything. The Akkitos boy approached and threatened him. Kairos tried to leave without a fight. Then the Akkitos boy cast a spell. Kairos dodged, and beat him to defend himself.' She turned to the assembled crowd and glared. 'I swear this is the truth and let any person who says otherwise come up here and challenge me.'

Chaos broke out in the hall. Friends of the Akkitos family expressed their outrage, whilst those who disliked Vaughn, along with several dwarves who simply sided with Stella, roared their approval.

The magistrate turned to consult with the counsellors. They muttered amongst themselves for some time, then beckoned to representatives from Valour Keep to join them. The audience hall grew restless as they deliberated. One of the men from Valour Keep became red in the face as he argued with his colleagues, pointing an accusing finger at Kairos and slamming his hand down onto a desk to prove his point. He was quickly silenced by the magistrate.

Kairos turned towards Stella, as if to catch her attention and nod his gratitude, but she ignored him and faced forward, her eyes locked on the magistrate. He stepped forward and a hush descended upon the room.

'I have consulted with the counsellors and representatives and we have reached a decision. We find you, Kairos Azel, guilty of assaulting Vaughn Akkitos, son of Griffon Knight, Lady Naiya Akkitos. As repentance, you must pay Vaughn Akkitos the restitution of one Ordonian golden crown, or its equivalent value in silver.'

The hall filled with jeers and cheers. Supporters of the Akkitos family applauded the results. Those who sided with Kairos or Stella scoffed. The boy had merely defended himself against an unprovoked attack, a story validated by Stella, an employee of the honourable Dragon Knight, Galen Avenal, and a prominent member of the dwarven community.

Kairos's shoulders slumped at the news. One golden crown was a lot of money for a youth, and it would take him a long time to pay that off.

The magistrate held his hand up for silence. 'Moreover, we find Vaughn Akkitos guilty of initiating bellicose measures and casting combative magic against another person when there was no threat to the citizenry of Vadost. As repentance, he must pay Kairos Azel restitution of half an Ordonian golden crown.' The magistrate's hand shot up once again to suppress the murmurs. 'Additionally, the representatives of Valour Keep also find Vaughn Akkitos guilty of assaulting a fellow recruit of the order. As repentance, he must further pay Kairos Azel restitution of half an Ordonian golden crown, thus equalling one Ordonian golden crown in total, or its equivalent value in silver.'

The throng erupted, chattering about the judgement. Kairos stared at the magistrate in disbelief. Even in the cold hall, beads of sweat trickled down the sides of his face.

The magistrate continued, yelling to be overheard. 'The representatives of Valour Keep further deemed that since the charges negate each other, both subjects will be allowed to continue on as squires of the Mana Knights, however, under close supervision of their superiors. Kairos Azel, you are dismissed.'

Stella stepped close to Kairos, who saw her, and this time managed his grateful smile. He looked as if about to speak, but stopped upon seeing her face remaining severe and distant.

'Do not make me regret this day, Kairos Azel,' she said quietly, so that no one else could hear. 'You treat her well.'

Without uttering another word or waiting for a response, Stella turned and left the audience hall.

\* \* \*

'That's about everything!' Kairos said, tying shut a rucksack that was on the verge of bursting.

Jace Dubose rested a large, meaty hand on the boy's shoulder. 'I'd say I was going to miss you, but you're moving thirty minutes away, so instead, I'll just say don't come over here to eat all my food, shit, and leave.'

Almost a month had passed since the Hammerfall Festival and Kairos's visit to the magistrate. He was off to Valour Keep today, to start his new life as a squire. To become a Mana Knight.

Kairos cast one last longing glance around the workshop. He had grown fond of the place. It was like a second home, and just as he was starting to really enjoy it, he had to leave.

The days of working the forge had come to be some of the best of his life. He had spent entire afternoons hammering the iron and talking to Mr. Dubose. The dwarf was a wonderful listener, and Kairos found it easy to open up to him.

During these conversations, Kairos had touched on many difficult subjects, such as his lack of mana, or the possibility of being god-cursed. He even spoke a little of his time as a captive in Malus's army, but he never mentioned his homeland, or Farina. He was scared to say her name. Fate had brought him to this happy life, and he was frightened that to tempt fate would snatch everything away. Above all, Kairos was still ashamed when he had thought of Farina, of Thylar, and the other Einar that sailed with him. How he'd let them die when only he had lived. The thought that Hargonnas, the elf with the wing-crested helm, played a role in their deaths sparked a flame deep within him that he fuelled with this shame.

'Why are you staring around the workshop like you have your thumb up your arse,' Mr. Dubose snarled. 'Get a move on! Besides, you don't need to get in any more trouble with the Knighthood, being that you recently visited the magistrate and all.'

Kairos nodded, unable to say anything because he was choking back the tears. Mr. Dubose had been like a father to him, more than a father, actually, considering that his own, Karthok the Cruel, didn't care too much for him.

'Don't forget these.' The dwarf handed him the casting glove and the staff. 'You'll be needing them.'

A horse-drawn carriage, another gift from Mr. Dubose, awaited Kairos outside the workshop. He composed himself and turned back to the dwarf. 'Mr. Dubose,' he began, 'Thank you for every—'

'Ah, just shut it,' the dwarf said. 'I've been waiting for this moment for months — ever since you stepped through my front door. I think I'll celebrate your departure with a pint. Now go become a knight, already.'

Kairos nodded and waved, stepping into the carriage. Mr. Dubose returned the wave and stood there until the carriage carried the Einar away. Kairos looked back and saw the dwarf still standing in place.

He thought he saw something else, too.

A shadow flickered from behind a workshop. He gazed at the area for a long time until it disappeared into the distance, but saw nothing else. Perhaps it was one of the street lamps going out.

That was another reason he was looking forward to Valour Keep. He always felt that something or someone was watching him in Dwarfside. He never saw anyone whenever he turned and looked, but he always felt a nearby presence.

His ride through Vadost made him forget his premonitions. Other thoughts occupied his mind.

He wondered how the Einar at home were faring. When he could return. But most of all, he wondered when he could face Hargonnas again. Not as a captive, but as a knight.

# PART THREE

## VALOUR KEEP

# CHAPTER SEVEN

## Badger's Tail

*The Order of the Mana Knights consist of four main classes: Wolf, Lion, Griffon, and Dragon. Wolf Knights comprise of the majority of the Knighthood, followed by the higher-ranking Lion Knights. Griffon Knights command a given post and answer only to the highest rank, the Dragon Knights.*

'*The History of the Mana Knights*', Sir Edwin Rosal

I t was cold in the classroom. The late autumn air blew through the open windows, chilling the students into a miserable state.

Instructor Jomur's voice droned through the cold, his breath forming a mist with each sentence spoken. He looked comfortable, bundled in thick furs.

Kairos didn't mind the cold as much as the other recruits did. He would have enjoyed it if he had not had to train for several hours, working up a sweat during the morning's obstacle course. His sweat-damp clothes, combined with Jomur's dull lecture, made him bored and uncomfortable.

No one liked Instructor Jomur's class. He was an incompetent teacher. They also felt that *An Introduction to Magic Theory* was useless and impractical towards becoming a Mana Knight, but no one dared to tell Instructor Jomur that. So the squires sat on their stools and shivered. Some dozed, but were unable to fall asleep due to the cold. A few speculated that this was the very reason Jomur kept the windows open, to freeze them beyond comfort.

The same could not be said for Kairos. He had lived a lifetime in discomfort; he slept huddled in a longship at sea in the rain and gale; he slept outside on the hard ground when Malus's army had pursued him. This was nothing compared to those harrowing circumstances. He thought he had suffered all varieties of hardships in life. Pain, death, torture, starvation. But Instructor Jomur introduced him to a new form of suffering: boredom. As Kairos listened to the instructor drone on and on, he never knew he could be so bored. He stared out the window at the surrounding scenery of Valour Keep, wishing he could be counting blades of grass.

'Lillanthia Mardon, of the now-defunct House of Briarrose,' Jomur said in his monotone, reading a passage directly from a book, 'first theorised the continued existence of Murasa, the Lost God, years after the Celestial War, or Godfall. She postulated he had not fled this realm because his seers could still sense his presence, albeit weak and suppressed. Furthermore, the lack of any godshard suggests the Lost God did not perish like Zemus or Thelos. She mentioned Murasa may be biding his time in recovery, but her research was abruptly cut short when she had begun exploring another hypothesis on a new compound glyph…'

Kairos's eyes drooped, and he had to pry them open to stay awake. He looked over at Althea, who was furiously scribbling down notes as the instructor prattled on. He wondered how she could enjoy this rubbish. At first, he thought he lacked interest due to not having any magical abilities, but a glance around the classroom showed he wasn't alone. The other squires shivered in misery.

With a great yawn, Kairos put his head down on his arms and closed his eyes. He couldn't tolerate this class much longer. The instructor's voice lulled him into a pleasant nap.

'Squire Azel! What is the meaning of this?'

Kairos lifted his head in a daze. Instructor Jomur was staring at him and frowning, which caused his receding chin to recede even further. Kairos stared back, did not answer. The other squires sitting nearby responded with smothered giggles. This was the most entertainment they had yet had.

'Do you mean to make a mockery of my lecture?' Jomur asked.

'No,' Kairos answered. He just wanted the lecture to end.

'You must say, 'No, Instructor Jomur,'' the instructor corrected.

Kairos sighed. 'No, Instructor Jomur.'

'Look at me when I'm talking to you!' Jomur put his book down on his desk, his hands on his hips, and took a deep breath.

Kairos saw the posture and knew the instructor was about to launch into another one of his diatribes. He yawned without bothering to cover his mouth, much to Jomur's chagrin and the other squires' further amusement.

'How would this rubbish help us in a fight?' Kairos asked.

The quiet laughter halted. Althea, who sat to the right of Kairos, gasped.

Jomur squinted, which Kairos had learnt was an indicator that he was angry, and opened his mouth to speak. At the same time the bell tolled outside from the courtyard, signalling an end to the class and drowning out whatever he was saying. Kairos stood up and walked out, leaving the instructor standing there and sputtering in impotent frustration.

Apart from Jomur's class, though, the rest of the Mana Knight Academy was enjoyable for Kairos. The other recruits accepted him and treated him well. He had been worried that after the beating he'd given Vaughn he would have enemies, but apart from the usual vulgar humour amongst the youth, no hostility was apparent. Vaughn had recovered before starting the Academy (Kairos later learnt that was thanks to Sir Flain's healing spells) and acknowledged Kairos with a nod whenever their paths crossed, but neither spoke after the fight. The rest of the squires displayed reserved admiration for Kairos and his candid honesty.

The instructors and professors expressed the opposite. Professor Bumbershoot, who taught the rules and regulations of Knighthood, complained how Kairos lacked focus. Instructor Jomur openly expressed his desire to remove him from the Order. However, as a mere instructor, all Jomur could do was take out his frustrations in the classroom.

The smallest class Kairos had was *Rudimentary Spellcasting* with Professor Argent. It was a relaxed class, and the only other squires in attendance were Althea, Shah, and Squire Urzen, a shy and quiet squire who seemed friendly enough. Kairos did not need to be a genius to understand that this was a class created for the cast-offs – those who demonstrated little aptitude for magic.

Kairos knew he was the worst of the lot.

At first, he feared the professor would reveal his secret (if he had not already) to the others. But much to his relief, that was not the case. Professor Argent said nothing when Kairos brought the casting glove and the staff Mr. Dubose made, only raised an eyebrow for a moment, and then coolly ignored him.

Kairos would have liked Argent's class more had he carried the ability for magic. Argent took a pragmatic approach to teaching, showing the students a demonstration and expecting direct results – just like a warrior. Thus, Kairos learnt which glyphs created fire, or which summoned a torrent of water. Much to his amazement, he discovered that each element of magic had its own unique pattern of glyphs when it came to forming the spell.

Under the watchful eye of Professor Argent, Kairos, along with the other pupils, practised their spellcasting in the courtyard. Or rather, the other students practised casting glyphs while Kairos merely pretended to do so with his casting glove and staff. Their objective was to hurl spells at a row of straw dummies, which stood on the other side of the yard.

Kairos used his glove to trace the glyphs, then activated the trigger in the staff, which detonated the gnome powder inside, sending a fiery projectile sailing across the courtyard and into the dummy, incinerating a portion of it. He had practised his aim with Mr. Dubose all summer, and it didn't take him long to look like a natural in the class. Despite the strong odour of gnome powder wafting out the hollowed end of the staff, none of the students were ever the wiser.

They had their own concerns.

Althea could cast a fire spell, but only to light a candle or start a cooking fire, not to incinerate an enemy from a distance. For some unknown reason, Squire Urzen was afraid of fire, and all of his fire glyphs fizzled out. He could summon a gust of wind, but that only caused the straw dummy to sway on its stand. Then there was Squire Shah, who set himself afire.

After Professor Argent doused him with a deluge of water, he subsequently banned him from using fire magic for the duration of the class.

Thus, Kairos's 'curse' had gone unnoticed by the others, and he was able to perform the spellcasting portion of his training without problems. It was only a matter of time, though. Each time he attended Argent's class, he felt like a fraudster living a big lie. Galen and Mr. Dubose had told him to keep it a secret, and Kairos knew he would not benefit from telling anyone, but sometimes it was too much. He wanted to tell Althea in private, but they never had much time together alone.

So, he continued his façade of sorcery in silence.

\* \* \*

By the afternoon of their fifth day, the squires had finished their classes, and met at the training grounds – a large field located near Valour Keep. The afternoon sun did little to warm the twenty recruits, as they formed two ranks of ten, all of them clutching a wooden spear.

It was here the squires met the man they all feared and dreaded the most: Sir Flain.

Sir Flain stood before the recruits, his fierce eyes studying them, and his face grew disgusted by what he saw. Of all the professors and instructors, he was the only one who was an actual Mana Knight. At fifty years old, he stood tall, and proudly wore the emblem of a silver lion that designated him as a paladin, as opposed to the ordinary lion that represented the typical Lion Knight. His hair, close-cropped, was iron-grey. His face and exposed arms bore scars from various wounds, and he wore a perpetual scowl, as if his only emotion was anger.

Sir Flain introduced himself with a voice that would have carried over the din of the daily hammering inside Dwarfside. 'Listen up, squires. I am Sir Flain. You may call me 'sir' or 'Sir Flain', but don't ever call me 'Flain'. I am here to instruct you ladies on how to use a mana lance—'

'But sir,' came a voice. All eyes turned toward Shah. 'This isn't a real mana lance, Sir Flain. It's a wooden stick with a padded tip.'

Kairos discreetly hefted his wooden spear and realised that it was weighted, much heavier than any spear he had ever held.

Flain marched right up to Shah's face, touching him nose to nose like lovers, except Flain looked as if he wanted to chew Shah's head off.

'Squire Shah! That is a fascinating observation you have made about my weighted spears. We give these to you squires, because the Knighthood deems you too worthless to waste a fine mana lance.' Shah blanched and dipped backwards, but Flain leant forward to continue pressing his nose into the hapless squire. 'And don't you ever interrupt me again, squire. If I hear one more word out of your mouth, I will set you on fire and put you out by beating you with a wet flail. Understood?'

Barnaby Shah nodded.

'What's that?' Flain shouted. 'I cannot hear you!'

'Y-yes, s-s-sir,' Shah stammered.

'Louder!'

'Yes, sir,' Shah said.

'That's better,' Flain said with a look of satisfaction. 'Now eat some dirt.'

The recruits soon learnt that 'eating dirt' meant fifty press-ups, and they stared forward awaiting further instructions as Shah dropped down to do press-ups.

'Now.' Flain hoisted his own wooden spear upwards. 'I will demonstrate how to use this weapon, which is supposed to simulate a mana lance.' He took a stance and lunged. 'Now you try – and put your weight behind it. When I say 'strike,' you step forward and ram that spear forward with your best roar! You hold that position.' The paladin stopped a moment to allow Shah the time to finish his press-ups and gather his spear. 'When I yell 'recover,' you return to the original position. Strike!'

Sir Flain's command at the tail of his instructions tripped up all but the most observant squires. Half the recruits thrust, whilst the others faltered. Kairos caught on before the others and gave a powerful thrust with a hearty yell. Althea's attack followed shortly after. Shah thrust, lost his grip on the spear, which flew forward and almost struck Flain, who barely dodged in time.

'Recover,' Sir Flain hollered, and the squires returned to their starting position. All except Shah. 'Missing something, Squire Shah?'

'Oops,' Shah said, walking sheepishly out of formation to retrieve his spear under Flain's baleful stare.

'Squire Shah,' Sir Flain began quietly.

'Yes, Sir Flain?' Shah asked nervously.

'I don't even know why the Knighthood allowed you here. I've been watching you for ten minutes and I pray to Zemus for the future of the Knighthood. You are more useless than a one-legged cat trying to bury shit on a frozen pond!'

Kairos cast a sidelong glance at Althea, who smirked back at him. He almost broke out into a laugh. He was not alone, either. Several other recruits snickered at Shah's expense.

'Quiet in the ranks!' Flain thundered.

The recruits snapped back to attention.

The older knight eyed them as a hawk hovers over its prey, waiting to seize an opportunity to strike. No squire wanted to attract the paladin's attention.

'Strike!'

This time, everyone yelled and attacked.

'Hold that position,' Flain shouted. 'Don't move!'

The squires held their spears extended at an awkward angle. Soon the horizontal rows of spears began to wobble as the arms holding them began to tire. Kairos held his spear strong and steady, and he silently thanked Mr. Dubose for the back-breaking manual labour during the summer. He looked over at Althea whose spear trembled and dipped lower and lower. She bit her lip as sweat trickled down the sides of her delicate face. Her strength was draining fast; her spear tip about to touch the ground.

'Recover!'

Every squire breathed a sigh of relief and returned to their original positions. Kairos's blood was flowing. For the first time all day, he had no time to think about his mana-less situation. Or the losses of his recent past. Before he could contemplate his problems, he readied himself for more of the exercise. Flain noticed his eagerness, but made no comment.

'Strike!'

'Recover!'

After an hour of the session, the squires could barely raise their spears. Kairos was the exception, although even his muscles were beginning to tire. Sir Flain stalked in front of the ranks of recruits, told them to be still.

All listened except Shah, who fidgeted.

Sir Flain was on him in a flash. 'Squire Shah! I don't care if a hob bends you over and starts humping you. You don't move at the position of attention. You let him finish! Understood?'

'Y-yes, sir!' Shah stammered.

With a look of pure disgust mixed with hatred, Flain resumed his place at the front. 'I bet some of you are wondering why we're training with spears, huh? I bet some of you are wondering why we even bother with weapons when you can toss around your flashy spells.'

Several recruits nodded. Everyone, except Kairos, preferred magic.

Flain raised his spear and lunged at Claudius, who flinched a moment after the spear tip stopped within an arm's width from his face. Flain swung the spear downwards, sweeping the squire's feet, knocking him to the ground. Flain then charged at the other squires who turned and ran. They scattered before Kairos, as he saw the paladin levelling the spear towards him. Kairos took a stance to parry the incoming thrust, but it never came.

The paladin spat and turned and faced the squires, who now milled about in disarray.

'That's why we use weapons. Because they work. Most of you would have been dead. The enemy, especially dwarves, aren't going to sit around playing hounds-n-jackals whilst you're casting a spell. That's why we train with weapons over and over. Because the body remembers what your addled brains forget! Now fall in!'

Everyone shuffled back into their ranks.

'Strike!' Sir Flain shouted, resuming the exercise. 'Recover! Strike! Recover!'

The exercise continued until the sun began its descent into the Gloaming Peaks of the West. When the session finally ended, most of the squires flopped onto the cold grass and lay panting. Sir Flain directed them to return their weapons and head back to the barracks where they could eat and sleep. Everyone readily complied.

Kairos felt an unbearable hunger. He returned his spear and was about to leave with Althea when Sir Flain pulled him aside.

'I know about your little spat with Vaughn,' he told Kairos in a low voice. 'I was in the audience hall next to the magistrate that day, and I voted to bar you entry to the Academy. I was out-voted. We don't need a reckless, cocky bastard like you coming into the Knighthood, botching things up.' A leering grin spread across Sir Flain's face. 'But now, I'm rather glad you made it in here, because I'll be watching your every move. There's something not quite right about you. I don't know what it is, but I will find out soon enough.' The paladin pointed a threatening finger level with Kairos's nose. 'And remember this, Squire Azel. You cannot do anything without me knowing about it. I can hear a rat piss on cotton from a league away. Now get out of my sight, squire!'

'Yes, sir!' Kairos yelled, trying to hide his smile.

Another instructor who did not like him. But Kairos decided that he liked Sir Flain, and looked forward to tomorrow's training session.

*   *   *

Two weeks had passed since the Mana Knight Academy started. Althea was wondering if she had made a mistake by joining.

Ever since she was a child, she had wanted to follow in her father's footsteps. It was her dream. Her fantasy. But so far, the Knighthood had doomed her to disappointment. She had come here to become a Mana Knight, and what did she find? Waking up before dawn each day for gruelling training sessions in the cold, followed by long-winded lectures and tedious classwork. Mean and bullying instructors who belittled and yelled at her daily. Magical exercises that expected her to cast spells beyond her ability.

To make matters worse, the accommodation was lacking. She had to bathe in freezing water and the straw mattresses made her itch all over. The only reason she could fall asleep was due to sheer exhaustion from the constant activity.

She also became homesick. She missed her comfortable routine at home, and Stella's cooking. She missed her father. She had not seen him for quite some time, but she had received a letter from him a week ago. He was still out in the field, fulfilling some unspoken quest. If he were at home, she would have quit the Academy right then and there to see him.

In fact, Althea had begun toying with the idea of quitting the first time she found a dead cockroach in her soup. When she reported the problem to the cooks, they laughed in her face. Her dejection increased each day. She wanted out. But what would her father say? Her peers would see her as a failure, of course, and the thought sickened her. She would leave in shame, but she could find another occupation, such as becoming a lecturer like Instructor Jomur. 'For those who cannot do, they teach,' she mused.

'Althea!'

Kairos's shout snapped her out of her brooding thoughts. A rope with a large knot at the bottom swung to her. She was supposed to grab it with her hands, stand on the knot, and swing across the mud pit to the wooden platform on the other side. To her dismay, the rope had already started its return trip without her. With a yelp, she tried to snatch it. She managed to grab the knot with one hand, but she was unbalanced and the rope pulled her off of the platform she had been standing on. She lunged for the knot with her other hand and missed as her grip gave way. She cartwheeled into the thick mud, landing headfirst with a loud splat.

Althea frantically kicked with her legs until she flopped over onto her back. She spit out a mouthful of the filth and sat up in the squelching mud. Everyone was laughing at her. And in case anyone hadn't noticed her little tumble, Sir Flain made sure they were brought up to speed.

'Why, Squire Avenal, I must say, that is an interesting technique for dismounting the rope swing obstacle! However, it did not achieve the stated objective of placing you on the opposite platform from your starting position. Or is this part of your cleverly devised two-step process to achieve the objective?'

Althea hated him. She and several of the other recruits had nicknamed him 'Flower Flain' from the rumours of his large flower garden he secretly tended. An oddity for such an angry man.

Now he stared at Althea with an expectant look, waiting for an answer to his question.

She glared back at him and yelled as loudly as she could, 'No, Sir Flain! I slipped and fell.' She tried, with limited success, to clean the mud out of her eyes.

'So you decided to soil my beautifully and finely crafted mud pit with your presence? This is unacceptable. Remove yourself from there and return to the obstacle's starting position. And if you leave any personal articles in my mud pit, I will personally see that everyone here is punished on your behalf. Do I make myself clear?'

'Yes, Sir Flain.' She managed to crawl out of the mud pit and climb the stairs to the first platform. Kairos stood on the other one, waiting to swing the rope to her. His eyes held the only compassion she would find on the obstacle course.

Sir Flain wasn't done humiliating her yet. 'Everyone pay attention! Squire Avenal will now demonstrate the Academy-approved method of traversing this obstacle.' Laughter and eyes aimed in her direction. Kairos swung the rope to her again. Althea reached to catch it.

Out of the corner of her eye, Althea saw Nacole grinning in anticipation. She was enjoying this, she wanted her to fall again. Althea wrapped her hands tightly around the rope and clinched the knot with her feet as she began her second attempt. She was determined to not humiliate herself again.

She barely succeeded in crossing the mud pit and moved, with the other recruits, to the next obstacle. Sir Flain always seemed close by, yelling words of encouragement along the way.

'Why are you lagging, Squire Avenal?' he bellowed. 'You are softer than a boot full of puppy shit!'

No amount of verbal abuse could hasten Althea on to the worst part of her day: the run to Banshee's Lookout. The ruined fortress loomed upon a distant hill, daunting and foreboding.

Althea had heard stories of Banshee's Lookout from her father. Long ago when soldiers garrisoned the fortress, a large and powerful dragon came and attacked it. The soldiers retreated, save for one young man who happened to be trapped in the east wing, after the corridors collapsed from the dragon's initial assault. His young wife – her name long forgotten – pleaded with the Knighthood to save him, but to no avail. They were no match for the dragon and refused to help. She set upon the fortress alone to find her lover, and soon afterward, her screams could be heard throughout the surrounding area. The screams eventually stopped until one night, a heavy fog enshrouded the land. A high-pitched, lamenting wail pierced the night, and no one saw the dragon again. Now on dark, moonless nights, some claimed to hear a keening sad song from the fortress. The Knighthood had classified the interior as off-limits, and only those associated with the Knighthood were even allowed to approach the vicinity.

Unfortunately, the squires were associated with the Knighthood, and running up the steep hill, circling the fortress, and running back were all part of the training.

The exercise not only took its toll on Althea, who collapsed halfway up the hill on the first day and vomited, but it frightened her very soul. Whenever she limped, exhausted and footsore, up the hill, the entire atmosphere darkened as she neared the fortress, as if a ghost's presence lurked nearby. She could almost hear a woman's whisper echoing from the crumbling walls. No matter how hot and sweaty the run made her, Althea would shiver uncontrollably. Even after two weeks of running to and from Banshee's Lookout, the feeling did not dissipate, and she begged Kairos to slow his pace to accompany her.

Sir Flain seemed to enjoy spending his time with stragglers, berating them for their incompetence. Although Althea found herself, more often than not, one of the laggards, she wasn't the worst. Four other recruits could not make the run to Banshee's Lookout at all, and their limitations drew Flain's attention off her back — until they dropped out of the Knighthood after the first week. Her only saving grace was Squire Shah.

Barnaby Shah liked to ask questions a lot, much to Sir Flain's ire. He failed miserably at the obstacle course, always falling into the mud pit, and always getting lost on his run to Banshee's Lookout. According to Sir Flain, Shah must have been dropped from the tallest mountain in the Gloaming Peaks as a baby and struck every jagged rock headfirst on the way down, because he often made poor decisions, such as trying to enter Banshee's Lookout seeking a shortcut, or stumbling into a bear's den off the beaten path.

Because of his inept behaviour, Shah required Sir Flain's constant attention to avoid dangerous or fatal accidents.

Today, however, Althea fared worse than Shah, who managed to miraculously cross the mud pit and stay on course for the run. She had not even reached the top of the hill when her breathing became painful. She bent over with her hands on her knees to catch her breath.

'Why are you stopped, Squire Avenal?' Sir Flain seemed to materialise behind Althea, causing her to jump. 'You're not thinking about quitting, are you? Because if this is the effort you plan on giving, you may as well go home. Don't think I'm going to cut you any slack because your father is a Dragon Knight. You disgrace his good name.'

Althea was tempted anew to quit. Her easy life would return. She could sleep in a nice soft bed again and enjoy Stella's cooking over the bland food in the mess hall. Her father wouldn't mind, either, because he had always tried to talk her out of becoming a Mana Knight anyway. She would miss Kairos, of course. Being around him daily was the only reason keeping her going in this awful place, but he could always visit her.

The thought was increasingly tempting... But Sir Flain's words stirred an anger inside her that she didn't know existed. With a firm resolve, she clenched her jaw and continued up the path.

She did not want to be like those four failed recruits.

* * *

Several more weeks passed, and the training and classwork continued relentlessly. The temperature plummeted further, and a thin blanket of snow covered the land, the classrooms providing a warm respite from the cold. Even Instructor Jomur broke down and cast a fire spell into the fireplace, pleased to show off his meagre talent as he bored the students to sleep with his lectures on theories.

Today, however, the squires did not have Instructor Jomur's class. Instead, they stood out in the field in front of Valour Keep, wrapped in their cloaks.

Kairos stretched languidly, eager for today's practice. He, along with the rest of the recruits, could execute the manoeuvres blindfolded now, and was hoping for something new. Althea huddled miserably next to him, very close, but not so close as to draw Flain's ire. Displays of affection were forbidden in the Academy, and neither of them dared to encourage the ribald conversation amongst the other squires. Some had already speculated, but they were keen to keep the comments to themselves. They had heard stories of what happened to Vaughn.

Sir Flain came today with the cart of wooden spears. Seeing the paladin in the distance, the squires assembled into formation, and Sir Flain nodded in approval. 'You rotters are learning. Now come and get your damned spears.'

The squires retrieved their spears in an orderly fashion and returned to their respective places among the ranks.

'So who here has killed before?' Flain asked the class. 'And I'm talking about battle, not murder confessions.'

The recruits exchanged uneasy glances. Only Kairos, Vaughn, and Claudius raised their hands. Vaughn's eyes met Kairos's, and their gazes locked for a moment.

Sir Flain raised an eyebrow at the three. 'Oh? Who were you fighting,' he asked after a pause, 'a pack of drunken gnomes?'

'Brigands,' Vaughn said, exchanging knowing glances with Claudius. 'We had to kill two of them, Sir Flain. And the third surrendered.'

Kairos looked at Vaughn and Claudius with newfound admiration. He had heard about Vaughn's talent for magic, but did not know that he and Claudius had fought brigands before.

Sir Flain did not look impressed, he glowered. 'And you?' he asked Kairos.

'It was an elf, sir,' Kairos answered, his face grim. 'A soldier from Malus's army.'

Flain grimaced and spat. 'A bloody elf and some cowardly brigands! Bloody easy to kill, they are!' He pointed at Kairos. 'You, come here.'

Kairos did as he was told and stood in front of Flain, who hoisted a wooden spear for himself.

'We're going to spar today,' he explained. 'Squire Azel and I will demonstrate, then the rest of you pathetic lot will follow. Prepare yourself, Squire Azel.'

They proceeded to have a practice fight where Flain quickly overwhelmed and knocked Kairos into the ground, leaving a welt on his forehead along with an aching head. The paladin stood over him, spear levelled at his throat. 'Guess what – I'm no bloody elf, you maggot!' he snarled, kicking Kairos in the midriff for good measure.

The Einar heaved and slowly rose to a sitting position, taking care not to smile. He liked Sir Flain even more.

Each squire found a partner and sparred. Each developed cuts, scrapes, bruises, and welts. One squire quit after falling and breaking his wrist. Sir Flain cast a healing spell on it, but the wounded boy decided that there were better things in life than standing in a cold field and getting yelled at and whacked with a spear.

Kairos fought a variety of opponents, none posing much of a challenge. Cassie's moves were predictable. Shah defeated himself, tripping on the butt of his spear and tumbling onto the padded point of Kairos's. He faced down Claudius, who fought back viciously, and Flain called an end to the match before either could gain the upper hand. One opponent Kairos did not tackle was Vaughn, and he suspected that Flain did not want them to stir up any bad blood again.

Althea fared almost as poorly as Shah, losing all her matches to everyone else.

When Kairos faced her, he stifled the power of his attacks. Whenever Flain was watching, he pretended that Althea struck him a powerful blow that would make Jace Dubose proud. He wanted Althea to succeed, but her delayed reactions and stiff movements proved she was no warrior. He also saw something else in her eyes: fear. She flinched away from the padded spear, even though it was a harmless sparring prop. At the end of their match, it became evident to Kairos that Althea would die if she found herself in a real fight. He was doing her no favour.

The sparring matches continued every day for several more weeks. Flain mediated, interrupted, and taught a few more moves, pivots, and attacks. He berated them relentlessly, and two more squires quit, until only twelve remained.

Kairos enjoyed Sir Flain's harsh training. His physical prowess gave him the upper hand over the other squires. Though he was a runt amongst the Einar, he excelled with the Ordonians. Even Flain muttered a comment about Kairos having the strength of a griffon and Kairos's opinion of the paladin improved even more.

He couldn't say the same for the other staff. Instructor Jomur continued to demonstrate how much smarter he was than his pupils, whilst Professor Bumbershoot became ill — much to the delight of everyone since they found the legalities of the Knighthood as almost as boring as Jomur's lectures. Professor Argent was a very capable teacher, but Kairos was only learning glyphs he couldn't use, and he always left the class feeling like a failure, despite the professor's praise of his 'resourcefulness.' The curse of the gods always weighed heavy on his mind. Would the others find out? It was his biggest fear. He considered himself unlucky, not resourceful.

He also grew more concerned for Althea.

She was becoming more and more withdrawn. She was often the last person to stumble into each class (only followed by Shah) and her eyes were frequently downcast. She cheered up slightly whenever she was near Kairos, but mostly she slogged through the day carrying a look of defeated sadness with her, like a hound separated from its master.

Kairos predicted she would drop out soon. The thought appalled him, and he immediately felt guilty for thinking it at all. But her suffering also caused him grief. He felt so helpless watching her struggle. He wanted to be near her, but he reasoned that she would be better off going back home to Stella and her father. Judging by the way she fought, she would be killed or get someone else killed. He couldn't bear the thought of losing her.

He would have a talk with her, he decided. It would be for the best.

\* \* \*

'Are you sure it was him?' Hargonnas asked eagerly.

The rotund dwarf glanced around, making sure no one was eavesdropping. 'Aye. I'd never forget this one.' He moistened his lips with his tongue. 'He's got quite bigger since then, but there's no doubt it's him.' The dwarf grinned, combing his chestnut hair with meaty, dirt-stained fingers. He was balding, Hargonnas noticed, and constantly brushed his hair forward to cover the thinning patch at the front.

The light elf disliked the dwarf. He smelled like a rancid mixture of a horse stable, acrid body odour, and ale. Hargonnas recoiled when he saw him pull a louse from his beard, study it for a moment, and then flick it away. There was also a sly nature about the dwarf that he found particularly disconcerting, as if he were plotting against Hargonnas while pretending to work for him. But the dwarf was instrumental to retrieving the boy – alive rather than dead – and while they were deep in enemy territory, Hargonnas would take all the help he could get.

He had greatly underestimated the young Einar and the Mana Knights, and by Dia's golden hair, it wasn't fair!

Hargonnas visualised the ambush over and over again in his mind. He had been careless and over-confident, his own arrogance and premature celebration leading to his downfall and demotion. He should have kept Sergeant Selkis and the griffons around, but he'd sent them ahead, thrilled at capturing the boy – and Henrik, who would have been his first slave! He was so sure the Mana Knights would blunder in far behind like they always did, but they had despatched a Dragon Knight, of all people, and struck quickly. Hargonnas had barely escaped with his life, lost favour with Malus, and so his position as captain of the Grimaldi Flying Squadron, and now he was reduced to living incognito here. The elf clenched his fist, nails digging into flesh. Rage burned through his veins, stoking the heat of his mana. He was destined for greatness; he *would* rise above his parents' meagre status, above a commoner. But first he would destroy Kairos.

A curse on that Einar boy. He had caused Hargonnas so much misfortune, ruined everything for him. But he would soon feed Kairos's charred body to the griffons, and again take his rightful place as captain... or perhaps higher.

'Did anyone see you?' he asked now.

'No,' replied the dwarf. 'I have always remained hidden amongst the brambles and rocks. I have been careful. For a time, I watched the class train in the fields, then I returned here. Nobody saw me.'

'Excellent. Well done.' The elf handed him a purse filled with silver crowns. 'There is much more than this when you succeed. We shall strike soon.'

Hargonnas stared back at Valour Keep, dreams of death and vengeance burning in his eyes. He did not see the dwarf shudder at the look on the elf's pale face.

\* \* \*

Kairos cleared his throat and pulled at the side of the collar where it rubbed his neck. He wrinkled his nose and scratched at his arm. He didn't like it. But it was the dress uniform for the Mana Knights, so there wasn't anything he could do about it.

The squires all wore the deep blue woollen garbs of the Knighthood. The sleeves and legs were unhemmed. They hadn't completed training yet, but he and his class were being fitted with the uniforms they would wear for graduation. A swell of pride and accomplishment burned within him. He really felt like he belonged with the knights now.

Stephon, the tailor, measured them, calling out numbers to his assistant who wrote them down as each squire stood at attention in front of him. He marked the material with a bit of chalk so he could finish the sizing and tailoring later. It was almost Kairos's turn. He had already seen Stephon glancing at him. No doubt the elf would have some disparaging comment.

'Stephon,' whispered Althea from behind Kairos, when the elf approached.

He beamed at Althea and bowed with a flourish. 'Althea! A pleasant surprise to see you.'

'What are you doing here?' Althea whispered back as loudly as she dared.

Stephon covered his mouth, which hung open in mock surprise. 'Oh? You haven't heard? The Knighthood happened to notice my booth at the marketplace, and they offered me a contract. They have good taste, after all.' The elf's gaze moved from Althea to Kairos. 'With an exception, of course. It seems like you still keep boorish company, Althea. I say, he will burden you. Mark my words, darling.'

'Just measure me and get a move on,' Kairos said.

'You will be silent!' shouted Jomur, pointing an imperious finger at Kairos. 'Maintain your bearing, Squire Azel, this is not a rainbow ice social!'

Kairos didn't know what that even meant, but he cleared his face and stared straight ahead. He seethed with frustration and embarrassment, but barely let it show. Jomur never let a chance to humiliate Kairos pass him by. He even invented them, as necessity dictated. Now, he noticed Kairos's frustration and smirked. So did Stephon.

The moment was broken by a soft *fwoosh* and a startled scream. Glancing back, Kairos saw that Shah had somehow managed to set his uniform on fire. The too-long sleeves and legs flapped like broken wings as he ran around screaming. The flame wasn't bad, but Shah was going to make it so, fanning it like he was. Other squires were diving out of his way as he ran through the ranks.

Jomur's smirk changed to a look of horror as he shouted, 'Squire Shah!' What are you doing? Stand still! Someone stop him!' His voice rose a few octaves in his near-panic.

He pushed through the unsettled squires, hurrying over to Shah and began casting glyphs. Even Kairos could tell he was doing it incorrectly. Jomur may have meant to conjure water to put out the flames, but he transposed the water and fire glyphs. Several instructors shouted for him, also, to stop, but it was too late. A stream of scalding water jetted out of the glyph, parboiling

Shah. Jomur had managed to put out the flames, at least, and later he would say it was part of his plan, interrupted before he could finish. Still later there would be some idle speculation on whether Jomur's plan was to kill Shah. No one reached a definitive conclusion.

'S-s-should we call for Sir Flain?' Jomur's assistant asked.

'No!' Jomur yelled too quickly. Watching Shah scream in pain, though, he suddenly seemed unsure. 'I-I don't know! Yes! Go fetch him! Squires, break for one hour.'

The squires cheered – much to Jomur's further dismay – and scattered throughout the grounds of Valour Keep. For the past several months, every waking moment of their day had been dedicated to serving the whims of an instructor, or reporting to a specified location at a specified time. Kairos never had time to see Althea one-on-one. He and the others rarely had time alone.

Taking advantage of the momentary distraction, Kairos and Althea took off in a separate direction to the other squires. He planned on having a talk with Althea today, and was gathering his thoughts on their walk. They came to an abandoned temple on the outskirts of Valour Keep, hidden from view of the main roads. She pointed to the crumbling building and watched for Kairos's reaction.

It was a Temple of Zemus, she explained. Whilst the city of Vadost had many such temples dedicated to the god, this one was different, as it was older than the Celestial War itself.

Kairos was impressed. The walls were made of stone, perfectly cut rectangle blocks, and the entire structure sat on a podium with a raised portico. Two pilasters flanked each side of the entrance, containing scenes of Zemus's deeds throughout the history of mortals. There was a pillared walkway and several smaller rooms inside. The main room had a large mosaic on the floor, and Kairos gaped at the image of Zemus – as Althea told him – descending from the heavens, whilst lightning flickered around him and above a large gathering of humans. Dragons populated the skies, looping through the series of clouds, and there was a miracle or some sort of magic being performed in the centre of the picture, but it had faded or been discoloured by the elements over the centuries.

'This was a time when the gods existed in Alban,' Althea marvelled, studying the mosaic with fervour.

'How long ago?' Kairos asked.

'About a thousand years ago in the very least,' she answered. 'It's the year 964 now. I don't think they built this after the Celestial War.'

They wandered through the temple and Kairos wondered that humans could no longer build like this. The Einar worshipped Rudras, but they only knew how to build houses consisting of wooden beams and rafters with thatched roofs, which had rotted and decayed within decades. Without any maintenance, this temple stood the test of time throughout a millennium. 'Was Zemus a powerful god compared to the others?' he asked.

'Yes,' Althea answered. 'One of the most powerful.'

'But he is dead?'

'Yes. All gods have either fallen or fled our world.'

'Do you suppose that some might still be alive? Jomur spoke of a lost god or such.'

'I don't know,' Althea said. 'Some in Ordonia believe Zemus still lives – that he was greatly injured during the Celestial War and has been resting since then... But the godshards are proof of their death.' She paused, looking thoughtful. 'Why do you ask?'

'Just wondering,' Kairos said, but he had been thinking that powerful gods rewarded their followers with more luxurious lives. It appeared Zemus had looked after the Ordonians rather well. He thought of the Einar and Rudras and wondered if his race really was 'god-cursed'. He flushed with guilt, knowing that such a thought was blasphemous, but he couldn't help thinking of how much better the Ordonians, and even the elves and dwarves, thrived over the Blight-stricken Einar. He also wondered if a godshard of Rudras existed somewhere.

Althea no longer paid him heed. They had found a staircase near the entrance leading upwards to another room filled with many murals of Zemus, detailing the creation of humans and the god's interactions with them. Althea walked over and began examining each one in detail.

'Don't take too long,' Kairos said. 'We have to return soon.'

She looked disappointed, as if wanting him to join in. He was disappointed in himself. He wanted to talk to her about her struggles in the Academy, but his courage had failed him. She seemed happy today, especially on this walk, and Kairos did not want to ruin the moment. He walked down the stairs back to the main room, looking at the images of Zemus, wondering if the god was still alive watching from somewhere, or broken off as pieces of godshards. Everyone said that Zemus's main godshard was housed in Valour Keep – the Sapphire Shard. Maybe all the gods *were* dead–

Kairos jumped; he whirled around. Expecting Althea – where was she? – he came face to face with an unexpected visitor.

Togram the dwarf stepped through the entrance of the temple. He stopped just inside and stroked his beard, head nodding, then half smiled. 'Missing a weapon, Kairos?'

'No,' Kairos said.

'Mr. Dubose sent me,' he said. 'He has a gift for you.'

Kairos nodded, but said nothing, knowing Mr. Dubose would have delivered the gift himself.

'Here.' Togram put his hand in a leather pouch that hung on his belt. 'A silver crown for you. Now come along.'

Kairos nodded again, but did not move.

Togram's brown eyes glanced at the temple walls, then at the large mosaic on the floor. 'Do you worship Zemus?' he asked.

'No.'

'In Dvergar,' he said, 'we dwarves worship Thelos.' He walked towards Kairos, who moved back in tandem, keeping the pillars of the walkway between them. The dwarf looked better dressed than the rags he had worn when he first came to Dwarfside. He wore leather padded armour and proper boots, and a sword hung on his belt. 'Which god do you worship, Kairos?'

'I don't want to talk about the gods,' Kairos said sullenly.

'I do,' the dwarf said, grinning. He tossed the coin aside and drew the sword, its blade grating on the scabbard's wood, and he stepped forward, the sound of his boots echoing on the walls. Togram was no longer looking at the mosaic, but at Kairos, who did not move. For some reason, he could not move. He was dumbfounded, and yet not surprised. He had never liked Togram from the very beginning; the dwarf had the untrusting eyes of a serpent ready to strike.

Since his initial meeting with the dwarf, Kairos realised he had always been in the company of others. Now he and Althea had strayed from Valour Keep, Togram had his opportunity. The dwarf flashed his teeth and moved down the walkway, sword raised, and finally Kairos found his feet. He ran back into the interior of the temple and behind a broken pillar. He hoped Althea had the good sense to run.

'What's the matter, Kairos,' Togram called. 'Afraid of the gods?'

'What do you want?' Kairos asked.

Only the broken pillar separated them. It was low enough for Kairos to see the dwarf on the other side, but high enough to prevent the dwarf from jumping over it. Kairos feinted right, darted left, but the dwarf was much quicker than he looked, his sword flashing from side to side, lethal, blocking any chance of escape.

Kairos was trapped.

The dwarf knew it, too, and he smiled showing all of his teeth. 'Captain Hargonnas sends his regards, boy,' Togram said, stalking the pillar.

'H-Hargonnas...' Kairos repeated in disbelief. It should have been obvious. That elf still wanted him dead, and Kairos was a fool to think he was safe in Vadost, or in Valour Keep.

'Lord Malus wants you dead, as well,' Togram said. 'And the reward should help me buy a new home in Dvergarberg. You've been a tough bastard to kill. I almost tracked you that night near the Grand Forge in Dwarfside, but you reached Mr. Dubose before I could catch you. Then there was the Hammerfall Festival where I almost hit you with an axe, but you ducked. This time I have you. Hargonnas wants you to suffer, but as Thelos as my witness, I'll make it quick.' He sliced an arc over the broken pillar and the blade whipped in front of Kairos. 'There's no honour in killing an unarmed boy,' he said. 'But you humans spread like a plague, so I suppose honour doesn't matter here.'

Kairos tried to circle the dwarf around the pillar, but the sword hissed, almost cutting him and causing him to stumble backwards. The dwarf smiled and moved in, cornering him. 'Don't move boy,' he said. 'I'll make it quick—'

Suddenly, a small ball of fire struck his head from behind, cutting him off mid-threat. It was a weak spell, but the unexpected flame found a fuel source in the dwarf's oily hair, and it ignited instantly. The stench of burnt hair filled the room. Before Togram could react, a second fireball struck him in the head again, and he was horribly transformed into a dwarven torch with flailing arms.

From the stairs near the entrance, Kairos heard Althea's voice. 'Run,' she shouted. 'Run!'

Kairos ran from the dwarf, who was now beating his own head with an open hand, in an attempt to douse the flames, and headed for the temple's entrance. Althea rushed down the stairs, and together, they raced along the path that took them back to Valour Keep.

Togram – head still smoking – burst forth from the temple in pursuit, pumping along with all his might, but his short dwarven legs could not keep up with the taller humans, and soon he gave up chase and disappeared.

Kairos and Althea continued running until they saw Valour Keep in sight. Then, Kairos slowed his pace so Althea could keep up, but, surprisingly, she ran faster and harder today than any other day on the obstacle course. As they ran into the courtyard, the squires, Instructor Jomur, and Stephon all turned to watch them. Even Sir Flain was there.

'You're late!' Jomur shrieked in a high-pitched voice. 'Explain yourselves.'

'Someone tried to kill us, you idiot!' Kairos yelled. He balled his fists and approached the gangly instructor. He was furious and was not in the mood for Jomur's belligerence. He drew his fist back, intent on shutting the instructor up.

'Stand down, squire!' came a voice, and a strong arm grabbed Kairos's wrist. It was Sir Flain. 'Tell me what happened.'

Kairos knew only one thing – Hargonnas was nearby, waiting to kill him. He glanced over at Althea, who was on her knees in tears, and the grip of terror seized his chest.

Life would never be the same at Valour Keep.

\* \* \*

'This is madness!' Sir Flain could hardly contain his anger. 'You heard the boy. One of Malus's men tried to kill him and you fools want to sit there with your thumbs up your arses!'

A series of murmurs swept across the men and women in the meeting hall. Flain and Professor Argent sat at one end of the table, whilst Lady Naiya and Professor Bumbershoot sat at the other, leaving Instructor Jomur and the other knights and faculty members along the sides. Some of them looked wistfully out of the window, wishing to be anywhere but there.

Flain was exhausted and outraged. He was also genuinely concerned about the safety of Valour Keep.

Lady Naiya slapped the table with her palm and stood up. 'Silence! You forget your place, Sir Flain.'

Even the instructors and knights who had been feigning disinterest in the conversation turned their heads and stared.

Flain knew he had overstepped his boundaries. No one yelled at Lady Naiya. She was a First Class Griffon Knight, next in line to become promoted to Dragon Knight. 'My apologies, my lady. You are correct. But I only speak this way because I fear that Malus's men are close by, watching our every move. I have reason to believe that the boy is speaking the truth. We found a silver coin that was minted in D'Kari, and wide boot prints in the snow going in the opposite direction of Valour Keep. There *was* someone else there.' Flain felt helpless as he watched Lady Naiya clench her jaw and look away, he knew she wasn't listening. 'I am doing my duty by speaking out in this regard.'

The meeting hall was silent. The professors cast nervous looks at each other, except for Argent who seemed aloof from the entire argument. One of the knights nodded along to Flain's words, but dared not voice his opinion, for fear of Lady Naiya's displeasure. She outranked Flain, and there was more to lose by incurring her wrath than in agreeing with Flain.

Flain had believed something was wrong the moment Kairos and Althea came running back to Valour Keep, trembling and out of breath. The fear upon their faces was real. To his dismay, Instructor Jomur dismissed their stories as 'contrived alibies' in order to avoid punishment for tardiness. Flain summoned a few knights, much to Jomur's protests, and scoured the area where the squires had been. Finding a D'Kari coin in the ruined temple of Zemus was no mere coincidence and he would not back down from this.

'Sir Flain,' Lady Naiya began. She was angry, furious at being dishonoured in front of the other knights and professors, especially by a lower-ranking knight, but she spoke in a calm voice. 'Malus was defeated years ago. His armies were decimated beyond recovery. His elves can wave a few spells and his dwarves can shake their axes, but it's all mere threats. We do not need to resort to paranoia because one dwarven brigand trespasses upon our lands and threatens a squire who's wandering *beyond* his given boundaries.'

'It's true the boy was in the wrong,' Flain conceded, 'but I think Malus is up to something. He's been quiet for far too long, and he has recently attacked Milbrooke.'

Lady Naiya shook her head. 'A measly raid on the outskirts of Ordonia. Even if he were to launch a full-scale war, he cannot stand up to the combined might of the Knighthood. We have nothing to fear from him or his armies. He has not declared war and he refuses to face us. The dark elf is a coward, nothing more.'

Flain remained unconvinced. He had fought against Malus alongside Lord Avenal. He knew first-hand that Malus was no coward. 'If Lord Avenal were here, he would agree with me. His daughter's word confirms the boy's story—'

'Lord Avenal is not here, and what do squires know?' Lady Naiya's words were like ice, and Jomur smiled and nodded along in agreement. 'They lack the training to differentiate between the common bandit and a member of Malus's army. And speaking of bandits, we've had increasing reports of our farmlands being raided this past season. This is due to the Knighthood allocating its valuable resources towards Milbrooke and Gersholm.

'Do you see where I'm coming from, Sir Flain?' she continued. 'I'm thinking that we should focus on our more immediate problems close to home. If we focus abroad on what Malus is doing, we'll allow the bandits and hobs to raid us dry.' She slammed her hand down on the table again and glared at Flain, who knew it was pointless to argue further. 'Enough of Malus. Let's talk about the squires – Professor Bumbershoot, tell me how the recruits are doing?'

Professor Bumbershoot, who was staring at the ceiling, jumped upon hearing his name. 'Wh-what? Oh yes, right – the recruits. Yes. Most know the basics. Your son, Vaughn, is a prodigy, my lady,' said Professor Bumbershoot with a bow, causing the lady to smile. 'Claudius is gifted, as well. I would say Cassie is very well rounded. Nacole is a hard worker. A good bunch, if I do say so myself.'

'Good to know.' Lady Naiya turned to Professor Argent, who looked as if he would rather be anywhere else. 'And your class? How fares the badger—' the Griffon Knight caught the derogatory comment. 'How fare your squires?'

Professor Argent eyes narrowed. 'The 'badger tails' as you like to call them are doing well enough, I suppose. There is nothing much to report.' He stifled a yawn.

'Take this seriously,' the Griffon Knight ordered, her tone taking on an edge at the mockery.

'I am serious,' Argent replied in an even voice. 'I have nothing remarkable to report, unless you count the fact that Barnaby Shah has a bit more mana than everyone thinks. He just cannot control it well.'

Flain studied Argent's face. It was impassive, like the granite walls of the meeting hall. To his surprise, the professor turned towards the paladin and their eyes met. They stared at each other for several tense moments.

They were interrupted by Lady Naiya asking Instructor Jomur for his report.

Jomur bowed, and shuffling a stack of papers, stood and began reading from the first page. 'These squires are not studious. Several, such as Kairos Azel, continue to show disrespect towards my knowledge and towards the literary material presented—'

'Yes, yes, thank you for the report, Jomur,' Lady Naiya said, much to the instructor's irritation. He sat down and stared at his lap with a reddened face. 'Sir Flain, I believe it is your turn.'

Flain knew she wanted a report, but he continued to argue his point in a forced low tone. 'Again, my lady, my apologies for overstepping my boundaries, but I think this attack on my squires was calculated!'

He expected Lady Naiya to become angry, but to his astonishment, she suddenly relaxed and nodded. 'If that is so, then you must train them harder.'

Something in her voice gave Flain reason to pause. This was unexpected. 'What do you mean?'

The Griffon Knight smiled. 'I have orders for their first campaign.'

'When is that, my lady?' Professor Bumbershoot asked eagerly. 'And where?'

'After Yule, by the beginning of spring,' Lady Naiya replied. 'As I mentioned before, we have been receiving disturbing reports about an infestation of hobs attacking the farms on the outskirts of Vadost. Currently we have despatched a few knights to deal with this problem, but we are understaffed, and most of the hobs have hidden away in hibernation for the winter. We were hoping to have your recruits ready by spring to assist them.' She raised her hand upon seeing the looks of concerns. 'They will have supervision, of course. We will divide them into units and place a seasoned knight in charge. We believe the hobs have settled in the area and won't be leaving any time soon. Their inactivity for the remainder of winter should give you a little time to prepare. Will your squires be ready by then?'

Instructor Jomur and Professor Bumbershoot looked at each other with uncertainty. Professor Argent did not show any interest in the conversation.

'My lady,' Flain began, 'They will not be ready. There is not enough time between Yule and spring time, and they need much more training, otherwise some of them will certainly die. And danger still lurks—'

'Then train them harder from now until then,' she replied icily. 'These squires signed up willingly for the Knighthood, knowing the dangers involved. Spring is when the hobs will stir from their hibernation, and this matter cannot wait any longer, unless you want them pillaging our countryside and farms. So I will ask you again. Will they be ready by spring?'

'Yes, my lady,' Flain answered in a measured tone.

# CHAPTER EIGHT

## Yule

*The celebration of Yule traditionally involves decorating yule trees with lights, treats, and small runestones to entice Thelos, the god of the earth and stone, to awaken from his slumber and warm his forge for the coming spring. Therefore, we imitate this by burning a yule log. In the past century, however, this celebration has become a holiday of feasts, mead, and debauchery — with some gift-giving in between.*

'Dwarven Traditions: Vol. III', Lysandofer Galatius

It was winter of 964 A.C., the first day of Yule.

The first day of the squires' winter holiday marked Althea's fifteenth birthday. A snowstorm had swept through the previous night and whited out the landscape. The leafless trees stuck out of the snow, looking like darkened skeletons in the bleakness of white and grey. The cold whitened Althea's skin and reddened her cheeks, as she and Kairos traversed the grounds of Valour Keep.

In the barracks, many of the squires were packing to travel home for a week. Instructor Jomur checked on them periodically, reminding them to study their theories during the holiday, to which one squire muttered that he'd rather plunge into the icy waters of Lake Turquoise and freeze to death. Eventually Jomur decided it was too cold to trek back and forth in the snow to the barracks and shut himself in his study, much to everyone's relief. Sir Flain paid them one last visit and stated that the training would recommence in a week. The squires noted that his yelling seemed more subdued than usual.

Althea was thankful for the holiday. At least it was a break from the intense routine. She wanted to spend time with Stella, her father, and especially some alone moments with Kairos. They rarely had any time alone during days filled with training and classwork. Yet, she and Kairos did not walk three paces from the barracks when they encountered Flain and another knight waiting for them.

'This is Sir Hugo, a Wolf Knight,' Flain explained. 'Given the recent attack on you, I'm not taking any chances on your safety. He will escort you to Vadost and stand watch.'

Sir Hugo saluted and stood at attention. Althea and Kairos returned the salute half-heartedly. Althea did not want the knight around, but she could not argue with Sir Flain's reasoning.

'Show him your utmost respect,' Flain growled upon seeing the lack of enthusiasm. 'If you need something over the holiday, send word to me immediately.'

Flain departed, and Sir Hugo offered to help carry Althea's belongings, which was a rucksack full of her clothes. Squires were not yet permitted to carry weapons home.

'I can carry my things,' Althea snapped. 'I'm not helpless, you know.'

'Forgive me, my lady,' Sir Hugo said with a bow. 'I'm only trying to assist.'

They neared the gate entrance of Valour Keep when they ran into Stephon, who was pulling a sled burdened with linens and wool.

The elf smiled and waved. 'Greetings, Althea! Greetings, Sir Hugo. Oh my, that armour looks fabulous on you!' He looked Sir Hugo up and down, then glanced at Kairos and frowned. 'Oh, you're here, too. At least you're better dressed than when I first saw you.'

'Hello, Stephon!' Althea said, placing a restraining hand on Kairos's arm. 'Why are you working? It's a holiday!'

'For you lot, perhaps,' he said with a longing sigh, 'but I have extra work. You squires and knights are always ruining uniforms, so I'm either repairing old ones or making new ones, and there's many of you and only one of me. So I won't have much free time, I'm afraid. Otherwise, I would invite you, and especially Sir Hugo there, for a glass of wine. Unfortunately, I cannot... What about you, darling?'

'I'll be going home, of course,' Althea said. 'If my father is there, we're going to celebrate with a big Yule feast. I'll be inviting Kairos along, because he said he never celebrated Yule before, so this will be his first—'

'Althea!' Kairos said, glaring at the elf. 'Let's go.'

'Kairos, please!' Althea said with exasperation. Then she turned to Stephon. 'I'm sorry for his lack of manners. He means no harm.'

'Of course not.' The elf bowed to Althea. 'I'm not bothered by barbarians. Now if you'll excuse me, I have to take care of this order. Enjoy Yule.' He grabbed the cart and began pulling the sled through the snow. Sir Hugo appeared relieved at his departure, but said nothing.

Once the elf was out of earshot, Althea sighed. 'Honestly, what is your problem with Stephon? I think you offended him. Are you still holding a grudge because he made some comments about your clothing?'

'It's not that.' Kairos looked down in thought. 'Forget about him. Do you think your father will be home for Yule?'

The mention of her father made Althea feel hollow. She had not seen very much of him during the past year, and with each day, she felt as if he were becoming a stranger. He had been around much more when she was younger. Ever since he became a Dragon Knight, he rarely had any time for her. She wondered if he would make it home for this year's Yule celebration. She didn't receive many letters at the Academy, but maybe Stella had got some news.

Althea was destined to disappointment.

They arrived at the Avenal Manor in the late afternoon, but only Stella greeted them at the door. Galen had sent word to her that he would be in Ordon, the capital of the Kingdom of Ordonia, which was almost on the other side of the country. Apparently, he was meeting with the king and the other Dragon Knights for something important. His letter was short, concise, and overly formal. Althea sighed again.

However, she was glad to step through the front door of her home. Stella hugged her so tightly that her back made popping sounds.

'My, how you've grown, lass!' the dwarf exclaimed.

'Stella, you're going to break my back!'

The homecoming raised everyone's spirits, including Stella's — she actually invited Kairos and Sir Hugo inside.

Althea's burning frustrations with the Academy drifted away like ashes on the wind when she settled down at the dinner table. Stella took to pampering her like old times and had cooked a large meal. Even though she still regarded Kairos with the occasional suspicion, she served him and Sir Hugo dinner, which was a large slab of beef, gravy, mashed fire potatoes, candied carrots, and star-apple pie. The Wolf Knight initially denied the offer, but after Stella's insistence (which was more of a demand), he graciously accepted the invitation as if he wanted nothing more in life. Kairos happily cleaned his plate and wanted more.

Stella dominated the conversation at the table, asking many questions about the Academy. She said very little to Kairos during the meal, except that he could stay overnight, but had to be off to Mr. Dubose's workshop in the morning.

Althea felt a wave of nostalgia as she looked around her home. Even though half a year had passed, it was the same as she left it before the Academy. Nothing had changed. She looked by the doorway and noticed that her father's helmet was still missing. The dwarf still fussed over her as if she had never left at all.

Althea spoke of the Academy, though most of it concerned how awful a human being Flain was, and elaborated on her daily classroom activities. Kairos didn't say much, only ate and listened. Stella moved on to talk about the latest gossip in Vadost, the problems of taking care of the manor, and the new restaurant in the city: Milliways. The dwarf made a point of not bringing up Galen, however, much to Althea's relief. The absence of her father made her sad, but she vowed not to dwell on matters that she could not help and decided to enjoy her holiday.

After dinner, Althea helped Stella with the dishes. When the dwarf wasn't looking, she gathered the plates on the table and whispered to Kairos, 'Shall we sneak out into the city tonight for the Yule Festival?' She grinned at him mischievously.

'Yule Festival?' he asked.

'Yes!' Althea looked over her shoulder as if expecting the dwarf to come swooping into the room at any moment. 'There's dancing and singing, and—'

'Won't Stella get angry?' Kairos cast an uneasy glance towards the kitchen. 'Remember how she was last time.'

'Althea,' called Stella, herself, from the kitchen. 'Hurry it up, lass.'

'Yes, Stella. I'm coming.' Althea hurried back, but she stole one more glance at Kairos. 'It's also my birthday, in case you've forgotten.'

He gave a rare smile and nodded.

* * *

The two moons, Paollus and Vay, had climbed high into the night sky, causing the snowy landscape around Vadost to sparkle like glittering mounds of gold and silver. Stella had finished cleaning the dishes with Althea, and sat in the parlour to relax. She was exhausted, having spent many long hours preparing the welcoming home dinner for Althea. Her heart ached for the girl, considering her father would not be here, but Stella did what she could to make her happy. Althea and Galen were all the dwarf had.

Stella had come from a rural mining town in the mountain range called Yeti's End, which was on the border of Ordonia and Salforia. One night a horde of minotaurs swarmed the town, setting fire to every building, cutting down the dwarves as they ran out to escape the flames. Stella's husband, Thorok, was one of the first to die, shielding Stella as she ran out with a few of the surviving townsfolk. They scattered, some getting overtaken by their pursuers and dying gruesome deaths. Stella escaped and made her way into Ordonia where she eventually came to Vadost, with nothing but the clothes on her back and the loss of her entire family.

She met Galen, who listened to her story and immediately hired her as a nanny.

Althea's mother had just passed, and the grief-stricken girl had locked herself in her room and wouldn't come out to eat. Galen tried everything to coax her out — from gifts to sweets — but nothing worked. Then Stella came along and tried a different approach: she threatened to break down the door if Althea didn't come out. Althea opened the door, and ever since, Stella had loved the girl like her own. They had both experienced the painful loss of a loved one and they found solace in each other's company.

How much Althea had grown! It would only be a matter of time before she, too, would be gone. Despite Stella's best intentions, Althea had already attached herself to that foreign boy who lived with Mr. Dubose. Stella had disliked him from the moment Galen brought him back to the manor. She knew he'd be trouble. Still, Althea could do worse, though Stella would rather drink elven wine than admit as much to the girl. Kairos was strong and driven – like a dwarf – and she knew he would risk his life to protect Althea from harm.

Stella closed the book the in her lap and set it on the table next to her. She wouldn't get much reading done tonight. She was already thinking of what to cook Althea and Kairos for breakfast. Maybe she would go and ask Sir Hugo if he wanted anything to drink. She was rather surprised to see the knight escorting Kairos and Althea, but he showed her his orders from the Knighthood. She had meant to enquire more about his presence, but seeing Althea again after a long absence had distracted her. She would find out more in the morning when everyone was well rested.

It would be a long, busy week, consisting of chores, errands, and shopping, but Stella was pleased about the activity. Ever since Althea had left for the Academy, the dwarf had little to do to occupy her time, and the manor had been lonely. Lord Avenal had stopped in twice during Althea's absence, but that was only for a night; he was off again the next morning. Everyone was always so busy! Even now, Stella knew that Althea and Kairos had slipped out the secret doorway in the back of the manor to enjoy the Yule Festival.

She thought of alerting Sir Hugo and going out to find them, but changed her mind. The poor knight was exhausted, working during the Yule holiday. Instead, Stella offered him a slice of star-apple pie and told him to make himself comfortable. The dwarf told herself that Kairos and Althea would return later that night. They were already in the Academy training for dangerous situations. She had to let that little girl act on her own someday, and now was as good a time as ever. Stella shook her head and sighed. Perhaps she was getting soft now. But the young pair did remind her of her youth.

She thought of Thorok. What would he have made of Kairos? But she knew the answer already. He would have liked him. Stella could almost hear her late husband saying, 'He's not bad for a human, and he can work a forge!' She smiled at the thought, remembering the mischief she and Thorok got into so many years ago. Perhaps that was why Stella was so protective over Althea. She did not want the girl repeating her mistakes.

She stood up, looking for something to do. She would not be able to sleep knowing that Althea was out in the city, so she decided to pour herself some mead and sit out on the veranda. It was Yule, after all.

It was cold outside, even for the dwarf who was used to the much colder temperatures of Yeti's End. But she enjoyed the pleasant view of the city below. The hundreds of colourful street lamps illuminated the throngs of people parading through the streets, the lights reflecting on the surface of Lake Turquoise. The sounds of cheering and laughter carried up the hillside to where the dwarf sat, and the smell of roasted meat and baked pastries was strong. She sipped the sweet mead and relaxed, enjoying the sights and smells from the festival. Compared to the jubilation below, it was very quiet around the Avenal Manor.

So quiet that Stella heard the distinct sound of something crashing inside.

She quickly stood up. The dwarf always tidied up to the point where things simply didn't 'crash' on their own. She stood still and listened, but there was no further sound.

'Sir Hugo?' she called. 'Do you need something?'

No answer. A feeling of unease settled on Stella like an ominous shadow.

She slowly peered around, looking into the surrounding darkness. Her dwarven night vision could distinguish shapes in the darkness much better than a human's, but she had been staring at the radiant festivities in the city below and her eyes needed time to adjust. She crept quietly to the door and listened. She heard nothing, and everything appeared normal. But surely Sir Hugo would have awakened with such a racket.

She quickly grabbed a kitchen knife from nearby.

'Sir Hugo?' she called again. Maybe Althea and Kairos had come back sooner than expected, and one of them clumsily bumped into something. Stella felt foolish to be so nervous.

She went into the next room and saw that the front door was ajar. Althea would have slammed it shut. The hair on Stella's neck bristled, and she gripped the knife's handle tightly, her knuckles becoming white.

Then she saw the inert form of Sir Hugo. His body was contorted in an unnatural position, blood covering his clothing and forming a puddle around him. A broken plate – the source of the crash – lay in pieces nearby.

Movement in the corner of her vision made Stella turn, and she let out a loud gasp of surprise.

Another dwarf began to approach her slowly from the parlour. He looked very rough and said nothing, only brandished an axe and smiled.

Stella backed away, but a voice from behind made her spin around.

'Where's the boy?' It was another dwarf blocking the path to the front door, Stella's escape. The bandage around his head hinted that he had seen better days, but the dark shadowed eyes, along with his drawn sword, exuded a malevolence of what was to come. He bared his yellow teeth in anger. 'Or better yet, where's the girl?' He pointed to his bandaged head and edged closer. 'She did this to me, you know. It's time I repay the favour.'

Stella shuddered, and raised her knife.

Her hopes sank when a third dwarf emerged from the hallway leading to the bedrooms. 'The boy and girl are not here,' he called.

Stella was painfully aware that she was trapped, but she faced the fearsome dwarf with the bandaged head and stared him in the eyes.

He levelled his sword at her. 'Tell us where they are,' he said, 'and we'll let you live.'

Stella spat at him. 'I'd rather die.'

The dwarf with the bandaged head sneered. 'So be it. We'll have some fun with you.'

Despite her fear, Stella smiled, an inner smile at her fate – she would finally join Thorok soon.

But first, she wasn't going down without a fight.

*　*　*

Kairos and Althea made their way through the crowd in front of Lazio Fountain.

They did not feel cold. They walked close together, hands intertwined. The mass of people around them sang and danced to the various musicians performing in the city square. Kairos found a bench on the outskirts of the fountain plaza where they sat apart from the crowd, watching the fireworks and festivities in companionable silence.

'Are you sure you shouldn't pay Mr. Dubose a visit?' Althea asked after some time.

'I'll go tomorrow.' Kairos grinned. 'I fear if I visit him first, he would burden me with so much work that I would not have time to enjoy the festival.'

'This is the first time we've been truly alone since the Hammerfall Festival, isn't it?' Althea asked.

They sat close together, not quite touching, but close enough that the other's physical presence was a constant distraction.

'There was the temple of Zemus,' Kairos began, but regretted bringing up the unpleasant memory when he saw Althea stiffen. He hastily added, 'But that place doesn't count.'

Althea turned towards him. 'You never did tell me much about your homeland.'

Kairos swallowed. He had still not spoken to anyone about Logres ever since his conversation with Galen. He wanted to tell Althea everything about himself. About Logres. The Einar. The events at Cape Caipora and Milbrooke. His suspicions of being god-cursed. But, then again, he did not want to frighten her away.

'You don't have to say anything if you don't want to—'

'I come from a land far away from here,' said Kairos, figuring he could tell her a little without the extraordinary details. 'The Blight came and everything began to die, so, many of us — including my father, brother and I — set out to find somewhere better. We ran into Malus's army, instead, and they killed everyone else, and now I'm alone.' Before he could say anything more, Althea reached out and grasped his hand. Her touch made him breathless. It was agonising to be so near her at the Academy, but so distant at the same time, and now they were finally alone.

'Do you plan to go home?' she asked – as she recalled doing once before. She wondered if this time, he would be more forthcoming.

'Someday. I have sworn to take revenge for my family, but first I need to become a Mana Knight. They're the only ones fighting Malus and his army... And Captain Hargonnas.' Memories of the elf stirred a sudden rage that Kairos tried to quell immediately. He was together with Althea. This was not the time nor the place for anger.

'I'm sorry,' Althea said. 'I did not mean to bring up bad memories.'

'It's okay,' Kairos said, offering a wan smile. 'I'm quite happy here, and after I finish everything, I would like to live here.'

That was true, he realised. He had been happier in Vadost than his entire life in Logres. He cherished being close to Althea and working for Mr. Dubose. He enjoyed the rigorous training of the Mana Knight Academy (with the exception of Jomur's class). The citizens of Vadost seemed cheerful and optimistic compared to the dole-faced expressions the Einar usually wore. And they weren't always trying to kill each other, either! He was even warming up to Stella, although he figured his standing with the dwarf had not much improved since their first encounter.

The sudden thought of Stella alarmed him.

'Shouldn't we be returning soon?' Kairos asked. 'Remember last time? Stella will be looking for us, and I don't want her hitting me with a frying pan.'

Althea also looked startled for a brief instant, but threw her head back and laughed. When she stopped, her features took on an alluring expression.

'Stella can wait,' she said, and her lips parted expectantly. Oblivious to the music, the dancing, and the merrymaking around them, Kairos leant forward...

There was a flash of light in the distance.

The sounds of carousing took on a fretful air, and the change in the atmosphere drew Kairos's attention away from Althea.

'Look!' a man shouted, pointing. 'On the hill!'

A shower of red sparks spewed high into the air. Its brilliance did not dissipate, but hovered in place.

'That's a strange firework,' Kairos muttered.

'That's not a firework,' Althea said in a hollow voice, on the verge of panic. 'That's the spell that signals distress.'

Kairos did not need to ask why Althea was upset. The spell flared directly above her home. He was about to say more, but Althea was off, racing towards the manor with fear and adrenaline spurring her onward. Kairos made haste to keep up with her in the crowded streets. He was not sure what was happening, but he hoped to find the Avenal Manor in one piece.

If not, he had a premonition that their happiness would soon come to an end.

\* \* \*

Sir Hugo did not sense danger until it was too late. There should have been nothing to fear. His mind dwelled on his parents back at home while he was stuck here on escort duty during Yule, his body languid from over-indulging in the abundant feast Stella had provided.

Therefore, he turned too slowly. He barely glimpsed the dark figure surging towards him from the front door—now wide open. He twisted, but the hammer landed a glancing blow on his head, knocking him back against the wall. He tried to pull his mana lance free of its sheath, but he was disoriented and in his panic, he could not grip the weapon.

Another dark shape joined the fight, this one lunging with a sword. The blade bit into Hugo's side, where his armour did not protect him, and the first figure delivered another stunning blow to his head. Hugo tried to cast a spell, but his vision was blurred and he wasn't sure what was happening. His mana fizzled away as he traced an illegible glyph, and then he saw a blinding flash of light as another blow struck his skull, sending him crashing to the floor.

Hugo tried to rise, to alert Stella of the danger, but his body wouldn't obey him. He felt the sharp blade plunging into him again, and soon darkness overwhelmed him.

When he came around, he thought he had dreamt the entire event, but his head throbbed and each breath brought pain. He bit his lip to avoid crying out, and lay there for some time, feeling faint. The sound of rough, grating voices slowly pervaded his awareness.

His attackers were still nearby.

Hugo tried to open his eyes, but found he could only manage one of them. No wonder the attackers had left him for dead. He probably looked horrible. With his left eye, he slowly looked around the room, making sure to lie still. He couldn't move much anyway, because even looking around brought him a jolt of unbearable agony. He saw enough, though.

Stella was dead.

The sight of her corpse nearly made Hugo gasp aloud in horror. She had been brutally murdered, hacked to gory bits. Clearly, she did not go down without a fight.

The attackers were still in close proximity to her. To Hugo's surprise, they were also dwarves. One of them, wearing a bandage on his head, nursed a wound on his left shoulder. Another sat against the wall, clutching his stomach and grimacing in pain. He had been stabbed. The third dwarf helped tend to the dwarf with the wounded shoulder, whom Hugo assumed was the leader.

He lay still and tried not to breathe loudly.

'I'm telling you, Togram! She fought like a rabid beast. We should have taken her by surprise like we did the knight.' The voice was rather high-pitched for a dwarf.

'Yes, she was a fighter,' the dwarf named Togram agreed. He applied a cloth to his shoulder and winced. 'Orvid didn't expect such ferocity. Now the whoreson might bleed out before those kids get back, and then it will be just us two against them.'

Orvid did not reply, only stared at his comrades with glassy eyes and nodded.

'Damn it!' said the dwarf with a high-pitched voice. 'Let me look through the house, see if they have a healing tonic or something!'

'Hurry it up, Jarvis,' Togram said, 'I'll stay here with Orvid just in case those kids come back.'

The high-pitched dwarf known as Jarvis walked past Hugo without a glance at the knight and marched upstairs. Soon the sounds of him rummaging through the rooms reverberated throughout the manor.

Hugo tried to get up carefully. He felt dizzy at once and searing pain caused a wave of blackness to overtake his vision. He was on the verge of collapsing, but if he didn't do something, not only would he die, but so would Althea and Kairos.

He managed to get to his knees, using the wall for support. His armour creaked as the joint plates jostled. He paused in horror, sure that the dwarf near the front door had heard.

'Keep it down up there, Jarvis!' Togram shouted. 'I'm sure that half of Vadost can hear you making a ruckus!'

Hugo finally managed to haul himself upright without making more noise, but the effort caused him a wave of nausea and dizziness. He leant against the wall for a few moments, trying to stifle his panting. His throbbing head felt on the verge of exploding, and he thought, again, he was going to fall. The dizziness passed, though the nausea and pain didn't. He had to move. One of the dwarves was bound to find him soon.

He knew that if he tried to go out the front door, the dwarf called Togram would strike him down, even with the injured shoulder. He remembered Stella going out on the veranda earlier in the evening – if he could make it there…

It took Hugo a long time to reach the veranda. His head reeled with every step, and pain shot through his torso with each breath. He shuddered at the thought of how much blood he had lost, and he felt consciousness slowly slipping away like sand running through his fingers. It would be so much easier to just sit down and rest. He thought of his family, his mother and father beaming at him with pride when he became a Mana Knight. They would be missing him by now, sad that he was away for Yule. His little sister would be expecting a gift. He missed them more than anything.

He clenched his teeth and trudged on. Thankfully, the door to the veranda was open. He staggered out, unaware of his surroundings.

His thoughts turned to his career as a Mana Knight. He wasn't the best of the best. In fact, he had barely passed the Test. He received the easy tasks such as guard duty at Valour Keep, or mere escort duty with civilians. He shied away from the battles and the high-risk assignments. It was unfortunate that this one turned out to be the most dangerous of all.

Without realising it, he stumbled against the rail overlooking the city below. His vision clouded and the lights of the festivities dimmed in and out. He focused his remaining effort into one spell. He vaguely heard a dwarf cry in alarm from inside, which now seemed so far away. They would be looking for him. He had to hurry.

Hugo traced the glyph and a bright, red flash blinded him. He slumped to the floor. As his injuries pulled him into the darkness, he gave a fleeting smile of triumph.

He had managed to fulfil his duty.

*  *  *

Kairos and Althea arrived at the manor to find it partially in flames, with a crowd gathered around. Althea and Kairos, along with the City Watch and Mana Knights on duty, had to wade through the horde of onlookers to reach the home. At the sight of all the commotion, almost everyone within the vicinity who wasn't excessively drunk had come running to stare at the burning structure with mingled horror, concern, and curiosity.

The knights and several citizens were using water magic to douse the flames. Althea tried to rush inside the manor, but several knights stopped her.

'I have to go in!' she cried in a shrill voice. 'Stella is in there!'

The leading knight, a tall and broad man, shook his head in sympathy and spoke to Althea in soothing tones. She broke into tears. The people standing nearby began to murmur, and Kairos looked to see what they were excited about. Four men carried a stretcher with a man covered in wounds. Kairos did not recognise him, but as the stretcher drew closer, he felt a weight in the pit of his stomach.

'Sir Hugo!' Althea cried.

'Make way!' one of the knights said. 'We have to take him to a healer. He doesn't have long to live.'

Kairos examined the injured man and knew immediately the knight was right. How Sir Hugo was still living was a mystery. His face looked like a sodden mass of blood. It was no wonder Kairos had not recognised him immediately.

Althea rushed over to Hugo. At the sight of the terrible injuries, her already pale face became even whiter. 'Hugo!' she said. 'What happened?'

'Stand back!' one of the knights barked.

At the sound of Althea's voice, Hugo had stirred and lifted a feeble hand. 'Lady Avenal and Squire Azel,' he muttered in a voice so weak that Althea and Kairos had to lean forward to hear. 'You're both safe.' He coughed, blood bubbling from his lips, and he squinted his eyes shut against the pain and panted. 'Forgive me... I couldn't save Stella.'

Althea sobbed and covered her face with her hands.

'What happened?' Kairos asked. 'Who were they?'

'Dwarves,' he managed to whisper. 'They came for you. Orvid, Jarvis, and To-Togr–' He tried to say more, but a tremor of pain shook him.

The knight standing next to them stepped forward. 'Get him to a healer,' he ordered.

The bystanders bowed their heads in respect as the four men carrying the stretcher moved on.

Kairos felt numb. Was Stella truly dead? He was just beginning to get along with the dwarf. Suddenly he became very concerned for Althea. 'We should find a way to tell your father,' Kairos told her.

But upon turning, he found Althea was not listening. She made a rush for the manor. The knights intercepted her again and she threw herself against them, but they were stronger and held her back. Defeated, she collapsed onto the ground in front of her home, where she shook, convulsing in sobs. Kairos approached and rested his hand comfortingly on her shoulder.

Althea's small tender hand closed tightly around his. They found comfort in each other's touch.

One of the knights at the door urged them back.

'She lives here,' Kairos said. 'Her nanny is inside.'

'All the more reason to stand back,' the knight began, his eyes full of sympathy for Althea. 'She does not want to go inside and see what we've seen. We're doing her a favour by keeping her out.'

'Let me go then,' Kairos offered. 'I know Stella, too.'

The knight hesitated, but upon seeing Kairos's grim and determined face, he nodded and stepped aside.

Althea peered up at Kairos with puffy eyes. He squeezed her hand reassuringly. 'You stay here with the knights. I'll be back.'

It did not take long for Kairos to find Stella. Once the knight escorted him through the front door, he found her – or what was left of her – lying in a gory mess near the parlour. Her murderers had mutilated her, smashing and chopping her up beyond recognition. Kairos could only identify her by her red hair.

The knight turned away. Kairos did not blame him.

He stared for a long time at what was left of Stella. With her death, his hopes of happiness fled.

He heard the knight whisper a prayer to Zemus on Stella's behalf. He thought of the time when Gulliver had prayed to Zemus, and wondered if the god was truly dead, his spirit encased in a godshard, or if he was merely resting in the shard as some believed. Either way, Kairos didn't think much of this god, who allowed his faithful's enemies to murder them so easily. He preferred Rudras, who honoured the strong and scoffed at the weak. Rudras never offered false hope.

After extinguishing the flames, the knights searched the rest of the manor — what was left of it. They found another dead dwarf, whom Kairos had never seen. It wasn't Togram. This dwarf had been stabbed.

The leader of the knights, who Kairos recognised as Lord Cyr, signalled to the others. 'Take this body, along with...' He struggled to remember the name of Althea's nanny, 'Stella. We will see to it that they all get a proper burial.'

'Only Stella,' said Kairos evenly.

'What?'

'Only Stella should get a proper burial.' Kairos stared intently at the body of the dwarven male.

'What are you saying?' asked Lord Cyr.

'This is one of the murderers.'

'How do you know?'

'Because I have never seen this dwarf before,' Kairos said, his voice taking on a lethal edge. 'And Hugo told me that the attackers were dwarves. Their leader is Togram, and when I find him, I will kill him myself.'

\* \* \*

The run-down house, located next to the Pinch and Tickle in the seedy part of the city, had been avoided by prospective tenants for years. Everyone knew the area attracted a shoddy variety of vagrants, drunks, and shady business men, so they looked elsewhere for real estate.

After renting the house and living in it for a day, Hargonnas soon discovered why: between his new home and the ill-reputed tavern, he found a corpse in the alley, covered in stab wounds. As time went on, his opinion of the place only sank further. The homeless and pub-goers alike constantly urinated all around the house, resulting in a perpetual smell of piss. The elf occasionally found drunks sprawled out at the front door, having, gingerly, to step over them whenever he left the premises.

He eventually became used to these antics, however.

What he couldn't get used to was the constant noise of prostitutes shrieking, moaning, and squealing through the darkest hours of the night, or the yells, fights, and crashes caused by the tavern's patrons. The humans, especially drunken ones, disgusted him beyond rage. Whereas elves preferred peace and quiet, Hargonnas's human neighbours enjoyed mayhem and malarkey.

Thus, the elf yearned for the day he would leave this heap of rubbish. Yet the house was cheap and offered him the ideal location to stay hidden from prying eyes. No one ever questioned his comings and goings. Everyone, except the beggars, left him alone. He could invite suspicious guests, engage in all sorts of nefarious activity, or make the most awful of noises, and it all paled in comparison to what the Pinch and Tickle offered on a daily basis.

Therefore, no one bothered wasting a second look when two dwarves came to visit, or when an elf answered the door and invited them in, or the ensuing shouts that came from within the house.

'Imbeciles!' Hargonnas shouted indignantly. 'You were tasked to kill or capture a mere boy. Not only do you fail to do so, but you kill another dwarf, burn her home, and now bring the probing eyes of the Knighthood down upon us! I cannot fathom how someone could be so stupid to concoct such an idiotic plan... Wait – I know. Your father must have swived a troll, and then you popped out. That's the only explanation for your stupidity.'

Togram stared at the stone floor as he knelt before the elf, who outranked him, though his scowl continued to deepen under the elf's tirade. He apparently didn't take too kindly to hear his mother being referred to as a 'troll.' His companion, Jarvis, slunk away in the shadows.

'We had no choice,' Togram replied. 'We set up the ambush as planned, but the kids were not there. They must have left without our notice.'

'So, you killed the dwarf and the knight, instead of waiting,' the elf said mockingly.

'We took out the knight first, because he was the biggest threat. The dwarf heard the commotion and put up a fight. She stabbed Orvid... He didn't make it.'

Hargonnas spat, something that only humans and dwarves did, and elves abhorred, but this particularly foul habit was the only suitable way to express his disgust with these two. 'Damn Orvid! May he rot eternally. So you two wretches fled and did not wait for the boy to return?'

Togram's dark eyes flashed in the gloom of the house. 'We thought the knight was dead, but he managed to go outside and cast a distress signal. We had to flee, otherwise the City Watch and the knights would have caught us.'

Hargonnas made a face of pure exasperation. 'I've been getting nothing but failure after failure from you, Togram.'

'That makes two of us then,' Togram answered with gritted teeth.

'What do you mean?' Hargonnas demanded, rising so fast from his stool that it toppled over.

'I meant that if you hadn't botched your job in the first place,' the dwarf retorted, 'then we wouldn't need to be chasing this cursed boy at all, cleaning up after your blunder.'

'How dare you!' the elf growled, his hands taking on a deadly glow.

Jarvis, who was hiding behind a wooden beam, emerged to step between the elf and Togram, who had drawn his sword halfway from its sheath.

'Captain, I-I mean Hargonnas,' Jarvis said, correcting himself on the elf's demotion. 'He didn't mean it. He was distraught over the loss of our friend.'

'Silence!' screamed the elf, raising his hand to invoke magic.

A cloud formed around Jarvis and erupted into a fountain of ruby-coloured flame. The air sizzled and crackled around him, searing his flesh as he screamed. The wooden beams groaned under the intense heat. The dwarf stopped screaming, and the fire spell stopped, leaving a charred, blackened husk that fell to the floor with a thud.

The elf flashed a wicked smile and raised his hand to cast another spell. 'Farewell, Togram. I detested working with you from the very beginning.'

But Togram was no longer there.

Using the diversion of his comrade's death, Togram rushed out of the decrepit house as fast as his bulky dwarven legs would carry him, knocking over potions, spell books, and an ink jar in his wake.

'Curses!' Hargonnas swore.

He followed in pursuit, but the dwarf was already out the front door and in the street, shoving pedestrians aside in his effort to escape. Several turned and shouted angry threats, and a bar wench, who was flung into a puddle, bellowed several derogatory slurs aimed at dwarves. But such shenanigans around the Pinch and Tickle were common, and everyone soon returned to their daily business, except the bar wench, whose skimpy dress was muddied; she demanded the dwarf's head.

Hargonnas hastened in pursuit, but quickly gave up. The short dwarf had disappeared into the crowd of tall humans, and all he could do was yell – to no effect. The only response he got was from a drunken vagrant who shouted back that some people were trying to sleep, and the bar wench who wanted someone to buy her a new outfit.

Without a word, Hargonnas ignored the wench and returned to the house. It didn't matter if Togram escaped, he supposed. The dwarf would not report him for murder, especially after the incident at the Avenal Manor. The elf had more important things on his mind than a disobedient dwarf.

'If I want to leave this accursed city and bloody house,' Hargonnas said to himself, 'then I'll have to take matters into my own hands.'

He walked back inside where the smell of cooked meat permeated the air. First, he had to dispose of the body. A wicked grin slowly crept across his face. He knew just the right spell to use.

236

'You may have been useless in life,' he said to the blackened lump on the floor as he channelled currents of purple light into it, 'but you may be of use to me in death.'

*       *       *

On the same morning that Jarvis faced his fiery fate in Hargonnas's house, Stella was buried in the Passage to Thelos, a tomb located in the further depths of Dwarfside. A hammer, the symbol of Thelos, was placed on her grave, as was customary amongst the dwarves, and the priest of Thelos read the final rites and offered his condolences, stating that Stella would now return to become one with the stone. Kairos and Althea were at the ceremony, but the majority of those who attended were dwarves. Jace Dubose was amongst them; he did not say anything until after the ceremony, only glared. Most of Stella's family had died prior to her arrival at Vadost, and she did not befriend many humans during her tenure at the Avenal Manor. In turn, the few humans who knew her felt uncomfortable attending a funeral ceremony in an underground cavern. A despatch had been sent to Lord Galen Avenal, but there was no response, yet.

When the attendees filed out of the tomb and onto the streets, Mr. Dubose rounded on Kairos.

'WHERE THE HELL HAVE YOU BEEN?' he thundered, his voice ringing out through Dwarfside.

Several dwarfs peered up from their work to stare, as Mr. Dubose marched towards Kairos, his hair and beard looking wild like an enraged lion.

'Let me explain,' Kairos said. He told the dwarf about Sir Hugo escorting them to the Avenal Manor because of Togram's recent attack near Valour Keep, and how the dwarf attacked again, but they survived by sneaking out for the Yule festival.

'Sneaking out? You prowled the streets of Vadost? Togram and his goons were trying to kill you, and you thought it would be a good idea to traipse around the city?' Mr. Dubose screamed. 'You were supposed to have come straight here yesterday!'

'I know, but I was ordered to stay near Sir Hugo!' Kairos hollered back. 'If I had left, then Althea would have been in the house when Togram…'

'It's true,' Althea said, coming to Kairos's defence. Though her face was red and swollen from the tears, she could not bear to see Kairos punished on her behalf.

'No, you don't know,' the dwarf yelled, ignoring her. 'You should have sent a message to me. Then I would have come over, and if Togram still came, I would have cut the bastard's head off and pissed on his corpse!'

'He might have killed you, too,' Kairos said.

'Bah! That coward could never best me – to think that I even gave him work here!'

'He had help,' Althea said. 'Togram was working for Malus. Besides, why isn't my father here to help?'

Silence fell over the room.

Finally, Mr. Dubose said, 'You should have told me about all of this. That way I could have done something! I didn't know any of this was going on. You both were careless and the only reason you're alive now is because of pure, dumb luck.' The dwarf turned towards Althea. 'And leave your father out of this, lass. He is doing what he can. He cannot be everywhere at once, and even *he* could not have anticipated this from Malus.'

Kairos suddenly realised why Mr. Dubose was angry, so he apologised, explained that he had become complacent in the face of danger, and outlined all the reasons why his actions were stupid.

'Okay, okay, I get it.' The dwarf interrupted Kairos's tirade of self-deprecation. 'You think with your prick more than your head. It's not the first time, and it certainly won't be the last.' He motioned Kairos over. The boy cautiously approached, expecting a hard cuff to the face. To his surprise, the dwarf grabbed him and hugged him fiercely. Then he motioned Althea over and did the same. 'You bloody idiots,' he said. 'Losing Stella was too much. I don't want to lose both of you, too. I don't know how I could face Galen if something else happened. You can stay at my workshop until Yule is over. I'll let the others know about

Togram. He won't show his face around here again.' Mr. Dubose released Kairos and Althea from the hug — much to their joint relief as they drew in large breaths.

They made their way back to Mr. Dubose's workshop. Once inside, the dwarf cleared space for Althea in the spare room. Once he was done, Althea thanked him, went into the room without another word, and shut the door behind her. Kairos stood by, waiting anxiously. He never had seen Althea so upset before and was unsure of what to do.

'Leave her be, lad,' Mr. Dubose said, reaching into a leather purse he wore on his belt. 'Take these. I need you to go into Alberich's grocer and bring back some fire potatoes, goat blood sausages, and whatever else you think you can eat.' The dwarf fished out several silver coins and tossed them to Kairos.

Kairos departed. Of all places to be after Stella's death, he was relieved to be back in Mr. Dubose's workshop. The bustle of the workshops and the sound of hammers ringing through the streets brought back a profound sense of nostalgia he did not know he had. Even as he walked through the streets, several dwarves briefly stopped their work to yell out a cheerful greeting to him. Some displayed eagerness for conversation, but Kairos did not feel like talking to anyone today. Not now. He was more concerned about Althea. He rushed to Alberich's and bought what he needed and returned.

The door to the spare room was still shut.

'How is Althea doing?'

Mr. Dubose turned from the forge. 'She is well enough, considering.' Then, after a pause, 'Stella was the closest thing she had to a mother. Her real mother died and the Knighthood keeps her father away.'

Those words sent a pang through Kairos. He knew what it was like to lose family, and the despair of losing his own was still raw. He had seen how close Althea was to Stella, and his heart ached to think of the pain she must be suffering.

Mr. Dubose approached and rested a hand on Kairos's shoulder. 'So you care for her, I see. It's good to feel the pain of others. Warriors who do not learn compassion end up becoming cold-blooded killers.'

Kairos suddenly realised there were tears streaming down his face. He did not feel like a good person. The Einar lived to fight, to kill others. Malus's army seemed no different. There seemed to be little good in this world. He had come to this foreign land, to Ordonia, only to find a place filled with more evil, death, and sadness than he could ever have imagined.

And now his presence, his association with Althea, had caused Stella's death. Althea had saved his life at the temple, prevented Togram from cutting him down. And he had repaid her kindness by bringing danger to her home. The gods had truly cursed him. Everyone who showed him benevolence had either died or suffered dreadful consequences.

The images of Farina's scalped corpse and Stella's mutilated body flashed in his mind. The blood. The gore.

If he had never come to this land, they would both be alive now. Gulliver would still be unharmed at the lighthouse, and Sir Hugo would be enjoying Yule with his family. Kairos wondered if everyone would have been better off if he were dead. He wished he had fallen in battle, next to his brother.

'Do not blame yourself, lad.' Mr. Dubose spoke gruffly, but his look of concern hinted that he understood what was troubling Kairos. 'We dwarves are said to have come from the stone when Thelos breathed life into us. Stella merely returned to the stone. Althea, nor anyone else, holds her death against you.'

Kairos said nothing. He turned away and faced the forge fire, the tears running unchecked down his face.

\* \* \*

Kairos woke to the sound of the hammers pounding throughout Dwarfside. Being inside the mountain, he could not tell if it was dawn or dusk, but he assumed it was the former. Dwarves often put away their tools at dusk and headed for the taverns – or home, for the ones who had strict wives.

He lay on his cot and noticed the lack of snoring in the room. Mr. Dubose was already up. It was surprisingly quieter than usual in the workshop, as the dwarf was wont to start the forge early. He heard voices in the other room. The dwarf's booming bass tones reverberated off the walls, but Kairos had to listen carefully to discern the other.

It belonged to Althea. She was up and out of her room, picking at the poached eggs and scones Mr. Dubose had made. That was a good sign, Kairos thought as he ventured over to join them.

Mr. Dubose took notice of him. 'By Thelos's beard, do you ever comb your hair, boy? It looks like two crows landed on your head and started fucking.'

Kairos smiled. He had forgotten what it was like to live with the dwarf's daily insults.

'I could say the same about your beard,' Kairos said, poking at it. 'It looks like a vulture's nest.'

'Don't touch my beard, boy!'

Althea giggled. Another good sign.

After breakfast, Mr. Dubose thrust a few silver coins into Kairos's hand and told him to treat Althea to some food. 'Go on. I have work to do.'

'I can help,' Kairos offered.

'You obviously cannot take a hint, can you?' Mr. Dubose growled. 'I want you two out of my house for the day. Now stay in Dwarfside, mind you. It should be safe here. Unlike the rest of Vadost, there's only one way in and out of here, and we monitor that carefully.'

Kairos finally took the hint and left with Althea. They walked around until they found a stone bench next to the bakery where it was warm, and the aroma of bread and pastries was pleasant. Althea did not say anything. Her sad expression caused guilt to tear at his conscious.

Kairos was silent for a moment, before deciding to speak. 'I'm sorry.'

Althea looked up, startled. 'For what?'

'Togram was after me. If I hadn't come here, you wouldn't have got involved, and he wouldn't have tracked us back to your house. I put you in danger and cost Stella her life.'

Althea shook her head. 'Togram is an evil man. It's not your fault.' She paused, and looked up in thought. 'I do wonder why he was going to such great lengths to bring about your death. Why does he want you dead so badly?'

'I don't know,' said Kairos. 'But when I find him, I'll kill him.'

Althea squirmed uneasily. 'You can kill so easily?'

Kairos stared straight into her innocent, blue eyes. He remembered stabbing the elf in the neck to protect Farina. 'Yes,' he answered in a steady voice. 'I can and I will.' He saw that his words had shaken Althea, and he was immediately sorry for causing her more distress. But it was the truth, and he would not lie to her. Life was harsh, and vengeance was the Einar way. He would not forgive his enemies like Zemus's followers did.

'Why do you want to kill?' Althea finally asked, her voice so low that Kairos had to lean in close to hear. 'That's an odd thing to say. I've never heard anyone talk like that.'

Kairos turned towards her. He was not surprised at the question, though it would have been an odd question in Logres. It was ironic how he was not violent enough to be an Einar, but he was too violent to be an Ordonian. 'To protect myself and those I care about.' He clenched his fists, seeing the images of Hargonnas and Togram in his mind. 'There are those who deserve death. If you could kill the dwarves...' He caught himself, not wanting to say the words that would cause more agony. But Kairos felt compelled to get his point across to her. 'If you could kill the dwarves who killed Stella,' he continued, 'wouldn't you do it, too?'

Althea sat in silence for a long time, pondering his words. She remembered the first time the motherly dwarf had come to the house, and how poorly Althea had treated her then. She had taken out her frustrations of losing her mother on Stella, but the dwarf persisted in caring for her, comforting her when the other children teased her, or when her father went away for a very long time.

Althea remembered the dwarf's jokes, the times they cooked together, shopped together. Stella was always around to soothe the turmoil in Althea's mind, and now she was gone. She could not stop the tears now as they flowed freely down her cheeks.

Finally, Althea turned her tear-streaked face towards Kairos. 'No, I wouldn't,' she said with conviction. 'I don't want more death. Killing Togram won't bring her back.'

'But killing him will prevent more murders,' Kairos returned.

For a long time, Althea only stared back at him. 'That's where we differ, Kairos. I don't want to kill anyone.'

Althea stood up quickly, and before Kairos had a chance to reply, she walked away towards Mr. Dubose's workshop, leaving him sitting alone on the stone bench.

* * *

The week of Yule had ended. Under the impatient stares of four Mana Knights stationed outside the workshop, Mr. Dubose packed some provisions into a rucksack for Kairos and Althea's journey back to Valour Keep. After what had happened to Sir Hugo, the Knighthood was taking no chances this time; they increased the escorts.

'What happened with Althea?' Mr. Dubose handed the bag to Kairos.

Kairos had been absorbed with his thoughts on the upcoming classes at the Academy, and it took him a moment to respond. He put down the rucksack and turned his head towards the dwarf.

'She is angry with me,' he replied.

'Why?'

'She thinks I like to kill.'

'Don't you?' Mr. Dubose put a sword in a scabbard and tied it to the rucksack.

Kairos did not answer, staring at the sword.

'That's why you train,' the dwarf prompted. 'To kill. Those moves you learn are not exactly gestures of friendship.'

'No, I don't like to kill,' Kairos conceded. 'But I won't hesitate to defend the innocent, or to exact revenge on the wicked.'

'Spoken like a true warrior,' said Mr. Dubose in a rare compliment that astonished Kairos. The dwarf continued, 'And you'll make a fine knight. That is your niche in life. Mine is to work this forge and build things. Yours is to protect the innocent around you. That is fate.'

'What about Althea?' Kairos glanced outside. She was waiting by the knights, quiet and morose.

'She'll find her way. She can be a great knight without resorting to killing anyone. She can help you in other ways. One thing I know for sure – she's not angry with you.'

'She's not?' Kairos asked, surprised.

'No, she's just concerned for you. She doesn't want you to put yourself into unnecessary danger.'

'How do you know that?'

The dwarf lightly cuffed Kairos on the head. 'Trust me, boy. When you've been alive for more than ninety years, you tend to learn these sorts of things.'

Kairos rubbed his head. The blow was meant to be playful, but it felt like someone had struck him with a rock. 'Okay, I get it!'

Mr. Dubose handed the rucksack and the sword back to Kairos. 'Give the sword to Flain immediately upon arriving at Valour Keep. Otherwise, you'll be disciplined for carrying a weapon. And give him this letter, too.' He handed over an envelope, which Kairos almost dropped as his hands were already busy holding the rucksack and the sword. 'Well, you'd better get going. Those knights don't like being here, and the dwarves don't like them here, either.'

'Thank you for everything, Mr. Dubose,' Kairos said.

The dwarf snorted. 'Don't thank me. Go become a knight so you can start repaying me for all the food you've eaten from my pantry.'

# CHAPTER NINE

## Knight Academy

*The line between a healer and necromancer is a very thin one, indeed. Both users manipulate the mana of the surrounding nature to do their bidding. One encourages the stabilisation of the injured or dying spirits, whilst the other contaminates and corrupts.*

*Treatise of the D'Kari Arts'*, Acolyte Clovis

It was 965 A.C. Spring had come early this year. The melting of the snow and rivers, and the blooming of the flora and fauna brought new excitement to Valour Keep.

The squires were in good spirits upon their return from Yule, all eager to complete their training and pass their test. They were well past the halfway point of the Academy, and now they all knew each other, the pranks and jokes ran freely. Kairos and Vaughn still did not speak, but they nodded a silent greeting whenever they passed by each other. Each squire knew that their time at the Academy was nearing an end, and with each passing day, they tried to enjoy what remained.

The only person not enjoying herself was Althea.

She seemed more forlorn and serious than ever, since her return from the Yule holidays. Everyone in Valour Keep heard about the incident at her home and offered their obligatory condolences, which caused Althea to withdraw even further. Everyone recognised her grief, and left her alone, partly out of sympathy, but mostly because they felt awkward around her.

Only Kairos lingered, but even he did not understand the turmoil in her mind.

For most of her life, Althea felt as though she walked in her father's shadow. He was a great and powerful Dragon Knight, while she could not even muster up an average spell. She felt like a failure. Though she never admitted it to anyone else, her father was the only reason she was allowed into the Academy. Despite the advantage of nepotism, some instructors tried to weed her out – and they almost succeeded. She couldn't do the lessons, and the physical training was too demanding. She had been on the verge of giving up since day one.

Until the skirmish with Togram.

She saw the dwarf trying to kill Kairos. Althea witnessed their exchange from the second floor of the temple, as she hid up the stairs and listened. When the dwarf approached Kairos and drew his sword, her heart lurched, she couldn't bear the thought of losing him. Summoning her mana and willing her hand to not shake, she had traced the fire glyph that singed the dwarf's hair and allowed Kairos to escape.

That was when Althea realised that up till that moment, she was trying to become a knight for all the wrong reasons. To her, being a Mana Knight was all about parading around in fancy armour, showcasing one's authority, and basking in a hero's praise from the grateful populace. She fantasised about the image and adulation her father had.

The encounter with Togram shattered that image. She finally began to understand the high stakes for which she gambled, stakes that would make her feel a sense of accomplishment, but would also kill her. The position of authority came with responsibility.

Then Togram returned and murdered Stella.

When Kairos mentioned that killing Togram would have prevented more murders, he unknowingly cut into Althea's soul very deeply with his sharp words. She knew that he was speaking the truth and meant no harm, but she felt that killing *anyone* was wrong. Doing so would cause her to stoop to the dwarf's level. Vengeance was against her very beliefs.

It took several days for Althea to speak to Kairos again, and they had avoided talking about Togram and Stella – although their shadows seemed to lurk in the background of any conversation, out of sight, but always nearby.

In Althea's case, time was the panacea. The passing weeks made her sadness recede, to be replaced by a new resolve. She vowed to improve herself, both in her magic and physical abilities, until she completed the Academy. She would prevent more wanton killings.

Word of Sir Hugo's recovery also offered her a sense of ease. She felt guilty about the Wolf Knight's injuries, and his death would have eaten away at her conscience.

Althea made progress for the remainder of winter, aiming for faster times on the obstacle course and swift victories when sparring with the others. She persisted in her magic practice with unrelenting fervour. Whenever she had a free moment, she traipsed off to the training hall where she could practise spells on the corzite targets without fear of hurting anyone. During these training sessions, she replayed, over and over, the scenario of Togram attacking Kairos. She decided it was pure luck that the dwarf's hair had caught on fire. The spell was weak, and had she not been lucky, Kairos would have died. Althea would be better prepared for next time.

Flain took notice of her recent improvements.

'Squire Avenal,' he said one day after Althea completed the obstacle course faster than most of the others, 'I used to think you were the most useless human being I had come across in all my years on Alban, with no chance at redemption, but I realised I was wrong. It seems that you actually *can* polish a rusty sword.'

'Um, thank you, Sir Flain?'

Sir Flain did not respond, only took his place before the recruits in the Commons. He regarded them with a sour look on his face, as if he were about to make a very bad decision. His customary frown had deepened more than usual, if that were possible.

'Listen up, you worms,' he said. 'Henceforth, we will train with real weapons. As some of you may already know, our standard issue weapon is the mana lance. These are the easiest to use and carry around.' He drew a crystal-tipped rod from his belt and hoisted it high. 'All you do is channel a little of your mana into it like this—' Flain's hands glowed and the mana lance began to extend to four times its length, 'and now you have a weapon that should protect you, should your magic ever fail. Now you try.'

The paladin and another knight handed out the weapons.

Althea hefted her mana lance. It was lighter than she thought it would be. Just as Flain instructed, she willed a portion of her mana into the staff, and the shaft extended into the length of a normal spear, but she barely had enough mana to extend the crystal-pointed tip a foot.

That was the one thing she didn't improve much upon — mana. She wondered what she was doing wrong. She wasn't alone. She looked over at Kairos, who stared at his mana lance with a darkened expression, making no attempt to activate it for combat.

She wondered what was ailing him. Was he not feeling well today? No, that wasn't right. He had excelled at the obstacle course, as usual, running about with an air of contentment like a child during playtime. No, he was fine until he was asked to channel mana.

Flain also noticed. 'Squire Azel, why aren't you engaging your mana lance?'

Kairos acted as if he didn't hear anything.

Flain's scowl deepened, and he marched towards Kairos to confront him. 'Squire Azel! I asked you a question. Now you—'

A glowing crystal tip grazed Flain's hair as he ducked, just in time.

'Oops,' said an embarrassed Shah, sheepishly clutching the mana lance that had almost skewered his instructor. 'Sorry about that, sir.'

Flain rounded on Shah and snatched his mana lance away. As he continued berating the hapless squire, Althea saw Kairos breathe a sigh of relief. A murky understanding began to coalesce in her mind. The answer was fuzzy, but the more she thought about his strange behaviour since their first encounter, the clearer it became.

Her thoughts were interrupted, because Flain was apparently finished yelling at Shah.

'Attention!' Flain yelled, directing the squires' focus back towards him. 'You received those mana lances for a reason. As you all may well know, due to recent and unfortunate circumstances, we have a shortage of knights in the field. Therefore, we have many unfulfilled quests from the citizens of Vadost and its surrounding region. Thankfully, the Knighthood has allowed us the honour of performing that deed – though looking at you pathetic lot, I would say that honour is well undeserved.' The paladin fixed his recruits – who now stood aghast – with a scathing eye. 'Don't worry. The Knighthood knows that you aren't big enough to wipe your arses yet – especially you!' He cast a fiery gaze on Shah, who slunk his head. 'That's why you'll be getting the easiest of assignments. And you'll have a seasoned knight coming along to help in case you botch the job miserably. Any questions?'

The class was quiet. Shah raised his hand.

'Good.' Sir Flain looked at everyone and nodded. 'There is no need to fear. The key to success is constant training. You are free to spend the remainder of the day doing just that. Train.'

The squires began chatting excitedly with each other as Flain walked away. Almost every squire was eager to stab a mana lance into something. They practised channelling mana into the weapons, along with the jabs and swings that Flain had made them do thousands of times over. The mana lances were much lighter than the practice spears. Everyone marvelled how easily they could fight with them. As they drilled themselves for the next hour, some began trading jokes and good-natured insults, and a few imitated Sir Flain in the act of berating the other squires, though they first made sure to look around to check if Flain was still in the vicinity.

Shah joined in with his own humour. 'There is need to fear,' he barked in perfect imitation of Flain as he puffed his chest out and pretended to admire the backside of Squire Urzen. 'Flower Flain is at your rear!'

No one laughed. A few of the other squires coughed and shuffled their feet uncomfortably.

'What's wrong?' Shah asked. 'That's funny!'

Kairos tried to hiss a warning, but Shah remained oblivious. He finally noticed several squires looking past him.

'Oh... He's right behind me, isn't he?' Shah said, defeated.

'Yes, Squire Shah, he is,' came Sir Flain's low, deadly voice. 'You must really like running until you puke.'

Slowly turning, Shah said, 'N-no, Sir Flain, I was just—'

'Oh, I know what you were doing.' Looking at the silent squires, Flain asked, 'Don't we have something better to do? Find a partner and resume your training.'

As the squires scattered, Flain said to Shah, 'Oh, not you, Squire Shah. I have another task for you.' The knight flashed a wicked smile.

Shah swallowed hard, trying to keep his knees from knocking together.

As Althea found Cassie to practise, she turned one last time and saw Flain doling out physical punishment of the worst kind on the unfortunate squire, who looked like he was facing his own doom. In a way, she envied Shah. She would trade places with him in an instant, if it would rid herself of her worries, her fears, and the memories of Stella's death. The physical pain of Shah's punishment seemed to pale in comparison to the mental anguish raging inside of her soul.

The time of the Knight's Test was nigh approaching and she wasn't ready. She needed more power. Her mana level was insufficient and she didn't know what she would do in combat. She could only think of one person who could help her: Professor Argent.

During the storm of her internal struggle, she had forgotten about Kairos, who still stood near Flain and Shah, hopelessly gripping the still-retracted mana lance.

* * *

The mana lance felt cold and lifeless in Kairos's hands.

He watched the other students and attempted to copy them. It was no use. He could not activate the weapon and he already knew why. He knew before he had even touched the weapon: he was god-cursed with no mana.

He felt numb as he stood there, unaware when the class had been dismissed. He didn't notice that Althea had also left. He could only see the mana lance in front of him, and, try as he might, he could not channel anything into the weapon. If he couldn't activate a standard-issue weapon, the Knighthood would eventually discover his shortcomings and kick him out. Why had Professor Argent even allowed him entry into the Academy if wielding a mana lance was a prerequisite?

'What are you still doing here?' a stern voice demanded. 'I said that class was dismissed ten minutes ago.'

Kairos looked up as if he were in a daze. Sir Flain stood in front of him, looking angry, as usual. Shah lay on the cold ground, out of breath and covered in sweat.

Flain continued, 'I also said to give back my mana lances, so if you don't hand it back over right now, I'm going to snatch it from you and clobber you over the head with it.'

'Oh, right,' Kairos said contritely, handing the weapon over and inwardly bracing himself for a scolding. 'Sorry, Sir Flain.'

Flain eyed him. 'Do you know what your problem is, Azel? You think too damn much. That's my job. Your job is to take orders from me. If you did only that, then your life would be much easier.'

'Yes, sir,' Kairos said hastily, suddenly self-conscious that the paladin could read his troubled mind. Perhaps his tormenting thoughts appeared on his facial expressions. He decided to heed the paladin's advice. 'Yes, sir,' he said again, turning to follow the other squires who had already left.

'One more thing, Azel.'

'Sir?'

'Is there something you're not telling me?' Flain affixed him with a scrutinising gaze.

*He knows.* Kairos couldn't meet Flain in the eye. *This is it. I'm done.*

'Answer the question!' Flain yelled.

'Yes, sir,' Kairos said dejectedly. He might as well tell the truth now. It was bound to come out sooner or later. 'I'm afraid that I cannot use the mana lance.'

'Perhaps a different weapon would suit you better then.'

Kairos looked up. 'Sir?'

'Did I stutter, squire?' Flain gestured to the mana lance. 'You looked more awkward than Shah, holding one of these. Would you prefer another weapon – such as a sword?'

Kairos was unsure if he had heard correctly. 'Is that allowed, sir? I thought the mana lance was the standard issue weapon of the–'

'See? That's your damn problem! You think too much. So a sword, it is, then. Very well, starting tomorrow, you will use a practice sword for training.' Flain turned to leave but paused. 'And to answer your question, it is allowed… Using swords, that is. During my great grandfather's time, most Mana Knights carried swords, though that tradition has long disappeared. The invention of the mana lance changed that.'

'How so, sir?'

'Because a sword requires a lot of training to become skilful. Mana lances and spears don't. Even an untrained spearman can easily defeat a skilled swordsman if he utilises the advantage of reach. Mana lances are also lighter and easier to carry around. But if you want to carry a sword, I won't stop you.'

Kairos bowed. 'Thank you, sir.'

'Don't thank me,' Flain said gruffly, pulling out a letter. 'Thank Mr. Dubose. According to this letter, he vouched for your

252

swordsmanship. So, starting tomorrow, you're going to start training like a barrel of gnome powder has been shoved up your arse with a burning torch.'

Kairos wiped the sweat from his brow as he walked back to the barracks, fatigued with sudden relief. He did not know how much longer he could go on with this ruse. It was only a matter of time before somebody discovered that he was god-cursed.

But for now, he had managed to avoid yet another problem.

\* \* \*

Althea thought of turning back once she entered the Gauntlet, the row of living quarters for the teaching faculty — instructors, professors, and scholars — at Valour Keep. According to Shah (who was a frequent visitor), the place earned its name due to the punishments professors doled out to squires, after hours. Even Flain had his own quarters here, complete with a large garden and a greenhouse, accommodating many colourful varieties of flower, thus earning him his much-loathed nickname, 'Flower Flain.'

It was a beautiful garden, Althea thought, as she strolled past. She wondered why the tempestuous and foul-mouthed paladin took such a passionate interest in gardening. It was such an odd contrast to his hot-headed demeanour. She forced her wandering thoughts to focus on her current task; she had questions and needed answers.

For a long while, Althea had kept her shortcomings pent up inside. It was no secret to everyone else that her mana was lacking, but pride compelled her to avoid seeking help. There were other reasons, too. She didn't want to be labelled as incompetent. Mana Knights were not supposed to beg for help; they were supposed to render help. After extensively deliberating her options, along with a strong dose of desperation, she came to the conclusion she would ask Argent.

The professor acted aloof during class, rarely engaged anyone in conversation, and he seemed like a loner outside of the classroom. But whenever she had a question or concern, he always helped. She figured the anti-social professor would keep her request private, even if he refused to assist. What did she have to lose? Pride, maybe. And she had already lost so much of that during her tenure at the Academy.

She approached his quarters and saw candlelight flickering from within the window. Perfect, she thought. As she raised her hand to rap on the door, the sound of voices from inside made her hesitate.

'But he is! I've seen him before he came to Ordonia!' said a man's voice. It sounded very familiar, yet very brutish.

'There *are* other methods,' said another voice – Argent's. 'Don't forget I've toiled long and hard for this position. I'd rather keep it.'

Althea knew it was rude to eavesdrop, but it was also rude to interrupt another's conversation. She should have turned around and headed back to the barracks. There was always tomorrow, she reasoned to herself. But she did not leave. Curiosity and intrigue overpowered the desire for politeness. Who was Argent talking to? He sounded so strange. Dangerous even. She put her ear against the door.

'So have I!' the other man responded. 'And I've been living in a shit pot this entire time, too. At least you have these quarters where it's nice and quiet. I'm tired of hearing whores, drunks, and street urchins during all hours of the night.'

'You can always look for another place,' Argent replied complacently. 'No one has bothered you, yet.'

Althea held perfectly still, not even breathing. She wanted to know what was going on. She realised that she, along with everyone else in class, knew very little about Professor Argent. The man she was hearing now sounded very different to the man who stood at the front of the classroom making her cast rudimentary battle spells.

'I'm almost at the end of my patience,' the other voice growled. 'I'll deal with him soon enough on my own, and then I can leave this bloody cesspool of filth.'

'I have my own methods regarding the god-cursed one,' Argent returned coolly. 'Do not interfere. You will do your job and— Wait! What was that?'

Althea had adjusted her position against the door to relieve her quivering legs. The day had been a long one of training, and her muscles were beginning to cramp. She tried to shift her weight, ever so slightly and silently. Unfortunately, the wooden door on which she leant upon creaked loudly when she moved.

The door flung open inwardly, almost causing Althea to fall inside.

'A spy!' Argent's companion said in a harsh voice.

A colourful cloak fluttered, and a strong hand reached out, gripping Althea's cloak. The mana on her fingertips evaporated in the heat of terror. The man dragged Althea inside and shut the door, his pale blue eyes full of blood lust.

Althea's eyes widened in surprise. The words for mercy died on her lips. She stared, not at a vicious brute like she had imagined, but at Stephon who immediately released her and smoothed the wrinkles on her cloak. The elf's expression showed that he was just as surprised to see her.

'Why Althea! Fancy seeing you. What brings you here at such a late hour, milady?' The tone sounded friendly and inviting, but Althea thought she could detect a trace of venom lying underneath the honeyed words.

'I might ask you the same!' Althea countered, still in shock. There was something wrong with the elf, but she was so flustered that her thoughts jumbled around in a hurry.

'How long have you been there?' Argent demanded, sitting behind an oak desk, looking irritated, as if disturbed from something important. 'And what are you doing skulking around my door in the evening when you should be back at the barracks?'

Althea tried to look stupid, copying Shah's blank stare and dumbfounded expression. 'Not long,' she answered. 'I came here to ask you a few questions about class. I had just got to the door when I realised you had company. I wasn't waiting long.'

'My dear,' Stephon began, 'it's a terrible thing to lie. You have been snooping, haven't you?'

'N-no, I have not, Stephon.' Althea replied hastily, fear churning her insides. 'I'd just finished my classes and training for the day, and I came to see Professor Argent.'

'That's quite enough,' said Argent. 'Stephon and I were just discussing business.'

Althea glanced from Stephon to Argent in puzzlement. 'Do you two know each other?'

The elf turned and his gaze met Argent's, as if an unsaid message passed between the two. He suddenly raised both open hands as if warding off an attack. 'Oh heavens, no! It's nothing like that. He's definitely *not* my type! Too human for my tastes, if that's what you're thinking.'

'Stephon was taking a custom order for a new robe.' Argent did not look amused. 'He's not pleased about living in Ordonia, so this may be my last chance to have him make something. Stephon, if you have no further business with me, I shall see Squire Avenal now.'

'Yes.' Stephon sighed and gave a wan smile. 'I wanted to keep my leaving a secret, but I suppose it's best that you know, Althea. You have always been one of my best customers. It was a pleasure! By your leave, milord, milady.'

The elf bowed to Argent, then to Althea. He seemed tired and dishevelled, not groomed to his usual standards. His cheerful voice sounded strained. He left through the front door, his cloak swirling around him. Althea watched him leave, not knowing quite what to make of the elf. She had never seen this side of him before. She tried to think, but couldn't grasp a coherent thought. Maybe he hated living in Vadost. Most elves did. She didn't ponder on the matter for long, because she felt like she was going to be in trouble with Argent.

After the elf shut the door, Argent gestured to the lone chair across from him. 'Have a seat, Squire Avenal,' he said. The desk was tidy except for a quill, ink jar, parchment, and an acorn carved of stone. Argent picked up the quill and began scrawling notes on the parchment in front of him. 'What brings you here? You're performing sufficiently enough in my class.'

Althea averted her eyes and shifted her feet. She had almost forgotten why she'd come. The words of the professor's conversation with Stephon still burned fresh on her mind, but the professor didn't seem about to punish her for peeping in on his conversation. She forced herself to relax. 'Well, I wanted to talk with you about something.'

Argent continued writing without looking up. 'Go on and say it then. Let's not tarry on the matter.'

'Sir, I have a problem,' Althea began, struggling with the words. 'It's my mana…'

'What about it?' The quill continued its strokes across the parchment.

'No matter how much I study or train, I barely seem to improve.' Althea opened up her bottled-up feelings. The words poured freely now. 'I've always had low mana, you see. Ever since I was little. I know the glyphs and their combinations, but whenever I try to draw upon the magic to cast the spell, I feel as if the well is almost empty.'

Argent paused briefly, then continued writing. 'And what makes you think that I can help?'

'Because you're powerful,' said Althea.

The quill stopped. Pale, piercing eyes looked at her, appraisingly. 'What gives you that idea?'

Althea shrugged. 'I've been around my father my whole life, and he's powerful in magic. You give off a similar aura.'

The professor regarded her with an approving eye, evidently impressed. 'You flatter me, Squire Avenal. My abilities are not that remarkable. Your father is much more powerful.'

'But surely you have some advice for me!' Althea said stubbornly.

Argent put the quill into the ink jar. Whatever he was writing was going to wait.

'Please, professor,' Althea pleaded.

'You mentioned your father,' Argent said suddenly. 'What about your mother? Magical abilities often lie in lineage.'

Althea looked at the floor and swallowed. Talking about her mother was painful, and she rarely ever brought her up. 'I don't know much,' Althea admitted. 'My mother died when I was young. Father hardly ever talks about her, and I don't know the extent of her abilities. I was too young to remember, and I never asked father.'

'I see,' Argent said. 'And now you lack the mana to cast intermediate spells, and the spells you can cast seem weak, correct?'

'Yes, sir.'

'I can theorise what your problem is,' Argent replied.

Althea brightened, sitting up in her excitement. 'You have a solution?!'

'I did not say that,' he snapped. 'I'm merely theorising here. Your problem may lie within yourself. Negative emotions and stress. A lack of self-confidence can constrict the flow of mana throughout your body, limiting your spell-casting abilities.'

Althea sat up straight. 'I don't understand. I know the glyphs and I feel confident casting them.'

The professor pursed his lips. 'That's not what I meant. When you cast a spell, you memorise the glyph, channel your mana into it, and expect the result, correct?' Without waiting for an answer, the professor continued, 'Well, spellcasting is like solving math equations – but it's not. You have to know your glyphs and how much mana to funnel into the spell, but sometimes your emotions get involved.'

'My emotions?'

'You get flustered easily, Squire Avenal,' Argent said. 'And that's not a good thing when you're casting spells.' He added, 'It's just my personal observation. You could have a low mana pool, too. Some people are born unlucky.'

Althea leant back in the chair and contemplated the professor's words. She had always assumed she lacked a significant degree of mana. Emotional distractions were a new concept.

'Self-doubt hinders your abilities greatly,' the professor continued. 'Focus on removing that, first. I know it's easier said than done, but know this: when you cast a spell, you have to envision that the end result will be powerful, and then you train to attain that level of power.'

'I've tried that.' Althea's shoulders slumped in defeat. 'Believe me, I've tried!'

'Is that so?' Argent raised his head to glance at Althea. 'Well, then.'

'Please, sir,' Althea pleaded again. 'I don't want to be useless. I've been useless my whole life. The other kids have always picked on me. I feel like a burden. For once, I would like to be of some use.' A tear flowed down Althea's cheek. 'Please. Surely you know some training method or exercise I could do. A spell I could practise.'

The professor's face regarded her like a mask of stone.

Althea felt humiliated. She had been plagued by self-doubt ever since she came through the door, had been on the verge of admitting she was mistaken in coming here. Professor Argent seemed like the right person to ask, but his indifferent responses hinted otherwise. Althea was going to look a fool, especially in front of a professor whose respect she wanted to earn. She was about to excuse herself from his quarters and retreat back to the barracks with what little dignity she had remaining, when she noticed the professor's eyes flicker.

Or was it her imagination? Ever since their first meeting, the professor had never displayed any emotion. Surely he wasn't going to start now.

'I'll just take my leave then,' Althea mumbled, rising from her seat. 'Please pardon my intrusion.'

'Stay seated,' Argent said, rising. He ambled over to a bookshelf tucked into the corner of the room, and reached up to grasp a worn, leather-bound book from the topmost shelf. 'I think I may have a partial solution to your problem.'

259

This was a surprise.

Althea clamped her teeth over her lips to keep her excitement from bursting out. Spellbooks were a valuable commodity, and few owners passed them around casually due to the possibility of them falling into the wrong hands. Althea had to join the Mana Knight Academy to study the classroom spellbooks that were sanctioned and approved by the Knighthood, and those spells were not allowed to be used outside of the Knighthood. Spellbooks dealing with other professions such as farming required an apprenticeship before one could simply peruse the pages. She knew that this book was not sanctioned or approved by the Knighthood, and Argent could face dire consequences for merely showing her its contents.

She teetered on the edge of her seat.

He set the spellbook down upon his desk and spent a moment opening it and examining the pages as if he found it all uninteresting. Althea gazed at the book as well, but with a ravenous curiosity to see what wonders it might contain. She had already suspected that the book was illegal, and the notion made her heart pound rapidly against her chest.

Argent confirmed her suspicions by closing the book and showing her the angular lines of the elven alphabet. Other than that, the book looked rather ordinary, which was common for spellbooks. No owner in their right mind would want a gaudy book that brought unwanted attention to itself. 'Just so you know, this book deals with spells of healing and necromancy. It was written long ago, before necromancy was outlawed by all the nations of Alban.'

The book was indeed old. The brown leather of its binding was frayed and showed heavy signs of wear. A small part of her mind told her to be wary when Argent mentioned 'necromancy', but the prospects of power drowned that caution with a tidal wave of excitement. Althea reached forward.

Argent placed his hand over the book, halting her movements. 'This book is very difficult to comprehend, and it's written in the language of the dark elves. This magic focuses more on drawing the mana from the nature around you, and less on the mana inside of you. However, there are consequences of its misuse.'

'Such as?' Althea whispered, scarcely daring to breathe as she clung to Argent's every word.

'You must be careful how you draw the mana for these spells, even the simple ones, because if you force it, then you devolve into the art of necromancy.' Argent cast Althea a stern gaze. 'And you know the consequences of that.'

Althea nodded. She knew that all nations captured practitioners of necromancy and sentenced them to death. Few users of the forbidden art had the temerity to boldly cast their magic out in the open, most conducting their evil acts in caves or abandoned structures, away from prying eyes. Even healers such as Sir Flain had to earn approval under strict supervision for the use of his healing abilities. Thus there were very few paladins and healers in the Knighthood.

'Keep this book hidden from others,' Argent said, 'Do not tell anyone about it or where you got it from, and keep a low profile on these spells. Use only the healing spells when necessary. Understood?'

'I understand,' Althea said reverently. And she meant it, though a small sliver of her conscience told her that her actions were wrong. The Knighthood wouldn't condone such an act: concealing a forbidden power. That sliver of reasoning was weak, however, and she countered that she was using this power for good. She would benefit the Knighthood with it, rather than burden it with a lack of power.

'Good,' Argent said. 'Now I suppose you should be on your way.'

'I'll return this to you when I'm finished with it,' Althea said.

'Keep it.'

Althea was about to stand to leave, but paused. 'Why are you doing this, professor?'

The professor's usual impassive face flickered with bemusement for a moment. 'What do you mean?'

'Why are you giving this to me?' she asked. 'You're risking your position and your well-being by entrusting me with this book.'

Argent gave a slight, half smile – the only time Althea had ever seen him coming close to smiling. 'You remind me of a child I once knew.' His hand reached out and touched the stone carving of the acorn on the desk, and his eyes glazed over, as if seeing something far away. 'Only I couldn't provide her help at the time... And she was unable to defend herself when danger came.'

Several silent seconds passed. Althea did not respond. It was very brief, so brief that Althea had almost missed it, but she saw a look of infinite sadness on the professor's face. The look vanished instantly.

'Sorry,' Argent said in a stiff voice, nodding off a memory and focusing back on the present. 'Let me return to my work.' The professor picked up his quill and began writing again. 'Is that all?'

'Yes, sir.' She stood up.

'Good,' he said, not looking at her. 'I'll see you in tomorrow's class.'

Althea walked towards the door, but stopped again. There was one other thing that had been bothering her, tugging at her mind lately.

'D-do you believe that someone can be god-cursed?'

The quill fell onto the parchment, splattering ink in a few tiny droplets that seeped into the page. Argent stared at Althea in long silence, causing her to wither before its intensity. 'What do you mean?' he finally said.

Althea did not expect such a serious response to what she deemed a flippant question. The sudden severity of his expression frightened her. 'I-I mean that someone who has no trace of mana whatsoever...'

'So, you did eavesdrop on my conversation with Stephon,' Argent said coldly.

'No, I haven't, sir.' Althea replied in a conciliatory tone. 'I just came to the door and heard mention of a god-cursed one, so I stopped to listen. I couldn't help myself. I have read stories about the god-cursed ones before, and I have always found them fascinating.'

'They are interesting stories,' Argent agreed. 'Do you believe them?'

The question startled Althea. She did not expect this, either. The stories about the god-cursed people were just that. Stories. No one had ever seen the god-cursed. But here was Argent, asking her in earnest. 'I-I just thought they were legends,' she stammered.

'I see,' he said, picking up the quill and tossing the ruined parchment aside. 'As much as I would love to talk, you should run along back to the barracks. It's getting late, squire. Focus more on your new spellbook and less on stories. I'll see you tomorrow.'

Althea bowed. Muscles stiff and aching, she exited Argent's quarters and made her way back to the barracks. Hearing sounds of footsteps, fearing that someone was following her, she glanced back.

It was just a pair of Mana Knights patrolling the keep.

She mulled over the conversation between Stephon and Argent, trying to ferret out its meaning, but her mind was too dulled with fatigue to make any sense of it. The introduction of the spellbook had left her body and mind drained from the excitement. She forced herself back to the barracks in a daze, placing one foot in front of the other, only seeing the recent events swim around over and over in her mind.

Her instincts told her that something was off. She would think more about it later, when she had had sufficient rest.

*　*　*

*This is it. He knows. I'm done.*

Kairos cleared his throat roughly as he tried to think of something to say. Something to do. Anything! But he was frozen in place.

'Well, Squire Azel?' Jomur said. 'Shall we all watch you just sit there gaping stupidly or will you demonstrate how to light the candle as instructed?'

Snickers chased around the classroom as some of the other squires enjoyed not being the target of Jomur's ire. Kairos walked as a man to the gallows.

'Oh, and leave your glove and staff,' Jomur said. 'This isn't a tactical scenario. I just want you to light a candle.'

Jomur knew it all. Kairos was sure to get kicked out of the Mana Knight Academy – and that was the best he could hope for. He didn't know if they would arrest him for his deception or ostricise him for being god-cursed. Either way, he was finished with the Mana Knights, he was sure of that. He looked at the candle on Jomur's desk, saw everyone staring expectantly.

'Well?' Jomur demanded. He didn't even bother to conceal his smirk at Kairos's discomfort.

Kairos took a breath. He slowly raised his hand. There was no mana to conjure forth. The candle remained unlit.

'Hurry up, Azel.'

The door at the back of the classroom slammed open. Lady Beatrice, a Wolf Knight, strode in purposefully. 'Sorry to interrupt, Instructor Jomur. Sir Flain has ordered all squires to assemble in the Commons. Training mission to rid the hobs plaguing the farmers.'

Kairos tried to conceal his utter relief as he walked back to his desk. He gathered his things and filed out with the rest of the squires.

As he stepped out of the classroom, he heard Jomur say softly, 'This isn't over. Not by any stretch.'

At first, Kairos wasn't sure who Jomur was talking to, but he saw the instructor's dark eyes, shadowed by a thick unibrow, boring straight into him.

\* \* \*

The advent of spring moved the squires into the field for more drilling with Sir Flain, much to the collective misery of the class. Kairos, on the other hand, was thankful. He would continue to avoid Instructor Jomur, who seemed eager to expose him to the world. Kairos had once thought of the instructor as a weak, pompous coward of a man, but suddenly he had good reason to fear and avoid him.

'I miss Instructor Jomur's class,' said Althea to Kairos one evening in the mess hall, after a gruelling day of sparring in the field. 'That was the only class where I performed rather well.'

Kairos sneered. 'Jomur is a snivelling shit, who doesn't deserve a position here. Performing 'well' in his class doesn't exactly transfer to excellence in battle. I mean, what has he taught us that would be of practical use as a knight? Theories, formulas, and essays on rubbish! I say that his entire class is a waste of time, and I'm not sure why he is even here in the first place.'

'I suppose,' Althea responded, looking uncomfortable. She never liked to speak badly of anyone if she could help it, especially in the vulgar way Kairos usually did. Her father had taught her better.

'I'm not sure why we are taught by instructors and professors instead of actual knights. Like Flain,' Kairos said, with emphasis on mentioning the knight. 'I've learnt more from him than all the other classes combined. The instructors and professors here are boring old fools who love nothing but the sound of their own voices echoing across the classroom. Though I suppose Argent isn't that useless.'

'I like Argent,' Althea said defensively, thinking that Kairos's words disparaged their professor. 'He's a good teacher, and his lessons are easy to understand. He's even gone above and beyond to help me with my magic.'

'Of course. I like Argent, too.' Kairos thought of the Badger's Trial, where the professor had discovered his darkest secret. To this day, Kairos still didn't understand why Argent hadn't told anyone. Maybe the professor was practical enough to understand that wielding magic did not equate to being a good knight – Shah was proof of that. 'He's different to the other non-knights. At least he teaches something worth a damn.'

Althea was about to argue, but Kairos became focused on his meal, eating voraciously and consuming everything on his plate and wanting more. Althea shoved her plate towards him with a sigh. She was a picky eater, cutting away the bruised portions of her fruit and vegetables, or removing the gristle from the meat. Kairos was always happy to finish whatever she didn't want.

He finished and carried the wooden plates away to be washed and went back to the kitchen for a second visit. He returned to the table with more food. Most of the other squires in the mess hall had already retired to their barracks for the evening.

'I went to the Gauntlet the other day and sought out Argent for help,' Althea said, looking down and fidgeting with her cup of water.

'Althea, you're spilling water on yourself. Be careful! Or the cook will yell at us for making a mess again.' Kairos paused to shovel some potatoes into his mouth. 'As for Argent, did you learn any new spells? He's quite standoffish, you know. I can't imagine him helping anyone outside of the classroom.'

'Stephon was there,' Althea said. She used her sleeve to wipe the spilled water from the table, then inspected her clothes, wiping her shirtfront.

Kairos snorted. 'As if I care about that bloody elven bastard. He can rot at the bottom of the sea.'

Althea tried to explain her discovery. 'You were right about him before, Kairos. Something is off about him. That flamboyant friendly act of his is a façade.'

Kairos stopped chewing and looked up swiftly. 'What happened?'

Althea's face reddened, ashamed about what she was about to admit. 'I was eavesdropping on their conversation. Stephon was talking to Argent, and he sounded *evil*,' she said with a strong emphasis on the last word. 'They were talking about dealing with 'the god-cursed one' or such. Argent told him not to act on whatever he was intending. When I made a sound, Stephon opened the door and found me there listening in on his conversation. I thought for a moment that he was going to kill me, Kairos! The look in his eyes and the sound of his voice... He would have enjoyed it. Then when Stephon realised it was me, he reverted back to his warm and friendly self again.'

Kairos was pale. 'What else did they say?'

'Nothing much. I didn't listen that long. I played dumb, and he and Argent seemed to relax. They gave each other odd looks, then Argent said he was ordering a robe, or such, from Stephon.'

'What happened next?' Kairos prodded her.

'Stephon left and Argent invited me to sit down. We talked about my low mana level, which was the original reason why I went to him. I was too scared to ask about what they were talking about...' Althea hesitated and looked around to see if anyone was within earshot. Satisfied no one was, she continued, 'Argent also gave me a book on healing magic. He's not supposed to do such a thing, Kairos. It's forbidden for us to study healing magic without permission. But I took the book and read it anyway. Please don't get mad at me.'

'Why would I get mad?'

'Because reading such a book is forbidden.' Althea frowned and paused. 'And also because I didn't believe you before about Stephon.'

'It's no bother. Stephon was very friendly with you, so it's understandable that you didn't believe me. Besides, that was clever of you to play ignorant,' Kairos said, regarding Althea with admiration. 'Somehow, I don't think Argent was requesting a tailor's services in his private quarters. And their conversation sounds very odd. You don't suppose that book is dangerous then?'

'It can be. There is a thin line between healing magic and necromancy. And the Knighthood denounces all use of necromancy.' Althea shivered. 'So I must ensure I study the book properly... and not get caught.'

'I still wonder why Argent gave that to you,' Kairos said, thoughtfully. He remembered the magicus measuring his mana level. He thought Argent had kept it secret, but if Stephon knew...

'Eh?' Althea was bemused. 'What do you mean?'

'You are certain that you heard him mention the 'god-cursed one?'' Kairos asked quietly. He was glad that the mess hall was almost empty.

'I am certain,' Althea said with conviction, her expression solemn and troubled. 'I thought it was such an odd thing to talk about. What should we do? Should we say something about it?'

'No, not yet,' Kairos said. He hesitated a moment, then added, 'We continue playing dumb. They're planning something strange, and if we act suspicious, then we will lose the element of surprise. I always knew that there was something off about that bloody elf.' A brief vision of Milbrooke formed in his mind. He saw Farina's pleading eyes, and remembered Captain Hargonnas's search for the god-cursed one. He pushed the memory away.

Althea misread Kairos's facial expression. 'What shall we do about Stephon?'

'We watch him, Althea. And we watch our backs very carefully.'

*　*　*

Gulliver travelled alone as he walked through Syphax, the capital of Numidia, which was a small kingdom situated to the south of Ordonia. Despite the intense heat of the tropical climate, he shook with excitement and nervousness as he neared Gala Fortress, the Mana Knight stronghold located in the centre of the city.

His arrival had not gone unnoticed. Almost every Numidian in the streets stopped what they were doing to stare unabashedly at him. Most regarded him with considerable suspicion, which by now Gulliver was accustomed to. His pale skin contrasted sharply to the onyx hue of the Numidians. There was no such thing as blending into the crowd here. However, his pale skin was not the only reason why they stared.

Long since the Godfall, Numidia had shut its gates to problems of the outside world. The inhabitants studied their magic and prospered in peace, treating all outsiders like potential thieves, murderers, or disease-ridden vermin. Numidia was a nation of the magical elite who lived in isolation, neutrality, and strict lawfulness; everyone followed the rules. The woes of the world rarely affected them.

The Numidians' attitude towards Gulliver did not bother him. It was his upcoming meeting at Gala Fortress that left his nerves taut.

Gala Fortress was the only exception that Numidia made for outsiders. It housed the headquarters of the Mana Knights, who were the only non-Numidians allowed to travel freely in and out of the country. The Knighthood was led by a mysterious Numidian by the name of Eribus, or 'Grandmaster Eribus' as the Mana Knights called him.

Thus, the reason for Gulliver's visit: he was summoned by Grandmaster Eribus, himself.

He sometimes had to pause during his walk to gather his flagging courage. He did not know the true reasons for his summons, though he had several assumptions. The main one was that that he had failed his duty at Cape Caipora, and his failure had incurred the wrath of the Knighthood's highest-ranking member. Another scenario in the young knight's mind was punishment for abandoning Tanton. He had come up with a profuse apology and a multitude of excuses for his actions, including the loss of the fingers of his casting hand, which still ached to this day. He hoped the Grandmaster would take pity and mercy on him, so he could go on with his life. Gulliver had been a nervous wreck ever since getting the summons, and he dreaded the outcome of this meeting.

The wild imaginations of youth.

Gulliver stated his business truthfully to the authorities at the front gates of Syphax. Even the most suspicious of the knights yielded the outsider knight a grudging bit of deference in return and pointed him in the correct direction of Gala Fortress. Several of these men hinted at where the exit was as soon as Gulliver had concluded his business. Gulliver hoped that he lived through this ordeal to see the exit. Apparently, Eribus was held in the same regard as the king of this nation, Gulliver thought.

He saw the tall ivory buildings and marvelled at their beauty and quality. They reached for the clouds, looking much more majestic than anything in Ordonia. The streets looked clean enough to eat from, and the citizens went about their daily lives in an orderly manner that seemed almost mechanical to the knight. The only break in this organised ritual were two young women staring at him and whispering with lowered eyelashes. As soon as they saw him look their way, they giggled and turned away. His cheeks burned as he walked by, and it wasn't from the glaring sun. Under ordinary circumstances, Gulliver would have enjoyed all the above, but he was too entrenched in his own despair to pay but a moment's notice.

He was drenched in sweat by the time he arrived at Gala Fortress, which was taller than anything in Vadost. If Gala Fortress were side by side with Valour Keep, it would tower more than three times the height of the Ordonian stronghold. This bastion also housed the Ruby Shard, the godshard of Numidia, evident by flickers of red, magical energy pulsating from its many towers.

Gulliver greeted and saluted the knights at the entrance, who returned a perfunctory salute and greeting that was expected, but also demonstrated that he was to conduct his business in the quickest manner possible and leave. A Lion Knight came and escorted him to Eribus's chambers, which were situated on the highest floor of a very tall tower. Gulliver rode a magical lift that carried him with dizzying speed to the top, where the Lion Knight led him to the door, knocked lightly, and announced Gulliver.

'Please enter,' came a deep voice within the chamber.

The Lion Knight escorted Gulliver into the room and bowed. Gulliver did the same, as was standard procedure for a Mana Knight addressing his superior. He looked up to steal a quick glance at the most-esteemed knight, but could not see much. The room was dark, due to all the windows covered with curtains shutting out the light, and Eribus was leaning back in his chair, lost in the shadows.

'Thank you, Sir Vasteras,' came Eribus's deep voice. 'You are dismissed.'

The Lion Knight bowed and left the room, plunging Gulliver into wild fear – the moment of reckoning had come, and the darkness of the room only added to the effect. Gulliver lowered his head. His litany of apologies and excuses fled his mind.

'Welcome Sir Gulliver Swift. You must be thirsty from your long journey,' Eribus began, his face still hidden in the darkness. 'Have a seat. Drink with me.'

'S-sir?' Gulliver muttered. The young knight paused and stared at the shadowed figure in speechless amazement. Whatever he had expected, it wasn't this. He had envisioned banishment from the chivalrous order, at the very least. He had even taken some time to go to the library to research the fates of knights who failed horribly at their duties, and the lists of punishments gave birth to several creative scenarios in Gulliver's mind. Perhaps this was the Grandmaster's way of 'priming the cow before the slaughter.' He cautiously sat down.

'It appears that you did not understand me,' Eribus said, speaking in a warm pleasant tone. 'I was offering you a drink to quench the thirst of your travels. I understand that some of you Ordonians may find the heat here quite oppressive.'

Gulliver heard the soft rustling of robes, saw a trace of light, and suddenly several candles flared to life. A face – calm, ageless, with gleaming dark eyes – looked at him from across the table. An invisible energy like a hot wind struck Gulliver, causing him to lean against the back of his chair, and suddenly a glass of water materialised on the desk in front of him. Gulliver almost gasped. The man before him looked as every bit majestic as he had imagined.

Yet despite the awe-inspiring aura the Grandmaster emitted, there was something off about the man... Eribus appeared worn out, haggard, frail. Was he ill?

'My apologies,' Eribus said. 'I haven't had many guests lately, so I forget my manners. Most people are not used to the dark.'

'I-it is quite all right, my lord,' Gulliver replied hastily, then with a tone of nervous concern, he asked, 'Um, a-are you well, milord?'

Eribus chuckled. It sounded like a deep rumbling rasp. 'Do not fret about me, Sir Swift. My malady is not contagious, and the symptoms should recede within due time if everything proceeds as planned. Please, drink.'

Gulliver took a quick sip from the glass, more because he didn't want to offend his host rather than for quenching his thirst.

'Now let's skip the formalities,' Eribus said. 'You know who I am, and I know who you are. I'm here to ask you for your first-hand account of the events at Cape Caipora. You will tell me everything.'

Gulliver's shoulders slumped. He felt like a little boy caught in a forbidden act and confessing to his parents. Now he *would* tell everything to Eribus. For some reason, it felt satisfying. The pent-up guilt from many months spilled forth from his soul, and the Grandmaster listened in silence, only interrupting when he wanted clarification on something.

The young knight told of spotting a shipwreck and finding Kairos in the woods. He noticed that Eribus leant forward and listened eagerly at the mention of the boy. He mentioned arguing with Tanton over lighting the signal fire, as instructed whenever anything of significance came from the sea, and how Malus's army attacked a short time later. Gulliver was unable to hide his shame when he admitted abandoning Cape Caipora and Tanton to the enemy. He began to weep.

'I tried to convince him to leave, my lord.' Gulliver sobbed. 'But he wouldn't budge. I took Kairos and ran like a coward. I know it wasn't honourable, but I thought at least I could help him survive...'

Eribus held up a hand for silence. 'I beg to the contrary, Sir Gulliver. You did what had to be done. Do not let anyone else judge you for your actions. If they must, then I will vouch for your integrity and honour. Your deeds were, indeed, heroic. You lit the signal fire and saved the boy.'

Gulliver wiped his eyes and stared in astonishment. 'Truly?'

'Proceed with the rest of your account,' Eribus merely said.

Gulliver nodded, and he let out a sigh of relief. He told of the escape into Milbrooke only to be ambushed by Captain Hargonnas. He did not want to conjure up the horrible memory of the dead bodies everywhere, or of Farina. He still had nightmares about that incident, and that was only when he was able to sleep at all. Insomnia was a large problem for him lately.

'The elves cut off the fingers of my right hand – my casting hand,' Gulliver said sadly, holding up the scarred stumps. 'I'm adapting to casting left-handed now, and I'm alive, so I suppose I should be thankful.'

'And I presume Lord Avenal rescued you the next day?' Eribus asked.

'Yes, my lord.'

'I have a few questions,' the Grandmaster began, his eyes boring into Gulliver, as if reaching for his innermost thoughts. Gulliver briefly wondered if anything else was being called into question. 'You mentioned a ship. You believe the boy named Kairos came here on a ship?'

Gulliver blinked. He did not expect this, either. Knowing that he wasn't in trouble, he relaxed enough to gingerly lift the glass of water from the desk and drink. 'Yes, my lord. He mentioned that Malus's army attacked his people at sea.'

'Did he say anything about his people?'

'No, my lord.' Gulliver looked elsewhere as he tried to remember. 'Come to think of it, the boy didn't say much. He was a quiet sort of lad.'

'How was his magic?' Eribus asked in a carefree tone, but his eyes showed intense focus.

Gulliver shrugged, then caught himself in the midst of the informal gesture. 'That was rude of me! Forgive me, my lord.' Upon seeing Eribus's casual wave, he bowed and continued, 'I never saw him cast a spell. He attacked an elf with a dagger, which I thought was odd. It worked, though.'

'Some people have very low levels of mana, and some never train in battle magic,' Eribus said offhandedly. 'Some rural citizens are ignorant of many spells and revert back to the primal methods of survival in lieu of magic.'

'Yes, milord,' Gulliver answered. 'The thought had crossed my mind, but there was something else...'

'Go on.'

'The boy was not only surprised, but seemed rather–' The young knight paused in recollection of the memory, 'rather perturbed when I cast a mere windcutter spell. You should have seen the look on his face, milord. It was as if he had never seen magic in his entire life.'

'Did he say anything?'

'No, milord,' said Gulliver. 'It was a mere observation of mine. Forgive me for speaking out on such a trivial matter.'

Eribus nodded and bared his teeth, which the young knight realised was supposed to be a warm, friendly smile, but looked more like a cunning grin. 'Quite the contrary, Sir Swift. You have done quite well, in fact.'

'I have, my lord?' It was on the tip of Gulliver's tongue to ask the Grandmaster about his fascination with Kairos: why the unknown boy was of interest to someone as important as the highest-ranking knight in existence. The voice of stern reasoning stopped the words in his throat. It was not his place to ask such questions, and his natural curiosity had also got him in trouble many times before. He decided to keep his mouth shut on the matter. As far as he knew, the Grandmaster was supposed to know everything that went on around him – even if it was about a lost boy from the middle of nowhere. He was the Grandmaster, after all.

'You fulfilled your duty at Cape Caipora to the best of your abilities and you displayed true courage and helped rescue a boy from the evil clutches of Malus. Now this very boy is seeking to become a Mana Knight, himself. If everything goes as planned, our ranks will welcome another exceptional member. This is all due to your perseverance and bravery.'

'I seek your pardon, my lord,' Gulliver said, forgetting himself again. The praise horrified him, and he felt the need to let the truth out. 'I was only trying to survive with the boy. I had no honour or bravery in any of this. I was sent to Cape Caipora because I fought with an archduke's son. Then I let the lighthouse fall into the enemy's hands.'

Eribus waved his hand for silence again. 'I've heard. You self-remonstrate too much, Sir Gulliver. If you had not fled Cape Caipora, you and that boy would be dead. No, you saved him and fulfilled your mission. You succeeded where Tanton had failed.' Eribus's expression darkened for a moment – so quick that Gulliver had almost missed it– 'And for that, I am offering you a promotion to Lion Knight, with your own quarters here in Gala Fortress. You will reside here in Syphax and answer directly to me.'

Now Gulliver was quite sure he was dreaming. He came here thinking he was going to the chopping block, and instead, he was getting rewarded with a promotion on top of that! He became so dazed with jubilance he didn't notice that Eribus was still talking to him.

'Did you hear my terms? I ask that you keep this matter of Cape Caipora and Kairos between us.'

'Oh, sorry,' Gulliver said, bowing apologetically. 'My lips are sealed, my lord,' he said emphatically, and meant it.

'Do you accept this offer?'

Gulliver hesitated. He hadn't exactly received the warmest of welcomes in Syphax, and he wasn't quite sure how the locals would accept him over time. Even with a promotion, his prospects of happiness seemed slim. But he dared not refuse the offer. The thought of offending the Grandmaster seemed the most terrifying of all, and what other choice did he have? His career as a Mana Knight, before coming to Numidia, had seemed bleak; it was only a matter of time before the Knighthood sent him to another whipping post like Cape Caipora.

'In case you were concerned about your status as an outsider, you will be accepted by the citizens of Numidia and treated with the utmost respect,' Eribus said, as if reading Gulliver's mind. 'The public ceremony of your promotion will ensure that. And as long as you're near me, that archduke will have no influence over you here. I will personally see to that.'

The young knight quickly thought the situation over. He didn't have much to consider. Less than a year ago, he was sleeping on a straw mattress in an old cottage at Cape Caipora, now he would have his own sumptuous quarters in the mecca of the Mana Knights – and near Grandmaster Eribus, of all people! Not to mention the image of the dark-skinned Numidian girls giggling coyly, which sent a shiver of excitement running through him. Perhaps he would enjoy it here; it was worth losing a few fingers for all of this.

'I accept,' he said graciously.

'Splendid,' Eribus responded. 'I shall make arrangements. Now if you'll go down and see Sir Vasteras, he'll show you to your new quarters. You are dismissed.'

Gulliver made a deep bow to the Grandmaster, a bow that was full of humility, gratitude, and sincerity, for his fortunes had suddenly changed for the better.

Eribus made no response or acknowledgement, but went back to the stack of parchments on his desk. His business with his guest was concluded.

Gulliver did not mind.

The now ecstatic knight walked (almost joyfully skipped) from the Grandmaster's quarters and shortly met with Sir Vasteras, who seemed equally surprised at the news of the promotion. However, if he had an opinion on the matter, he kept it to himself, and showed Gulliver to his new quarters, which were located in the north tower, and had a large bed with silk sheets and carpeted floors!

Only when Sir Vasteras had departed and shut the door behind him, Gulliver danced with joy, prancing around the room and whooping in delight. He planned to write to his family immediately. They would be proud; his friends would be surprised, and his rivals jealous.

Throughout the mixture of relief and joy that flooded Gulliver, he had one nagging thought at the edge of his mind. Why was Kairos so important to Eribus and Malus?

He quickly forgot the question when he walked into the washroom and realised that he also had his own bath tub.

# PART FOUR

## KNIGHT'S TEST

# CHAPTER TEN

### Star-apple Orchard

*Hobs love to attack unsuspecting travellers and raid hardworking farmers. They attack in large numbers and kill for fun. But you always know when they're about to ambush you, because you can smell them from a league away.*

*Ellie's Journal'*, Ellie the Adventurer

When he thought no one was looking, Kairos bit into a star-apple.

The star-apple trees grew exclusively in Ordonia and were harvested during the height of spring. The Ordonians, particularly the farmers of Vadost, exported the star-apples to neighbouring nations each year, thus the fruit was an important source of income for the economy. Kairos had learnt this during their briefing, but all of it bored him to the verge of sleep. The only thing that interested him about star-apples was the taste, which he was currently savouring in secret. Or so he thought.

'You're not supposed to be eating that!' Althea whispered.

'I'm hungry,' Kairos complained.

'You're always hungry,' she replied. 'If you get caught, that's considered stealing. They explicitly told us not to eat any star-apples found around the orchard because they belong to the farmers.'

'I won't get caught unless you keep it up,' he muttered, but he tucked the partially eaten star-apple into one of the pouches suspended from his belt. 'Besides, it was already on the ground.'

Kairos, Althea, and the rest of the squires gathered around Sir Flain near the star-apple orchard farm on the outskirts of Vadost. The sun had begun its descent, its light shining down upon the squires, their weapons gleaming in the rays. Most of them carried mana lances and wore leather cuirasses, though they did not bear the rank insignia found on knights; they were not knights, yet.

Only two squires did not carry the lances.

Shah proudly wore his wooden boomerang at his side. Sir Flain barred him from carrying a mana lance, deciding that anything with a sharp or pointy edge would be a safety hazard to Shah and everyone else in the class. The wooden boomerang was not lethal, Flain had determined. It had a blunt edge that might not even kill, or so the rest of the recruits hoped.

Kairos, on the other hand, demonstrated enough proficiency towards dismembering straw dummies, that Sir Flain allowed him to carry the sword on the expedition in lieu of the mana lance. Kairos grasped the hilt of the blade for reassurance. He could not stop shaking at the prospect of battle, not knowing whether it was fear or excitement. Unlike straw dummies, hobs dodged attacks and fought back.

Now Sir Flain stood in front of the squires, glowering at them with his cold blue eyes. The squires ignored him, focusing curiously on the three other knights standing behind him. Flain introduced them as Lady Beatrice, Sir Angevine, and Sir Sigfried. The three knights said nothing and regarded the class coolly. Sir Sigfried, the oldest-looking of the three, appeared bored and about to fall asleep.

'Listen up,' Flain yelled, jolting the squires' focus back towards him. 'As I have previously explained, we're here to kill hobs today.

They've been terrorising the farmers each year, and they multiply like rats. The Knighthood is overburdened with tasks by the local populace already, so they somehow passed this task onto you sots. First order at hand – Squire Shah! What are you reading?'

Shah looked up from a letter he was holding and saw that everyone had turned and was staring at him. He attempted to covertly tuck the letter away, but Flain waded through the mass of squires and appeared in front of him in an instant.

'You have a letter, eh?' He snatched the parchment away, much to the pudgy squire's horror. 'Why, it must be a really important letter for you to ignore my briefing. Let's see who it's from… Oh, it's from your mother.'

'Sir Flain, please,' Shah pleaded.

Flain cleared his throat. 'To my dearest Honeybear,' he read.

The other squires began to laugh. Even the three knights smiled. Kairos tried to suppress a grin, but failed.

'No laughing!' Flain yelled, his angry gaze burning into the squires. The laughter ceased, though several of them covered their mouths with their hands. Flain continued reading, 'How is my little strong knight doing? I am so proud of you! Have you been eating your peas and carrots like Mummy told you? Don't forget to brush your teeth before bedtime and check under your pillow for those vicious spriggans that like to bite you while you sleep. Everyone at home is doing well, except for your Uncle Debias. He cut down another tree that fell on top of him and trapped him. This time we did not find him for three days. Your cousin, Tarey, went to Vadost and caught the itch from a girl at the Pinch & Tickle. His wife is not happy about it, because he also spent all of his money there.'

The squires' cheeks bulged with stifled mirth. Sir Angevine and Lady Beatrice shook their heads in disbelief. A trickle of laughter escaped Kairos's mouth, and he instantly felt bad upon seeing Shah hang his head in shame. When Sir Flain finished the letter, he handed it back to Shah with a look of disgust, and marched back in front of everyone.

'Enough of this,' Flain said. 'We will patrol the star-apple orchards in divided groups. These ugly bastards can't see too well at night, and they're too cowardly to skulk about in broad daylight, so they usually come out just before sundown.

'We will divide the class into four expedition groups of three to four squires,' Flain continued. 'Each group will be led by a senior knight – as you can see behind me – to provide you with direction and assist you should the situation get out of hand. Just remember,' Flain said, seeing several worried faces in the group. 'It's okay to be afraid and scared, but it's panic that will kill you, not fear. Any questions?'

A few hands shot up.

Flain pointed. 'Yes, Claudius?'

'Can we choose our teammates?' he asked, looking pointedly at Althea, which for some reason irritated Kairos. Althea did not notice. She seemed too absorbed in her own worries.

'No. For the sake of balance, we will choose your team for you.'

There were some whispers of disappointment. Kairos was hoping to partner with Althea, watch over her. Maybe luck would pair them together.

'Any other questions?'

Kairos raised his hand.

'What is it, Squire Azel?' Flain demanded.

'Can the hobs use magic, sir?' Kairos was genuinely curious because he had never seen a hob before.

A few squires laughed, presumably at the ignorance of the question. Sir Flain slammed the butt of his mana lance into the ground. 'Silence! This is no laughing matter. No, they cannot use magic, but that doesn't mean you let your guard down. Now are there any more questions? No? Good. Now, fall in. We'll divide you into groups. From there, we separate and take our positions.'

The other three knights stepped forward to assist Flain in creating the groups. They began announcing the first team, which would be led by Sir Flain. Almost every squire cast furtive glances at Shah. Kairos knew what they were thinking. He was thinking the same. No one wanted to group with Shah. Kairos felt badly for him, but he knew the bumbling squire was a liability. As Flain said, Shah excelled at being creative with stupidity.

'The first team led by me,' Flain announced, 'will be Squires Akkitos, Azel, Urzen, and Shah.'

Vaughn silently worded a string of swear words, and Urzen looked to the sky dejectedly. The rest of the class breathed a sigh of relief, thinking that their chances of success had vastly improved.

Shah beamed with pleasure and sidled next to Kairos. 'H-hey Kairos, looks like we're on the same team. That's good, but I really didn't want to be under Sir Flain. He's really mean to me... He didn't have to read my letter to everyone, you know.'

'Yes, that was quite mean of him, Shah,' Kairos agreed, noticing that Althea was watching the knights and not him. He pulled the partially eaten star-apple out from his pouch and took a big bite.

Flain paced in front of the ranks, calling out more teams. Kairos tried to listen, but Shah continued mumbling. He looked quite nervous, scared even.

'What's wrong?' Kairos asked.

Shah looked around to make sure the other squires were out of earshot. 'D-do you think we could die today?' he asked in a low voice. 'Those hobs have weapons and what not.'

Kairos shrugged. 'It's a possibility.'

Shah paled. 'I-in that case, I'm glad to be on your team.'

'Why?' Kairos asked in surprise.

'Because you're the only one in class who isn't mean to me. Well, you and Althea, that is. But I get too nervous around her, so I'll just stick close to you.'

Kairos thought of the potential outcomes with Shah by his side and gave a long, deep sigh. He finished the star-apple without even tasting it and tossed the core onto the ground.

If any of the gods had survived the Celestial War, they were surely laughing at him.

                    *   *   *

'Keep it quiet,' Flain hissed. 'You lot make more noise than the damn hobs!'

Flain could barely control his anger. He constantly harangued Kairos's group from the start, griping about everything from their appearance down to their behaviour. Kairos assumed that Shah's presence put the knight in a foul mood, but Flain had enough irritation left over to yell at everyone else.

They sat on a hill in a copse of trees, waiting for the sun to dip behind the western mountains, bathing the landscape in a warm, orange hue that contrasted with the cold wind. The star-apple orchard looked peaceful and inviting now, perfect for a picnic, but as the dusk came, the trees cast long shadows that promised a more foreboding scene at night. Hobs would soon come out in numbers, looking to loot, maybe even murder.

The group was an odd combination, yet Kairos's heart swelled with pride in their presence. Gazing at them, he felt a kinship closer than anything he had ever felt with his fellow Einar. They had suffered through many trials together in the Academy, and now they would face danger together, maybe even die.

Vaughn nodded to Kairos when they took their position, but kept his distance. The friction from their fight still created an invisible boundary between them that neither dared cross. This was the closest contact Kairos had with Vaughn since their encounter during the festival.

Squire Urzen said very little. His quiet demeanour made him blend into the background, and Kairos knew very little about him; his previous attempts at conversation with the squire had resulted in one-worded answers or awkward grunts.

Shah made up for the lack of conversation with incessant prattling of his own, much to the consternation of Flain, who grabbed his neck and told him that he would crush it if he didn't learn how to quiet himself. Kairos paid little heed to them. Self-doubt clouded his mind. Could he contribute to the upcoming fight without mana? Or would he be useless? He traced his fingers on the triggering mechanics of his staff, remembering how helpless he was against the elves. He felt like a fraud, deceiving his team with his so-called fake magic.

The watching and waiting were making them increasingly anxious and irritable.

Below them were rows of star-apple trees, and a large red barn, surrounded by grass and heather. A small brook trickled nearby.

Flain broke the silence suddenly. 'Over there!' he pointed. They peered into the distance, and saw several figures darting from tree to tree.

The hobs had come out of hibernation for their springtime raid.

As they neared the barn, unaware of their observers from the hill above, Kairos was able to get a good view of them. He had never seen a hob before, and he immediately concluded that they were one of the ugliest creatures in existence – uglier than a kobold from Logres, even. The green-greyish skin gave them a sickly appearance, and large canines, protruding from their lips like venomous daggers, were stained dark yellow from rot. The hobs brandished clubs and various farm tools, such as scythes, knives, and hoes, which were apparently scavenged from previous raids. A small breeze from the northwest blew towards Kairos and his group, carrying the stench of the hobs with it. Kairos gagged even at this distance. The worst of latrines smelled better.

'Hold!' Flain whispered, raising his hand. 'Wait until they enter the barn. We may still have the element of surprise.'

The hobs lumbered along the gravel path towards the barn, muttering amongst themselves. One of them devoured a star-apple as he walked, and tossed the core into the trees where Kairos and others lay hidden. One by one, the hobs entered the barn. Kairos counted at least a dozen of them. Two remained by the door as lookouts. Their occasional backward glances towards their comrades demonstrated that they found more interest in what was happening inside the barn rather than outside. They voiced their displeasure in their strange guttural language.

The knight and the squires stood. Their enemies were within their grasp now. They could hear the sounds of crashing and breaking from inside. They would defeat the hobs and fulfil their task.

'Move forward,' Flain whispered. 'Now, while they are looting!'

Kairos looked around the star-orchard field one last time for any signs of other hobs, but saw none. He did see Flain's look of approval. He nodded and gripped his staff as the others brandished their mana lances. Shah wielded his boomerang and tried to adopt a serious expression, but only looked like he had stomach cramps.

As they approached the barn and the two hobs posted outside, a feeling of disquiet wrapped around Kairos like a warm blanket. He finally had a chance to mete out the pent-up rage that had been building inside of him.

Only Shah saw the look on Kairos's face, and he trembled.

\* \* \*

It was just before sundown.

Althea channelled mana into her mana lance, barely extending the crystal tip from its retracted length. She didn't want to waste her mana to experiment with it like the other squires in her squad were doing. 'I want to be at full strength when we meet the enemy,' she told them when they asked her about it.

Claudius made some biting comment towards her. Althea made a rude gesture she had seen him use when no instructors were looking. Her other squadmate, Cassie, laughed. She didn't like Claudius any more than Althea did. Claudius was about to make some retort or other when Lady Beatrice returned. They fell silent and came to attention.

'Listen up. We are patrolling the north end of the star-apple grove, by the bend in the river. Squire Carrow,' she gestured to Claudius, 'you take point.' Then, she pointed to Althea and Cassie. 'Squire Avenal, you're left flank. Squire Lee, you're right flank. I'll be rear guard. Take it slowly and communicate with the rest of us. Remember that you will probably smell the hobs before you see them. We'll eventually meet up with the other squads patrolling the grove along the western edge. Any questions? Now's the time to ask. None? Then move out.'

Althea moved to her position, about three metres to the left of the formation. Her leather cuirass creaked softly with every step. She hated wearing armour. She knew she needed it, but it smashed her boobs down. It wasn't usually too bad, except when she had to breathe, which she frequently had to do. Right now she was very nervous, this being her first real mission. She was doing more breathing than usual. She tried to keep it to shallow breaths.

Althea knew Claudius was point because he was the best in the squad at magic. He was also the strongest fighter. She and Cassie were expected to hold their own, but the point position was usually the first to run into trouble. She didn't mind the idea of Claudius being the first in trouble. She would come to his aid, of course, just as he would for her. But that didn't mean they liked each other.

As they slowly crept along, to their right the sound of the river grew until it burbled softly beside them. The smell of star-apples reminded Althea of Stella, and the thought saddened her. She would never again taste one of Stella's homemade star-apple pies. Althea took a deep breath, catching herself in her reverie. Thinking of the beloved dwarf now would do her no good, she had to focus.

They eventually found tracks. And another smell.

Claudius froze. Everybody froze, tension crackling in the air. 'Shit,' he whispered. 'I stepped in shit. Hob shit, I think.'

'I don't give a shit,' replied Lady Beatrice. 'Keep going. We're here to kill hobs, not worry about our pretty boots,' she hissed.

Nodding, Claudius continued slowly forward.

The grove was made up of dozens of neatly ordered rows of star-apple trees. Althea appreciated the symmetry, the way the trees lined up as they walked. The wind shifted, and the smell of ripening star-apples was replaced by the stink of body odour and rotten cheese. Even at a distance it was so strong she could taste it in the back of her throat. 'I smell hobs!' she said in a breathless whisper. Lady Beatrice made a few hand gestures to the squad, and they turned as a unit to follow the smell.

In the fading light, about thirty metres ahead, they could just make out several hobs huddled together against a pile of brush that was waiting to be hauled off to be burned. Claudius tensed. 'Wait,' said Lady Beatrice in an urgent whisper, 'get closer before you attack.' Claudius relaxed his shoulders a little and kept moving forward on silent feet. Althea wasn't surprised he was so good at being sneaky.

At ten metres away, they could clearly see half a dozen burly male hobs and several females. They were sleeping. Claudius began casting his lightning glyph. Althea quickly traced several symbols in the air, layering one on top of the other. Her knowledge of glyphs was top of the class, her artistic ability was in the top five. But her mana was probably last. She had to work to conserve mana. That's what this spell was for.

The crackle of Claudius's lightning broke the silence, making her jump. Clods of dirt fountained skyward and the screech of hobs dying filled the air.

'Avenal! Lee! Close in!' came Lady Beatrice's orders.

Her spell wasn't as quick or as flashy as the others, but as she finished the glyphs of the spell, the hob she was casting on thrashed on the ground, spasmodically clawing at its throat. A small crystal of ice blocked its trachea. Assuming the spell was a little tricky, but it only took a little knowledge of hob anatomy and a trickle of mana to do. Lady Beatrice seemed impressed, but her classmates less so.

As that hob died, another dropped from a low-hanging branch, landing in front of Althea just as she levelled her mana lance towards it. The hob had a crude spear, which it swung at her face. She managed to deflect the blow with her mana lance and, with a clumsy counterstrike, she cut into its forearm. It dropped the spear and turned, running away from the fight. Althea didn't want to look like a coward, running away from a lone injured hob. She followed.

Lady Beatrice called after her, 'Avenal! Stop!'

I can do this! I'm not afraid! Althea told herself. It was a single hob! She would finish it off and re-join the squad. She wasn't really prepared, though, for how fast a hob could run when death was on its heels, and she was having trouble breathing in the stupid armour. She was just about to catch the hob, she thought–

She didn't even see the rope as the hidden hobs pulled it tight. Her feet swung out parallel to the ground as she hit the rope with her neck, partially crushing her windpipe. She was seeing stars before she hit the ground. Flat on her back, she was helpless, and the hobs who set the ambush closed in. They were grinning, sharp teeth gleaming against their dark silhouettes.

Althea panicked, shut her eyes, and braced herself for the worst.

\* \* \*

'Remember, no fire magic.'

Flain was adamant about this; he had repeated the order many times throughout the day. Kairos's hopes sank, since his staff could do little else besides fire.

'Can we cast it away from the trees?' Shah asked.

'No!' Flain snarled. 'Don't use it anywhere. We don't need to destroy the farm.'

Shah rubbed his chin in thought, then opened his mouth. 'What if the hobs ran off the farm– Oof!'

Urzen elbowed Shah in the side, cutting him short.

'Hush, Shah,' Vaughn said, eyeing Flain's furious visage with trepidation. 'We're nearing our quarry. No more talking.'

As Flain's group approached, they almost gagged from the stench emanating from the two hob sentries by the barn door. Vaughn, who led the front of the group, pointed and signalled for the men to prepare themselves.

'Now!' Flain hissed, his moustache creasing upwards in a flicker of a smile.

Vaughn and Urzen cast first, drawing glyphs aimed at a set of boulders on the side of the main path. Kairos watched in wonder as two large rocks levitated into the air. It was great being on the side using magic. Another glyph by each squire sent the boulders flying toward the sentries at a high rate of speed.

Neither of the hobs noticed.

The first died upon impact; the rock slammed into his face with a sickening crack, crushing flesh, bone and brain. The other boulder fell short, crashing into the dirt and rolling to a stop in front of the second hob, who heard the sound and said something in the hob tongue. Upon hearing no answer, he walked over to his inert partner and knelt, scratching his head in puzzlement.

Urzen cursed under his breath.

'Dammit, you missed, Urzen!' Flain said quietly, no longer whispering. 'All right, Shah! You're up!'

The pudgy squire did not move. The remaining hob studied the boulders that had mysteriously appeared from thin air, and understanding dawned on his dull face as he looked around in alarm. Kairos wanted to move in, but Flain ordered him to wait. He clenched and unclenched his sweaty hands around the staff anxiously.

'Attack, you imbecile!' Flain yelled, very loudly, pushing the bumbling Shah forward.

The squire, plainly lost in terror and confusion, raised his boomerang and gave a haphazard toss toward the hob. Kairos watched its flight. It homed in towards the target in a figure-eight pattern, but the hob turned, suddenly noticing the boomerang and nimbly side-stepped out of the way. The boomerang began the return trip back with startling accuracy and speed. Under normal circumstances, a typical handler would have been prepared to catch it, but Shah stared at it dumbfounded, with his arms by his side, as the boomerang thwacked him in the head, knocking him onto his back. He lay unmoving, with his eyes rolled into the back of his head.

Flain pulled on his own hair and swore loudly, no longer caring whether the hobs heard him or not.

Kairos had already charged forward. He felt the cold, clarity of battle descend upon him. The remaining hob screamed something indiscernible at his friends inside the barn. Now the element of surprise was gone, and the squires were drastically outnumbered. Their only advantage was magic, which Kairos did not have, but he did have the staff. There was no time to think clearly about what he was doing. He'd made the decision almost before the idea had formed in his mind.

Flain yelled something in the background, as Kairos charged forward with no intention of stopping.

At the last moment, Kairos bore down onto the lone hob at the barn door, who stared at him with the realisation of imminent doom. The hob tried to jab his spear, but Kairos knocked it aside with his staff and slammed it into the unprotected head with a crushing sound.

As Kairos recovered, more hobs streamed out of the barn, surrounding him. He raised his casting glove up, pretending to trace a glyph in the air. The hobs paused, wary; they had apparently seen magic before. Kairos used their hesitation to raise his staff. He remembered Flain's warning: *no fire*. A bright light burst forth at the end and the hobs shrieked and backed away expecting the worse, but it was only a flare effect. Still, the hobs did not know the difference.

Kairos drew his sword with his other hand. There was anger in him – the image of Togram and Hargonnas flashed in his mind – and he brought his sword down hard onto the hob's neck, slicing through leather, skin, muscle, and bone. Blood splattered as Kairos pulled his sword towards him to free it, leaving the hob almost decapitated with its neck dangling by skin and a thin sinew of muscle. The body pitched forward onto the ground.

The other hobs, noticing that the flare did nothing, cautiously edged closer. The nearest lunged with a look of pure savagery, aiming his spear at Kairos's neck. Kairos parried the hard stroke with his sword and countered by slamming a fist into the hob's face. He followed with a powerful sword thrust into the abdomen. The blow was so vicious that Kairos was sure he stabbed completely through the hob. The hob's enraged expression changed to horror as it opened its mouth, revealing yellowed, rotting teeth, and then bright blood bubbled and spilled out. Kairos could smell the hob's putrid breath as it slumped to the ground.

More hobs surged forward before Kairos could extract his sword. He was outflanked at the barn entrance, and his teammates were still behind him. One hob swung its club, and Kairos barely raised his staff in time. He managed to block the attack, but the force of the blow nearly knocked the staff from his hand. Another hob grinned and thrust its spear at Kairos's unprotected midriff.

Something flashed. A crackling sound filled the air, and the spear-wielding hob dropped to the ground, charred and smoking with a revolting stench of burnt meat. Another burst of magic and more hobs dropped. The other foes looked beyond Kairos and then at each other. Kairos dared a look behind him and saw Vaughn, Urzen, and Flain casting spells. One hob yelled something, which Kairos assumed meant, 'Retreat,' and the hobs suddenly scattered, but not before Kairos freed his sword and chopped into the neck of one of them.

'After them!' Flain hollered. 'Don't let them escape!'

The battle dissolved into a pursuit. Only half a dozen hobs remained alive, but they dispersed and took off in opposite directions. Kairos chased after a pair, who were fast, but Kairos was faster, though he was beginning to breathe heavily. He caught one, slicing his sword into the hob's legs. The blow carried months of pent up aggression and shame, and the hob's legs buckled as it crashed into the turf, and Kairos began hacking away at the flailing creature.

The other hob continued running, but Vaughn suddenly appeared, traced a series of glyphs, and sent a lightning bolt into the back of a retreating hob. It gurgled and fell to the ground motionless.

Kairos gave a nod to Vaughn. 'Thanks.'

'You can thank me later,' Vaughn said, then raised an eyebrow when he saw the mangled hob that Kairos had killed. 'Wasn't that a bit excessive?'

'No.' Kairos chopped his sword down into the dead hob's head for good measure. Better to ensure it was dead. He was panting heavily, both from the exertion and the adrenaline rush.

Vaughn's hand involuntarily touched his face, his nose crooked since the fight with Kairos, as he stared at the mutilated hob. 'I'll say one thing for you, Azel,' he said solemnly.

Kairos looked up from the hob and met Vaughn's gaze, expecting trouble. 'What?'

'I'm glad that you're fighting on my side.' He smiled wryly. 'Come on,' he said slapping Kairos's shoulder. 'We have some hobs to finish.'

\* \* \*

Althea was on the verge of losing consciousness. She had trouble breathing from where the rope struck her windpipe. *I'm going to die*, she thought, expecting the rain of attacks to come.

The blows never came.

She didn't understand why the grins on the hobs' ugly faces became looks of anger and horror. She didn't understand what it meant when a large silhouette was suddenly standing atop of her, fighting off the nearest hobs. When she saw a hob aiming a makeshift arrow at her, she did remember that they liked to use poisoned weapons whenever they could. She tried to scramble to her feet. She heard the twang of the bowstring and the dull thud of the impact, but she didn't feel any pain. Assuming it hit her armour, she didn't worry about it right then, not that she had the time. Hobs were everywhere. She managed to stand and realised that Lady Beatrice had cleared a large circle around them.

Althea cursed her stupidity as she stood back to back with Lady Beatrice, levelling her mana lance at her enemies. She remembered that hobs liked to lay ambushes almost as much as they liked using poison. Now the hobs were grinning as they surrounded the pair. Lady Beatrice summoned forth magic, but one of the hobs lunged at her, forcing her to parry and interrupting the spell. The hobs were toying with them now, poking and prodding with wooden spears and clubs. It was only a matter of time before the pair would tire enough to drop their guard, Althea realised, and that's when the hobs would move in to kill. Lady Beatrice was already breathing labouredly behind her.

There was a flash of bright light. The hobs turned away from them in confusion. Their grins shifted to open-mouthed horror as myriad glowing projectiles tore into them like arrows. Many of the hobs screamed. Some fell to their knees whilst others collapsed. Althea seized the opportunity to lunge forward with her mana lance, piercing the belly of one of the vile creatures still standing. She stole a glance in the direction where the projectiles came from and saw Claudius and Cassie. She had never thought she would be happy to see Claudius. Another volley of glowing missiles – this one not as brilliant as the first – burst forth from Cassie's glyph and struck the remaining hobs.

All of the hobs were dead or severely wounded, except for one, which was limping away with a maimed leg – the lone survivor. It didn't survive long, because Claudius caught up with it and plunged his mana lance into its back with enough force that the tip protruded out its chest. The hob twitched and dangled as it choked on its own blood. Claudius flung the dying creature down and plunged the mana lance into its neck. Althea looked away, feeling sick.

'We tried to get here sooner, but we had to finish the other hobs back there,' Cassie explained.

'Sorry,' Althea muttered.

'Why'd you run off like that?' Claudius demanded. 'Didn't Lady Beatrice tell us to stick together?!'

Althea couldn't look at them. She was ashamed she had left her squad like that. Claudius's eyes held nothing but disgust. Cassie looked at Althea with disappointment.

As Althea turned to face Lady Beatrice, the pit of her stomach sank. She saw the arrow meant for her. A lucky shot, the arrow hit the seam in Lady Beatrice's armour; it had sunk several inches into her side. Even without the poison, this was a deadly wound. Lady Beatrice had crumbled to the ground and lay still.

Her eyes on Lady Beatrice's unmoving form, Althea said to no one in particular, 'This is all my fault.'

'Of course this is your fault,' Claudius bellowed. 'If you hadn't run off like that, then none of this would have happened!'

'I'm sorry!' she shouted, fighting back tears.

He glared at her, then, his voice dripping with venom, 'Your apologies won't fix this if she dies, Avenal. You never should have been out here. You'll never be a knight because of this, and it won't matter who your daddy is!'

'That's enough, Claudius,' Cassie intervened. 'Standing around and yelling about it isn't going to solve anything. We need to get help.'

'I'll go,' Althea offered.

'No!' Claudius yelled. 'You've done enough damage already. The last thing we need you doing is botching up another job. You stay here with Lady Beatrice and do nothing. Cassie and I will go and get Sir Flain. Maybe he can do something.'

Althea watched as the two split up to canvas the whereabouts of Sir Flain's group. She knelt down by Lady Beatrice and checked her vital signs. She felt a faint pulse, but her breathing was very shallow. The poison was spreading fast, Althea thought. Sir Flain was not going to make it in time.

With her finger, she began casting the forbidden glyph. She had studied the book Argent had given her and practised the technique in the late hours of the night. With the first stroke of the glyph, she could feel the mana hidden, trapped in the plants around her. She called out to them – to the lives she could feel thrumming with the power she needed to heal this injury. Almost of its own accord, the elven glyph continued to build, its rounded edges so different, yet so similar, to Ordonian glyphs. The wound. The poison. So much to heal. She knew she could do this.

She silently called on the life all around her. There was so much life around her. It responded! Power filled her – much more power than she had ever experienced. Her senses sharpened to a painful clarity. She could see and count every one of the fine hairs along Lady Beatrice's jawline. She could hear the slowed heartbeat within her chest. Althea felt the breath, almost gone, as it moved in and out of Lady Beatrice's nostrils. All that life she pushed into the glyph. As she completed the spell, the glyph flashed so brightly that Althea was blinded. The joy of it was ecstasy.

All of her doubts washed away.

She had done the right thing.

* * *

Sir Flain was drenched in sweat. All the squires were, except Shah, who still lay unconscious at the edge of the copse of trees near the barn. No one had bothered to check on him.

'I thought I was clear about fire magic?' Flain glowered at Kairos.

They all stared at the charred hob corpse, small wisps of flame still flickering about the blackened mound.

'You could have set the whole orchard ablaze, Squire Azel.' Flain was not happy with Kairos's breach of discipline, but he had to admit that the squire's action had prevented the hob from escaping. Urzen and Vaughn had drained most of their mana on the other hobs, and Flain had been too far away to finish the job himself, so Kairos used a fireball from his staff to strike the last retreating hob from a distance. It had been a foolhardy thing to do, but Flain knew the gods – if any were still around and watching over them – smiled on the brave.

'Should we tend to Shah?' Urzen asked.

'Yes,' Flain answered. 'Go check on him. Make sure his head injury isn't too serious, though I doubt he can further damage that addled brain of his.'

The hob corpses lay scattered about the orchard. Urzen had found some shovels in the barn, and Flain made Kairos bury them all. It seemed fitting, as he was the one who disobeyed orders. Still, the expedition was a success, and all the squires except Shah had performed so well that Flain's anger had already dissipated. He said nothing when Vaughn began helping with the burials, moving mounds of dirt with his remaining magic.

Flain eventually went where Urzen hovered over Shah and roused the unconscious squire with a minor healing spell. He woke with a start.

'W-what happened?'

'Well done, Squire Shah,' Flain said, his voice dripping with sarcasm. 'You successfully defeated yourself in combat.'

Shah smiled, uncomprehending and dazed. 'I did?'

Flain did not answer. He looked up at Urzen, who stood by attentively. 'Squire Urzen, keep watch for the rest of us,' he ordered, peering off in the distance. 'There may be other hobs around. Otherwise, good work.'

'Yes, sir!' Urzen shouted, then ran up the hill where he had a better vantage point.

The paladin nodded to himself. These squires were coming along, except for Shah, whom Flain decided was going to clean the entire barracks with a toothbrush after this. The other three still had much to learn, but they were ready to become knights. The only thing that was left was the test. His gaze fell on Kairos, more especially on his glove and the staff. Something was suspicious about those items. He was about to question the squire, when a shout interrupted him.

'Sir Flain!' It was Squire Urzen. 'Someone approaches from the northeast.'

They all turned their heads towards the approaching figure – except Shah who scanned the west.

Whoever it was ran with urgency. Flain felt a sense of unease as he waited. He could see, in the evening light, the glowing tip of a mana lance bobbing as the figure ran towards them. Was someone in trouble? The other squires stopped what they were doing and approached Flain. They, too, were concerned.

Then they saw it was Claudius. He stopped short of Flain, panting heavily and pouring sweat.

'What's going on, squire?' Flain demanded. 'Report.'

'It's...It's...' Claudius paused to catch his breath. 'It's... Lady Beatrice!'

Flain took a step forward. 'What about Lady Beatrice?'

'S-she's been gravely injured... Hobs ambushed us!'

'Where are they?' Flain asked.

'The north end of the star-apple grove, near the bend in the river. Squire Avenal fell into an ambush when she—'

Kairos took off.

'Wait, Squire Azel!' Flain called, but Kairos continued running.

The paladin swore and ran after him, towards Lady Beatrice's group. First Shah, and now an ambush. He was getting too old for this.

* * *

Lady Beatrice sat up, shock painting her features, as she picked up the arrow that had nearly killed her. The healing had pushed it out of her side.

Something fell, startling Lady Beatrice and Althea. It hit with a wet thump, smelling like rotten fruit. Then more of the things fell, like ripples in a pond when a stone is thrown in. The ripples were travelling out from where Lady Beatrice and Althea were.

Althea realised, with curiosity, that the star-apples were falling. She looked up to see that the leaves had shrivelled and blackened, their branches twisted and curled in a sickly manner. The star-apples had all suddenly rotted.

'Althea!'

Althea looked up. The voice belonged to Kairos, and she felt a swell of warmth rush through her upon the sight of him.

'Althea, are you all right?' He ran up and embraced her tightly.

'Y-yes,' she said, returning the embrace, still looking around in confusion.

As she tried to make sense of it, Sir Flain strode up to the pair, taking long strides. His plate mail gleamed in the last remnants of the sunlight. 'Oh, no, no, no... You stupid little girl! Do you have any idea what you've done?' The abject disgust on his face confused Althea.

'What do you mean?' she asked, feeling rather hurt and offended. 'She would have died otherwise. I saved her!'

'You have used the forbidden magic.' The force of his eyes falling on her made Althea flinch back in fear. 'You've destroyed the life in this orchard. Destroyed! Your forbidden magic has tainted this grove.' Then his eyes widened. 'Where did you learn this magic from? Tell me where!'

Althea did not answer. She lowered her gaze, refusing to meet Flain's penetrating stare.

*　*　*

Althea's boots clicked softly as she walked the Gauntlet. Sir Flain had ordered her to report to his office. That was hours ago. Now, she could hear him shouting at Shah from the small building. Even the other instructors had fled before the storm of his anger, and Althea would rather have been going to her execution.

'I've never seen someone as inept enough to knock himself out with his own weapon. Did you train to be so stupid, Squire Shah, or does it come naturally?'

In the brief silence, she heard Shah's voice, sounding very small, 'Well, I...'

'The question was rhetorical, Squire Shah! You can't even stand there and get chewed out properly? Don't answer that! Shut your mouth! Do you have any idea that your mere existence is a liability to this Order? Don't ignore the question, Squire Shah! Answer me!'

'I...'

'Shut it! You obviously haven't a clue!'

This went on for several more minutes. Althea's knees were shaking, and she thought she might faint.

When the door opened, she gave a small squeak of surprise. She had been so consumed by her thoughts, she hadn't noticed Sir Flain had quit yelling.

As Shah walked out, Althea walked in. He whispered to her, 'I think he's angrier than usual, Avenal.' His eyes held worry for her.

'Could you please shut the door, Squire Avenal?' Sir Flain asked softly. 'And have a seat.'

Althea froze. She had expected a different kind of greeting. A louder one. A more insulting one. One more like... Well, more like Sir Flain. She sat in the wooden chair across the desk from the paladin.

'I know you think you healed Lady Beatrice. Where did you learn to do that from?' he asked.

Althea thought of the spellbook that Argent had given her, but she would say nothing of it. 'From a book,' she said quietly.

Sir Flain asked, 'What book? Do you know the crime you've committed? That the elves would take you away, question you at length, and execute you if they ever found out what you've done? You have committed unsanctioned use of a forbidden art and have done so in such a blatant manner.'

Dumbfounded, Althea could only blink. *All that because I healed someone?*

'If it was allowed, don't you think the Academy would teach classes on healing?'

'I didn't... I never...'

Sir Flain lifted a hand, stopping her from continuing. 'I understand. You chased the hob to show you were brave and useful. So brave and useful that you ran straight into a hob ambush. A hob ambush I, myself, taught the class on how to recognise and avoid. But you did not recognise it. You did not avoid it. You did not show yourself to be brave or useful. And, in the process, you got Lady Beatrice seriously wounded. Your squadmates had to clean up your mess. And, worst of all, you tried to heal Lady Beatrice.'

Hurt and angry, Althea looked Sir Flain in the eye. 'I did heal her. You saw she was healed. She would've died otherwise.'

'No. You are not sanctioned to heal because you are not trained to heal. Had you been trained, you would have known that improper healing – what you did – can cause your spirit, and hers, to rot. The living body with a rotted soul can become a terrible thing. You irrevocably destroyed a major section of the star-apple grove you were supposed to protect. You could have corrupted Lady Beatrice's soul along with your own. What you performed back there was tantamount to necromancy. What in the names of the gods of creation do you have to say for yourself?'

Althea sat in silence. She couldn't breathe. Everything she had tried to do she had worse than failed at. The walls of the office seemed to close in on her, trapping her. Vaughn, Claudius and Nacole had been right about her all this time. She was dangerous to those around her. She decided she had to leave. Leave the Mana Knights. Leave Valour Keep before she hurt anyone else.

She had to run.

Flain recognised the pained look on her face, saw her feet move towards the door.

'Stop right there, Avenal!' he commanded, his booming voice freezing her in place. 'Since you insisted on travelling down this trail of stupidity, there's something you should know. Now follow me.'

Althea listened. She had no other choice. All Flain had to do was write up a report of her unsanctioned use of healing magic and her prospects of becoming a knight would come to an end. She could run away or face her fate head on, so she decided to see everything until the end.

The paladin opened the side door of his living quarters, which led into his infamous flower garden, the literal root of the 'Flower Flain' moniker whose mention caused veins to bulge out of the knight's neck in large, pulsating branches. They walked amongst neat rows of flowers and all varieties of exotic plants that Althea could not name. He opened the door to the greenhouse which housed the plants more sensitive to the colder weather.

'What's this?'

'Isn't it obvious?' he said caustically. 'It's my flower garden.'

'I know that, Sir Flain,' Althea said with the utmost respect. 'But why are you showing it to me?'

'Training,' he said, picking up a trowel and a watering can.

'Training?' Althea was confused. She was half-expecting to till the soil and water the plants in lieu of expulsion from the Knighthood. But how would this suffice as training? Unless he was going to teach her gardening because he was too lazy to tend it himself. That sounded like something Flain would do, Althea decided. He probably hated her with a passion.

But Flain had other plans.

'You're going to cast that healing spell and draw upon the inherent mana residing within these plants.' Flain pointed to a cluster of common Ordonian daffodils. 'Starting with these.'

'You want me to–' Althea began, shocked.

'Did I stutter, Squire Avenal?' Flain shouted. 'You will practise your healing spell – and don't overdraw, mind you! Doing so will kill them, and if you do that, I'll have you dig me some new ones from the forests outside of Vadost, so I suggest you draw carefully.' As he yelled at Althea, he watered a few of the plants, and inspected a row of dragon lilies, whose petals looked like scales. His rough, calloused hands gently caressed each plant like a loving father. Althea thought the tender gesture contrasted with the scowl on his face and almost giggled aloud, forgetting her dire situation.

'So that's why you have the flower garden!' Althea said in sudden understanding. 'It was for training because you're a paladin and you needed to practise your healing magic! All this time, everyone called you Flower Flain because they thought you were some daft looney who enjoyed flowers too much and–' Althea suddenly stopped, horrified at what had she blurted out. 'Oh dear, I'm sorry–' she began.

'That's not *at all* why I have a flower garden,' Flain snapped, his voice taking on its usual irritated edge.

'I didn't mean...' Althea couldn't finish. She had to open her loud mouth; Stella had often told her that she couldn't keep it shut enough.

'And I know what you meant, and I know what the others say behind my back, and I don't care.'

GODSHARD CHRONICLES: VOL. 1

'Why did you start this garden then?'

Flain stopped his inspection of the dragon lilies and stared in Althea's direction, although he seemed to be looking off somewhere else. The moustache quivered, and she thought she detected a faint smile. His next words surprised her. 'I didn't,' he said. 'My wife did.'

'Your wife?'

'Hilda. She loved collecting flowers from throughout the world. You should have seen her garden at our old house in Ordon.' Flain smiled at the memory. 'She would make me accompany her on these outlandish excursions to find the rarest species.'

Althea felt uneasy. 'Sir Flain, you mention her in the past tense.'

Flain nodded. 'She fell ill one day. The doctors couldn't do anything and the closest healer lacked the skill to remove her sickness. I summoned a high-ranking cleric, but he couldn't arrive in time.

'Before she died, she made me promise to continue tending her garden,' he muttered sadly. 'She said it would break her heart to see all of her plants wither and die.'

Althea nodded and thought of those many horrible jokes of 'Flower Flain' she had made behind his back to the other squires. The memory made her burn with a profound shame, and she dearly wished she could unsay those cruel words.

'I wasn't very good at gardening,' he continued. 'Many of the flowers died. So I took to the library to study botany, and I visited the numerous gardens around the capital. I eventually became better, and soon, I had one of the most impressive gardens in Ordon. A healer came by one day and asked to train in my garden, and that was when I took an interest in healing.' He paused and looked at Althea. 'Because, had I known some good healing spells, maybe my wife would be here today.'

Althea was silent for many heartbeats. She didn't deserve to be here, and she hoped that Flain's wife hadn't been watching from the afterlife, hearing all those horrible things she had said about him. 'Sir Flain, I don't deserve to train here,' she said finally.

'Nonsense,' he snapped. 'Hilda would want this. You see, after all these years, I came to the realisation that she made me tend to this garden so I wouldn't mope around after her death. I think she knew that I would take up healing to help others, and sure enough, I did. I became one of the few paladins in the Knighthood.'

'Is that how you came to Valour Keep?' Althea asked.

'Yes, I came here as a healer,' Flain said, then added brusquely, 'Although I once again lost many flowers during the move. Still, I managed to save several lives with my healing spells here, including Sir Hugo's. That's why you need to study healing the *appropriate way*.' He gave her a menacing look as he emphasised the latter part of the sentence. 'I just wonder where you obtained knowledge on that spell you cast.'

If there was such thing as having a bucket of guilt, Althea's would be overflowing by now. But for some reason, she could not bring herself to utter Argent's name. The professor would face dire repercussions if word got out that he had given her access to forbidden magic.

'Bah, there's no need to say anything for now,' Flain said. 'We're here to train.'

Guilt quickly changed to horror. 'But Sir Flain, I don't want to kill the flowers! You saw what happened at the star-apple orchard.'

'And that won't happen this time, I assure you,' Flain growled.

'But your wife's flowers—'

Flain cut her off. 'She would be happy knowing that her garden helped you train towards a greater cause. Now hurry. We have a lot of ground to cover and very little time until the Knight's Test.'

The knight gestured to the daffodils. Though he appeared irritated, Althea saw something else in his eyes: concern.

'Now cast the same elven glyph that you did at the grove,' he ordered.

Althea turned inward, to the very core of her being, and traced the forbidden glyph. She silently vowed to be as delicate as possible. *Feel the energy. Do not force it!*

As the spell took effect, small tendrils of mana rippled faintly around her. She grasped towards the direction of the Ordonian daffodils – gently, taking care to not harm them – and allowed a trickle of the mana to flow into her being. This time was different to the last. Instead of 'ripping' the mana from her surroundings, she felt a sense of harmony.

'Go easy,' Flain urged. 'Now trace the next glyph and return the mana.'

Althea's senses sharpened to where she could feel every petal, the pollen, and the dew on the flowers. She traced the glyph and a soothing wave flowed from her back into the daffodils, taking her breath away. She slumped forward and panted.

The transfer was complete.

Althea raised her head, feeling quite drained. Perhaps she had made a mistake. 'How was it?' she asked.

Flain nodded approvingly. Another rarity for Althea. 'Well done, Avenal. You're a quick learner.'

'What's next, then?' asked Althea. She was tired. It was late. She had fought hobs, drained herself with magic, and came to the Gauntlet for a tongue-lashing from Flain. She wanted nothing more than sleep.

'We train some more,' barked Flain, taking on the commanding voice he used for class. 'Now cast it again. This is your punishment detail.'

* * *

It was early morning in late spring. Too early.

The squires peered bleary-eyed at the bundle of sealed letters on a table in the training hall. The very sight jerked most of them awake. Those squires knew that, rolled up and bound together by a wax seal, with the crystal emblem of the Mana Knights imprinted on it, their fate awaited. Others, like Kairos and Shah, were ignorant of that fact and stared sleepily ahead, annoyed at the early morning interruption.

Sir Flain stood next to the desk and addressed the class.

'As you all know, not everyone can be a Mana Knight. Few have the strength of character to even try. Many with the strength still don't finish training. Even some who finish are deemed, for one reason or another, to be unfit for final testing.'

He scanned the gathered squires, making eye contact with each one of them.

'Shortly you will each receive a letter – either a letter of invitation to the Trial of the Chair, or a letter of dismissal.' Several squires murmured and shuffled their feet. Sir Flain glowered and continued on more loudly. 'Understand that dismissal at this point is not a reflection on your character or ability. It is strictly for your safety. If you are dismissed this morning, you are to pack your belongings and move out of the recruit barracks by this afternoon.'

A solemn air descended upon the gathered squires. Most looked glum. Shah yawned, looked around, saw the serious expressions on his classmates' faces, and took on what he believed to be a stern expression.

'Is there a problem, Squire Shah?' Flain asked, noticing the squinted face. 'You look like you need a latrine break.'

'No, sir!' Shah responded shamed-face.

Flain continued, 'If you receive your letter of invitation, you must schedule your test with Sir Agama, who will conduct the Trial of the Chair. You must be tested within three days from today. Deciding not to do so will be taken as a sign of your resignation.'

He held up a sealed letter and announced, 'Squire Carrow.'

Claudius straightened, pompous and smug, and walked forward to retrieve his letter. Upon returning to his place, the squire broke the wax seal and opened it. He gave no reaction, only stared at the letter quietly. One by one, the rest of the squires followed when their name was called.

'Squire Azel!' Flain shouted. 'Are you listening?'

'S-sir!'

Kairos's thoughts swirled as he stepped forward. He knew failure during the Trial of the Chair meant death. That was what 'for your safety' meant. He knew his letter could only be a letter of dismissal. But how could he help the Einar if he didn't test? And, if he did test, how could his death help anyone?

'Squire Azel, kindly approach any day now, take your letter, fall back into your position, and *then* you can continue to look like a poleaxed grass carp. A few more people, the entirety of the class, in fact, would like to receive their letters so that they may get on with their lives,' said Sir Flain.

Everyone was looking at Kairos.

'Sorry, Sir Flain.' Kairos hurried to collect his letter. He didn't open it. Why even bother?

*   *   *

'I'm thinking of testing tomorrow,' Althea said to Kairos later that day.

They sat in straight-backed, wrought iron chairs outside the barracks, and avoided talking about the ones who had been dismissed.

Claudius had already packed all his belongings. Kairos decided he wouldn't miss him. Another squire he didn't really know was gone, too. He thought her name was Le'Anna Verdona. He wasn't sure.

'Well? When are you testing?'

'I…' Kairos shifted uncomfortably before continuing. 'I don't know. I haven't opened this bloody thing yet.' He produced the letter, showing Althea the unbroken wax seal as proof. He didn't meet her stare.

'Why ever not?'

'Because it's a letter of dismissal.'

'How would you know that?'

'Because I know it's a letter of dismissal!' He stood and paced with frustration. 'I can't be a Mana Knight.'

'Kairos, I don't understand,' said Althea, now looking considerably concerned and visibly upset. 'What are you on about?'

'Would you quit asking me questions? I told you that I can't be a Mana Knight. Look – I have no mana.'

There. He'd said it. He had finally let it out. No more harbouring secrets. Now she would know that he was god-cursed, and hate him for being a liar.

Althea looked around. No one was within earshot. 'Well maybe you had better explain to me,' she said more quietly.

'Did I ever tell you where I come from?' Kairos didn't wait for her answer. He knew he hadn't told her. He leant in closer. 'I am an Einar. From across what you call the Dark Sea. That is why everyone here thinks my accent is strange and different. It's because I *am* different. To you Ordonians, I'm quite big, tall, and fit. Amongst the Einar, I'm scrawny – 'the runt of the litter', as you would say.'

Althea blinked. She looked stunned by this new information. Kairos forged ahead.

'Shortly after coming here, I took the Badger's Trial. Professor Argent told me that I'm god-cursed. I can't cast spells because of it. I don't have mana because of it.' He paused. 'That's why I cannot be a Mana Knight.'

'And it's not just me,' Kairos continued. 'No other Einar can use magic. The first time I witnessed this miracle was when I came to this land – this beautiful land full of greenery and life. I've also learnt that people like me are called the god-cursed. And after seeing your people cast miracle after miracle, I believe it. Your land and people are thriving whilst mine are dying. Maybe that's why Malus and his men attacked us. Maybe that's why they're trying to kill me – because I *am* cursed. I've brought nothing but misfortune since coming here.'

There was a long moment of silence. Kairos felt a strange sense of calm after telling his story, as if a suffocating pressure had dissipated. Even in his melancholy, his breathing became easier. Althea regarded Kairos with a look of horrified wonder.

'I see.' Her expression suddenly changed to indignant. 'You idiot! Are all Einar, as you call yourself, so stupid? You couldn't have mentioned this earlier?'

Kairos regarded her in astonishment. Of all the possible reactions Althea could have had, this wasn't one he had prepared for. 'Well, no! I didn't tell anyone.'

'I'm not anyone!' Althea seethed. 'You should have known you could trust me!'

'Galen told me not to tell anyone.'

At the mention of her father's name, Althea grew quiet. 'He said that?'

'Yes. I wanted to tell you a long time ago.'

She punched him in the arm. He grunted for her benefit. 'You still could've told me. Father is not always right, you know.'

'Well, now I have. What are we going to do?'

She smiled softly before smoothing her features. 'First, we're going to open your letter.' He held it up. Althea took it and broke the seal.

She read the letter quickly, gravely. Kairos didn't breathe. She lowered the letter, serious eyes meeting his. 'I don't know why I'm still amazed by how much of a fool you are.'

Kairos stared back.

She showed him the letter and said excitedly, 'You made it — you're in!'

Kairos blinked, and snatched the letter back. 'Let me see. That's not possible.'

'Well, it says so,' Althea stated. 'They know what they're doing. They may not know your background, but they know you're the proper material for becoming a Mana Knight. And so do I. Now let's get you scheduled with Sir Agama to be tested.'

For the first time since he had crossed the sea, Kairos's spirits soared. Elation and hope bubbled inside him for once—elation he did not deserve. Many lives had been sacrificed so he could get this far: Thylar, Karthok, Farina, and the entire crews of the *Wolf Fang*, *Sea Serpent*, and *Grenda*. He dared not let them down now, leave their sacrifices in vain.

'There is one thing I'm curious about,' Althea said, pulling him from his reverie. 'I have seen you cast spells in class.'

'You're right,' Kairos agreed. 'I did.'

'They were fire spells to be exact,' Althea observed. 'Quite a number of them, actually. They always came from that shoddy-looking staff.'

'They did.' He looked sidelong at Althea. 'Are you ready for it?'

For the first time since Stella's death, Althea began to laugh. Joyous laughter full of mirth and merriment bubbled up. When she caught her breath long enough to speak, she started laughing again. 'I am,' she said, 'though I'm sure Jomur wouldn't be too pleased that you duped him for so long.'

'Gnome powder.' Kairos pretended he was holding the staff and performed a demonstration. 'Mr. Dubose gave me the staff, and he placed triggers on it that detonated the charges.'

'And he made the glove that helped you draw glyphs,' Althea finished for him.

'Yes.' Kairos grinned. 'Tricked you all this time, didn't I?'

'Me and the whole lot of 'em!' said Althea, laughing some more.

# CHAPTER ELEVEN

## Trial and Test

*In order to become a Mana Knight, a squire of the Academy must take the Knight's Test, which is divided into two phases: The Trial of the Chair, and the Test of Valour. Failure of either phase can result in the death of the squire, but that is the risk the Knighthood imposes to weed out the weak and the corrupt.*

*The History of the Mana Knights',* Sir Edwin Rosal

**K**airos swallowed hard. He stood in a large chamber on the highest floor of the tallest tower of Valour Keep. Two other squires accompanied him: Vaughn and Shah. They all wore the ceremonial robes that was mandatory for testing. Before them was a chair made of orichalcum, and above them was the Sapphire Shard.

They were the last of the squires to take the Trial of the Chair. The others had already taken it, and everyone so far had passed and was awaiting further instructions. Kairos and Vaughn stared wide-eyed and awed around the chamber. Only Shah seemed oblivious of his surroundings, his feverish gaze focused solely on the chair.

The chamber was an eerie place. Eddies of magic pulsated and swirled about the room in a spectacular show, accentuated by an occasional flare from the Sapphire Shard. The squires could feel the intensity of the magic energy, and Kairos was almost brought to his knees in such a raw display of power. The other knights had told them that the energy came directly from the godshard, which was suspended directly above, but that knowledge provided little comfort to the squires.

The power of a fallen god awed and frightened them, as was evident in Vaughn's pallor and Shah's uncontrollable shaking. Kairos knew that the godshard, which glowed a bright sapphire colour, was part of Zemus's essence. Gazing about the room in wonder, he wondered if the god was even dead. He felt that the energy could coalesce back into some supernatural form at any moment and come to life. Even the room felt alive.

The older, more experienced knights who administered the annual Trial had grown accustomed to vibrant strands of magic that flowed unchecked around them. One of knights in attendance was Sir Flain, who consulted with another knight, Sir Agama, for preparations, and several others, whom Kairos did not know, assisted. There were no instructors or professors here, as the Knighthood did not allow non-knights to enter the chamber.

The three squires stood, waiting for what they hoped would be the beginning of their new lives as a Mana Knight. They tried not to think that it might be the last day of their lives.

When one of the magical eddies collided with the chair, causing a brief flash coupled with a loud crackling sound, Shah jumped, with the flailing of white robes, and let out a high-pitched squeal.

'Hush!' Sir Flain's voice was booming and echoing in the chamber.

'D-d-do people die in that chair?' Shah asked in a quivering voice, oblivious to Sir Flain's command.

'Yes, Squire Shah, people sometimes die in the Trial of the Chair.' Sir Flain said with a sigh. 'It has been a few years since anyone died, though. We have long disallowed the unqualified from taking the Test – to prevent unnecessary deaths – but that doesn't mean a few slip through the cracks. Don't worry. You might make it out alive.'

Shah was not satisfied with the answer. 'Sir Flain, what does the chair actually do?'

Sir Flain's face became a blank mask. Kairos knew this meant he was irritated, but not yet enough to start yelling.

'The chair has abilities beyond our understanding,' Flain said tersely. 'Some speculate that it judges one's life as a whole. Those who live good, honourable, and righteous lives will survive.' He shrugged. 'Those who do not, will die. It is the only way to become a Mana Knight. No one will be forced to undergo the Trial of the Chair. When it is your turn, you either take the Trial, risking death, or you do not, and are expelled from the Mana Knight Academy.' Shah was about to ask another question, but Flain cut him short. 'We have been through all of this in class. Expulsion is permanent, Squire Shah.'

Shah bit his lip. He was sweating profusely now.

Sir Flain's gaze lingered on him, and after a moment, the paladin decided to elaborate – one *more* time – for the benefit of the squire. 'I want to stress that expulsion in this manner is not considered a black mark on your record. It's not easy to face death. No one will think less of you.'

'B-b-but is this actually n-necessary?' Shah asked. 'I-I mean, I lived a good, and honourable, and righteous life. I've never stolen anything. I don't see why–'

Kairos elbowed Shah in the side. One of the veins on Flain's neck began bulging out, and Kairos wondered if the paladin was about to murder the bumbling squire before he had a chance to sit in the chair.

Sir Flain took a deep breath. 'If you must know, Squire Shah, the Trial of the Chair not only judges you, but it gives out your next quest: the Test of Valour. That quest is more dangerous, resulting in more deaths than the chair.' Anticipating another question from Shah, Flain hurriedly answered, 'It *is* necessary, Squire Shah, as your quest is decided by a higher power than what we mortals can provide. It has been this way for centuries. You may consider this a blessing, as it removes all decisions of politics that are commonly associated with mortals. This has been ordained by the founder, Grandmaster Burise.'

If Sir Flain had intended to calm Shah, his words had the opposite effect. Kairos was concerned that Shah might faint right then and there in front of the chair. He tried to ignore the squire's presence, whose nervousness was infecting Kairos's own fears. There was no reason he should be afraid. He was chosen to partake in the test, and the letters siphoned out those who were likely to fail. He had performed the best he could in the classes, and Professor Argent and Sir Flain explicitly told him that he had no reason to fear.

But Kairos alone knew his own doubts. And secrets.

The Knighthood was unaware he had no mana; that he was a liar who had slipped into the ranks of the Mana Knights undetected, deceived everyone on a daily basis in the Academy, and was only using the Knighthood as a means to an end. That end was to bring his people, the Einar, to the mainland, where he knew they would continue their warring ways. He felt trapped. There was no way to trick this chair. No way to trick something operating under a higher power.

According to Professor Jomur, the chair was a celestial artefact crafted by Zemus, himself, because only the gods could make or work with orichalcum. No one really knew how the chair came here, and Kairos often questioned the authenticity of Jomur's research. Other accounts show that the founder of the Mana Knights, Grandmaster Burise, had introduced it as a method of discerning the loyalty of the initiates and offering the Test of Valour to assess a candidate's courage and skill. There was speculation that he made a pact with a god (assumedly Zemus) before the Celestial Wars to receive the chair, but no two historical documents ever came to the same conclusion.

The chair did not look extraordinary. The yellow metal appeared rather uncomfortable. It gleamed and shimmered under the swirls of magic in the chamber, but appeared lifeless and incapable of 'judging' anyone.

Yet, people had died sitting on that chair. The fates of many squires were decided upon that chair.

The reputation of the Trial of the Chair had soon spread across the kingdoms of Alban. The Knighthood flourished with virtuous candidates, thus earning the trust of most of the populace. Even the Salforian elves recognised the Knighthood as a prominent order, and accepted it into their kingdom, opening a Mana Knight stronghold near the elven capital for their own to join the prestigious ranks.

There were only two races that the chair did not recognise: dwarves and gnomes. Whenever they attempted to sit on the chair, an unseen force would propel them off. Apparently, the chair needed a person with mana to subject him or her to the trial. Therefore, the leaders of the Knighthood could not establish whether a dwarf or gnome was a proper candidate, so they banned the two races from entering the Knighthood altogether. Most gnomes and dwarves were not bothered in the least. Their attitude about the matter was simple: why bother to become a Mana Knight when one has no mana in the first place?

How did Grandmaster Burise ever come up with the idea for the Trial of the Chair? No one could say. Certainly, none of the knights living today. The only thing the Knighthood could say for sure was that there were only two such chairs in existence: one here in Valour Keep and the other in Gala Fortress.

So Kairos pondered the history of the Trial of the Chair. In his mind, he was already doomed. But he could not turn back now. He could only wonder if the chair would reject him outright from the beginning like a gnome or dwarf, or strike him dead during the trial.

Sir Agama raised a hand indicating that he was ready, and Flain nodded his head in acknowledgement. The paladin took his place next to the chair and moved briskly on to the business at hand.

'When your name is called, step forward and take a seat on the chair. That is when your testing will begin. You should, by now, be familiar with the procedures,' said Flain, giving Shah a sharp glance, 'But the Knighthood dictates that I explain everything one final time so no one can later claim that he or she entered this unknowingly or unwillingly.

'Once you take a seat on the chair, Sir Agama here will cast a spell and the Trial will begin. His spell allows us to see your thoughts and memories, in addition to whatever vision you will have. During this vision, you will be given the details of your next test, the Test of Valour. If for any reason, you die during this Trial, your next of kin will be notified, and your belongings will be given to them, as indicated in the waiver you signed upon entering the Academy. Do you have any questions?'

Kairos and Vaughn did not. Shah appeared eager to ask many more questions, but he was too flustered to find his voice and only managed to mumble.

'Without further ado,' said Sir Flain, 'I call forth Vaughn Akkitos to sit on the chair and start the Trial.'

Vaughn stepped forward, met by Sir Flain. He lowered himself onto the chair of orichalcum, sitting upright stoically, but his pale visage betrayed his feelings.

Sir Agama traced a glyph, and suddenly the chair flared a bright blue. Vaughn's eyes remained open, yet unseeing.

Kairos watched in horror as Vaughn's head lolled forward over his chest. Was he dead? He suddenly feared for the young squire. They had been adversaries once, but they had fought hobs together and formed a sort of kinship. His first instinct was to go forward and help his comrade, but looking around the room, he noticed that the other knights seemed unfazed. Each knight had cast a spell that allowed them to see the same vision as Vaughn. One knight was writing something down on a parchment. Fear soon melted into curiosity, as Kairos wanted to know what they could see.

Only Shah seemed distraught, as evident by the growing puddle of piss forming at his feet.

The blue glow continued to envelop Vaughn as he sat, slumped over in the chair. Kairos assumed he wasn't dead, because he could see an arm or leg twitch occasionally. The seconds dragged on into the longest minutes of Kairos's life, and very soon, he became bored. Nothing was happening. Kairos's mind began to drift, and he wondered if the other knights could truly see Vaughn's memories. And if they could, would they see that night of the Hammerfall Festival when Kairos pummelled him to a bloody pulp? Kairos's eyes darted from knight to knight, as he suddenly felt very self-conscious, very ashamed.

Then the blue aura vanished.

Vaughn stirred and lifted his head. Sir Flain and another knight helped him off the chair and steadied him upright. Kairos breathed a sigh of relief upon seeing that the young squire was alive and well.

'Congratulations, Squire Akkitos,' Sir Agama said. 'You have passed the Trial of the Chair. You will report to the Commons tomorrow for a briefing regarding your Test of Valour. You are dismissed.'

Vaughn still appeared dazed, as if coming out of a trance. As another Mana Knight escorted him from the chamber, he seemed oblivious to his surroundings, off in another world. After he left, Sir Flain noticed the puddle beneath Shah and swore, his voice sounding unnaturally loud in the quiet chamber.

Sir Agama's lip curled downward. 'It appears we had an accident.'

Kairos stepped forward.

'Squire Azel, please wait until you are called,' Flain admonished, his eyes staring at Shah, instead, with open disgust.

'If I may, Sir Flain,' Kairos began, 'I would like to take my turn before Squire Shah.'

Kairos was afraid. Very afraid. These may be his last moments alive, and his sweaty hands were clenched into fists beneath the sleeves of his robes, but he wasn't going to take a test and die on a soiled chair.

Sir Agama and Sir Flain looked at each other and shrugged. Neither could fault him for the breach in etiquette, and Shah was certainly not going to protest.

318

'Very well,' Sir Agama said. 'Please step forward and sit on the chair, Squire Azel.'

Once Kairos was ensconced on the yellow throne, Sir Agama traced a glyph. There was a blinding flash.

Kairos slowly breathed in and out. Then he muttered a quick prayer to Rudras and closed his eyes...

\*    \*    \*

The day was beautiful. The city was perfect, utilitarian, and clean.

Dwarves walked through the well-paved streets, conducting their business much like they did in Dwarfside. Except here the sun shone brightly overhead in the clear, azure sky. There were many more dwarves here, and the city stretched out further than Vadost.

Kairos watched as a trio of dwarven children ran past him, unaware of his presence. It seemed that the other dwarves didn't notice him, either. No one stopped to gawk like they did in Dwarfside. They passed by him as if he were invisible.

As he was about to take a step to explore his surroundings, everything suddenly changed.

A strange energy, silver lightning with lines of black, erupted across the city. A foreboding image loomed in the sky, shadowing everything. Thunder shook the streets, and a building crumbled. Fires broke out. Dwarves ran in a panic, some screaming for their lost loved ones.

One of the dwarven children he'd seen earlier now ran towards Kairos. He tripped and fell at Kairos's feet, crying for his mother. Kairos tried to help him, but he could only watch as lighting struck the child. He shielded his eyes against the flash, yet the brightness seared his sight. The sound deafened his ears.

Other dwarves fled, screaming. They, too, were struck down. He watched a fire consume a little dwarven girl alive; her screams pierced the raging gale. Kairos tried to look away as her flesh blackened, but he couldn't. Kairos could only watch helplessly as the scene of horror unfolded before him.

The winds intensified, becoming the roar of another great creation, this one bright and lustrous, more brilliant than the darkness that threatened the city. It doused the flames and calmed the lightning. The darkness tried to fight back, but was losing ground.

It was too late, though. The city was destroyed, its citizens all lying dead. Only Kairos remained standing in the ruins and he could sense the fallen, the thousands of tormented souls crying in pain.

The radiant deity, angered and saddened by such devastation and massacre, channelled its vengeance and hurled it against the one who devoured everything. A flash brighter than a thousand suns whited out everything. Kairos could no longer see. No longer hear. But he felt the raw emotion of anger, loss, hurt, and betrayal, many times more intensified than any mortal could feel. He screamed. He could not even hear himself, though his throat hurt.

Then the vision vanished, only to be replaced by a darkness so thick that Kairos thought for a moment that he had died and entered a void of nothingness.

'Shatteraxe.'

The darkness spoke. Kairos not only heard its voice, but knew its intentions. A brief image flared into his mind. It was a large creature with no substance, transparent, dwelling in the ruins of the dwarven city. Kairos had no idea what it was, but it appeared formidable and foreboding.

Then the grip of pain, sharp and sudden, seized him. It tore at his mind, his soul. His head exploded in agony. Something was wrong.

He just wanted it all to stop.

\* \* \*

Kairos woke. He was drenched in a cold sweat. There were several Mana Knights staring at him, eyes wide with fear, mouths open in horror, and Sir Flain was casting a glowing green glyph over him.

Kairos didn't care. He tried, with shaking limbs, to rise, but couldn't. He gasped, unable even to take a full breath.

'Help me up!' he screamed. 'Get me out of this thing.'

Helping hands grasped him briefly, letting him fall to the floor. He scrabbled away from the chair, gulping deep breaths of air, his throat sore from screaming. His head throbbed in time with his heart. It was a few moments before his breathing began to slow.

'What the hell happened?' he asked, looking at Sir Agama.

'I-I don't know!' said Sir Agama. He leafed through a book, showing it around the room, as if it would make sense to anyone else. 'I did everything I was supposed to do. I followed the instructions to the letter. And then you started screaming. The godshard flared, bright and hot. It's never done that! I've never even heard of it doing that.'

Sir Flain completed his spell, green motes dancing in his eyes as he looked Kairos over closely. He lingered around the head, frowning intently. 'There's no harm to the body or spirit. You're fine.' He released the spell and the green motes faded.

Sir Agama remained as bewildered and tousled as a cat plunged unwillingly into a stream. 'Tell me what happened, Squire Azel.'

'Er...' Kairos, felt as dazed as Vaughn had seemed.

'He survived,' Sir Flain said over his shoulder to Sir Agama. 'He passed the Trial of the Chair.'

Sir Agama was not deterred. 'Yes, but what happened?'

At first, Kairos tried to explain the dwarven city, but he soon stopped. The memory was too painful, and he dared not mention the souls who died. He wanted to banish the image of those dead dwarven children from his mind forever. 'That city was called Shatteraxe,' was what he did say.

Sir Agama looked annoyed. 'Yes, yes! I know that. We all saw a brief vision of your upcoming quest.' He gestured to the knights behind him, who all wore troubled expressions. 'What we didn't see were your thoughts and memories. Your motives. This has never happened before!'

Kairos didn't know what Sir Agama was talking about and didn't care. His head still hurt. His voice was raspy and hoarse from screaming, and it was difficult to talk.

'Leave him be,' said Sir Flain, leaning forward to examine Kairos again.

'I will not!' Sir Agama stated indignantly. 'How do we know that this boy does not have ill intentions? The Trial of the Chair exposes the inner mind of all potential knights. We didn't see a thing at all from this lad. This was abnormal, I tell you. Absolutely abnormal!'

'We have the vision of the quest,' Flain said in a controlled voice. 'That is enough. It's in Shatteraxe.'

'But it was a partial vision,' Sir Agama insisted. 'The squire must have seen more, and he's withholding the information from us.'

Flain turned and faced Sir Agama, his face darkening into a fierce scowl. Agama took an involuntary step back. 'What would you have us do, Sir Agama? Make the boy retake the Trial of the Chair? That's never been done before, either, and I'm not about to start doing it now. Besides, we still have to administer the Trial for Squire Shah.'

Sir Agama stood speechless. For the first time since Kairos's Trial had ended, everyone noticed that Shah was still in the room. He had apparently fainted when Kairos started screaming, and he was still lying near the same spot he had wet himself. Some of the knights looked at each other. No one wanted to help the squire, but after a few moments of realising that something had to be done, they awkwardly shifted forward to offer a hand.

Finally, Sir Agama broke the silence. 'I'm going to double check the book later, and you can rest assured that I will notify the Council of this. Until then, somebody help me clean this mess and wake that squire so we can recommence the Trial.' He stomped off in high dudgeon, pushing past the cluster of knights gathered near the centre of the chamber, in search of a mop and a bucket.

'You do that,' Flain said, looking back. Once Sir Agama was out of earshot, Flain leant forward and asked, 'So what *did* you see?'

Kairos did not want to answer, but upon seeing the paladin's concerned face, he reluctantly decided it was best to tell Flain. Something wasn't right, and he thought that maybe the older knight had answers.

'I saw a darkness overtake a dwarven city...' Kairos began.

'Shatteraxe,' Flain said.

Kairos nodded. 'Yes... And it destroyed everything entirely. Something else, large and powerful, came to fight the darkness, but it was too late. Then I saw a strange creature, an apparition of some sort.'

Sir Flain listened in awed silence, his eyes wide. Kairos had never seen the paladin so unnerved before. He thought nothing could faze the man. In a quiet voice, almost a whisper, he asked, 'Sir Flain, what does it mean?'

Flain took a moment to answer. 'I'm not sure,' he murmured. Then, in a voice loud enough to address the whole room, he said, 'It means you have passed the Trial. Congratulations, Squire Kairos Azel. You can now proceed to the next phase of your testing.'

The paladin helped Kairos to his feet. Kairos took a few unsteady steps and massaged his pounding head. He knew where his Test of Valour would be, but he was not sure if he wanted to go.

\* \* \*

'Squire Azel. Please come in and sit down,' Jomur's mouth twisted like he had bitten into a raw fire potato whenever he called Kairos's name. 'Your first assignment has been determined, according to the Trial of the Chair.'

The instructor and several knights – those present at the Trial of the Chair – sat at a long table with Jomur in the Commons Hall. Sir Agama and Sir Flain were also in attendance. Jomur gloated in self-satisfaction whilst Flain looked more livid than usual – if that were possible. Kairos was nervous when he entered, but upon seeing Jomur and his haughty demeanour, his unease gave way to annoyance. Everyone was looking at Kairos expectantly.

The silence had grown uncomfortable. 'Oh?' Kairos said, not knowing what else to say.

'That's 'Oh, Instructor Jomur,' Squire Azel.'

Kairos took a calming breath. 'Okay, Instructor Jomur,' he replied in a level voice.

Jomur nodded. As self-important as he was, Kairos happened to know Jomur failed his Professor exam several times. What he didn't know was why he had such a large involvement in reviewing each squire's Test of Valour. As far as Kairos was concerned, that task should have been solely left to the Mana Knights. Even if Instructor Jomur was responsible for part of the Academy.

The instructor cleared his throat and smiled. 'In the dwarven ruins of Shatteraxe is an air elemental. You should recall seeing such a vision of it when you took the Trial of the Chair. This particular one, however, is a magical anomaly. No summoned elemental has persisted for so long. Primarily, you are to dispel it, destroy it, or unsummon it. As a secondary consideration, you must try and learn why it remains. Given the distance of Shatteraxe, you have two fortnights to complete your Test. Questions?'

Kairos looked at Jomur narrowly. 'I have a question, Instructor Jomur,' he said. 'The Test of Valour is different for every squire, correct?'

Jomur rolled his eyes in exasperation, which made Kairos clench his fists under the table. 'Yes, Squire Azel. We went over this in class several times. Or were you not paying attention as usual?'

Kairos ignored the remark. It would do him no good to throttle the instructor after he had come this far. 'I was just wondering who determined that I must get rid of this air elemental from my brief vision,' he said.

'I didn't,' Jomur sneered. 'I wasn't there. These knights saw the vision, and they have deduced from the details provided that this is your Test of Valour. I mean, it wasn't that difficult. They heard the words 'Shatteraxe' and saw the image of an air elemental. Even the most uneducated knight here knows about the air elemental at Shatteraxe.'

A few knights shot Instructor Jomur scathing looks.

'Just for the record,' Flain shouted, 'I stand opposed to this folly. Shatteraxe has been cursed and uninhabited for centuries. This air elemental is too powerful, too dangerous, for an army to take on, let alone an inexperienced squire. Not even our most powerful Dragon Knights could rid us of this 'anomaly'. We are sending Squire Azel to his death. I absolve myself of all liability resulting from this.'

'I'm sorry you feel that way, Sir Flain,' Jomur remarked snidely. 'But you were present during Squire Azel's Trial of the Chair, so you know that was the vision received for his Test. We cannot change it. It was ordained by the Trial, not chosen by any of us. If he doesn't like it, he can submit his resignation now. Every squire knowingly enters the Test of Valour knowing the danger, along with the possibility of death.'

Flain remained standing and slammed his hands down onto the table. The instructor jumped in surprise, causing his glasses to slide down to the tip of his nose.

'The Trial of the Chair has never given such an impossible task before!' Flain thundered.

'That is not my problem, Sir Flain.' Jomur tried to look composed as he pushed his glasses back onto the bridge of his nose with a shaky hand.

Flain looked as though he were about to reach across the table and grab Jomur by his scrawny throat, but to everyone's astonishment, he gave a long sigh and sat down.

Jomur shrugged. 'Any more questions?'

Kairos nodded. 'How long has the air elemental been there? And what's it even doing there? It doesn't make any sense.'

Jomur smiled. 'These questions are what you are to discover on your own. Like I said earlier, you have two fortnights to complete your Test. If you don't have any more questions of importance, then you are dismissed. There are other squires waiting to receive their despatch for their Test of Valour, Squire Azel.'

Kairos was clearly not finished, but he decided to walk out before he lost his temper. He hated Instructor Jomur enough already, and that hatred was coming to a boiling point under the instructor's discourteous dismissal of him. He would figure out this problem when he arrived there, he decided. Beating up Jomur would yield only more problems.

First, he would talk to Althea and see where her Test was. He was suddenly very worried about her. Maybe she wouldn't have an 'impossible task'. Flain's words and his worry unnerved Kairos.

He hoped the paladin was wrong.

$$* \quad * \quad *$$

'You are doomed to fail!' Althea was hysterical.

They were standing in front of the quartermaster's desk at the weaponry, waiting to receive equipment and supplies for their journey. This was the first time they would wear their Mana Knight uniforms, complete with the plated armour. A few of the other squires, who came before them, had already departed for their journey. The quartermaster, a bored and tired-looking knight, took the parchments from Kairos and Althea and disappeared into the storeroom.

'Sir Flain is correct,' Althea said, checking if the quartermaster had returned. He had not. 'That is an impossible task. Even my father and a battalion of knights wouldn't succeed.'

Kairos did not completely understand. He had only seen one of these so-called 'elementals' since his arrival to Ordonia, and it was in a field tilling the soil. Mr. Dubose had been taking him to the farms to get eggs and produce when he encountered the beast working alongside a human. At first, he thought it was some type of dangerous rock monster, but Mr. Dubose assured him that it was an earth elemental tending the fields alongside its master, who had summoned it solely for that purpose. Kairos had wondered aloud if the earth elemental could fight, and the dwarf cuffed him and told him attacking one without magic would be tantamount to suicide. Apparently, even farmers in Ordonia could be powerful summoners.

'I recall that an elemental stays near its summoner,' Kairos said now, remembering how that earth elemental did not stray far from its master. 'So I could just kill the summoner, correct?'

Tears of frustration welled up in Althea's eyes. 'An elemental is a creature summoned from a powerful spell. They exist as long as the summoner allows. There are only four ways to rid of them: the summoner dispels it, remove it from the summoner's presence, we kill it, or the summoner dies. But those who can summon elementals are very powerful on their own.'

'All people can die by the blade,' Kairos said in a nonchalant manner, hoping to cheer Althea up with a confidence he did not feel. 'I'll just need to defeat the summoner.'

'But there is no summoner,' Althea replied, her voice hollow and desolate. 'I've read about this particular elemental in my father's library.' She choked, as though mention of the library conjured the memory of the manor burning. After taking a moment to compose herself, she continued, 'It has resided in the ruins of Shatteraxe for centuries. There have been no signs of its summoner, and no one, not even the most powerful Mana Knight, Eribus, can defeat it. Many have tried and failed.'

'That might explain why Flain looked like he wanted to murder Jomur.' Kairos forced a smile. 'Perhaps he liked us after all... Flain, that is.'

Althea did not return his smile. 'You shouldn't go.'

'Nonsense,' he said, embracing her. 'It's fate that your father saved me. Fate that brought me to you. Perhaps this quest, too, is my fate. Only time will tell. I did not come all this way to give up. I will see this elemental first.'

Althea leant into Kairos's embrace and nodded, stifling her sobs. He could feel her tears moistening his tunic. She mumbled something. He could not discern the words, so he pushed her gently away to see her face. It was puffy from the weeping, but her beauty still radiated as it had on the first day they had met, brightening his dark and hopeless world.

'What was that?' he asked.

'It was nothing,' she said. 'You just run if it's too dangerous, okay?'

'What about *your* Test?' Kairos asked, trying to lead the subject away. He did not want Althea to worry about him, especially when she needed to focus on her own quest. 'You haven't told me about it.'

Althea's eyes were downcast. 'My Test is in Chendre.'

Now it was Kairos's turn to worry. He imagined a horde of hobs or brigands. Something beyond Althea's skill level to fight. 'What sort of monstrosities lie there?' he asked.

'None,' she said, as if embarrassed. 'Chendre is a small village a few days' travel northeast of here. I'll be healing the sick there. During my Trial, I had a vision of an epidemic breaking out amongst the villagers. It was ordained that I take the path of a healer. Sir Flain has been training me in private,' she explained, upon seeing Kairos's puzzled expression, 'and even allowed me special permission to study and use healing magic.'

'That's great!' Kairos said in relief. Now he wouldn't have to worry about her dying in combat, though the thought of her walking straight into an epidemic seemed rather disturbing.

'What's even better is that it's on the way to Shatteraxe.' It was Althea's turn to force a smile. 'I mean, it's only a few days from the ruined city by foot. We can travel together in the meantime. There's nothing in the rules that says we can't. We just cannot help each other with our own individual Test.' Althea's face lit up with a sudden idea. 'Maybe we can see if any other squires are travelling our way. Safety in numbers, and all.'

Kairos shook his head. 'That will take time. Then we have to wait around for them to prepare. The day is still early enough, we should leave as soon as we can. My journey is far, and I'd like to get started sooner rather than later.'

'I suppose you're right.' Althea straightened up and was wiping her face as the quartermaster returned with a bundle of rations.

He deposited them unceremoniously onto the ground in front of Kairos's feet without showing any concern for the fragility of the contents. He ignored Kairos's scowl as he leafed through his parchments until he found the one he was looking for. He raised an eyebrow. 'It says you are using a sword,' he said. 'Is this a mistake? Standard issue for all recruits are a mana lance and a dagger.'

'It is no mistake, sir,' Kairos said, still glaring at the bored-looking knight. 'I was given permission by Sir Flain. My sword should still be back there.'

The knight regarded Kairos with a tired gaze and shrugged. 'An old-fashioned choice, but this Academy class has been quite different. I issued a boomerang earlier. Very well, I'll be back.' He sauntered back into weaponry with the air of having all day to complete his task.

Kairos fumed.

'Kairos?' Althea asked, looking around.

'Yes?'

'You don't plan on fighting that air elemental with a sword, do you?' Her voice was almost a whisper. 'That's not going to be of much use.'

'I'll bring the staff,' Kairos answered with as much reassurance as he could muster but judging by the look on Althea's face, it wasn't enough. He couldn't even convince himself. 'I suppose I could stop by Mr. Dubose's house and get some extra gnome powder.'

'That's not going to work. Only magic attacks work on air elementals, and fire attacks are not very effective against them.'

Kairos took a deep breath.

'You're never one to plan much, are you?' Althea said, with a smile. 'Now here's what we do.'

Kairos looked across the desk and saw that the quartermaster still had not returned, so he leant towards Althea and listened to her plan.

\* \* \*

Stephon preened himself on a stone bench outside the Commons, putting on a grand show of brushing his long, flowing blond hair. Squires passed by, some looking glum, others excited. Few paid him any mind. That was to be expected. The elf knew they were on their way to take the second phase of the Knight's Test: the Test of Valour.

One squire did take notice. Shah walked by and cast him a look mingled with fear and malice.

'Good day, Shah,' Stephon called out in a pleasant voice and a flourish of his hand.

Shah's eyes widened in alarm, and he looked at the ground and rushed away without a word.

Stephon shrugged. He chuckled at the memory of the incident where Shah set himself afire when he tried on his uniform. Perhaps the bumbling squire was clever enough to suspect him… Stephon shook his head. No, he thought. Judging from the human's stupid and vacant expression, there was no way he could detect a louse stuck on the tip of his big nose. The elf almost laughed aloud at the memory of the other humans who blamed the hapless squire for the incident.

The day grew long, and the air took on a sudden chill. The elf pulled his cloak tighter and swore. This was taking too long and he was in a foul mood. He had been sullen all day, rubbing his temples as if his head ached. Upon spotting the knight known as Flain leaving in an angry huff, Stephon's temperament improved.

The academic faculty was nearing the end of doling out quests, and the squires were already departing. He recognised Kairos and Althea when they emerged from the barracks at last, and he pulled his cowl over his head so they wouldn't see him. Their morose expressions showed that they probably wouldn't have noticed him anyway, so absorbed they were with their own problems. They walked by without a glance in his direction.

Stephon followed them at a great distance. He could not hear most of their conversation without being seen, but he did pick out the words 'Shatteraxe' and 'elemental.'

The elf stopped following, astounded at what he'd heard. His surprise was so great that he paused for a good few moments. 'Well, well,' said Stephon to himself in a low, icy voice. 'It seems like Malus was completely right *after all*.' When he looked up, he saw that Kairos and Althea had vanished, already moving on far ahead. No matter. He knew where they were going.

\* \* \*

Kairos and Althea's journey to Chendre took them five days. They had expected it to be shorter, since the weather was fair, but they had to travel on foot. The Knighthood did not issue horses to new recruits; Sir Flain explained that 'walking builds character'.

They briefly stopped by Dwarfside and visited Jace Dubose, who had received word that Galen Avenal was to return to Vadost within a month. The Dragon Knight had finished his business in Ordon and letters would be forthcoming prior to his arrival. The dwarf had also restocked Kairos's supply of gnome powder and sharpened his sword. He asked where they were bound. Althea replied that they were going out to take their Test of Valour, but could not share the details.

Mr. Dubose looked very solemn at this, and wished them luck, hugging them both. He gave a long, deep sigh when they left.

They continued their journey and travelled northeast along the main road from Vadost. Although they were within days of Valour Keep, they could not relax their vigilance. The lands beyond the city were wild and desolate. On the second day, they were set upon by outlaws, and on the fourth day a horde of hobs marched so close that Kairos could smell their putrid stench.

The brigands had planned to ambush two defenceless travellers, as Kairos and Althea wore hooded cloaks that concealed their knightly regalia, but they soon faced the wrath of Althea's mana lance and Kairos's incendiary projectiles, courtesy of Mr. Dubose's gnome powder. They fled when one large fireball singed three of their number, and they realised too late that they had picked a fight, not with hapless wanderers, but with armed members of the Knighthood. The hobs far outnumbered the pair, however, so Kairos and Althea had to hide in the dense thicket off the roadway until the horde meandered off into the distant hills.

Near the end of the fifth day, they trudged into Chendre. The locals greeted them with the obligatory welcome due to those associated with the Mana Knights, but warned them that three members were bedridden in the town's small temple with high fever and chills. One was even bleeding profusely from the nose.

For Kairos, the news brought back memories of the Blight in Logres. He wondered aloud if the same thing was happening here. The outbreak frightened him more than the prospect of any battle, for disease and pestilence were an unseen enemy that could not be fought with a sword. Althea quickly allayed his concerns when she took to questioning the villagers about their activities: any travellers coming and going, and their hygiene. By the end of the day, she discovered that the three villagers had contracted the plague, with a fourth, a little girl, beginning to fall ill, as well. She used her healing magic to alleviate the symptoms of the ill, and soon they began to show signs of recovery. By the next day, she finally found the culprit: a bale of damp clothes infested with fleas.

'This is no Blight,' Althea explained, after she had incinerated the clothes with a quick spell. 'This bundle of clothes was recently brought in from a merchant, and they contained the disease-ridden fleas. I'll instruct the villagers how to take precautionary measures against the spread of the disease. Once that's done, I can accompany you to Shatteraxe.'

Kairos absentmindedly rubbed his arms and looked around. The mention of fleas gave him the impression that he was itching all over. Yet there were no bites or bumps. He could not wait to leave this village.

Althea saw his dilemma. 'You're not infected, Kairos,' she said. 'So you can stop worrying. I know the proper sigil of protection, and it doesn't use much mana, either. And on the off-chance that you start showing symptoms, a simple spell would reverse the condition.'

'You can do that now?' Kairos asked, amazed. She had come a long way since they had first met. He knew she was very intelligent, but now she had proven herself resourceful. Her words and knowledge on the subject had assuaged his fears.

'It's not that difficult, really,' she answered, and resumed her tasks with the villagers.

She deserves to pass the Test of Valour, he thought. Although there were no dangerous monsters that needed slaying, or outlaws that needed to be served with justice, this work was equally important. Althea had probably saved the whole village on her own.

After finishing her duty with the village, Althea announced that she was ready to depart to Shatteraxe and vowed to come back on her return trip to Vadost to check on the villagers. Everyone gathered to send her off with a warm farewell, offering gifts of baked goods, silver, and various trinkets. Althea politely refused everything. Not one to turn down free food, Kairos accepted two loaves of bread on her behalf.

Finding Shatteraxe proved more difficult.

Kairos and Althea spent almost a week searching for the ruined city. Kairos was no longer nervous, but frustrated, stating that they were on a 'false treasure hunt.' He consulted two maps, one provided by the Knighthood, and the other given to him by Mr. Dubose. Both showed the ruins on the southern portion of the Yeti's End mountain range, but that encompassed many miles. Neither map showed Shatteraxe in the same location.

Althea tried to calm Kairos's concerns, but she too began to show signs of worry. They had left Valour Keep almost two weeks ago, and only had four weeks to complete their Test. Well, Kairos had four weeks; Althea was essentially finished with her testing.

They made camp in a cleared grove at the foot of the mountain range. Using the casting glove, Kairos precisely traced the glyph for fire, and then struck a spark from his flint and steel. The spark landed on the tinder and started to glow.

'Why are you using the glove?' Althea asked, slightly amused. 'There's no one out here to convince.'

He had known that would distract her. He gestured vaguely into the falling gloom. 'You never know,' he said airily. 'And if no one's out here, how would the Knighthood know if I defeated the air elemental? I could just as easily conjure up a story and lie.'

'Remember the Trial of the Chair?' Althea said. 'It reads our thoughts and motives. Well, we have to sit on it again after returning and making our report. The Council verifies the validity of our story with the chair... And refusal to sit on it counts as failure.'

'So if you assisted me, they would find out?' Kairos asked.

'Yes.' Althea forced a smile. 'But there's no rule saying I can't accompany you prior to taking on your Test. I just cannot assist you *during* your Test.' She gave him a mischievous wink. 'Hence my plan that we talked about earlier.'

Kairos nodded. It was a good plan, but if this air elemental was as powerful as everyone claimed, he doubted that any plan would work. It was no use worrying about that now, however. He was hungry. He sat down wearily and pulled out rations from his rucksack, sharing some with Althea. They ate in silence, and afterwards, Althea cast a few alarm spells around the perimeter of the camp should an intruder stumble upon them during the night.

The next morning they awakened to find themselves in the midst of a thick fog.

Kairos wanted to leave immediately. This was no ordinary fog. He could hear spoken voices in the ghostly mists and an eerie melody in the distance. The Einar associated the fog as Rudras's way of collecting the souls of the dead, and Kairos knew that those voices were no longer living. Though he couldn't understand them clearly, they seemed to be warning him to leave.

He and Althea broke down the camp and gathered their belongings in terrified silence. Althea was extremely pale, appearing on the verge of fainting at any moment. Kairos regarded the impenetrable fog warily, summoning every ounce of his courage, as the mist seemingly parted in one direction, forming a clear path that led towards the source of the haunting melody.

Althea attempted to follow, but the whispers of the fog paralysed her. The voices hissed in anger. Her courage faltered, and she stopped, almost stumbled. 'Kairos!' she cried out.

Kairos turned. Seeing Althea's pallid face, he reached out and took her hand. 'I'm here, Althea.'

Hand in hand, they walked through the fog together. After a week of searching, they had finally found the ruined city, or rather it found them.

*   *   *

Kairos and Althea walked cautiously between the tumble-down, ivy-covered remains of the squat, dwarven stone houses of Shatteraxe. The midmorning light was obscured by the thick blanket of fog enshrouding the city. Here the many voices echoed across the alleys and streets but whenever Kairos looked for the source of one of them, he could see nothing. He could only think of the thousands of dwarven souls unable to find eternal rest.

Althea had told him earlier that Shatteraxe was the site where two gods had battled during the Celestial War. No one knew which gods fought or why, but historians concluded from the devastation that only a god could have destroyed an entire city so quickly. An entire population of dwarves decimated in moments; no survivors and no one to tell what happened, only the crumbled buildings of proud dwarven architects told their story.

Shatteraxe, with its elusive location and the fact that it was covered in perpetual fog, had earned the reputation of being cursed. Grave robbers and treasure hunters alike had sought to plunder the dead, seeking dwarven wealth lost to the centuries. However, many who attempted to find Shatteraxe often found themselves turned around and headed back the way they came, and those who entered were never heard from again. Only the most powerful of the Knighthood were able to roam its streets and leave alive, Grandmaster Eribus being one of them. Even then, rumour told that he barely survived the journey, and refused to ever go back again.

The city itself had an oppressing and sinister air, as if the souls of its denizens roamed about in an afterlife of limbo. Every time Kairos passed a building, he thought he glimpsed movement in the doorway or a window. When he turned, nothing was there. The sound of disjointed whispers came from all directions now. His surroundings combined with the knowledge of his vision deeply unsettled him; the ruined city only reaffirmed that the vision actually happened. He expected the ghost of the dwarven child to leap out at any moment.

Then there was the song.

'What's wrong? You keep looking around as if something's out there,' Althea said softly.

'Something is here!' Kairos said in a terrified whisper. 'Don't you hear it?'

Althea looked very afraid. 'Hear what?'

'It's a song. It sounds like it's coming from the heart of the city, beckoning us to come.'

'We should leave.' Althea looked around fearfully, for Kairos's words unnerved her. 'There is more at stake than your life out here. There is a feeling of dread in the air. I don't like it.'

Kairos's steps faltered. The idea was tempting.

'No one would fault you for abandoning this quest,' Althea continued. 'We don't have to throw away our lives, Kairos.'

Kairos thought about the outcome of giving up on the Knighthood. He could turn back now. He could return to Vadost and find another way to make a living. It would be so easy in this rich land! He would have to forget about the Einar, the Blight in Logres, and all of those lives sacrificed in vain...

He shook his head, knowing there would be no way he could live with himself. He had come so far, and he had a duty and an obligation to fulfil – the end was so close that it would be a shame to admit defeat on the threshold of his dream. The Mana Knights were the only ones fighting Malus, and he could not abandon his people. He needed a ship and the backing of a powerful force, and this way was his only option. It always had been.

'I cannot,' he said, looking at her.

He ignored the wails of torment and pleas for help coming from the mists, concentrating his focus on the song.

Althea said nothing. Only swallowed and nodded.

As they continued, the fog surrounding them became darker, the air colder. Althea and Kairos had quit talking, for fear that their voices would disturb whatever lurked here. The former city plaza of Shatteraxe came into view as they crept across the broken flagstones.

Though the light was dim due to the enshrouding fog, they could see the plaza was empty. There was only a crumbled fountain in the centre of the square, its features long-since eroded to shapeless lumps. Kairos could still hear the song, the sad haunting melody seemed to be coming from the other side of the plaza. He had no clue where to find the air elemental. He only had the song to follow. He focused on it, hoping it would lead him to where he needed to be.

Just as they were about to enter the plaza, a strong wind gusted. Althea clutched Kairos's arm in a death grip. Kairos could not see far ahead, but he felt the presence of something else. The tension of hostility rent the air.

'Althea, your spell,' Kairos said, just loud enough for her to hear. He attached the staff to the baldric on his back and drew his sword.

Althea nodded in understanding. She traced a glyph, aimed at the sword. Blue sparkles of light gathered around the blade, causing it to glow. Frost began to form on the weapon, and Kairos could feel his hands becoming cold as he clutched the handle. He stared at his sword in wonder, momentarily forgetting his surroundings. 'Are you sure your plan will work?'

'I don't know,' she admitted. 'Air elementals are prone to ice magic. It can freeze their essence, making them fragile like glass. I've seen one shatter under an ice spell before. I don't know about this one... But this is the best plan I have.'

'It's worth a try,' Kairos said, taking a step towards the plaza. 'You should stay here.'

Althea shook her head. 'No, I'm going to—'

Whatever she had planned to say was lost in a roar of wind. The fog around them coalesced, forming into a large, semi-transparent being.

It was five metres tall, with a head that was nearly level with its hulking shoulders, because it had no neck. Massive, reaching arms ended in thick hands, and its body ended in a tail of sorts instead of legs. This body was pale blue and white, as if cloud and sky had merged to constitute its flesh, which Kairos supposed is exactly what had happened. Its eyes were violet sparks fixed on Kairos. It hovered about a foot off the ground, roaring like a storm as it charged him.

Kairos raised his sword – enchanted with Althea's ice spell – and slashed at what he assumed was the air elemental's left arm. The sword cut through a small portion of vapour, leaving a trail of ice in its wake. Without pausing the creature tried to swipe at Kairos, but he had darted beyond its range and continued running across the plaza. Once he felt he was far enough away, he turned to face towards the elemental to survey the damage.

To his dismay, the small cut he had made only left an icy line on the elemental's arm. The ice quickly broke off, and the air elemental turned towards him unfazed and unharmed. Kairos did not need to be an expert on elementals to realise that he had no chance at winning this fight. He took a defensive stance as he tried to gauge his opponent from a distance. There was the staff and gnome powder, but Althea had told him that fire would have little effect.

The air elemental made a punching motion at Kairos, which seemed odd because it was still facing him from across the plaza. The column of air that the elemental threw out hit Kairos like a giant pillow across his entire body. His breath whooshed from his lungs as he flew back through the air. He landed with a bone-jarring jolt, rolling a few times before skidding to a halt. His sword clattered against the fountain. Black spots danced before his eyes as he tried to focus on the air elemental, and each breath caused him to wince in pain. He was vaguely aware of the music nearby, though he ignored it. He had other more pressing concerns.

Althea shouted something he couldn't understand. He saw a flash of light in his blurred vision, and realised with horror that she had joined the fight. There was another flash of light.

Kairos struggled to his feet in time to watch Althea complete an ice spell, which struck the air elemental on the centre of its body. He saw two frozen patches of ice on the creature's torso where the spell had struck. Kairos's hopes sank when the ice shattered away, as though the elemental was shedding off an unwanted patch of skin.

'No, Althea!' Kairos shouted. 'Run!'

Althea either did not hear, or she ignored the command. Instead, she skipped forward and slashed with her mana lance. The glowing tip bit deeply into the elemental's side, passing through without effect. The air elemental turned to her and lashed out with a fist, but she had already leapt back. Its fist passed through where she had been. She circled around, trying to stab it in the back, but as she sprang in, it reared back; Althea was fast, but the elemental was faster. There was no way for her to avoid the fist this time.

The blow caught Althea on her left side, causing her to spin as she crashed to the ground. She did not get up.

'No!' Kairos cried hoarsely. This was supposed to be his fight. His Test of Valour. And Althea had to get herself involved to save him. He no longer cared whether he passed or failed. He would never forgive himself if something happened to her. He should have never brought her here.

As the air elemental drifted towards Althea's inert form, Kairos unslung his staff and launched a fireball. It struck the creature, the flaming ball erupting in a shower of sparks. The elemental didn't even notice. Still shaking his head to clear his vision, Kairos sprinted towards Althea and the elemental. He spun the staff around and ignited the end that extended a two-foot bar of flame.

When the air elemental raised its fist again, Kairos slashed the elemental across the torso with the bar of gnomish fire. The large mass of mist affixed its gaze – two glowing orbs – on Kairos, leaving Althea forgotten. Kairos lifted the staff, ensuring that the bar of flame waved in front of those lifeless eyes. Then he threw the staff across the plaza. The violet sparks followed the fiery arc, watching as the staff clanged against the flagstone, bright, orange flame still spewing from the end.

As the air elemental glided toward the staff, Kairos ran to Althea and knelt down by her. The strange music sounded louder than ever. It was coming from a nearby, ascending, staircase.

'Althea!' he whispered, not wanting to draw attention to himself from the air elemental.

Althea did not answer. In her unconscious state, her right hand clutched the now-retracted mana lance in a death grip. Only the song called out. There were words in its melody, beckoning him.

Without hesitation, Kairos hoisted her up and ran towards the stairs as fast as he could. He did not bother to check if the air elemental was pursuing. He no longer cared about the Test of Valour. His actions were centred on survival now.

He climbed up the stairs that led towards the music.

# CHAPTER TWELVE

### Murasa

*There are many gods of Alban, but only three are known as 'Creators.' The first is Zemus, who fashioned the humans in his own image. Thelos produced the dwarves and gnomes from his realm in the underworld. The radiant Dia created the light and dark elves. One god, jealous of this power of creation, was Murasa the Devourer. He could only consume, so he sought to steal what he could not create.*

'The Celestial Pantheon', Professor Coleridge

**T**he staircase was long and wide, much longer than Kairos had anticipated, leading up the mountain and away from the city. The stairs were carved of stone, and rocky outcropping extended on both sides. He shifted his grip on Althea as he moved as quickly as he could upwards. The climb was treacherous due to missing steps that had long since crumbled away. His leg muscles screamed in agony. His sides hurt with each breath. More than once he lost his footing, almost dropping Althea and tumbling down the mountainside himself.

But he did not stop. He dared not face that monstrosity below again.

At last his foot touched the top of the stairs. He chanced a look back down, to see the fog-enshrouded city looking small and diminished, a far distance away, almost as if he were looking at a painting of another realm. He could see a few buildings jutting above the fog, but there were no signs of the air elemental. It had not pursued him.

It was strangely quiet on the moutainside above the city. Kairos gently set Althea down and checked her for vital signs. She was breathing and her pulse was strong. She had some scrapes that he treated with an ointment he carried in one of his pouches. Satisfied, he collapsed next to her. He needed to rest his weary legs and catch his breath. As he lay on the cold, hard ground, he surveyed his surroundings.

They were above the clouds. He had climbed higher than he had imagined. Strong winds battered the mountainside, but Kairos was relieved to know that these winds were not from the air elemental. The path before him led to a shrine, which was oddly intact considering the condition of the rest of Shatteraxe. Perhaps this shrine was far enough away to escape the carnage that he saw in his vision. Several statues and carvings lined the shrine, but their details had long since withered away from the tests of time. As he was studying the outside of the building, Kairos was startled to hear the eerie melody coming from within.

Fear tingled throughout Kairos's body. He wanted to flee, but he forced himself to be calm about the matter. Whatever was making that song, he decided, had not hurt him yet, and, indeed, it had led him here away from the danger below. He could not turn back, because the air elemental was lurking at the bottom of the long staircase. There was only one way he could go, and that was forward into the shrine. Maybe there was a reason for the song.

A low moan interrupted his thoughts.

'Althea,' Kairos said. Despite trying to keep his voice low, it echoed unnaturally on the nearby rocks.

Althea opened her eyes and looked about with a tired, dazed expression. Her light blue eyes found Kairos and lingered on him. 'Kairos...'

'Don't worry,' he said. 'We're safe for now. The air elemental is far away.'

At the mention of the air elemental, Althea tried to rise. Kairos rushed to stop her.

'Easy there,' he said, placing a restraining hand on her shoulder. 'How do you feel?'

Althea obeyed, though she held a hand to her head and winced. 'My head hurts,' she complained, shivering from the cold wind. 'I feel nauseous...'

'A concussion,' Kairos answered. He had experienced a few himself from the severe beatings his father had given him. 'Rest here. I'll see if we can take shelter from the wind in that shrine.'

Althea nodded and managed – with some effort – to sit in an upright position.

'Maybe there's someone inside,' Kairos continued. 'Do you hear that music?'

Althea wore a puzzled expression. 'I don't hear any music, Kairos.'

'Never mind.' Kairos tried to hide his unease. 'Wait here. I'll see if it's safe for us.'

'Don't do anything reckless,' Althea said. 'I don't think anyone would be inside there.'

Kairos looked down at her and forced a smile. He could hear the distinct melody emanating from the shrine, but he said nothing else. He did not want to frighten Althea any further. She had been through a lot today, and her fear would only feed into his own.

As he left her behind and approached the shrine, he noted that it contrasted to the temple ruins of Zemus near Valour Keep. The few images that were still legible depicted fearsome and cruel expressions. They did not bother Kairos, because they were similar to the roaring serpentine visage of Rudras. Most Einar loved images that portrayed power, war, and violence.

He arrived at the door. The music was louder now, as if someone was playing a lute on the other side. The melody had a sad, haunting feel. Kairos stilled his shaking hand to control his fear and pushed on the door. It did not budge. At first, he thought it might be locked or sealed, although a brief inspection yielded no visible locks or bolts. Kairos concluded that the door was stuck from being held in place for many years. He heaved and pushed and eventually it swung open with a loud grating sound.

Air, warm and foetid as an infectious wound, flowed out of the darkness within. Kairos coughed and quickly covered his mouth with his arm. The music was now ringing loudly in his ears, as he peered into the gloomy interior. He couldn't make out anything in the darkness. He pushed the door open further to allow as much light as possible to stream in. The dim rays of light did not reach very far. Kairos stepped inside to allow his eyes to adjust. As he walked further in, the door suddenly slammed shut, leaving him trapped in a darkness so thick and impenetrable that he could have fallen into the Void of the Netherworld. The song stopped abruptly.

'Althea!' Kairos called, startled to hear only the sound of his own voice in the nothingness.

Kairos's first panicked impulse was to reach for his sword. His hand gripped nothing where the handle should have been. He realised that he had left his sword, along with his staff, in the plaza below. He took a deep breath to calm himself. As Sir Flain had always said: 'It's okay to be scared, but panic will kill you.'

So, Kairos thought his situation through calmly. Since he could not see, he would rely on his other senses. There was no other sound, except his own stentorian breathing and his heartbeat pounding in his ears. He moved his feet, relieved to hear the sound of the stone floor beneath him. He decided he would slowly shuffle back towards the door and get out of this accursed place as soon as possible.

He moved, as quietly as he could, towards where he thought the door was. Several long moments passed, and his breathing calmed and his sight adjusted to the absolute darkness. To his surprise, something came into focus in his vision. He was not alone.

It was no wonder he hadn't seen it earlier. It was a crackling flame, the same colour as the blackness around it, except it seemed even darker, as though it absorbed the darkness itself. Kairos realised this was the source of the warmth in here, in addition to the foul smell. The flame was from another world.

Kairos's initial response was terror. But the more he stared at it, the more pathetic it appeared. The dark flame flickered weakly and sputtered, as though it was consuming the last of its fuel source. His fear diminished by the second when he realised that nothing was happening to him. No fearsome beast reached out to seize him. No spectre appeared. No supernatural being attempted to feast on his soul.

Then a voice spoke from the dark flame. 'Welcome, young Einar.' There was a hiss and a pop, then, 'It's been so long since I've had a visitor. Come closer. Speak to me.'

The blackened flame flared a bright orange, revealing an altar and a bronze gong that lay on the floor near its frame. The cords that held the gong had long since deteriorated. One quick glance assured Kairos that only worship took place in this room. A corridor led further into the interior of the shrine, but rubble lay strewn in its path, blocking the way. Kairos turned his attention back towards the talking flame.

A face was almost visible in the flames. Blue tufts of fire formed the outline of a wicked visage that leered back at him. In the centre, he could see two little red glints looking at him, just like the pupil of an eye. Even though they were not human eyes, Kairos could see the cunning, the wisdom of countless centuries flickering in those cynical orbs. Near the foot of the dark fire, amidst the dust of centuries, rested a partial skeleton of a dwarf. Its clothing had long since turned to ashes. The bones of its left side were opalescent tan; the bones on its right side, what bones remained, were blackened as if burnt. The entire right arm was missing. The pommel of a weapon, darkened with age, protruded slightly from the dust and decay. The flames rested on this weapon, rooted in place.

Kairos did not move. The face of the flames burned with a passion born out of cruelty and ambition, hatred and spite. Fear seized Kairos's entire being. He would have preferred to have been trapped in this shrine with the air elemental. Thoughts of escape thundered in his mind, but he could see the flames dancing with mocking, scornful laughter. Though they sputtered pitifully now, they once had burned with infinite power.

The darkened fire understood his thoughts well, Kairos knew. Those small rubies stared at him, piercing into his very soul.

'Come forth, young Einar. You who were lured by the melody of my hymn. Come, sit down and speak to me.'

Kairos froze in place. The mention of being lured here unnerved him.

'You have no choice in the matter, young Einar.' The fire cackled with mocking laughter. 'You are trapped here until I say otherwise. Just remember. You came to me. It is fate.'

Kairos measured his predicament. He could rush towards the door and attempt to pry it open, though the more he thought about it, the more that seemed futile. The door had closed on its own, probably by magic, and he would look like a cowardly fool beating at it. He also thought about standing his ground defiantly, but he figured this flame could outwait him; time was not exactly on his side here. Or he could try to maintain his dignity, and see what the strange fire had to say.

Kairos stepped forward and took a seat on the floor in front of the flames, placing himself far enough away from the dwarven skeleton. The ruby orbs of the fire watched him, and they seemed rather disappointed with what they saw.

'A runt! You, an Einar? You're not much larger than the typical human. What good will you do me with such mediocre strength? Here I was expecting the paragon of a warrior race, and all I get is a scrawny, castaway specimen.' The flames crackled and sputtered in anger, then they slowly receded. 'Yet, you alone made it this far from Logres. You alone journeyed across the sea and found Shatteraxe when the others have perished. Maybe I misjudge you. What are you called?'

Kairos had never given his full Einar introduction to anyone at Valour Keep, but in the company of this daunting being, he feebly answered, 'I am called Kairos, son of Karthok of the Azel clan.'

'Azel...' The flames hissed the word, savouring its taste. 'So the clan still survives to this day, eh? They served me well long ago, especially the great warrior called, Arvok. Do they still worship me?'

'We worship Rudras—'

'Rudras!' The flames flared again, causing Kairos to jump back in alarm. 'So he's the one who took my followers, eh? He was always the sly god, waiting for his opportunity from the shadows. Still, I don't sense his presence anymore.'

Kairos caught his breath. He felt like he was dealing with something much more than he could comprehend. Suddenly many questions burned in his mind, but all he could do was hold tightly to his flagging courage. He clutched his forearms to prevent himself from shaking.

'You mentioned that you lured me here...' Kairos began, but faltered.

'I did,' the flames said. There was a popping, blazing silence whilst the ruby eyes of the flames roved over Kairos. 'My Pariah also had a hand in bringing you here,' it said at length. 'We have planned this for a long time.'

'I don't understand,' Kairos said.

The flames helpfully explained. 'The Pariah are my immortal servants. One resides in Logres hidden amongst the Einar. The other works within the Knighthood. He has the ability to manipulate the Trial of the Chair to determine which quest a squire receives for his Test of Valour. For you, he gave the task to defeat the air elemental of Shatteraxe — a creature who was summoned by one whose power dwarfed any mortals. You came here quite willingly, and when you got close enough, you were able to hear the melody.' The fire flickered in amusement. 'The rest was all up to you.'

'I did come willingly,' Kairos admitted. In his mind, he had done what he thought was proper. He followed the melody because it led him to Shatteraxe when he was lost. When he encountered the air elemental, the song provided him a beacon of light in the ghostly mists. He thought that following the song was simply a better alternative than returning to the haunted maze of the city with an air elemental at his heels.

Kairos was silent for a moment, then said, 'There was no legitimate way for me to defeat the air elemental, was there?'

'No.' The fire crackled.

'And this whole ordeal was orchestrated by your P-Par–' Kairos fumbled over the word. 'Your servant, so I could meet you here?'

'Yes, my Pariah had planned this. From the start of your journey in Logres to here.' The flames wavered in irritation. 'Though Malus and his cohorts almost ruined everything.'

'Who are you?' Kairos asked.

'We will get to that soon. First there is something I want to ask of you.'

'All right, then. What do you want?'

The flames whined and popped in what seemed like a deprecating manner. 'Just a mere favour, young Einar. Nothing more.'

For the first time since Kairos had entered the shrine, he flashed his teeth in an ironic smile. 'I'm afraid I have nothing to offer. I'm – as you say – a 'runt' of the Einar. I also have no magic powers. You, on the other hand, seem to be a being of great power. There's nothing I can do for you.'

'That is where you are mistaken, young Einar.' The fire gleamed with a hungry, devouring light. A black light which consumed the darkness around it. 'There *is* something you can do for me!'

'I don't see how that's possible,' Kairos responded wryly. 'The air elemental is blocking the only way out, and I have no weapons and no magic. Althea is outside.' His heart burst with sudden concern for her. 'But she cannot harm the elemental, either.' Kairos looked towards the rubble in the corridor. 'I'm trapped here in Shatteraxe unless there's a secret passage behind this shrine.'

'There is one way to leave,' the fire sputtered. 'And your analysis of your situation is correct. The air elemental will kill you, if some wandering wraith doesn't. My song granted you and your friend safe passage through Shatteraxe, protecting you from the restless souls that wander the city.'

Kairos remembered the voices of agony and hatred he had heard, and suppressed a shudder to imagine what would have happened otherwise.

'You're not going to find another method,' the flames hissed.

Kairos stared intently into the blackened fire, forcing himself to lock eyes with the two red orbs. 'I was thinking about what you have said.'

'Don't think for too long, young Einar. The air elemental may not stray from the plaza, but it is only a matter of time before one of the undead wanders up here in search of a living soul to feast upon. I can only hold them at bay for so long. You are safe with me for now, but I cannot say the same for your friend outside.'

Kairos tried to quell the sudden urge of desperation welling up inside of him. He needed to help Althea and get out of this place. He should have never come. In his blind quest to save the Einar, he only jeopardised the one he cared about most.

'It is but a simple favour,' the flames sputtered softly.

'Just who are you?' Kairos asked.

'I was once called Murasa. Many others know me as the Devourer or the Lost God. Perhaps you've heard of me.'

'I have,' said Kairos, recalling the name from one of Jomur's longwinded lectures on theology. According to the history books and the ancient poems, Murasa was a god of darkness and destruction. Envious of the other gods' power of creation, the dark god wreaked havoc amongst his rivals' worshippers, as was evident in Shatteraxe. This eventually started the Celestial War.

Historian accounts and poems differed on what happened next, but most concluded that Murasa was one of the first gods to disappear, defeated by Zemus. The other gods became involved, some siding against Zemus for going too far, others joining him. A few of the minor gods, not wanting any involvement, fled to more peaceful realms in the heavens. In the end, none of the gods remained on Alban.

That is what Kairos had gathered from his brief time in Valour Keep from Instructor Jomur and Althea. He felt that there was more to the story, considering his upbringing in Logres. No Einar ever mentioned the so-called major gods or Murasa. They only spoke of Rudras, who barely received an occasional footnote in the Ordonian books. Kairos wondered what role the serpent god played in all of this. He had always wondered if any gods had somehow survived. Now he had an answer.

'Murasa — the Devourer,' Kairos said. 'The one who started the Celestial War.'

'Yes,' said Murasa.

'You are withering away,' Kairos noted.

The god did not like this one bit. His fiery form blazed in outrage. But the anger quickly sputtered out, leaving a weak flame. It was obvious to Kairos that Murasa was expending the last of his energy to hold this form together.

'You are correct. I am fading,' Murasa gasped in helpless frustration. 'My life essence is nearly exhausted. Some say that I tried to destroy Shatteraxe out of spite, out of jealousy of the other gods.' He flickered derisively. 'What a load of mortal drivel! I acted for a much greater reward than merely consuming some filthy dwarven city. My plan was ascension into the greater godhood. To rid the pantheon of Zemus once and for all!'

Kairos listened in awed silence. He could barely believe what he was hearing. This was more unreal than his vision from the Trial of the Chair.

'Zemus was always a jealous god.' The flames paused in their flickering, if that were somehow possible. 'He refused to allow his humans to worship any other god, even if they tired of his strict dogma. Eventually a group of his followers denounced him. You know this group well, for they are the Einar.'

'The Einar once worshipped Zemus?' Kairos asked. 'What happened?'

'I was getting to that.' Murasa fizzled, as if annoyed by the interruption. 'The Einar tired of going to the temples each Zemdag, and other such rules, so they refused to worship Zemus. They wanted to worship other gods, or worship no god. They wanted freedom. In return, he cursed them – stripped them of all mana. That made them a vulnerable target to all the other races and creatures, and as a result, they were almost wiped off the face of Alban completely. A few survivors prayed to me for help, so I took pity on them. I was unable to reverse Zemus's curse, but I managed to grant them other abilities beyond other humans: strength, speed, heightened reflexes, and resistance to magic.'

'I take it that Zemus did not take kindly to this?' Kairos asked.

'Correct. He tried to eradicate me along with all of the Einar, so I made a bargain with Rudras. The plan was that I attack Shatteraxe whilst Rudras would pretend to seek assistance from Zemus. Zemus would come just as I destroyed Shatteraxe, and we would blame him for the destruction. Thelos, the dwarven god, would have been angered enough to challenge him, but he would have lost. Zemus would have been weakened from the fight, and I would have merely finished him off. It would have worked perfectly, too.' The flames quivered. 'But Rudras informed Zemus too early. Before I could retreat from Shatteraxe, Zemus came...'

Kairos's eyes widened in sudden understanding. 'That vision I saw during the Trial of the Chair – that was the battle between you and Zemus!'

'Yes. I could not confront him alone. He defeated me.' The flames flickered in anger. 'My plan would have worked, because shortly thereafter, Thelos came and destroyed him – Zemus was weakened from his fight with me, you see – and you saw what was left of Zemus at Valour Keep. My plan worked, but not in the correct order.'

Kairos nodded, remembering the Sapphire Shard.

'And the rest devolved into what you mortals call the Celestial War. I later learnt that Rudras betrayed us all and fled, but not before summoning a powerful air elemental to prevent anyone from finding me here.'

Kairos gazed steadily at the dying flames. 'You said that Zemus defeated you. So why are you still alive?'

'Zemus did not kill me,' the flames said, diminishing in stature. 'He decided to punish me forever, so he imprisoned me into this sword laying here beneath me. The sword is indestructible and I cannot escape from it. Only a power equal to Zemus's can free me, and as you can see, there are no other gods around anymore. But there is a way, and only you can help me.'

Kairos looked at the dwarven skeleton in dismay. Judging from the corpse, the dwarf had died horribly. 'Does helping you entail ending up like that dwarf?' Kairos asked. 'I believe you killed him. Will I meet the same fate?'

'That is true I killed the dwarf,' Murasa admitted. 'I'm called the Devourer for a reason. I syphon life and mana away from others to feed my own power. That is why I remain untouched and forgotten. No other being can lift this sword — touch me — without having their life essence drained away. Even the creatures without mana, dwarves and gnomes, are susceptible to this effect. But you're different... You are an Einar. You have been blessed with my power. This makes you immune to my touch. That is why the Pariah chose you to come here from the Trial of the Chair.'

'Why me? Why not the Pariah?' Kairos asked. 'Why can't they help you then, if they're so powerful?'

'They have,' Murasa answered. 'For many years, they have calculated the events to bring about our meeting. Without them, you would still be in Logres right now. But to answer your question, they cannot touch me either, because they are made of mana. I would inadvertently absorb what little remains of their power. Only an Einar such as you can touch me. And you are the only one who crossed the sea unscathed. So, will you help?'

'What do I have to do?' Kairos asked.

'A simple task. Take me to Zemus's godshard in Valour Keep.'

Kairos regarded the flames with suspicion. 'That's all?'

'That is all,' Murasa said. 'You only have to carry me.'

'What's in this for me?' Kairos replied bitterly. 'This arrangement seems to benefit only you.'

'Life,' said Murasa. 'I can help you defeat the air elemental and save Logres from the Blight. My help is *your* only way out of here. You will become the greatest knight, and the most powerful Einar. We benefit mutually from this exchange, I assure you.'

Kairos looked away into the darkness, refusing to meet the god's ruby gaze that seemed to pierce into his soul. He remained unconvinced, knew that the god was hiding something else. He saw the altar in the weak firelight and thought of Logres. Was everything he had been doing up till now orchestrated by a nameless Pariah? The thought troubled him. He considered the odds he faced, thought about the air elemental and the vengeful spirits of Shatteraxe. He and Althea didn't stand a chance of getting out of here alive on their own. He wondered if the god was truthful about everything, or if he was being fed lies. He had more questions than ever. But Althea was in immediate danger.

Murasa sputtered impatiently. 'Time runs short, young Einar. The undead grow restless outside as my power wanes. I cannot maintain this form much longer. Do you accept my offer?'

Kairos turned towards the flames and met those ruby orbs. 'I accept. I will take you to the godshard. Now how do I get out of here?'

The flames regarded Kairos in what appeared to be a malicious grin. 'Excellent. All you have to do is pick up the sword and wield it.'

* * *

Althea's body ached. Her head throbbed in pain whenever she tried to stand. Her last attempt caused a surge of dizziness and pain, and she quickly found herself on her hands and knees, vomiting next to a boulder. Yet this pain was nothing compared to the anguish she felt staring at the door to the shrine.

When Kairos had entered and the door slammed shut behind him, she panicked. She called out to him until her voice was hoarse and the blood pounded in her head, but to no avail. She tried pushing on the door, and even spent precious mana casting a spell to force it open, but nothing worked. The door remained shut.

Eventually, she resigned herself to staring disconsolately at the shrine, hoping he would come out. Hours, which seemed like an eternity, passed. Althea listened for any sounds coming from inside, but she could only hear the wind. With nothing else to do, her thoughts centred on worry and regret.

The closed door trapped her chances at any semblance of happiness. With Stella dead, her home destroyed, and now Kairos gone, she wondered why fate was so cruel to her. Ever since her father had left again, her life had been a litany of sadness. She felt alone. Now she would die alone in Shatteraxe, despite having passed her own Test. The thought appalled her.

Having nothing else to do, she sat near the door. The stone floor was cold and hard, her mind full of despair. It was now late afternoon, and she dreaded being here past dark. The city below terrified her, and it was already frigid.

Althea began pacing to warm herself, fighting the wave of nausea that welled up within her. She peered at her surroundings, always wondering if there was something nearby. The gloomy atmosphere of this place reminded her of Banshee's Lookout. More than once, she jumped at her shadow.

She wanted out of here, but dared not leave Kairos behind. She did not want to travel back down to the city, either. She should have tried harder to talk Kairos out of this madness! This quest was suicide; she'd known it from the beginning. It wouldn't have bothered her if Kairos failed to become a knight. She would have done whatever she could to help him — even travel back to his homeland.

Thoughts of Kairos only made her feel worse. She ventured back to the long, descending stairs.

The ruined city of Shatteraxe rested below. The city of the dead. The fog thickened as the sun began its descent. She squinted, trying to catch a glimpse of the air elemental, but could see nothing from up here. She felt trapped. Hopeless.

Suddenly something grated open behind her at the shrine. Her heart leapt in her chest. She turned towards the shrine, and hope radiated within her.

Kairos emerged. He was alive.

\* \* \*

Kairos was ready for anything. His body still ached from the previous encounter with the air elemental, but he braced himself for the upcoming battle. He felt no fear. Only the sharp pain of anticipation.

He was relieved to find Althea safe outside the shrine. Together they descended the stairs to Shatteraxe. He showed her his new sword. It was a large, double-edged blade that looked tarnished and weathered. Althea was unimpressed. She had many questions, but Kairos only told her that the sword was magical and would defeat the air elemental. She remained unconvinced but said nothing more; there was little daylight left.

'*Say nothing about me!*' the voice in Kairos's head cautioned. It sounded weaker.

Murasa had vanished, returning to the sword. The god had abandoned the fiery form to conserve what little remained of his life force.

Kairos rushed though the failing light, trying to stay low and quiet, but hurrying to get into position at the bottom of the stairs. He held Murasa low and ready. Fog swirled thickly around the plaza.

Behind him, he knew Althea was setting up a simple spell that would launch a small fireball into the plaza. Fire had caught the air elemental's attention the first time, hopefully it would do so again, allowing Kairos to close in. He gripped the handle of the blade, hoping that the dark god would keep his word and help him.

It was a risky plan, but they had no other option.

Kairos stepped forward into the gloomy plaza, feeling the air change immediately. Althea moved into position nearby. Light blazed, a glyph of fire illuminated Althea's face. A flaming ball descended into the plaza and struck the fountain, erupting into a shower of sparks.

The air elemental roared as it charged towards the fireball. Finding nothing, it stood still, its arms swaying slightly, as the wind continued to circle. Then the creature faded.

To Kairos's surprise, the fog gathered around as the wind smote him full force. The air elemental materialised next to him. Its eyes flared with a menacing light as it closed in.

Kairos was not prepared for the elemental's sudden attack. He had imagined he would act first, but the creature lurched forward. Kairos instinctively raised Murasa up to protect himself, knowing that he was going to take the full brunt of the attack.

Kairos braced himself, holding his breath, hoping that the dying flame kept its promise – that Murasa kept his promise.

The elemental struck the sword with its vaporous limb. For an instant, bands of mana with glyphs etched into them flared around the elemental's arm. Kairos watched in disbelief as the transparent limb shattered into sparks that flew into the sword, streaks of light following behind them.

'*Attack! Now!*' the voice in Kairos's head commanded.

Kairos recovered from his astonishment and slashed forward. The sword struck true, right in the centre of the torso. A gap in the elemental's chest opened, and light spilled outwards, spiralling towards the sword. He noticed, as he swung again, that the sword's tarnished blade was glowing white hot, but he did not let himself get distracted by this phenomenon. He followed through with another swing.

The air elemental's wounds erupted in a shower of light. Deprived of mana from centuries of lying dormant, the sword drank deeply to slake its never-ending thirst. The light became blinding, and Kairos could feel the energy hum through the sword. He tried to pull away, but sword attached itself to the creature, refusing to let go. The air elemental exploded in a burst of mana, the concussive force knocking Kairos off his feet.

The light receded. The fog subsided substantially, though it still lingered around the outskirts of the plaza and throughout the rest of Shatteraxe.

'Kairos!' Althea called, running to him. 'Are you all right?'

Kairos picked himself up, his left hand fiercely gripping the sword, which was still glowing. The realisation came to him that the sword had protected him against the elemental's attack. He was still sore from his earlier battle with the elemental, and the fall ignited new pain within him. But he was alive.

Althea was staring at his sword, not in awe, but horror.

'Kairos, your sword...'

'Saved us from the air elemental,' Kairos finished for her.

'I-it's evil,' she said, taking a step back. 'I feel like it's pulling my energy away. W-what is it?'

'Just keep your distance from it, and you'll be fine,' Kairos said.

He was unwilling to talk about Murasa. He dared not to. Who would believe him? The voice in his head had gone silent. Kairos had the strange sensation the god was resting. He couldn't explain how he knew, but it was how he felt.

The air of Shatteraxe grew cooler and darkness set in the ruined city like a shroud. The shadows streamed long, and more voices whispered to them. Kairos thought he felt an invisible hand brush his back. He wanted to retrieve the staff and sword he had lost earlier, but a growing sense of dread compelled him otherwise.

'Let's hurry and leave,' Kairos said.

Althea did not argue.

\* \* \*

The night was never-ending. Kairos and Althea were so tired that each weary step brought pain, and yet they trekked on through the night. They wanted to put as much distance as possible between them and the ruined city. They dared not be caught in another fog by morning. And so they walked on.

They were too exhausted and fearful of Shatteraxe to talk much. They lowered their heads, hoisted their rucksacks on their backs and forced their feet to move them, one weary step in front of another, towards Chendre. Towards civilisation. Then towards Vadost.

Kairos walked side by side with Althea and tried not to think. He should have been happy. He had conquered the Test of Valour. Or had he? Althea had helped. Would the Knighthood disqualify him? The thought troubled him to an extent, but his worries swirled around the events of Shatteraxe. The flames of Murasa were etched in his mind's eye. He wondered what the god's intentions were. Murasa mentioned the godshard earlier, and Kairos wondered if he had made a bargain he would soon regret. There was now an invisible burden weighing down on him.

He had many questions, and tried asking Murasa with his mind. The sword remained dark and quiet. Asking his concerns aloud was out of the question. Not only would he appear foolish, but that would worry Althea. He felt guilty that he was hiding Murasa's existence from her, but it was for the best, he decided. She would only pester him with questions that he did not want to answer right now.

When the first rays of sunlight highlighted the billowing clouds in the eastern sky with red and pink, they stopped to rest at an abandoned farmhouse. Far away from the deathly atmosphere of Shatteraxe, the birds began singing once more. They sat down on a stone bench outside the house to rest their legs; the inside was too dilapidated to enter, and the roof had caved in a while ago.

'I've been meaning to talk to you about something,' Althea said, unsure how to phrase her next sentence.

The tone of Althea's voice and the look on her face told Kairos that this was not going to be a pleasant conversation. 'What is it?' he asked with trepidation.

'There is something odd about that sword, Kairos,' she said. 'Something sinister. Whenever I approached it, I felt my mana draining away like... like a necromancer syphoning life from the living.'

Kairos said nothing, only studied the blade in wonder. He twisted the handle, causing the tarnished blade to rotate.

'I believe that's what it did to that air elemental – sucked it dry of mana,' she continued. 'True, it helped us defeat it, but...'

'But, what?' Kairos asked, his voice taking on an edge.

The change in his tone made Althea peer up in concern. She closed her mouth and moved away from him.

'What do you want me to do?' Kairos demanded.

'Get rid of that sword,' she answered. 'We don't know what it is, but it cannot be good.' She glanced at the blade with unfettered revulsion. 'I sense nothing but evil from that weapon.'

Kairos regarded Althea with a grave expression. 'Get rid of it? This sword is the best thing that's ever happened to me.' He gripped the blade firmly, admiring the hilt.

'That sword is evil, Kairos!' Althea said. 'I cannot explain it, but there's more to it than meets the eye. Even now, I can feel...'

Kairos clenched his jaw and turned away.

'Don't ignore me like that!' she snapped.

Kairos rounded on her. 'Let me ask you this,' he said in a stern tone, his eyes burning feverishly. 'What would you do if someone offered you more mana than you have now? Would you take it?'

The sudden fury of the question stunned Althea, who had never seen this side of Kairos before. She only stared back at him with widened eyes.

'You would take it, wouldn't you?' he snarled, answering for her. 'You know how it feels to be weaker than the others. I've watched you struggle in class. Get bullied. You, of all people, know what it's like to feel insignificant. To be less than everyone else.

'I was like that with the Einar,' Kairos continued, taking on a dark scowl. 'I was the weakest, the smallest. Then I came here to Ordonia only to become the weakest in magic. Useless in impact, but did not feel the pain of burning. His sword had caught the spell and was now burning with its flames.

Now it was elf's turn to be surprised.

'I'm going to kill you, Hargonnas,' Kairos yelled. 'You're easy to kill when you're all alone!'

Did the elf just tremble?

Kairos approached him with the flaming sword, which he now wielded in his right hand. He was glad that Mr. Dubose made him work the forge and train weapons with both hands equally, for there was no hesitation in him. The battle fury was upon him now, melting away the pain in his shoulder. He would not be caught off-guard by another spell again. He sprang forward.

Hargonnas was wary now. His powerful spell did not work, its effect now evident on the sword. He began stepping back, assessing the situation. He tried to keep distance between himself and the Einar.

'*Cast the fire at him!*' came the sibilant voice inside his head.

Kairos obeyed, thrilled to hear Murasa again, and swung his sword. The inferno soared toward the elf, striking him, dousing him with flames. He pushed forward, swelling with confidence upon seeing his adversary engulfed.

However, Hargonnas remained unharmed, the flames vanishing around him in a sizzle.

'H-how?' Kairos said aloud.

'A shield spell,' the elf explained. 'You're not the only one with tricks, Cursed One.' He eyed the sword with caution, 'though that weapon may prove to be a nuisance.'

From the corner of his eye, Kairos saw another burst of light. He turned, expecting more enemies, but it was Althea hoisting her mana lance, the crystal spear tip shining a brilliant blue. She moved in on Hargonnas's flank.

The elf spun around to face his new threat, but upon seeing her, he threw this head back and laughed.

'It's too bad you had to get involved, sweet Althea. It was only the Cursed One who needed to die. Not you.' He sighed. 'Such a waste.'

Althea faltered upon hearing her name. Even Kairos paused, wondering how Hargonnas knew her. They had never met. Or had they?

Hargonnas removed his wing-crested helmet. Long blond hair cascaded down his shoulders. He flashed a charismatic smile to Althea, and for a moment, Kairos discovered that he resembled nothing of the cruel elven captain that killed innocents. Instead, he looked like the charming tailor who worked the clothing booth and sized their uniforms.

'Stephon?' Althea asked in disbelief, her mana lance wavering as she processed what was happening. 'Is that you?'

The elf laughed again. 'Oh my. That look on your face is splendid, dear Althea!' said the elf with a bow. 'Stephon Hargonnas, former captain of the Grimaldi Flying Squadron… Until this bloody fool escaped my grasp, that is,' he said with a maniacal gleam in his eyes. Then he turned to Kairos, 'Now it's time to die, you cursed bastard!'

'You want us to die?' Althea asked, confusion and fear etched on her pallid face. 'But you were always so friendly.'

Stephon Hargonnas's eyes narrowed to lethal slits. 'I was never friendly, Althea. I was merely tolerating you disgusting humans. Living amongst your kind has convinced me that Alban would be much better off if you were all wiped out.'

With a sardonic sneer, the elf cast a single, circular glyph. Althea and Kairos's every nerve ending filled with searing pain. Stephon laughed at their strangled screams. Althea collapsed to her knees, and the mana lance rolled from her limp grasp. Kairos managed to stay on his feet. He took a step towards Stephon, preparing to attack with Murasa.

Althea swiftly cast a glyph to free herself from Stephon's spell. It must have taken all her remaining mana, for she tried another spell only to produce tiny sparks of light that trickled harmlessly from her fingers. She fell to her hands and knees and glanced at Kairos, and realisation flickered in her eyes.

'T-that spell!' she stammered. 'He's a necromancer!'

That meant nothing to Kairos. He was fighting off the throes of torment coursing through him and concentrating on his foe before him.

Stephon ignored her, the lesser threat, and yelled at Kairos, 'How is it that you're still even standing?'

The pain throughout Kairos's body was slowly receding as Murasa drained the spell, but the pain in his shoulder intensified. He now watched the elf warily, knowing that he was not as invincible as he had once thought. Murasa, the sword, had limits. A well-aimed, powerful spell would end this fight instantly.

The elf put his hand, now glowing with a sickly indigo light, into the folds of his cloak and withdrew a mass of shadow. Tossing it on the ground between them, Stephon spoke in an unfamiliar language, its staccato pace flowing easily from his tongue. The shadow unfolded and stood. It was humanoid – dwarven – in shape, with glowing silver eyes.

Those eyes peered at Kairos, and he took in a sharp breath.

'Watch out!' Althea cried. 'It's a shadow spectre. Don't let it touch you!'

The warning was unnecessary. Kairos took one look at those silver eyes and knew that the spectre's touch would harm him more than a sword or spear ever could. There was suffering in those eyes, a silent plea to end the torment. And a hunger for a living soul.

He circled the spectre, staying out of its reach. His wounded and aching body was at its limit. His earlier fight and the gruelling journey through the night from Shatteraxe had drained him beyond fatigue, and now the blood loss from his shoulder was weakening him by the moment. His legs felt sluggish. His wound throbbed.

The shadow spectre slowly approached.

Out of the corner of his eye, Kairos saw Stephon casting another spell in the background. He tore his gaze away from the elf as the shadow spectre reached for him. He jumped back, barely avoiding the spectral hand.

A jagged boulder caught Kairos squarely on his chest. He was grateful for his armour, as it protected him from the brunt of the attack, but it knocked the air from his lungs and sent him staggering backwards. The shadow spectre swooped in as the elf howled with mad laughter.

Stephon Hargonnas had timed his spell perfectly. The boulder had distracted Kairos enough to divert his attention from the deadly creature. The spectre stretched out its ethereal hand and grasped a hold of Kairos's left forearm, which was hanging limp from his wound. Kairos's right hand brought up his sword, Murasa, and caught the shadow spectre on what was supposed to be its body. A normal sword would have passed through it; Murasa did not. The shadow spectre gasped a breathy whisper as the blade bit into it. The light in the silver eyes winked out, and the darkness around it transferred into the sword.

Kairos sank to his knees, agony overloading his senses. He clutched Murasa with his right hand to blot out the pain and squinted his eyes shut. It took all his willpower to open them, and once he did, he recoiled in horror at the sight of his left forearm. It was charred where the shadow spectre touched him, and the blackened wound was spreading towards the rest of his arm. He could feel himself rapidly growing weak.

Stephon stood, his face once more a wicked smile. He sensed victory. 'I will make you suffer,' he said. 'But first I will kill Althea like that human wench in Milbrooke. And I will scalp her all the same! Her hair will make a lovely trophy of my victory.'

Kairos was pale as tried to stand. He looked at his mutilated arm, unable to fully grasp what had happened. His arm burned with an icy pain. His grip on Murasa weakened.

He looked up at the elf, his vision becoming dimmer by the moment. They stared into each other's eyes with hatred. Vengeance clouded Kairos's mind. He shook his head to clear it. He had to focus.

'No!' he yelled. 'I'll never allow you to harm another person again. I'll avenge the Einar, the people of Milbrooke, and Farina.' With that, he leapt forward, Murasa held out before him.

Hargonnas laughed as he traced a glyph. The earth exploded in front of Kairos, sending a clod of soil raining down on him, followed by a series of jagged rocks pelting him like a hailstorm. He fell back.

Despite his courageous vow, Kairos could feel his remaining strength and stamina fading quickly. The wound from the shadow spectre now reached his shoulder. Only his vengeance combined with the desire to protect Althea kept him standing.

*'Get closer!'* Murasa's voice commanded.

Kairos tried once more to close the distance between him and the elf, so he could deliver the killing blow. Stephon nimbly backed away, he was quicker, fresh for battle, and powerful. Kairos held out his sword, hoping to draw more mana from his opponent.

Stephon Hargonnas was no fool. The elf knew the sword absorbed magic, so he directed his spells away from it. Instead, he used his magic to assail Kairos with physical objects, such as dirt and rocks. The elf even uprooted a large sapling and flung it at Kairos, nearly striking him and laughing maniacally all the while.

Kairos knew the elf was toying with him. He had to defeat Hargonnas soon, otherwise he would succumb to whatever injury the shadow spectre had inflicted upon him. It hurt to breathe. He was almost dropping his sword, and would not be able to swing it much longer. Was this the end? Pain and despair all but consumed Kairos. In the end, Stephon had far more power and experience in battle. Even with the godly might of Murasa, Kairos could not defeat him.

'Kairos, now!' shouted Althea, lifting him from his bleak stupor.

She tried to plunge the mana lance into Stephon's back, but his magical shield repelled the attack and threw her off balance.

The elf's cry of outrage echoed among the trees as he turned his attention on Althea. He cast a quick spell that sent her sprawling onto the ground, paralysed with pain. Another glyph brightened his face with an orange glow, giving him the appearance of a fiery demon of the Netherworld. This spell would end her life.

'Kairos!' she shouted. 'Help me!'

Althea's cry penetrated Kairos's despondency, and he rushed forward to save Althea. Stephon saw him coming and spun around to redirect his spell toward Kairos.

The elf began to smile, his malicious face hideous with glee at the prospect of incinerating Kairos.

But the moment of distraction had caused the elf to miscalculate, for he had forgotten to include the presence of Murasa in the equation as he loosened the scorching spell. Kairos raised his sword, channelling all of the anguish, pain, loss, anger and despair he had harboured since he had crossed the sea, and directed it towards the elf. He would avenge the Einar and Farina, even if he died in the process.

Stephon's magic burst forth in a large wave of flames. Kairos raised his sword, expecting to die in the attack. But he planned on taking the elf to the grave with him. He hurled himself at his tormenter.

Murasa's blade snuffed out the flames, smothering and inhaling them. It hummed with a white glow as it feasted on the spell, penetrated the elf's magical shield like it was a wall of fragile glass, and punctured the black leather encasing his torso. Kairos felt no resistance when the sword plunged into the elf's mid-section, splitting flesh, guts and bone. The sword continued travelling until the hilt pressed against the black leather of Stephon's suit, the blade protruding out of his back.

The triumphant smile had left Stephon's face. His icy blue eyes pierced Kairos with cold fury and hatred. In one final effort to bring Kairos down, the elf lifted his hand to trace a glyph. Kairos released Murasa and grasped Stephon's casting hand, crushing it. The spell fizzled away in trailing sparks of light that flowed towards the sword.

'You cursed human!' the elf spat. He tried to speak some more, but blood gurgled and bubbled out.

The elf continued to struggle. Even as he was dying, his power was shocking. But his struggles weakened quickly. Kairos watched Stephon's eyes as the shards of spells the elf had woven around himself were drawn into the blade.

'You killed the innocent and defenceless,' said Kairos, his words laden with fury. 'You took many loved ones from us.'

The sword glowed brighter, drinking the life essence within Stephon. Wrinkles began forming in the elf's face as the skin began to wither away. His cheeks sunk into his skull. The flowing blond hair faded to white.

'You will not have a proper burial,' Kairos continued in a low voice that only the elf could hear. 'You will be carrion for the vultures whilst your soul will live a cursed afterlife within Murasa.' Stephon's eyes bulged out in abject terror, his throat burbled something incoherent. He looked up at Kairos, his eyes pleading. Just like Farina's.

Kairos held his gaze and twisted the blade until the elf's eyes turned milky white, his skin grey and shrivelled – like an empty husk. His leather bodysuit hung limply from his dead form.

Kairos extracted the blade, which seemed to hum pleasantly, as if its thirst were quenched. The dried-up corpse pitched forward, held together only by the leather bodysuit. Kairos wiped the bloodstained blade on the black leather as best as he could, but could no longer hold the weapon, dropping it in the grass. With the last of his strength, he staggered towards Althea who was recovering from the effects of the elf's spells.

'Althea,' he said, breathing heavily. 'Are you all right?'

'I'll be okay, but you...' She paused, casting a horrified glance at Kairos's blackened left arm. 'The shadow spectre touched you.'

'I may be in need of some healing,' he said, managing a wan smile before collapsing.

\* \* \*

Althea cast the healing spell one last time for the night. Blue tendrils of energy wound their way over Kairos, seeping into his skin and soothing his fever. His body, tense and trembling, now relaxed in a peaceful slumber. Althea pulled the blankets over him.

They stayed at the inn in Chendre. How Kairos had lived through a shadow spectre attack was a marvel beyond her expectations. He had fainted, on the verge of death, after the battle with Stephon. His skin was sallow, and his life's blood was weak. Althea had drawn as much mana as she had dared from the surrounding nature for her healing spells, but it wasn't enough. She was losing Kairos fast.

In one last ditch effort, she had muttered a prayer to no god in particular and cast the spell to draw the mana. To her astonishment, mana surged into her, coursing through her veins. She had looked around in wonder, wondering where it all came from. Surely all of the plants in the entire area could not provide such a wealth of magical energy. Then she saw that the sword was gleaming nearby. She had not pondered why at the moment. For all she could tell, the mana was enough to stabilise Kairos. She had accepted it as a miracle. It was another miracle that he had managed to get up and trudge along, sword in hand, back to Chendre.

The town had fully recovered from the effects of the plague. Upon seeing Kairos in his diminished state, the villagers had grown concerned, expecting another calamity. Once Althea had soothed their fears, they had been more than happy to assist Kairos towards the inn.

For the next several days, Althea worked day and night to heal and tend to him. He tossed and turned in a restless sleep, speaking in the strong dialect of his homeland. She could make out some of the phrases: he spoke of his father, and of someone named Thylar. At the height of his fever, he screamed the name of Hargonnas. At intervals he would sob, apologising to someone named Farina. Or he cried, begging his father for mercy.

Seeing him in his pathetic and vulnerable state made Althea's heart ache for him. She did not know that he carried such torment within his soul, and watching his anguish made her sad.

She stayed by his side, barely eating anything. The innkeeper, a robust woman of later years, took sympathy and offered a hand, even cooking meals for Althea and changing the bowl of water every few hours for their room. A few of the other villagers — grateful for Althea's help with the plague — attempted to help, but Althea politely refused, stating that Kairos needed time alone. Althea spent her time praying to any god who would listen, for few people ever survived being touched by a shadow spectre. She did not even want to imagine what horrors would occur if the blackness had completely taken over Kairos's body.

During the evening, the innkeeper returned with a vial of amber-coloured liquid. She held it out to Althea. It looked like a typical potion.

'What's this?' Althea asked.

'A healing tonic,' the innkeeper replied.

'I'm aware of that, but where did you get it?'

'Someone from Valour Keep was passing by and got wind from the villagers that Kairos was ill,' the lady said.

Althea grew suspicious. After the fiasco with Stephon, she was reluctant to trust anyone. 'Who?' she asked.

The innkeeper shrugged. 'He wouldn't say, and I didn't get a good look at him. But he said it would help. He seemed like a nice sort of gentleman.'

Althea was not convinced. She cast a few quick spells that could determine the most common agents used for poison, but detected no trace of anything harmful. From her studies, it resembled the standard healing potion. Her mana was low, and she had exhausted the nearby plants to their limits. She dared not cast another healing spell, and Kairos's condition was still critical. She stared at the vial, swishing the amber liquid around. It was worth a chance at this point.

She funnelled the contents of the vial into Kairos's mouth that night, massaging his throat to get him to swallow. Nothing happened, but he continued sleeping.

The next morning, Kairos's fever broke. He had survived. He awoke and sat up slowly, looking around bleary-eyed. Upon seeing her, his lips formed a weak smile.

She wrapped her arms around him and tried to suppress a sob. She held him for a long time, and finally she pulled back to look at his face.

'You look horrible,' she said with a smile. 'How do you feel?'

'Hungry,' he croaked from the dryness of his throat.

For the first time in a while, Althea started to laugh. For once, everything was going well. Kairos even started to laugh himself, but laughter quickly devolved into a series of coughs. Althea fetched him some water and they sat in silence for a long time.

'We succeeded,' Althea said, breaking the silence. 'We'll become Mana Knights upon our return.' She managed a warm smile. 'And to think, you've done it all without a trace of mana.'

Kairos no longer smiled. 'You assisted me with the air elemental,' he said. 'Won't that disqualify me? Disqualify us?'

Althea shrugged. 'If that's the case, then it was worth it. I could never live with myself if I hadn't helped you.'

Kairos nodded solemnly, but said nothing.

'One thing that bothers me though is why Stephon wanted you dead,' Althea said with a shudder. 'And what sort of plans did he have in mind for me?'

Kairos's face darkened, the festive mood shattered in an instant. 'Let's not dwell on such things, Althea. That's the past now. We won. We're alive. That's all the matters.'

'You're right,' she said, trying to banish the disturbing memory away. 'We must leave for Valour Keep soon. Otherwise two fortnights will have passed, and our efforts will be for naught.'

Kairos nodded. 'Right. But first, let's eat.'

\* \* \*

There was a sombre air at Kinclaven Citadel that evening.

'Absolutely no visitors,' was the message Malus's steward told all comers, who included a diplomat from the Salforian Royalty, a prince from Dvergar, and even a baron from as far south as the Numidian border of Ordonia. They were all supposed to dine together in the citadel's great dining hall, which provided the most splendid view of the mountains. Some of the guests took offence, but what could they do about it? No one dared complain to the Dark Lord. Everyone knew that the 'walls had ears' in the citadel, and if they felt any ill will, they wisely kept it to themselves.

Malus did not spend the evening alone, however.

The General sat before him, bearing much greater news than the whole lot of superficial nobles who yammered about fashion, politics, and favours. His matters were actually of importance regarding the fate of Alban.

'The boy has the sword, my lord,' he announced with an air of indifference.

Malus listened, his red eyes gleaming with lethal interest. He was in an extraordinarily foul mood, but curious at the same time. 'And how can you verify all of this?' he asked.

'I was there, my lord,' the General answered in earnest. 'I saw Hargonnas take on the god-cursed boy, known as Kairos Azel. I saw the boy wield the sword.'

'The god-cursed was holding the sword?' Malus paused, frowning in thought.

'Yes, my lord.'

'Nothing happened to him?'

'No, my lord,' the General answered. 'It is as you surmised. The sword did not affect the boy in the least. I know this, because I saw him strike Hargonnas down.'

The dark elf raised an eyebrow. 'Captain Hargonnas is no more, then?'

'Captain Hargonnas is no more,' the General repeated, then corrected, 'Or shall I say that your former captain, Stephon Hargonnas, is no more. Not that you or I will miss his absence much. As we had suspected before, the pompous light elf was a liability corrupted by decades of misuing necromancy. It robbed him of much rational thought and made him a truly gruesome being. It makes one wonder how he used to be…'

'Yes, I thought the same. That foul magic addled his mind. He wasn't always such a fool. Well, do go on,' Malus urged.

'Hargonnas initially had the upper hand, attacking the boy and the girl with powerful spells. Even against the former captain's considerable magical prowess, the boy was able to cut him down.'

'Truly?' Malus was amazed.

The General, not often prone to strong emotional reactions himself, was quite surprised at the dark elf's response. Then again, he remembered that he, himself, had watched the fight with rapt curiosity.

'Truly, my lord,' the General said. 'The sword absorbs magic spells, thus confirming your suspicions of it being the Devourer. The sword consumed a variety of attack spells, and even a shadow spectre. However, it appears that magic spells that manipulate physical objects are effective. Hargonnas did use such spells, and they worked to great effect. Had he continued that line of attack, he might have succeeded. But as you presumed earlier, his arrogance proved to be his downfall in the end.'

'What happened next?' Malus leant forward.

'The boy impaled Hargonnas, my lord.'

The dark elf snorted and opened a bottle of wine. He poured two glasses and handed one to the General. 'Hargonnas had his uses, but that leather-clad buffoon was an imminent disaster, or shall I say, 'shit in the butter churn'. He always resorted to *his* way of doing things, so he deserved his fate.'

'Good riddance to that,' the General agreed, taking a sip of the wine. 'Excellent vintage, by the way. What's it called?'

'Salforian Summer, a deep red wine,' Malus said with a scornful smile and raised his glass. 'In honour of our fallen comrade, the late Captain Hargonnas.'

'To the former captain,' the General said, also raising his glass.

'Speaking of which, were you seen?' Malus asked.

'No,' he responded, then after a pause, 'I appeared before an innkeeper in Chendre, stating I was from Valour Keep and passed along a healing tonic for the boy. I wore my cowl to conceal my appearance.'

Malus nodded and took a sip of the wine, savouring the taste before continuing. 'Why didn't you attack them? Even with the sword, you could have defeated him.' The red eyes gleamed as they stared at the General.

The General shrugged. 'Two reasons. Firstly, I don't like to kill children. True, they are almost adults, but to me, they are children. Secondly, say that I did destroy the boy, then what do I do about the sword? I cannot approach it, move it. Even from a distance, I could feel the sword's hunger for mana.'

'That's because you have a much larger store of innate mana than the others, even Hargonnas,' Malus said. 'It's of little concern. What's done is done. The boy has the sword, but he doesn't know that he is merely a game piece for the Pariah, or his god. We may have lost the initiative, but we still carry the advantage. You're right,' the dark elf conceded. 'It's better that the boy carries the sword for now. Who knows what disaster would befall us if we allowed it to sit unattended in the wild?'

'My thoughts precisely, my lord.' The silver-haired man bowed.

The elf took another sip. 'Have you learnt anything else?'

'Yes, milord,' the General said, setting his glass of wine down. 'Lord Galen Avenal is on his way back to Vadost as we speak. I could never discover the nature of his mission. Grandmaster Eribus has kept that secret even from the high-ranking knights of Valour Keep.'

'Drat,' Malus said. 'He will be a nuisance.'

'Shall I prepare for the next phase of your plan?'

'Yes, General Argent.' A leering grin spread across the dark elf's face. 'Or do you prefer Professor Argent?'

Argent casually waved the question away. 'Titles are rather presumptuous, my lord. Either are fine, if you so insist.'

'Very well, General,' Malus responded. 'Let's make preparations.'

'Your orders?'

Malus poured himself another glass of wine. He offered some to Argent, but the General politely declined and looked out the window. The crescent orange of Vay hovered over the distant mountains, giving them the appearance of golden, jagged spikes. The dark elf sat back in his chair and took another sip, smiling.

'Return to Valour Keep. Here is what you will do...'

Argent listened intently, his face a stoic mask. After the dark elf finished speaking, the General reached for his wine glass. A hint of a smile formed on his lips, though his eyes remained cold and emotionless.

'An ambitious plan, my lord. Perhaps I *will* have another glass of wine.'

To be continued…

Godshard Chronicles: Volume II

# OTHER GODSHARD BOOKS

By Elmon Dean Todd

<u>Godshard Legends</u>
*Dark Pariah*

<u>Godshard Chronicles</u>
*Cursed Knight* - Vol. 1
*Blood Knight* - Vol. 2
*Volume 3 (Coming Soon)*

By J. B. Garner
<u>Godshard Odyssey</u>
*Goddess Tear* – Vol. 1
*Volume 2 (Coming Soon)*

# GODSHARD CHRONICLES

Our list of other titles is always growing, along with an action RPG video game in development for Steam and consoles. To find out more and to see our selection of titles, visit us at:

## www.godshard.com

### or visit:

Twitter: @GodshardRPG
Instagram: @GodshardRPG
Facebook: @Godshard

# ABOUT THE AUTHOR

Elmon Dean Todd is a former police officer and has also taught English in Switzerland and Japan. He attended the University of West Florida and University College Cork in Ireland, and graduated from the University of Florida with a BA in Literature. He is currently a full-time author and video game developer.

Made in the USA
Columbia, SC
06 May 2022

59854641R00231